AN IDLE WOMAN

Wendy Parkins

Legend Press Ltd, 51 Gower Street, London, WC1E 6HJ
info@legendtimesgroup.co.uk | www.legendpress.co.uk

Contents © Wendy Parkins 2024
The right of the above author to be identified as the author of this work has been asserted in accordance with the Copyright, Designs and Patents Act 1988. British Library Cataloguing in Publication Data available.

Print ISBN 9781915643278
Ebook ISBN 9781915643285
Set in Times.
Cover design by Sarah Whittaker | www.whittakerbookdesign.com

All characters, other than those clearly in the public domain, and place names, other than those well-established such as towns and cities, are fictitious and any resemblance is purely coincidental.

All rights reserved. No part of this publication may be reproduced, stored in or introduced into a retrieval system, or transmitted, in any form, or by any means electronic, mechanical, photocopying, recording or otherwise, without the prior permission of the publisher. Any person who commits any unauthorised act in relation to this publication may be liable to criminal prosecution and civil claims for damages.

Wendy Parkins was born in Sydney and now lives in Dunedin, New Zealand. She has held academic posts at universities in Australia, New Zealand, and the UK, where she was Professor of Victorian Literature at the University of Kent until 2018. Her memoir, *Every Morning, So Far, I'm Alive*, was published in 2019. *An Idle Woman* is her first novel.

Follow Wendy on Twitter
@WendyParkins1

Feathered darkness

(July 1845)

Frances

Farley Hill Court
Berkshire
July 1845

A nightjar rattles. Unbaptised children turn into nightjars if they die, it is said.

My new daughter, pink and plump and not yet two weeks old, sleeps in the nursery upstairs. When I was a girl in that same nursery, curtains drawn against the lingering twilight, a nightjar's strange churring would tell me I was not the only creature awake, impatient for dawn and for the freedom of park and wood once more.

The bird strikes up again, like a grating whirr within my own feverish head. All is quiet in the house. Earlier, I heard Mama's door close and Hester's soft tread pass quickly by. Mother retires early when John is here. No further sound will come from her room; she sleeps deeply after her black drops.

I turn over onto my back and stretch out each leg carefully, feeling that dark, sticky wetness between them. So much blood this past seven years! Worst of all, those glistening clots after a missed flow or two. At first, I had grieved those losses, like that time – in that other place – when I had lain on the floor of my chamber as a dragging ache took hold of me. By then I knew all too well what was happening yet I did not move, staying where John had pushed me down until Betty, my only ally, came to light my fire and found me. She stripped away the bloodied underthings past saving, bringing towels to staunch the flow and carrying away the terrible gobbets that made me shiver to behold, cold to my core.

The dark stain on the rug beneath me that day was so deep it had been a week or more before the rug could be restored to its place, the bare boards of my room a daily reproach. I cringed to think of the servants scrubbing and blotting, cursing me for their extra labours. Ever after, in the right light, I could still make out a shadow on the rug, the stain of failure, but also – tell no one – the trace of a life saved in the losing. Yes, a life *saved*, I truly came to believe. *She* who had left nothing but that shadow would never know what it was to walk that wretched house, to be bruised and betrayed there. She was free, unbound, just as her mother longed to be. Or perhaps *he* – an even more blessed release, if so. *He* would never be raised to be one of them.

* * *

Dr Bulley says Cecile must be my last, that the blood loss has been perilous and ought not to be risked again. There is damage, he says. He insists, too, that I consider a wet nurse, much to Mama's disapproval. She had deferred weaning her only child for so long that it was considered almost vulgar in a lady of her station but *you scarcely ever cried, everyone marvelled at that,* she always says. I grew up robust and fearless, a little wild even. I never sickened – unless from too much indulgence in the kitchen, where Cook knew my taste for all things sweet – until I left this home and went north to that place.

Strangely, my girlish strength seemed to return to me here in the months before Cecile was born. I walked out most days, taking a familiar path to a glade where I could lie at my ease among sun-warmed bracken. Late one afternoon, watching golden strands of web waft in the warm air above me, the flesh on my belly suddenly tightened and I knew my time had come. I lumbered back to my feet and slowly retraced my steps; Cecile was pulled from me with the first streaks of the next day's dawn.

* * *

When I looked out my windows this morning, having forced myself to get up and walk unsteadily about the room – I must get strong again, quickly! – I saw a row of bedsheets billowing in the breeze. It is Friday, I think, but there has been so much linen stripped from my bed that the maids have been firing up the laundry coppers almost daily. I hope they do not curse me here, too. God knows I am heartily sick of the mocking whiteness of freshly-laundered sheets that become clammy and soiled as soon as I lie in them, and of stale nightdresses, spotted rust-red below, with crusty yellowed patches across my breasts.

I seep, I leak, I cannot be contained. I am ebbing away like a foul tide, and yet John will not leave me alone, coming to my chamber last night after arriving from Scotland, still out of temper with my refusal to be brought to delivery in the house where those little never-babies dwell. A *go by*, I have heard such creatures called, as if merely passing shades that leave no mark, no pang, no scar.

He had cursed at the mess resulting from his efforts, but I squeezed my eyes shut and kept silent, straining to hear any night sounds from the feathered darkness beyond. After he had finished and gone, I had that dream again, waking with an acrid dryness souring my mouth and the sheet somehow twisted round my throat.

List! A step outside the door, too heavy to be Dinah, checking if I require a night draught or a change of linen. My heart thumps wildly, and, in response, I feel the throb of bruised flesh deep within, the hot sting of torn skin between my legs. I cannot suppress the sob that rises, even though I know that my weakness only inflames him. It is too much to bear. *He will destroy me,* of that I am certain.

And not me alone? Thoughts of my daughters flood my mind, like small apparitions spirited down from the floor above; the new babe and her three sisters, sleeping in their chamber beside the nursery. I see my own blue eyes staring back at me from their trusting faces and their presence is so strong I smell their young freshness like the first tart apples of the season. *Oh, my poor girls, we must take flight!*

1

What followed who shall tell?

(June 1838–January 1839)

Frances

Farley Hill Court
Berkshire
June 1838

After much reflection, I have come to the conclusion that Miss Austen was misguided. It would pain Mother's dear friend, Miss Mitford the authoress, to hear me say so. I usually bow to Miss Mitford's knowledge on all matters literary and she will brook no criticism of Miss Austen, but so I have concluded and so I commit to this page.

I understand that Miss Austen intended it as a witticism that *a single man in possession of a good fortune, must be in want of a wife* (I may not have that quite right, by the book) but what of a single lady in possession of a good fortune, like myself? Miss Austen's Emma had only a solitary unwelcome suitor in the form of Mr Elton to contend with, and she was twenty-one. I have been fending off dogged young men (and their mothers) from a tender age, and gentlemen of more consequence than a lowly vicar at that.

Nevertheless, since I was a girl with cropped hair – as Mother preferred for her tearaway daughter – I set my sights on becoming a countess. I wanted to be more than mistress of Farley Hill, leading a life of idle comfort, although I am sure I did not know quite how the lot of a countess might differ from that. Still, the idea of settling forever in the county of my birth was not one to be contemplated, even were I to find an obliging Mr Knightley of my own!

So I bided my time happily enough, awaiting my first London season when I believed a dozen eligible noblemen would vie for my hand, among whom – at last – would emerge the favoured one to whom I would yield, uttering a quiet but heartfelt consent to his impassioned proposal in due course. But even such a nobleman's son must have more than a title before I would consider bestowing my fortune on him. There must also be an abundance of curling hair and a loose cravat around a manly throat as he knelt to pledge undying devotion to *his love, his angel, his life*, with the promise of a corsair's life of adventure by his side.

I must say, in my defence, that such fancies of lords or dukes were not entirely preposterous. Was I not well acquainted with families of high rank and had I not been presented, at twelve, to Queen Adelaide at Windsor Castle? With my hair not quite grown out – so that it could neither be plaited nor curled in an acceptable style – and travelling seventeen miles in the carriage in my first ever white silk dress, I must have been a sight that day. The only child present, I recall being close enough to see that the circlet of diamonds on the queen's head was kept in place by an uneven row of black hair pins like a wattle hurdle, as if she had dressed in a frightful hurry and wouldn't sit still for her maid. That vision of regal disarray threatened to rob the event of all its enchantment until I beheld the dazzling spread of bonbons and sugarplums, merely picked at by court beauties ignoring the child secreting her bounty in a handkerchief when she could eat no more.

One noble family in particular courted the intimacy of the Dickinsons – by which I mean just Mother and myself, we two alone at Farley Hill Court since poor Father's death – and it was the daughter of that family, the brave and jolly Lady Penelope, with whom I later shared my plunder of royal sugarplums. Three years my senior, Penelope was a raider of birds' nests, a wader in rivers, a walker of rooftops, but despite her title was not an heiress like me. Her youngest brother, however, was heir to a considerable fortune through another branch of their family. This little gentleman of my own age was destined for me, I became aware, though we rarely spoke to each other when he was home from Eton as he considered girls of any sort, whether sisters or prospective brides, beneath his interest.

When I reflected, though, on how both my mother and Penelope's parents shared such a fond hope for our union, I came to feel a strong misgiving for holding so low an opinion of the little lord (for so I always referred to him in my head). I was very partial to his parents, who had shown me nothing but kindness on my visits to Easthampstead Park, and joining our families in marriage at some still far-distant time would secure me a place in their lives and hearts forever. And I might then have a sister, too, my dearest friend in the world, Lady P, and together we two might persuade the little lord to take us on travels who knows where! So while I cherished secret hopes for my first London season when it should arrive, I vowed to behave more charitably towards Penelope's brother in the meantime.

Thus it was that early last summer, I put this intention into action during a visit from Penelope's family to Farley Hill – a grand undertaking, as the Marquess's visits always were, with carriage and outriders fit for a state occasion. The day was fine and the visit had begun with a stroll in our grounds. While Lord Downshire engaged Mother in sustained conversation about farming, to which he was quite devoted, the Marchioness turned aside to inspect the contents of our glasshouse, a modest offering of tuberoses and other sweet-smelling plants and climbers in which Mother delighted. The Marchioness was a study worthy of Tintoretto as she swept gracefully through the greenery, trailing pale silks as soft as they were voluminous. I, to my shame, had already torn a rent in my dress and stained my sash by sliding down a green bank at Penelope's behest. Now, though, Penelope followed behind her mother as meek as a lamb, having managed to maintain a Parisian bonnet above her sleek black hair without any disarray from our brief escapade, even wearing unsullied gloves, something I baulked at in warm weather.

Penelope, however, was outdone by her brother on this occasion, Arthur being rather a slave to fashion, with his short-fronted tailcoat nipped so tight at his waist that it was as though he had been laced into it, and an abundance of linen at his throat that quite obscured his chin. When eventually the party passed indoors again and was sitting stiffly in our best reception room – Penelope looking as grave as if she had never fired off a pair of pilfered pistols in her life – I saw my opportunity to extend an olive branch to the little lord.

The day is still so fair. Would you care to take a walk further afield with me? I asked him, and was pleased to see expressions of delight on our elders' faces.

Oh yes, he replied, languidly. *Very agreeable, when there is plenty of game.*

Oh, I couldn't say. Perhaps then you would rather not go? Only it is very pretty, I assure you.

He looked at me then as if he wished me I won't say where, but I persisted with my mission, rising to leave the room, and was rewarded again by his father's smile as his son followed me.

Now Farley Hill Court is no Easthampstead Park, but the summer garden is always something to lift the heart, surveyed from where we both now stood on the stone terrace, ornamented in the Italian style with vases and festooned balustrades. Like the Boboli in Berkshire, I like to think, although I have never seen Florence. Beneath the terrace steps, garden beds with blooms of every colour punctuated swathes of lawn extending to an open sweep of parkland dotted with oaks and giving way, in turn, to a deep wood of pines.

Although I had gazed on this scene in every season, I thought I had never seen it to such advantage and I turned to my companion, forgetting for the moment his temperamental reserve. *Is it not beautiful?* I asked. *I am sure nothing can exceed it.*

The little lord looked quite astonished at my sentiment. *Very pretty*, he said coolly. *Certainly a good country for hunting. Do the hounds often meet here?*

Very often, I said, turning away in shame at my ill-advised display of enthusiasm. Still resolved on my course of action, however, I led the way across the park and out of the iron gates.

Where are you going? he asked.

I was going to take you across the common, and through a neighbouring park that is currently uninhabited. The family to whom the place belongs, the Anderdons, are abroad.

He did not demur, so we continued, soon entering the

Anderdons' gates to take a path canopied with chestnuts and bordered by laurels and holly, the whole rather unkempt and unpruned, allowing white anemones to dot the dappled shade. All this time as we walked, though, he uttered not a word until the prolonged silence became painful.

Do you think this picturesque? I asked.

Well, rather out of order, on account of the master's absence, I suppose, he said. *But what a hideous house!*

We had left the shelter of the trees by now and were crossing our neighbours' park, from which the façade of the empty house was visible. I had never thought it hideous but now I saw that its irregularity, reminding me so of something from Mrs Radcliffe, may not have appealed to an Eton man of more urbane tastes.

Is this all there is to be seen? he continued, stifling a yawn.

Well, the place I most wanted to show you lies beyond the rose garden, but I am afraid it will not please you.

He indicated with a languid gesture for me to continue and so I did, coming to rose beds riotous with blooms and heady with fragrance, surrounding a broken fountain in their centre.

My little lord cast a contemptuous glance around. *Why surely, Miss Dickinson, you don't admire this bear garden?*

I blushed, stammering something about old Mr Anderdon's passion for collecting antiquities and how he took little interest in anything beyond his collections, except of course for travelling to Italy each year and always bringing me back a trinket.

The little lord was unmoved. Still, I remained committed to my ill-considered expedition and, indicating the narrow path to a truly wild place, led the way until Arthur came to a halt, his coat-sleeve caught on a bramble.

What strange place is this? Had we not better go back? I am not exactly equipped for so savage an expedition. I see nothing ahead but an old gravel pit and this furze is most disagreeable.

Seeing my special place through his eyes now, I blamed myself for a fool. I begged his pardon and we turned back, reaching Farley Hill's terrace once more, where the Marquess was taking in the prospect.

Well, young people, he said, *have you enjoyed yourselves?*

Miss Dickinson prefers rather rough walking, I heard Arthur say to his father as I passed inside.

Penelope sprang from her seat and pulled me away from where our mothers sat talking over the tea table in the small anteroom we call the China Closet. *I thought you had eloped!* she said, taking my arm and turning me back towards the terrace.

No fear of that, I said.

Well, do come into the garden with me, I am tired to death of sitting among your mother's horrid china in that tiny room. Such ugly things she has, Fanny! Has your bailiff's dog had her puppies yet?

But the day had lost all its charm and I was impatient for the carriage to be brought to the door so the illustrious party could depart. Eventually the plumed horses stood pawing the ground, the outriders in liveried readiness. The Marchioness who never, even in her sleep I believe, forgot her status, advanced to the carriage with her usual slow dignity, accompanied by Penelope, bored once more, while the little lord mounted his horse and raised his hat in a manner that could not be more disdainful than if he had snubbed his nose at me. When the whole party was out of sight, I ignored my mother's urging to return inside with her to talk over the day, instead striking off across the park again, where I burst into a passion of tears. *If all the world is like Arthur,* I cried, *then I hate the world.*

* * *

I may have learned an invaluable lesson that day but I concealed my distress over Arthur's behaviour from my mother – a new sensation for me, used as I was to speaking my mind to her – and when the succeeding winter drew to a close, we travelled up to our place in Cavendish Square for my first season, where Mother and I were drawn again into the orbit of Penelope's family. Thus, I was often in the little lord's company and, under our mothers' eyes, the two of us were forced to be civil and to walk arm in arm.

Lady Downshire, no doubt anxious that the future wife of her youngest son make a good impression, undertook my induction into

London society in earnest, to some extent usurping my mother's role in that regard. Among other things, this involved lengthy shopping expeditions with Penelope and Lady D, turning over silks and ribbons and consulting with milliners and shoemakers until looking out upon the drab London streets from the carriage window seemed a restful diversion.

A further blow was soon to follow when Penelope became betrothed to the eldest son of a baronet. This was not, of course, *her* first season and while her fate was probably to be expected I felt as though some sleight of hand was being performed before my eyes: my beloved accomplice transforming into her mother the Marchioness, whom I could no more imagine romping than the little lord himself. I wanted to hear about Penelope's enviable wedding tour – a voyage on the wine-dark Mediterranean, no less! – but instead she only spoke about the china and linens to be ordered for her new Wimpole Street residence, as if a London life confined to streets and squares was all she had ever dreamed of.

At last, though, the dreaded morning of my presentation at St James' arrived, when even Penelope's imminent desertion paled into secondary consideration. After the visit by a French hairdresser to Cavendish Square, I contemplated myself in the glass to see ostrich feathers, white rosebuds and lace circlets miraculously rising from my impeccably-dressed hair. Only then could I put on the dress of spotless white silk that required such precise lacing and arrangements of voluminous sleeves and sweeping train that I feared I could never walk downstairs, ride in a carriage, and alight in a fit state to be presented. How could I be expected, in addition, to manage a bouquet of flowers *and* a fan, leaving no hand free? At that moment, I would gladly have swapped my court debut for any dare Penelope might set me in the woods of Easthampstead Park.

When I remember now the procession to the Presentation Chamber that took place that day – my Lady Marchioness, sweeping along in glacial grandeur; followed by her husband, quite eclipsed by the magnificence of his wife, despite the clanking sword at his side; Lady Penelope, demurely impassive, as if born to sweep a train and hold her head erect; my handsome mother, elegant in blue silk; and finally me, a cloud of white drapery and nodding feathers, quite a stranger to myself – I still feel the sick dread of the occasion and never wish to repeat it.

Of the ball that followed in the evening, however, I retain no such emotion, recalling instead a vaulted chamber, glowing with golden illumination and crammed with the season's finest faces. I plunged with giddy abandon into the din of music and conviviality and, free of my cumbersome train, gladly accepted every invitation to dance – until Lord Downshire led Arthur towards me.

If our brilliant little debutante is not engaged, he said, *will she dance with my son? I have told him of your splendid performance at court this morning, one he was sorry not to witness but for which he now wishes to make amends.*

Bowing, I accepted this invitation by proxy, determined to remain undaunted by Arthur's chilly silence.

Why do you dance so little? I asked him, after his father had left us standing together, waiting for the musicians to strike up again.

I am not fond of dancing, he replied. *I fail, in fact, to see the attractions of these events. The fineries on display are quite ridiculous, for the most part.*

Is that why, I said, tossing my feathers and lace, *I saw you standing by Lady Constance, watching her so closely? I never saw such loops of pearls as are threaded through her hair. She is a veritable mermaid!*

The little lord blushed, yes, really blushed, although with fury or embarrassment I could not be sure. Too nervous to approach a woman he evidently admired and instead reduced to standing up with me, the rustic heiress, he then propelled me into motion as the first notes sounded from the players.

And you allow your father to force you to dance? I persisted, revelling in my advantage as we turned and twirled. *How very disagreeable to be treated like a boy. For my part, I could not endure it.*

Again, he endured my remarks in silence and, when the music concluded, led me back to my seat by my mother without a further word from his bloodless lips. But that night I laid down my head – finally free of every pin and ornament – in utter contentment, not so much for my successful debut as for avenging myself for the shame of the gravel-pit walk. I knew with certainty that I would never allow myself to be humiliated again by one so unworthy of my affections. I was done with such boys.

I told my mother as much the following day and begged her that we might make our return home earlier than we had intended. Despite the evenings at the theatre, the glittering assemblies, the banquets with a footman behind every chair, the season had failed to live up to my youthful expectations. I was tired to death of the mutterings ever at my back as I passed – *ten thousand a year, they say,* a figure far from the truth but apparently the amount always attributed to unwed heiresses – and I longed to be just Fanny Dickinson of Farley Hill once more. After what seemed to me an interminable delay (some invitations simply could not be refused, Mother insisted) we set off for Berkshire at last.

Our early departure from the season, however, seemed to give rise to a rumour that an engagement with the little lord had, in fact, taken place. I squirmed at the thought but took a little comfort that the mistaken belief might keep at bay some of the more tiresome suitors who had pestered me in Town – none of them bearing the slightest resemblance to Lord Byron's curls and manly throat – and who now continued to write me equally tiresome letters.

Still, after our return home, Farley Hill palled on me somewhat. I was out of sorts and unsettled, discontented with the rustic pleasures of childhood, just as I had been with the brilliant ballrooms of London. Was this to be my life's orbit? The hubbub of Town for the season, the quiet country for the remainder of the year?

Observing my declining spirits, Mother then proposed we travel to Scotland to stay with old friends of hers whom I had never met, although from Mother's regular correspondence with Mrs Geils I knew they were a much-travelled military family. Scotland may not be the Mediterranean but I already felt such an affinity with the rugged glens and heathered hills of *Scotia* (thanks to Sir Walter Scott and Lord Byron) that the suggested journey quite ignited my imagination. From north of the Tweed, it might be *London*, with all its falsities and formalities, that seemed a foreign place. And military folk, I surmised, would more likely share my own inclinations for adventure; they would not settle for taking the air from a carriage in Hyde Park and calling it an outing. And what tales they might have to tell of their travels around the globe!

Amy Webb

Farley Hill Court
Berkshire
July 1838

Miss F has promised me letters from Scotland and says I must write in reply. It will be a *splendid opportunity* for my writing, she says, since I made so much improvement while we were in Town together for the season. Miss F had not had a maid entirely of her own before then and I had been so proud to be chosen, rather than some strange Londoner who wouldn't know our homely ways. That's what Miss F would always say to me in Cavendish Square, the morning after another of her dinners or balls or nights at the theatre, *We are both of us just little Berkshire rustics, Amy!*

Miss F had been like a stabled pony in spring when she had to sit quietly after the hairdresser had visited Cavendish Square, or while practising after another lesson from the Marchioness. Imagine learning how to walk or bow or hold a fan in Society! I couldn't have borne it.

So, whenever we could, Miss F helped me sneak up to the attics with her – *Come on, amiable Amy, I can't sit still a moment longer!* she would say – and wrestled and romped with me till we both looked like we had tumbled down a hill and through a hedge. One day as I tidied her hair after we were weary from our fun, she said, *Let me teach you some French. Would you like that? The Marchioness's maid can speak a little French. Say after me: juh swee Aimee.*

But I shook my head. I did not like to learn French, and not just because of the stories of Bonaparte that the teacher at the parish school had told us, about how so many Berkshire men had left never to return because of him. Besides, I did not want to be like the Marchioness's maid; such a stern person, not charming like Lady Downshire herself. And I had thought no more about it until Miss F returned from Bond Street with a small writing desk for me. Such a treasure! Beneath its polished lid, I found paper soft and creamy as unbroken curds, along with a bottle of blue-black ink, a lump of cherry-red wax, a jar of powder, a clutch of pens and the smallest knife I had ever seen, too dainty even to cut a switch of hazel.

Since you have no interest in French, Miss F had said, *we shall work to improve your hand, and write together. I feel there is so much to write down, my thoughts press on me so! I should like to spend my days putting everything I see into words, thinking it all over and over until I find just the right ones.*

Miss F would entreat her mother to have me cried off from work for an hour – much easier in Town, with fewer rooms to dust or fires to lay – and we would sit side by side at the table in the centre of the library. The Cavendish Square library is nothing like as grand as that at Farley Hill where Miss F's father's books line every wall, ceiling to floor. Old Mr Dickinson is long dead but four times a year each one of his books is taken down and dusted, its leather cover buffed, and put back just as it was.

One morning, a week or so before we had left for London, Miss F had led me into the library to gather some books for her journey and to show me its riches. She said this as if I had never seen them before, and did not come in every morning to sweep the fireplace ready for lighting again, if required. But I had said nothing, merely nodded and looked about me, and she said I might borrow something to take to London, too. She said she had always been told that she may read any book that took her fancy, even when she was so little that she could not reach past the third shelf, and I should not neglect my reading either. Not wanting to disappoint Miss F or seem ungrateful, I had then selected a small book, one that did not look as grand as some of the others, called *The Domestic Affections*, because I thought it might be about servant girls. When I opened it later, I saw that it must be poetry – short lines of words that left so much empty space on the page and the words chopped about so that I couldn't follow clearly, not like I could when Miss F recited poems to me, like songs without music that made me want to sway or tap my foot.

At the parish school, I had liked best the stories from the front part of the Bible, like the baby in the bulrushes. There are no books at Lower Cottage, even though Mother is a good scholar, Father says, with such a fine hand and head for figures that she helps with the estate accounts. In the big house, though, there is even a Bible for the servants in the little room beside the kitchen where Cook and Hester and old Matthew sit in the evenings. It is left open so that I sometimes see names from stories I remember, not like Berkshire names at all – *Potiphar* and *Jezebel* – but mostly Matthew seems to like the part of the Bible about vanities and lamentations to read to us.

While I swept the grate in that little room one day soon after I had borrowed the poem book, I stopped to read a row of Bible words. *As the deer pants for streams of water*. A picture sprang into my head of a hind standing in a running brook, bent down to lap at the water's surface, like a dream almost. Was that what words could do? And had not Miss F told me that poetry could be like a dream? So I thought I might try again with the poem book. And I found that once I had read them over a number of times, sitting with Miss F to tell me some of the words, they too brought pictures into my head, and made me feel a feeling that I did not have a name for but that I decided must be Domestic Affections.

So, any road, in that London square far from home, Miss F and I had often written together, or rather I blotted and wiped ink from my fingers and tried again while she scratched away like a demon, lines and lines so neat and flowing.

I will look back and laugh at these pages long after we have left London, she had said. *I will recall the alabaster face of that Joono I saw last night and the light of the candles reflected back tenfold in that mirrored ballroom, where even the floor shone like glass.*

And you must do the same, Amy! When you are back in Farley Hill, you may doubt that you ever saw that line of carriages stretching out of sight in the Park, more horses than in all of Swallowfield!

And on she had written, talking all the while, not at all upset about the beautiful sheets of paper I spoiled with my ill-shapen letters, my false starts and my words sloping across the page like a donkey track. She would laugh good-naturedly at my efforts, assuring me they would get better. And they did, so that my writing became round and regular, no longer wobbling or running away from me.

Miss F was so happy with my progress. Squeezing my hand one day as I held my pen, she had said, *Dear Amy, or perhaps I should call you Miss Webb since you write like a lady now, if ever I leave home – as I suppose I must or how am I to become a countess and travel the world? – I hope that you will come with me. I couldn't bear to leave you behind!*

But she *has* left me behind and now I must write things down here so that I keep my hand neat, as she likes to see it, and my letters will show that I have not forgotten her.

Dear Miss Dickinson, I shall write. *The weather here is wet. I wish you better weather there so you may walk in the glens, as you like to do.*

I fear Miss F has been won over by Scotland, like that Lord George who writes the poems that she swoons over (even though he is dead, she tells me). It sounds a place very different from Berkshire and she seems to do nothing but walk about with Lieutenant Geils. *Few are his words, but keen his eye and hand. That's poetry, Amy,* she writes. Poetry again. Miss F loves it so.

I never call her Miss F in my letters, of course, even though she has often said to me, *If you won't call me Fanny, as everyone else who loves me does, won't you call me Eff Dee?* But I couldn't do that, I told her, even when we were alone. It was already a liberty to call her Miss Frances rather than Miss Dickinson. *Nonsense*, she would say, placing a hand firmly on each of my shoulders. (She is as strong as a stable-hand is Miss F and can wrestle like a schoolboy but I am a match for her and can be stubborn like her too, when I need to be.) *Mama doesn't mind, you know she is fond of you,* she says to me.

But Father would never allow it, I know. Father thinks that Mrs Dickinson and Miss F may extend their stay in Scotland, may even shut up the house here for a time. And then what shall I do? I have known Miss F since Father brought us all to Farley Hill soon after Mr Dickinson died. Father had worked here when he was a younger man, before he married Mother. I do not know why he had left but after Mr D's death, Mrs D appealed to Father to return and Mother thought it best – it was just after Lydia was born and we were too many for our old place of two rooms. So we moved to Lower Cottage, as grand as a gatehouse it seemed to me, since it was near the main gates and looked over the lawns, smooth as velvet.

From our doorstep, I would see Miss F running there, with shaggy old Crab barking at her side; that always made her laugh. Then, when I was a little older and began to go with Mother to her work in the dairy and henyard, Miss F would sometimes join us, to see the new chicks or to let the calves suck on her fingers, but Mother did not like me to stop to talk, nor to have Miss F interrupt our work. *Mind your slippers, young mistress*, she would say but Miss F did not seem to mind the muck.

When her bonnet sometimes slipped back from her head, I noticed that Miss F's hair was shorter than my own. When I asked Mother why it was so, she said that Mrs Dickinson had firm ideas about the raising of young ladies and something in Mother's face told me that she thought Mrs D mistaken but I did not know why.

I had thought that I would always remain working alongside Mother with the hens or in the cool, dripping buttery, but then Father arranged for me to work in the big house instead. I began by taking Miss F's hot water to her of a morning. *Good morning, Amy*, Miss F would say, every day, sure as sure. And *Good morning, Miss Frances*, I would say, setting down the pitcher. I never needed to tie back the bed curtains – she would already have done that herself, and thrown the windows wide as well, if it was warm. It was then, up close in her chamber, that I could see the blue blue blue of her eyes, too.

We began to talk, Miss F and me, whenever she found me

shaking out a rug or emptying buckets in the yard, because she was out of doors so much herself. I did not want to seem to be shirking my duties but I could not resist those talks with Miss F. She seemed so keen to know about all I did, as if I were more than just an under-housemaid, the daughter of Webb the bailiff.

It was only during our time in London, though, that we could talk freely. At Farley Hill, I might go all day without seeing her again after my early morning visit to her room. While I was cleaning grates and laying fires, dusting and polishing the downstairs rooms, sweeping floors and brushing carpets, she and her mother might be dressing or at meals or on carriage rides or doing whatever ladies do. Since old Mr D died when Miss F was seven, it is just the two ladies here and Cook says there's many housemaids who would regard the duties given to Sarah and me as a spree.

I *do* like Cook though and, truth be told, would far rather work alongside her in her cheerful kitchen than dusting and scrubbing all day. Cook is almost as fond of Miss F as I am but then everybody loves Miss Frances Dickinson of Farley Hill, Berkshire, and Queen Charlton, Somerset. *Such a gift she is!* Cook says. *Her poor mother had given up all hope, after more than eleven years of marriage, Mr Dickinson having left it so long to take a wife, and then Miss Frances appeared, and never has she given anyone a moment's grief.*

But Miss F has given *me* grief now she is gone from home. There is nothing to distract me from missing Lower Cottage in the evenings. No light shows there by the time I climb to my attic room in the big house each night. At such times I almost wish that Sarah was my bedfellow, as much as her complaining prattle wearies me so during the day. Sometimes I even hear her grumbling to herself through the thin wall that divides us, until her snoring begins. But when I lie alone in the dark, rubbing my aching feet together to soothe them, I think about Miss F's vast empty room and wonder what it must be like to sleep beneath that feathered coverlet the colour of linden leaves, with damask curtains drawn snug against the draughts.

My fingers are clumsy tonight, the skin flaking and my nails rimmed with the grating black that has left every fireplace in the house shining. I know it is such a folly for me to write these pages.

I am sure Sarah would laugh at the sight of a servant writing of an evening – *like a lady*, she would say if she knew, meaning no praise by that.

But if Miss F does not return soon, there will be no more writing in any case. Mrs D may be generous with her candles but I am almost out of pages and rely on Miss F to share her paper with me. Such a supply she keeps! At least I have managed to copy out some lines from *Domestic Affections* to send with my next letter when it is done – with not a single smudge or blot! It makes me warm, somehow, to think that some poetry from Farley Hill will go all that long way to the north, to be with Miss F in that strange land. I shall write it here too, as a comfort.

There is a tear of sweet relief,
A tear of rapture and of grief;
The feeling heart alone can know
What soft emotions bid it flow!
It is when memory charms the mind,
With tender images refin'd;
'Tis when her balmy spells restore,
Departed friends, and joys no more!

Colonel Andrew Geils

Dumbuck House
Dunbartonshire
July 1838

25th July

My dear Mrs Dickinson,

It behoves me to state in writing what has been previously adverted between us in informal conversation here at Dumbuck. Therefore, I beg to inform you that I have been solicited by my eldest son John Edward Geils to apply to you on his behalf to sanction proposals of marriage to your daughter Miss Frances Dickinson, a Ward of Chancery, to whom, with the young lady's approbation, it is his as also my wish he should be united.

My son is 25 years of age and is Heir of Entail of the estate of Dumbuck in the County of Dumbarton, North Britain, of value about £1,200 per annum. He is a Lieutenant on leave of absence from Her Majesty's 4th Regiment of Light Dragoons in India. He is independent and free from any incumbrances, and with the prospect of early promotion.

As my heir he succeeds to this estate of 360 acres which I inherited from my father the late General Thomas Geils. He is also next Heir of Entail to the estates of Geilstown and Ardmore in this county and neighbourhood, failing the heirs of my late brother

Colonel Geils of the Guards and sister the late Mrs Kenny. In addition, I have promised to secure my son £600 per annum.

In case you should also wish to know his position relating to his family and connections, I beg to inform you that my second son Thomas is likewise a Lieutenant in the Queen's 4th Regiment, my third, Andrew (whom you know as Pitt) is a Lieutenant in the Honourable Company Madras European Regiment, and the fourth, William is at present a cadet at Addiscombe Military Academy, so that I may say John's brothers are all provided for.

If abilities of military skill were hereditary, my son is eminently entitled to them from both his mother's family and mine, though the former have shared the fate of many others in Scotland and from having had large possessions are now without an acre. My son's maternal uncle, whose nameson he is, was held in such estimation by His Grace the Duke of Wellington that could I lay my hand on a note I had the honour to receive from His Grace on the occasion of my excellent kinsman's death I would be gratified by transmitting it.

My son is truly a suitor for the hand of the young lady. Her fortune he has felt as an obstacle to be surmounted but as his affection, should he succeed, will make him cherish the beloved object, so his sense of duty will husband and guard her property for her gratification and advantage. He has himself no irregular habits or propensities. In the capacity of son, brother or other connection in his family, John stands pre-eminently distinguished, as I believe you will have had the opportunity to observe for yourself during your current stay in our home.

I remain,
Yours very sincerely,
Andrew Geils

Frances

Dumbuck House
Dunbartonshire
August 1838

1st August

Dear Amy,

I write in haste to tell you that I am to be married to Lieutenant Geils – John, as I may now call him! I *told* you Scotland would be an adventure better than London. Mother says please tell no one else at Farley Hill yet as the lawyers must first be satisfied (as if it matters whether anyone but myself and John should be satisfied though Mama, too, is delighted, as are all the family here). I will tell you all when I am back at Farley Hill next week. Thank you for your last. I do hope Lydia is now recovered.

Yours ever

F. D.

John Geils

Dumbuck House
Dunbartonshire
September 1838

8th September

My dear Mrs Dickinson,

The forenoon post brought me a letter from your solicitor, Mr Jennings, of the most satisfactory nature. I have not one wish regarding settlement ungratified and the only thing which now lays on my mind is that in the event of the mother's death our children – should Providence bestow them upon us – are to be entirely independent of me, and from the enjoyment of £3,000 or £4,000 per annum I would sink to the estate of £1,200. This is always likely to breed an unnatural jealousy between parent and children, who to my mind should not expect anything till the death of their father.

I do not mention this to cause further delay to my much-desired marriage to your daughter but you have always showed the utmost affection for me; nor has that been unreturned by me. I now entreat that if it is in your power to do anything on this head you will as much for the good and happiness of your own child as for the husband you have chosen for her. It is but natural and always usual that children should inherit through their fathers and I think it would be for their advantage and much more for my happiness that they should be allowed in the usual way to wait upon their father's death rather than usurping my stewardship over them.

Don't be displeased at this, my dear Mother, and if it strikes you as quite unreasonable say or think nothing more about it. Give this to my sweetest Fanny that she may see my worldly greed at full length and that there may be no secrets between us regarding her settlement. I trust to join you both at Farley Hill ere long and remain,

Ever your most attached and affectionate son,

J. E. Geils

Frances

Farley Hill Court
Berkshire
October 1838

I have a further quibble with Miss Austen's stories of young ladies, although Miss Austen is not alone in this regard. Mrs Radcliffe, Mr Richardson, Sir Walter Scott, even Monsieur Balzac from whom I had hoped for more – all these worthies lose interest in their heroines once their troths are plighted. Whatever pitfalls and dangers faced on the path to betrothal, their maidens fade from view once they leave the altar. Surely this is when life begins, in its fullest sense? I know that the appearance of orange blossom (only artificial, alas, for my autumnal nuptials) will not mark the end of *my* story. Like a young Edward Waverley, I will enter a new world of adventure north of the border. If only the laird of Abbotsford had told a story such as mine – A Hoyden's Highland Life!

But, then again, who better to tell my story than me? One day, perhaps I may find my way into print, not with translations like dear Papa but tales from my own life, beginning from my earliest years. *A First Visit to the Court of Queen Adelaide* or *Adventures of a First Season in London.* Stranger things have happened.

Nevertheless, how it was that John first caught my eye, and I his, would, I fear, offer nothing to engage a novelist's interest. There were no misunderstandings or reversals before a sentimental reconciliation swept away discord between us. Neither was there one sublime moment when true love suddenly dawned. Instead, there were merry rides and rambles around the neighbourhood of Dumbuck House, at first in the rambunctious company of Pitt and sometimes Isabella, and then, more often, with John alone. Up hill and down dale he led me, or perhaps up ben and down glen, I should say?

Mother had nothing to fear, I am sure, from John and I being alone in this way, so at ease were both families together. I almost think that Mother saw how things were before I realised myself the extent to which my affections were becoming entangled, as indeed did Mrs Colonel Geils. As before with the little lord, it was the two mothers who first discussed the possible alliance of our families – I subsequently learned – and it was then that Mother discovered that the Geilses had somehow heard the news of my supposed engagement and was able to assure them that no such hindrance existed, leading to the old Colonel's dignified letter of proposal on his son's behalf.

So, in the end, it may not have been the scene of manly curls and loosened cravat that I had long envisaged that sealed my destiny but, for all that, John did not lack gallantry when seeking my hand. It came about at the end of a day on which he and I had roamed alone like vagabonds through a woody glen carpeted with rosy-red campion and spikes of foxgloves quite as tall as me! He did not seem to mind my disordered bonnet or ungloved hands. Nor did he curb my exclamations at all, I observed, while we walked. Instead, in a quiet moment when we were almost upon the gate to Dumbuck House once more, he spoke his mind simply and freely – as he always does, whether to bestow a candid compliment or make his disagreement plain, such a welcome departure from the vain coxcombs of Town – and when he was done I was left in no doubt that it was the earnest desire of his heart to make me his wife.

Since then, the only complications have been of the legal, rather than sentimental, kind. Such a dreary back and forth of letters and interviews with our solicitor, Mr Jennings, all stemming from the fact that, upon Father's death, I had been left a Ward of Chancery. How peculiar I used to think it, that I – possessed of a wise and loving mother, as well as a secure home and fortune – should, in the eyes of the law, be at the mercy of the Lord Chancellor like some poor, defenceless orphan of the streets! My Lord Chancellor must be appealed to for anything on my behalf, money matters most of all, until I am of age – even now, when I am a grown woman of eighteen, on the verge of marriage. I confess I have never fully understood the constraints that Chancery places upon me, finding it all so tiresome. Mother, poor thing, bears all the burden of these legal niceties without troubling me and, indeed, still fears the consequences of having taken me to Scotland in the summer without first obtaining the Chancellor's leave!

At one point, it had seemed that the wedding might not take place at all *until I was twenty-one* but that was not to be borne, I told Mother, and she wrote to Mr Jennings immediately to say so. After all, are not John and I *both* heirs to estates? And, in the meantime, is my income not enough for us? What could be more natural than a wife's desire to share all she has with her husband? Mr Jennings took a rather different view, as I suppose he was obliged to do as our solicitor, but at last all was resolved to everyone's satisfaction. And very soon, the first significant chapter of my story will draw to a close!

Only a few hours remain until John is due to arrive at Farley Hill to join his parents, who with Isabella, Pitt and William came to us some days ago. What a jolly party we shall be here this evening!

Even in John's absence, though, Farley Hill Court has been a gay house, horses always at the door and people coming in and going out all day, in anticipation of my wedding. Poor mother looks a little pale, despite the comforting presence of her oldest friend, dear Mrs Ffarington, who travelled up from the Isle of Wight for my wedding with her husband, the Admiral, and their youngest son, Edmund, no longer the studious schoolboy I remember but a rather reserved young man, bound for the law rather than the navy like his brother.

Mother and Mrs Ffarington stroll in the grounds, arm in arm, whenever our northern guests are safely entertained elsewhere, but how she must miss poor Papa at such a momentous, happy time. I am delighted, though, that Mother has had the foresight to arrange a journey of her own – to Switzerland, no less! – after my departure for Scotland; she speaks glowingly of the restorative air of the Alps, where she first travelled on her own wedding journey. I sometimes catch myself wishing that *I* was going with Mother instead of her cousin Miss Allingham, an experienced lady traveller rarely on these shores, but that is only a moment of weakness on my part, a passing fear at the prospect of leaving Mother forever.

I shall miss dear Farley Hill, too, as I told Cook yesterday when I poked my head into her kitchen for a final visit to her domain. I have loved Cook like a second mother ever since I was a tiny thing and she would cup my chin with her flour-dusted hand to pop a raisin into my mouth. Whenever mother was absent or out of reach for any reason, it was Cook who opened her arms wide to let me weep my girlish grievances into her ample aprons, or counselled me as she stood at her sand-whitened table, her hands never still. When Crab, my beloved Newfoundland, wheezed his last in front of her kitchen fire, Cook let me lie at his side and never, never tutted that a young lady of fortune should not be crying over an old dog on a flagstone floor.

Poor Cook has been busier than I have ever seen her, baking and stewing, butchering and brewing, these past days. Amy, too, has been working in the kitchen from time to time, now that Jane McPhee is here to tend me. It was so thoughtful of John to send a girl for me from Dumbuck. She is to accompany us on our wedding journey to the Lakes, so that on my arrival in Scotland I will have at least one familiar face in service in my new home. Still, leaving Amy behind will be a hardship; she has been far more than a maid to me and has grown quite wise of late, since we have ceased our romping ways and spend more time in talk together, when we may.

She has not said so but I do not think that Amy likes Jane McPhee. On one occasion, I observed Amy quail when Jane came into my room bearing my freshly-brushed boots. It is true that Amy has not the full training of a lady's maid like Mother's Hester, or the Marchioness's Richards, nor does she have any strong interest in fashion. Jane, on the other hand, despite being raised in the wilds of Scotland, seems so accomplished, and quite towers over little

Amy. She has, too, the most extravagant head of hair, the colour and shine of rosewood and rippling with natural curls, which she knots and piles so expertly that it is a thing to behold. I can't think where she has acquired such skills living more than twelve miles from Glasgow! But such is her talent that I have no need now to summon the coiffeur from Reading, as had previously been intended for the dressing of my modest tresses on my wedding day.

How Jane darts about me, adjusting a ribbon here, fixing a pin in place there, if sometimes a little too vigorously so that I wince beneath her capable fingers. But I cannot deny the result, or the pleasure it gave me today when Isabella praised the loops of braided hair that Jane had securely contrived for me.

I have noticed, however, that in general Isabella seems a little uncomfortable here, even taciturn at times. I never once saw her in low spirits in the weeks I spent at Dumbuck where, as the only daughter of the family, she was always a hearty participant in her brothers' activities as well as an attentive companion to her mother. Even lively Pitt seems unable to rouse his sister's spirits! I am sorry to think she may not enjoy being away from home, but I confess I also take comfort from the fact that she may later call to mind what it is like to be among strangers, when *I* will be the one in a new place. It will be an unlooked-for pleasure to have a sister at last and one so loyal to John – I perceive he is her favourite among her brothers, at least the two that I have met. Thomas sent a very cordial letter from India, from whence he is shortly due to return on leave.

I long to ask Isabella about John, aware that I still know so little of him, just enough to have assented to his proposal without hesitation even if his hair *is* close-shaven. But when I think of what lies before me as a wife – the vista of our days together, first at Ambleside and then across the border in our new home, days when John and I can ramble together again as we did in the summer, and when I may accompany him shooting (he says he will teach me, how I should like to write Penelope and tell her) – I know there will be time enough to learn everything about him, and he of me!

Still, for now at least, I feel the absence of Penelope keenly, and cannot help but feel hurt that none of her family are to attend my wedding. News of my engagement to John brought a cooling of relations with Easthampstead Park, so there will be no Marquess or Marchioness to witness my nuptials, even though Mother and I travelled to Town to attend Penelope's soon after our return from Scotland. There is a part of me, although not my better self, that is sorry Penelope will not be there to see my procession down the aisle accompanied by nine bridesmaids – three more than at her own wedding – as well as a groom attired in impeccable regimentals to more than match her own military husband, many years her senior. *His* hair is quite grizzled – what remains of it!

* * *

Jane has just been in to my room to bring my new dress, the colour of celandines, that I am to wear to dinner this evening. It finally arrived from London this morning and she has aired and pressed it so that the flounces of lace on the daringly short sleeves cascade like froth, and the Indian muslin peeking forth from the split skirt bears no trace of creasing from being folded in its box. I was most insistent about that feature of *Indian* muslin, hoping it will not go unremarked by my new regimental family.

Jane's skills have even extended to making some minor alterations to my wedding gown, the sleeves of which I had feared were still a little too voluminous, rather than in the narrower style such as Penelope wore and that the fashion papers now recommend instead of a full gigot sleeve. Jane has pinned them, inserting a few invisible tucks, without in any way disturbing the whole effect of gentle pleating that features on both the bodice and sleeves. It is an absolute confection!

After gently laying out my evening dress, Jane could not leave me before lightly running her strong fingers along the lace of my wedding veil – so soft it is like touching air – where it hangs close by. I don't wonder that she marvels at it; she would look like a Greek goddess with such a fine gauze draped over her auburn coils.

I must return to my guests downstairs, much as I would prefer to remain undisturbed at my writing table while I await John's arrival.

I am so impatient to see him again that I cannot *think* of making conversation with Mrs Colonel Geils and Isabella, immured in the China Closet with mother. Like Jane, I am drawn to my nuptial veil. When I wind it around my shoulder and look at myself in the glass, I seem someone quite other than Fanny Dickinson, the girl with whom no sash was safe from harm.

In just one day more, I shall be clad in more silk and lace than I ever thought possible, more even than when I ascended to the Presentation Room with that train of ridiculous length, the hoyden debutante no longer!

Jane McPhee

Farley Hill Court
Berkshire
October 1838

You said it would be a treat for me, this journey. But there are nae walks in the gloaming, nae smoking rooms in this house of ower many ladies. And next we are to go and see a lake, as if we dinna have lochs enough to put their English puddles to shame. And I alone am to wait on your guidwife.

But all the time I am unpinning her hair or unrunkling her skirts, I will have the satisfaction of kenning what hersel does not – that you have been runkling *my* skirts this past year and more. J.

Amy Webb

Farley Hill Court
Berkshire
October 1838

It takes more than blue een to make a bonnie quean, I overheard Jane McPhee say to Mr Geils' manservant, Muirhead. At first I thought it might be the start of a Scotch poem, what Jane said, but then Muirhead said something in reply that sounded like *tocker* and other words about women's parts that made them both laugh. So it made me think it was of Miss F they were speaking, and not in a kind way!

When Jane asked me about my mistress the first night we shared a bedchamber here, she had laughed then, too, although mostly she does not strike me as a cheerful person. After I had told her a little about Miss F, Jane said that my cheeks were *glowing red as a Robbin Breestie*, which struck me dumb. And I'm sure I flushed even more then. But to think that Jane says *we* have a strange way of speaking! Like spitting pips, she says, or so I think she said. I do not always follow her. But Miss F does not seem to have any trouble understanding her new maid, praising Jane's efforts and skills until I feel quite ashamed of my simple ways.

In truth, though, none of the folk from the north are quite what I expected them to be. Old Mrs Geils seems mild enough, as does the Colonel, at ease with Mrs Dickinson as old friends should be, but Miss Isabella, Lieutenant Geils' sister, looks a sour kind of young lady, staying close by her mother and not at all warming to Miss F or her dear mother either, from what I can tell. Mr Pitt Geils is loud and lively, even more so than the youngest Geils boy, and not always kind or careful. But no one ever speaks against Mr Pitt, even when he blundered about on his first evening here and knocked a table over, shattering one of Mrs Dickinson's prized Severs candlesticks.

Of course, the one I had been most interested to see for myself was Lieutenant Geils and, when he had first come to Farley Hill for a day or two in September, I admit I was very surprised. He is not tall but very upright as you would expect of a soldier man, clean-shaven except for whiskers and a small moustache, both of a light brown colour like his hair close against his head, and with blue eyes like my mistress – but not a bit as striking as hers. I would not call him handsome, nor a man of good cheer particularly. He has a serious bearing and is slow to smile, although he is most courteous whenever Miss F is about. I have seen him guide her to the best chair before sitting nearby to listen closely to her spirited talk. At other times, though, he fidgets, always looking towards windows and doors as if seeking an escape. I know he is a sporting man so perhaps that is why he seems ill at ease inside.

But then again, Miss F, too, does not seem in her best spirits, on the brink of her new life. If I were to ever marry – which I have no wish to hurry about – I would be unlikely to move more than a mile or so from my mother, but Miss F is to go and live *hundreds* of miles away among strangers! So of course she might be a little teary or peevish, with such a prospect before her.

Perhaps that is why she has been so taken with Jane McPhee. Jane seems to find her way with ease in a new house, wasting no time gawping at the wedding preparations or the overstocked larder. She quite puts me to shame.

* * *

I cannot put my head on the pillow yet – although what a treat that will be now that Jane McPhee has departed with the bride and groom and I am alone in my little room where I may sit undisturbed with my pen, despite being so very tired.

All the household was up long before light. I helped Cook and Sarah in the kitchen, along with Mother and Lydia, summoned like others from the estate to work in the house this past week. Finally, at mid-morning, all of us were allowed to gather outside to watch the departure of the wedding party for the church. Such beauty and grace did the bride display in her white satin and blonde mantilla – even amongst her *nine* bridesmaids, all ladies of distinction from throughout the county, dressed in gowns of a far simpler style than Miss F, of course. Out they all processed from the house to the line of carriages to travel to Swallowfield Church, that I later heard was filled to overflowing.

When all returned once more for the wedding breakfast, our labours increased yet again, until the feasting was over and we gathered on the lawns – all the household, the outside labourers and tenants, all the nearby villagers – to cheer the couple on their journey, while the Swallowfield band played.

Lieutenant Geils, I only noticed now, was not wearing his regimental uniform as Miss F had hoped, but a simple blue coat. Nor was their carriage pulled by the grey horses Miss F had wished for but I am sure she cannot have minded, so happy did she look as her bridegroom handed her inside, and as Jane McPhee and the Lieutenant's manservant Muirhead took their positions outside the carriage with the coachman. As they drove away, Father threw an old boot filled with salt for good luck and we all laughed and clapped and shouted our good wishes. Even Mrs D's Hester, who is always so prim.

How strange it seems that on this special day, though, I spoke not a word to Miss F, and now she is gone without saying goodbye.

But tomorrow the fires must be lit as usual, the hot water and tea trays carried up for the houseguests who yet remain. Poor Cook must return to her stove, and the extra scullery maids and laundry girls and footmen will continue their labours for another week yet, until all is restored to how it was before. But not really as it was before.

Frances

Ambleside
Westmorland
October 1838

It is less than a mile to the top of Stock Ghyll Force, where the roaring torrent splits into two columns that cascade into a deep pool far below. Depending on how long a walker tarries at the top, the excursion may be completed in little more than an hour and certainly less than two. After that, questions might be asked about a prolonged absence.

When I am back on level ground in the town once more and passing the stream that flows by the little stone mill, it pleases me to recall the white surge so recently below my feet. To know that such untamed power lies so close to these cobbled streets, where squares of yellow light already show out from cottage windows, feels like some secret I alone possess.

I stood at the top of the falls too long today, thinking of that legend of another waterfall not far from here, that Mr Wordsworth retold. In his poem, a lady who doubts the constancy of her absent knight walks in her sleep at night, drawn back again and again to the *torrent-fall* where they had courted, until one night her errant lover returns to find her there and, reaching out his hand to draw her back from the ledge.

> *He touched; what followed who shall tell?*
> *The soft touch snapped the thread*

> *Of slumber – shrieking back she fell,*
> *And the Stream whirled her down the dell*
> *Along its foaming bed.*

I, too, feel woken from slumber. But I do not fall.

* * *

Something seemed to go amiss between John and I almost as soon as we had left behind the cheers of wedding well-wishers with their singing and waving of handkerchiefs at Farley Hill. I do not mean the minor vexations of the day – just a matter of horses and servants and a misunderstanding about John's attire – but something deeper, some disharmony that will not easily be put right.

Our first night together at an inn, John perhaps imbibed a little too much, which may account for the pronounced difference in his manner towards me when we were alone in our bedchamber. Mother's advice and my own reading in no way prepared me for what followed, how the flesh of a man could take such command of him that he could not be turned from his purpose; such a strange, indelicate purpose that felt as though it were nothing to do with *me* at all and I was a mere instrument for his – pleasure? I could not tell.

This, then, was marriage? Was *this* why Miss Austen left her heroines at the church door, venturing no further? (Did Miss Austen *know* what lay in store for them?) There seemed no more affection involved in the act than I had observed of the beasts in the field. John seemed almost to dislike me, even as his limbs entwined so tightly with mine. Was this the *love* extolled by dear Byron? And why did it hurt so?

The next morning, over breakfast, I found the courage to ask John whether it might be possible to call for a doctor before we continued our journey north and he had merely laughed. Yes, laughed! *Jane will attend you*, he said. *Jane knows all about it, you may be sure. Speak to her.* But of course I could not speak to a servant of such things.

When we stopped for luncheon that day, I was shown to a room to refresh my toilette before returning to the hostel's dining room by a different corridor, where I observed John in earnest conversation with Jane by the outer door. I would not have minded at all, I am sure I would not, if it had not been for his earlier advice to confide in her so that I wondered if it were *me* that they were speaking of. I blushed with shame and could eat little of what was placed before me. John did not seem to notice, though, nor was he troubled by my silence for the remainder of that day, dozing beside me in the carriage.

Then, on our first night in Ambleside, I was forced to request John leave me alone in the bedchamber, not wanting to tell him that my monthly flow had begun during the latter part of that day's travelling. I did not know quite what to say but he seemed to understand and slept in an adjoining room, although I heard that room's outer door close once or twice, as if he were unable to settle too, perhaps returning to the deserted public rooms below or taking a stroll further afield, since the night was mild and bright under a full moon.

For the rest of our stay, he has not used that room again other than for dressing and washing, even though, by the fourth day, the pain I experienced on passing water made my head spin and my brow feverish. I sat close to the fire, feeling by turns hot and cold, pulling close the fine Kashmiri shawl that had been John's morning gift to me, a garment of such impossible softness and delicate work that merely to look upon its beauty reminds me of my husband's true affection for me.

Still, I confess I often felt powerless to stop the tears that came unbidden and it was then that Jane brought me a special brew, a remedy favoured by the women in her family, she said, with a strange twitch of her mouth, not quite a smile. My throat had tightened at the first sip of the steaming liquid, yellow-green and bitter, but Jane was insistent and I was too weak to refuse. I drank it and she brought the tea again and again for the next few days, as well as cooling poultices that she told me to place in my underclothing.

Now I no longer need the tea, Jane says, and I can walk about easily, with little pain, but I begin to tire of the Lakes, finding them drearier than I had been led to expect by the poets. John has no interest in walking with me as he did when we were together in Scotland in the summer. He prefers to seek out the company of local men for shooting or fishing to fill his days, yet quite unfairly questions where I have been if I walk out alone. I cannot make him out.

Yesterday, he received word that the house he had leased for us, a place called Glenarbuck, was ready for our arrival sooner than expected and I urged him to cut short our journey. He is considering it, he says, and I must await his decision. I long to settle into our new home and hope that I will then find truth in the stirring words of Sir Walter Scott: *O Caledonia! stern and wild, Meet nurse for a poetic child!*

Rev. James Jaffray

The Manse
Dumbarton
November 1838

The parish of Dumbarton has not produced many men of eminence over the centuries and, even today, contains only a handful of landowners possessing estates of value. For this reason alone, it would not be surprising if the affairs of the family at Dumbuck House attracted my notice, but my official responsibility for the parish entry in the *Statistical Account of Scotland* also requires me to record any noteworthy developments in the neighbourhood.

On first meeting the new Mrs Geils just a matter of weeks after her wedding, while she was paying a call on Mrs Colonel Geils at Dumbuck House, I greeted the young lady with the information that Dumbarton is a corruption of the old name Dunbriton, signifying the fort of the Britons. *So you are joining a long line of antecedents who have made their home among us here*, I said with what I hoped was an acceptable degree of gallantry, rather than any unpleasant allusion to the more bellicose character of relations between those from opposite sides of the border in past times.

The young mistress Geils then entreated me to tell her more of Dumbarton so that she might learn as much as possible about her new home. She was *woefully ignorant of all things Caledonian*, she said, despite a deep fondness for its *blue hills and clear streams, in the words of my beloved Lord Byron*.

I kept to myself my reservations concerning the choice of that reprehensible libertine, George Gordon, as reading material for a lady of her tender age and made a mental note to bring some more appropriate volumes from the manse library for her edification on my next visit. In the meantime, heartened by young Mrs Geils' encouragement, I began by telling her of our most singular landmark, the Castle Rock, which stands on the southern extremity of the parish, on a small peninsula formed by the junction of the River Leven and the Clyde, an imposing feature made all the more so from the fact that the surrounding topography is almost entirely flat, or at most mildly undulating moorland.

But I find I am ahead of myself, I said. *First allow me to sketch out for you the ground from which Castle Rock springs so that you may build up a firm foundation, as it were, for knowledge of your new home.*

So I began my discourse with the Leven, the parish's only river, describing for my attentive auditor how it rises in Loch Lomond and flows seven miles thence before it joins the Clyde at Dumbarton Castle. The soils and stones of the parish I merely touched upon, surmising that of more immediate interest might be the climate hereabouts, which is on the whole moderate, though rather damp and variable. *Very heavy showers are frequent in spring and autumn,* I informed Mrs Geils, *such as we have experienced in the past week.* But I was able to assure her that the winters are generally temperate, frost and snow not continuing for any great length of time, although in the spring easterly winds persist, often doing much injury to early vegetation as a result. Soon, I concluded, she could expect to witness the dense fogs that unfortunately hang over the south part of the parish towards the close of the year.

I then considered it my duty to inform her – both for her current benefit and for the future when, the Lord willing, she will be blessed with responsibilities of a value incommensurate with their tiny size – that influenza tends to come with great severity when the fogs are at their worst. Without wishing to alarm her unduly, but again to forearm her with knowledge that any mother would want to possess, I could also not withhold from her that scarlet fever and typhus can prevail to an alarming degree, and that whooping cough and measles are common, too. I was able to mitigate these worrying tidings, however, by reassuring her that smallpox is mild and rarely fatal because of the widespread practice of vaccination in the parish.

Such is the sensitivity with which the Lord has endowed me, a blessing in my vocation for which I frequently give thanks, that I noticed Mrs Geils becoming restless at this point in our conversation so I sought a change of subject. After all, such a young Englishwoman, lacking in the rigour of education that she may have enjoyed if raised in these parts, might not possess the ability to absorb information in the degree and detail that I am able to impart it to her. So I asked after her mother and when we might expect to see her visit the north again, since I had not had the pleasure of meeting Mrs Dickinson in the summer when the two ladies had briefly sojourned at Dumbuck.

My inquiries after that gracious lady, however, had not the effect I sought. I believe I saw Mrs Geils' lip tremble until, with a shake of her head and a rather watery smile, she confided that she was missing her mother very much. Clearly, the daughter's first significant separation from the maternal bosom, exacerbated by a lack of regular correspondence from the Continent where her mother was currently travelling, accounted for the new bride's unsteadiness of feeling.

I promised Mrs Geils that her mother would be in my prayers and the eternal care of Providence and, thus comforted, the young lady seemed to regain her equanimity, saying that she feared she was keeping me from more important duties. So I took my leave from her and her mother-in-law, who had sat good-naturedly in silence for the most part during our conversation. I decided to save my advice about the prevalence of adders on higher ground for another occasion when it might be less likely to cause alarm to a new resident. In any case, young Mrs Geils will have nothing to fear in this regard until the warmer months.

* * *

On the next occasion I visited the new Mrs Geils – this time at her own home of Glenarbuck and armed with *The Border Antiquities of England and Scotland* and *Annals of the Parish* – I found her alone and troubled by the most recent letter from her mother, who was still abroad and apparently experiencing some disturbance of health in addition to inclemencies of weather in Switzerland. Mrs Geils had grown a little pinched about the face, I observed, with lines of darker pigment below her clear blue eyes that made them even more striking. The autumn's sudden cold could be felt even in the smart drawing room of Glenarbuck and perhaps that in part accounted for the lady's dispirited manner. As the fire had died down, I gently suggested that a person of the household might be summoned to attend to it, mindful that the young bride was still new to the responsibilities of household matters.

I am sorry, sir, she said, *but do not be alarmed on my account. Unless you are cold, Reverend?*

I assured her I was entirely comfortable. *And what of Mrs Colonel Geils and Miss Geils?* I then asked. *It must be such a comfort, during this time of concern for your own mother, to have a new family to fill this temporary void of feminine companionship? Dumbuck House is but a few miles away.*

Oh yes, of course, such a comfort, she said, *but could you tell me more about Dumbarton, pray? While this dreary weather prevents me from exploring my new surroundings, I may at least profit from your vast knowledge, Reverend, to bring the place alive for me. Is it true that there are signs of Roman occupation on the Castle Rock at Dumbarton, as Colonel Geils tells me?*

I was more than happy to discourse on the features of those historic fortifications, which led me, in due course, to the strategic importance of Dumbuck Hill, which rises directly behind Dumbuck House and that Mrs Geils had climbed during her summer visit, she said. It was from a vantage point on that hill, I told her, that the wily Wallace watched his opportunity for attacking the Castle, while concealing more than a hundred of his men in a place known ever since as Wallace's Cave (although really only a wooded hollow). But it was another feature I mentioned, Rhymer's Cave, named for the Thomas of the old ballad and found at the bottom of Dumbuck Hill's western precipice, that seemed to capture Mrs Geils' attention more fully so that, on my departure, I promised to bring her Sir Walter Scott's *The Minstrelsy of the Scottish Border* on my next call. She will settle in and become a fine Scotswoman in no time, I predict, with a deep knowledge and love of her new home, judging by her keen interest and quick mind.

Frances

Glenarbuck
Dunbartonshire
November 1838

Such an impressive place is Glenarbuck, standing on the southern slopes of the Kilpatrick Hills above the Clyde, with its daily traffic of sails and steamboats. So why does this house – with its columns and porticoes of such recent construction that the edges of the stonework are still sharp and clean – make me pine for the simple old rooms at Farley Hill?

We had a rough voyage from Liverpool and in our first days here John remained peaky from our travels – despite the fact that he has voyaged halfway round the world and back many times! I have begun to wonder if his health is not more impaired by his time in India than he has disclosed. When he had told me during the summer that he had no immediate plans to resume his commission, I had assumed it was because of his *father's* health – the Colonel depending so much on his eldest son – rather than his *own*. But Dr Reid has visited us more than once and although John says the new prescription does him much good, I observe bouts of breathlessness that give me some concern.

Nor did Dr Reid's advice to reduce the rigours and frequency of his favourite outdoor pursuits – shooting, riding and fishing – do anything to improve John's temper. But I, too, find that Glenarbuck offers limited occupation, with its meagre library and no instrument to play. John will not hear of hiring one, telling me to furnish one from my own income if I consider a piano so essential, which of course I cannot do while Mother is still abroad as I am unable to initiate an expense of this kind on my own authority until I am twenty-one. As John well knows.

We pay morning calls as duty requires (to a rather dull set of people hereabouts, truth be told), and the family from Dumbuck dine with us regularly, but a gloom prevails that I cannot seem to dispel. Even my maid here is a sullen young woman; Jane McPhee having been sent back to Dumbuck House where she was needed by Isabella, whom she had served before being brought to Farley Hill on my behalf. Of course, I have the comfort of John but it is as if there are several Johns and I cannot yet judge which one I may encounter at any given time: the lively, free-speaking man of the summer, or the surly one who barks at my smallest infractions concerning things I cannot possibly be expected to know, like the cost of the joint on the dinner table or the whereabouts of a favourite riding crop. Worst of all is the stranger he becomes in our chamber at night, a creature at the mercy of his basest impulses, incapable of a caress, a gentle word, before he takes hold of me, never once asking first of *my* feelings on the matter.

Am I not, then, to be a person with my own inclinations and wishes, now that I am a wife? Did I, in all innocence, forsake self-possession forever when I uttered those vows in Swallowfield Church? And can it be true that other wives – the Marchioness, for example, or Mother's friends like Mrs Anderdon or Mrs Ffarington – submit to these same rough crudities behind closed doors in their chambers? *Or is John not like other men?*

How can I ever ascertain whether the fault lies with him, or with my own ignorance or shortcomings? I cannot possibly speak of such matters to Mother, even were she not so far from me; I would blush to put such things down in a letter, to be seen by anyone's eyes. But surely *Father* never treated her thus? At Farley Hill, when Mama had spoken of a husband's *special embrace,* I had thought of this as something to be endured maybe once or twice – in the case of gentlemen, at least – and the event of a mere moment so that a child may result when the time was right. I had no comprehension of the surrender that would be called for, night after night, leaving me afterwards like a thing erased.

When I wake in the mornings after John has gone from my bed – his military training prompting him to rise before dawn – I lie with eyes closed, listening to my own breath, until gradually I return to myself, as it were. I cannot think how else to express it, except that with each breath, I will myself back to being Fanny, she who I have always known myself to be, until I can bear to rise and regard my face in the glass.

Perhaps, I think each morning, that has been the last time and John will tire of what he does to me, like a bad habit that loses all appeal with hollow repetition. But he does not seem to weary of his ways and with each passing day I feel more estranged, not only from him but from myself, as if it were not merely my name that I renounced on my wedding day.

* * *

We had only been at Glenarbuck a matter of weeks when my maid – also named Jane, as luck would have it – fell ill and was forced to quit the house, and John proposed fetching Jane McPhee to wait upon me once more. He was so often back and forth from Dumbuck, assisting his father on estate matters, that it was simple enough for him to bring Jane over in his pony cart, he said. At first, it was pleasant to be attended by Jane again; we spoke of matters at Dumbuck, things that John would think too trivial to pass on, and she quickly restored my wardrobe to the immaculate state it had acquired under her watch, unlike the less-attentive manner of Glenarbuck Jane.

Soon, though, I began to feel uncomfortable in Jane McPhee's presence in a way that I could not explain, except that I sensed a sulkiness in her as she dressed my hair, as if Glenarbuck was having a deleterious effect on *her* spirits as well. I came to dread having her lace my stays each morning, fostering a silly fear that she was deliberately pulling the laces too tight – one morning, she snapped them not once but twice – until I realised there could be another reason for my discomfort in that regard.

It was Jane herself, in fact, who raised the matter. I had woken feeling a little liverish and, further disheartened by the sight of a blanket of chill fog sweeping down the hillside to envelop the house, had remained in bed rather than rising to dress for my morning walk, as was my habit. Finding me thus, Jane had inquired whether I did not yet require my monthly clouts. She kept a steady regard on my face until I felt the first prick of a blush rising across my neck and cheeks as I called to mind how many weeks had now passed since that first night at Ambleside.

Do not say anything to my husband, or to anyone else, please, I said, and she gave me that strange half-smile, the only kind I have ever seen from her: one side of her mouth drawn in, her full lips puckering slightly while her smooth cheeks, dusted with freckles like nutmeg on hot milk, showed her dimples to advantage. I do not know why I asked for her silence but something in her manner told me that she would keep my secret, if that is what it was.

After she left me, I did not know what to do with myself, uneasy with this new possibility that Jane had raised. Could it be true? How might I determine it? I suppose Dr Reid might be summoned but I blanched at the thought of what form his examination might take. No doctor but Dr Bulley had ever touched me since the day I was born. Still, if confirmed as true, might not that mean John would cease his nightly attentions to me, having no reason to persist if I were with child?

What a strange notion that seemed – to be *with child,* something new and strange within my very being. Not in the manner that John is inside me, a painful intrusion, but instead a thing as yet unfelt, unsensed. But was I not still myself *alone*, my outline in the glass still that of a singular person? How could such a profound change be invisible even to me? Perhaps it was just a fancy after all and I should not set any store by the mere inkling of a servant.

The following day, however, was to bring a further unforeseen change. John came to me in the afternoon, wishing to speak to me on an urgent matter.

Jane has reported to me a case of smallpox in one of the kitchen servants, he said, *so I propose that we return to Dumbuck House without further delay. We had intended, in any case, to spend the Christmas season there and it is only a matter of weeks till then.*

I was taken aback by this announcement, having heard no such report myself from anyone in the household. My face must have conveyed something of my shock and confusion because, before I could organise my thoughts to make a considered reply, John rose from his chair with a dismissive gesture.

Come, come, my dear, he said. *Do not dissemble. I know you find this place unappealing, as do I, and now the threat of infection only adds to its deficiencies. But, in any case, if you will not be guided by my desire in this, I might have thought a concern for your own health might be uppermost in your mind at this time.*

How could he know, when I was far from certain myself? Was there some sign that he had discerned that I had not?

In any case, I immediately conceded to his proposal and he departed the room, apparently mollified. Instead of returning to my book, though, I gazed out at the river, the colour of polished lead on this dull day. I never used to be one for brooding but I had not long to sit idle before I was roused by John's return.

Why do you yet sit here? he asked.

I had assumed we would pass the night here before departing for Dumbuck in the morning but no, John said, he had no intention of dining here and the horses had already been summoned.

At this hour? I asked. The light was fading, as it did so early now, with perhaps the promise of snow in the rapidly-darkening sky. *Cook is already preparing dinner. Might it not be better to wait until the morning, Johnny dear? I am rather tired, and the weather so inauspicious.*

We are leaving this evening and that is an end to it, damn you! John said. *There is no need to tarry in this place another night.*

So I found myself in my room, as Jane gathered up my night things into a small valise. The rest of my belongings were to be packed and sent on tomorrow by the Glenarbuck housekeeper because Jane was to accompany us back to Dumbuck. I writhed inwardly at the thought she might detect my distress as she buttoned my gloves, her strong, warm fingers against my chill wrist. More than anything, I craved a cup of sweet tea and a morsel of bread to quell my delicate stomach but Jane brought my coat and hat and I submitted to her preparations like a child.

Despite my muffler and the blanket Jane threw over my knees in the carriage, the bitter cold penetrated everything; my feet were frozen inside my too-thin boots, my nose and ears throbbed painfully. John, however, seemed to experience no discomfort, even lowering the carriage window at one point to smoke a cigar – at which point the cold air was the only thing that kept a sudden faintness at bay.

Opposite me, Jane's face was impassive, her ungloved hands resting lightly on top of my valise that she held on her lap, as if the cold and our sudden departure meant nothing to her at all. The only apparent concession to the weather was that she rode inside with us, instead of on the box beside the driver. I wondered, then, at a life like hers. I had had no more say in the events of the past few hours than she did but she looked as though she could voyage any distance at a moment's notice without fear or doubt as to her destination. Perhaps, I thought, she has friends back at Dumbuck so that she welcomes our unexpected return.

Our progress was slow due to black ice already present on some of the more treacherous turns in the road and the horses became tentative, blowing out frozen clouds of breath and shaking their heads. At times they needed to be whipped to make them move at all, and the sound of each stroke carried so clearly in the raw air that I flinched as if my own flesh felt the sting.

When we finally reached Dumbuck, the house was already in darkness, signalling that all within had retired. It occurred to me that perhaps we had not been expected tonight at all, that John had sent no word, so impulsive was his plan to escape Glenarbuck. Only Colonel and Mrs Geils, together with Isabella, were currently in residence and since the old people had both been a little frail of late, it was not surprising that no one had been inclined to sit up on an evening such as this.

John, still in a dark mood and muttering imprecations, leapt from the carriage and rapped sharply on the door with his stick after ascertaining that it had been locked for the night. In the time it took me, with Jane's assistance, to step down – my limbs clumsy with cold and sick tiredness – he had rapped again, his curses growing louder, when a faint light appeared through the fanlight and we heard the sound of bolts being slowly drawn back inside.

When the heavy door opened, though, we saw not Crawford the footman but the smallest slip of a girl, her braided hair dishevelled and wearing only a thin nightdress, with not so much as a stocking on her white feet.

Well, who is this? John said, his ill-humour seeming to evaporate. *What a pleasant surprise on a cold evening to be greeted by a nice naked little thing like this! What a sweet little duck you are – how I should like to warm you up, darling!* And I watched in horror as he stretched out his hands towards her, motioning vigorously. The girl, all the while, held her candle unsteadily and never took her eyes, opened wide in alarm, from John's face, nor did she speak a word. He laughed at her fear like it was the merriest joke but did not move to cross the threshold, meaning that the little maid, who cannot have been more than ten or eleven, had to remain shivering in her station while I was left lingering outside in the frozen night, with Jane behind me.

So I stepped forward, grasping John's arm to force him to turn around to face me, and before I knew what I had done, struck him full across the cheek.

Run away to bed now, dear, I said to the frightened girl, taking the candle from her gently. *Bring my bag, Jane, and show me the way.*

Jane McPhee

Dumbuck House
Dunbartonshire
November 1838

When I first told you about your guidwife's clean clouts you looked proud as a cock on a midden, and grabbed for me like you would couch me down right there in the close of that dreich place Glenarbuck. And I felt the blood come into my face, that queer way it does that I half-like, even though I know you are a skellum.

But you have not sent for me since our return to Dumbuck. Shall I knock on the smoking-room door tonight when the others are all abed? J.

Frances

Dumbuck House
Dunbartonshire
December 1838-January 1839

Jane has just brought a book to me, left by the tiresome Reverend. At least being confined to bed means I am spared another protracted conversation with him; it is like taking tea with an almanack in human form. The book is Sir Walter Scott's *The Antiquary*, as if I had not devoured a steady diet of his novels from a very young age, encouraged by dear Miss Mitford, who held him before me as the pinnacle of literary achievement, alongside Miss Austen of course.

It is not books I want but Mother. Such a bitter blow to receive her letter saying that Dr Bulley has strongly advised against a journey north at this time of year. It is true the weather has been most foul of late; I wonder that Reverend Jaffray ventured forth at all today. I suppose he is a kindly soul, after all.

Seeing the book, though, Miss Mitford's favourite, has brought to mind such a strong recollection of the little authoress, one day at Farley Hill Court. I was perhaps twelve because I recall sitting eye to eye with the dear lady, not at all a literary lion in stature. She had called me over as I loitered in the drawing room while she and Mother conversed in the China Closet, probably to ask about my reading as she often did, and I no doubt replied with my latest enthusiasm – Mrs Radcliffe perhaps, or Miss Porter. What I remember vividly, however, is that, after listening to me, she turned to Mother and said, *Fanny is such a perfect pattern of childish simplicity, silliness and mischief, attributes that provide the very best foundations for a clever woman!*

Such praise from Miss Mitford, a demonstrably clever woman herself, was very gratifying, even if I wondered at the *silliness* she identified in me, but I knew that Miss Mitford shared Mother's views on my upbringing. They both held that girls were not to be kept quietly indoors, nor over-burdened with tedious feminine accomplishments, but instead permitted to read and speak and fancy as they desired. She had always encouraged my love of nature, too, telling me all about the rambles she took with her beloved little dogs around Three Mile Cross. *I cannot understand how anyone can live in a town*, Miss Mitford often said, even though she returned from her occasional visits to London full of wonderful stories of people and doings there.

So I set great store by Miss Mitford's pronouncement and from then on paid close attention for signs of emergent cleverness, wishing I might hurry up and be clever at once! But I certainly do not feel like a clever woman now, sick at heart and beset with a lassitude that will not lift. Dr Reid has advised bed rest until I feel stronger but each day I seem only weaker and more bilious, which in turn clouds my mind so that I feel quite unable to turn my thoughts to deeper things. It is all I can do to rise for dinner in the evenings, where the banter and horseplay of the family quite grates upon me.

Dumbuck is not at all like it was in the summer. Is it myself or this place that has changed? To find myself a person of *violence* – striking my own husband, and in front of servants! Strangely, though, John never rebuked me, nor spoke of it at all. That first night back here I had feigned sleep when he came to our bed and he left me undisturbed so that, the next morning, I almost wondered if I had dreamed it all. Never in my life before had I struck another person in anger! To think that I have feared at times that John might strike *me*, when it was *I* who struck the first blow. (I do not count what occurs between the two of us at night. I must cling to the belief that it is not harm that John wishes to inflict then; rather it must be something amiss with me that it upsets me so.)

Indeed, John has been in much better spirits than he had ever seemed at Glenarbuck since returning to his family, and they evidently delight in him being among them again, too. But nobody's delight seems to extend to *me*. Or rather, it is not that anyone is unkind but simply that they overlook me. The younger members of the family share their private jokes without me, leaving me to the Colonel's interminable stories while Mrs Colonel – Mammy, I must call her, John says – sits quiet as a mouse much of the time. I wonder if she is not a little deaf, or whether it simply suits her not to heed too closely what goes on around her.

For instance, it turns out that there is *more* to the household than I thought. There are two ladies, the Misses Margaret and Hannah Geils, who live in an upper, secluded part of this rabbit warren of a house. They were away from Dumbuck during our summer visit, but strangely no one so much as mentioned them to Mother and me then. It was only since taking up residence here that I have sighted them – very dark ladies, quite dusky complexions in fact – and it transpires that they are *natural daughters* of Colonel Geils, from the sub-continent! How can this be? The two, it seems, have been raised as part of the family from a young age, travelling the world with them, ever since the Colonel left India. I am quite unsettled by them, I confess. While I have never left the shores of these British Isles, I almost feel that I am now living in a foreign land, so strange is this place.

How I wish Mother were here.

* * *

John has insisted we move from our chamber upstairs to one on the ground floor which is larger, with a smaller room attached that he may use as a dressing room. He says it will be to the greater convenience of us both now that we are to make our home here; for me, as my health confines me much to bed, and for him, because his dressing room also connects with the office (by a queer little passage between the walls) that is called by all the smoking room. But a bedroom on the ground floor! It is quite unseemly and not in any sense congenial to me, whatever John says. I am sure it is damper than the upstairs rooms, as well.

Such noise, too, from the smoking room when the men gather in the evening, not to mention the pungent smell of tobacco. Worst of all, when bad weather prevents the Geils men from entering that room through a side door that opens directly into the forecourt, they must pass through our *bedchamber*, there being no other door that gives access from the smoking room to the ground-floor rooms or passages. What a house! How have changes and renovations not been made to better accommodate this large family over the years? I cannot think how Mrs Colonel Geils has borne it for so long, even if that resilient lady once lived in a primitive cottage in Van Diemen's Land and has passed who knows how many weeks in cramped ship's cabins voyaging from one posting to another with her husband.

I know I could tolerate things better if I were more myself, though. Never have I felt so weak, never so neglectful of food. Christmas came and went almost unnoticed from my sick bed, looking out from the low window into the flagged forecourt where the snow piled ever higher. I have rallied a little, though, and am in hopes of joining in the festivities of Hogmanay tomorrow. The house is filled with the bracing scent of juniper branches and there is a plan for us all to ride into Dumbarton to observe the children of the town at play (*guising* they call it) in the afternoon, before a large party is to gather here in the evening.

* * *

Alas, we woke today to reports of snow-blocked roads, ending all our plans for Hogmanay. Of most concern was the first-footing ceremony, a thing I had not heard of before. It has been explained to me that the first to cross the threshold after midnight is said to bring all the luck, good or bad, that will fall on a household for the year to come. There are so many rules about the kind of first-footer who will bring good luck – he must be dark, and bring the right kind of gifts, including a piece of coal to put on the fire. It goes without saying that he must be a man, too! Other guests usually follow the first-footer's entrance, sparking a night of song and revelry. But with no possibility of guests this Hogmanay, Bella proposed an unconventional alternative: *Why should John not be the first-footer?* she said. *He has until very recently been living elsewhere, and is practically a stranger in his new role as a married man!*

At first, objections were raised, not least by John himself, who feared to be the inadvertent cause of bad luck, he said. But with the prospect of disappointing the entire household – the servants and even the outdoor labourers traditionally being included in at least part of the evening's fun – Colonel Geils decided that perhaps the rules could be stretched under such exceptional circumstances, so that his son's new wife could celebrate her first Hogmanay.

And so, at the stroke of midnight, the Colonel opened the front door – no mean feat, as violent gusts of snow blew into the hallway, guttering the lamps – and John entered without a word, left foot first, bearing a lump of coal and a bottle of whisky, and affecting a dramatic demeanour befitting his role. We all watched in silence as John placed the coal on the already-roaring fire before pouring a glass for his father and proposing a toast. His father then poured a dram for John and, with that, the spell was broken; everyone could speak and raise a glass and sing. John played his part with gusto: the first-footer is entitled to claim a kiss from every woman present and none escaped, even the servants, till the house rang out with laughter and cheers! The two retiring ladies from upstairs came down to join us for a time, but spoke little and soon were gone again, in their quiet way.

Free of my dreary room and buoyed by the warmth and light of the house in revelry, I felt blessed to be surrounded by loving folk who wish me nothing but good. How can I fail to be content with my life here? I am no longer a child in the nursery shut away from the world, but a woman, a *wife*, and soon a mother! The dram I took seemed to bring with it a fairy-like vision of all that this new year promises like a series of tableaux, beginning with the Glasgow ball in a fortnight's time when, splendid in my new green velvet dress, I shall dance a reel or two among the finest society in Scotland!

2.

A false conception

(March 1839–March 1841)

William Buchan, M. D.

Domestic Medicine,
Or,
A Treatise On The Prevention And Cure of Disease,
By Regimen And Simple Medicines:
With Observations On
Sea-Bathing And The Use of the Mineral Waters.
To Which Is Annexed,
A Dispensatory,
For The Use Of Private Practitioners.
(Exeter: J. and B. Williams)

ABORTION, &c.

Every pregnant woman is more or less in danger of abortion. This should be guarded against with the greatest care, as it not only weakens the constitution but renders the woman liable to the same misfortune afterwards. Abortion may happen at any period of pregnancy, but it is most common in the second or third month. If it happens within the first month, it is usually called a false conception.

The common causes of abortion are the death of the child; weakness or relaxation of the mother; great evacuations; violent exercise; raising great weights; reaching too high; jumping, or stepping from an eminence; vomiting; coughing; convulsion fits; blows on the belly; falls; fevers; disagreeable smells; excess of blood;

indolence; high living or the contrary; violent passions or affections of the mind, as fear, grief, &c.

The signs of approaching abortion are pain in the loins, or about the bottom of the belly; a dull heavy pain in the inside of the thighs; a slight degree of coldness, or shivering; sickness; palpitation of the heart; the breasts become flat and soft; the belly falls; and there is a discharge of blood or watery humours from the womb.

To prevent abortion, we would advise women of a weak or relaxed habit to use solid food, avoiding great quantities of tea, and other weak and watery liquors; to rise early and go soon to bed; to shun damp houses; to take frequent exercise in the open air, but to avoid fatigue; and never to go abroad in damp foggy weather, if they can help it. Women of a full habit ought to use a spare diet, avoiding strong liquors, and everything that may tend to heat the body, or increase the quantity of blood. Their diet should be of an opening nature, consisting principally of vegetable substances. Every woman with child ought to be kept cheerful and easy in her mind. Her appetites, even though depraved, ought to be indulged as far as prudence will permit.

When any signs of abortion appear, the woman ought to be laid in bed on a mattress, with her head low. She should be kept quiet, and her mind soothed and comforted. She ought not to be kept too hot, nor to take anything of a heating nature. Her food should consist of broths, rice and milk, jellies, gruels made of oatmeal, and the like, all of which ought to be taken cold.

If she be able to bear it, she should lose at least half a pound of blood from the arm. Her drink ought to be barley-water sharpened with the juice of lemon; or she may take half a drachm of powdered nitre, in a cup of water-gruel, every five or six hours. If the woman be seized with a violent looseness, she ought to drink the decoction of calcined hartshorn prepared. If she be affected with vomiting, let her take frequently two tablespoonsful of the saline mixture. In general, opiates are of service; but they should always be given with caution.

Though we recommend due care for preventing abortion, we would not be understood as restraining pregnant women from their usual exercise. This would generally operate the quite contrary way. Want of exercise not only relaxes the body, but induces a plethora, or too great a fullness of the vessels, which are the two principal causes of abortion. There are, however, some women of so delicate a texture, that it is necessary for them to avoid almost every kind of exercise during the whole period of pregnancy.

Where abortion cannot be prevented, the next indication is to conduct the patient safely through the process, by directing our immediate attention to the haemorrhage; to check which, bleeding is resorted to by some practitioners; but, unless the vessels be above their natural force and strength of action, it is not likely to be of any service. Astringent injections, composed of alum, oak bark, or sulphate of zinc, and cold applications to the loins, &c., are often employed in floodings; and where the haemorrhage is slight, these immediately will prove beneficial; but in floodings without any remission, they do not appear calculated to afford much relief. In such cases it will be best to trust to the formation of a coagulum: enjoining rest, giving an anodyne at bed-time, and keeping the bowels open by some gentle aperient.

As soon, however, as the haemorrhage has stopped, give a dose of castor oil in order to prevent any bad effects from the action of these remedies on the coats of the stomach and intestines. The application of cloths dipped in cold water to the back and external parts will have a much better effect than internal astringents, and consequently ought never to be neglected. The introduction of a piece of smooth ice into the vagina has often a very speedy effect in arresting the haemorrhage. A snowball wrapt in a bit of soft linen will have the same effect; but neither of these should be continued so long as to cause pain.

Frances

Dumbuck House
Dunbartonshire
March 1839

It vexes me to be beholden to others about the slightest thing. Dr Reid has forbidden me to walk out while the weather continues foul and John enforces the medical man's instructions to the letter. Nobody consults me, minds me. It is as if I have never left my sick bed, as if I am as invisible as a wraith at the dining table or in the drawing room.

This afternoon, John has driven away in a temper after I had asked to accompany him, a request he said showed how childishly thoughtless I was, and the burden my ill-health has imposed on him and the whole household. If it were not so unfair to charge me so, it would be amusing, given that today there were none but him about the house in any case. The Colonel, Mrs Geils and Bella have gone to visit their Geilston kin overnight, Tom has taken Pitt to Glasgow to outfit him before his commissioning, and the mysterious Misses Geils are cloistered upstairs as usual.

It seems a dream now to recall that after the perilous Hogmanay storm was followed by an extended mild spell in January, all had been well in every way. With the approval of Dr Reid, I travelled with John, Pitt, Tom and Isabella to Glasgow, where we attended a number of receptions in addition to the Ball – itself quite different from English balls, with the inclusion of Scottish dances and music, and where I was introduced to an array of friendly people of spirited disposition and hospitable manners so that my heart quite warmed to them after the briefest of acquaintance. To be among kindly-inclined people, and conversation about matters other than hunting and regiments and the parish of Dumbarton – what joy! I hope I may soon return to that lively city.

As diverting as the delights of Glasgow were, though, they were almost surpassed by the excursions that John and I enjoyed after we returned home again and my good health continued. Just as in the summer when first we met, John seemed at his ease in taking me out, by cart or on foot, to his favourite haunts around the countryside, as the weather continued to be unseasonably benign. With the ceasing of his nightly attentions to me due to my condition, his manner became much more like that of a companion and I thought that perhaps if this was the way our marriage was to go from now on, there might be far worse fates. One crisp, bright day I had even walked with him to the top of Lang Craigs, with Loch Lomond stretched before us on one side while on the other lay the noble River Clyde like an inland sea. Stopping there to eat a simple meal of cheese and oat cakes on our laps, it was as if we were the sole inhabitants of some enchanted, elevated island, surrounded by ancient trees and rugged moorland.

Then came my mishap, unforeseen, without the slightest foreshadowing of danger, and once more the dreary bedchamber entombed me. Long, solitary days with only the nurse sent by Dr Reid for company. I scarcely saw John at all. Yet I was made to feel, somehow, that my illness was an imposition. In the evenings, as the revelry in the smoking room rose ever louder, I wondered what I had done to deserve this miserable isolation.

When he was not neglecting me, John was peevish, taking petty offence at anything so that my nerves frayed and I never seemed to find the right words on the rare occasion he came to sit with me (on his mother's insistence, I suspect). Whatever I said seemed to provoke him until I wept from sheer frustration. I have never before been a weeping, whining woman. Perhaps I should not marvel at John's desire to flee from me, as he has done today. I repel *myself* with my own misery.

Sometimes of late, I have felt so forsaken that I have sought sympathy from Mrs Colonel, or even Bella, although I well know that their affections are wholly with John, that in their eyes he can do no wrong. They hear me out when I say that I believe a husband should show greater charity towards his wife at such a time, but there is no true warmth in their response, no acknowledgement of the grounds of my grievance. Mrs Colonel will mildly say something about the need to protect my health so that my spirits may improve, but I see in Bella's eye a kind of contempt that almost makes me afraid for my state of mind. I must surely be imagining it, her antipathy, when I have done nothing against her, just as my growing discomfort around Jane McPhee must be fanciful. Has not Jane done more for me than anyone else in this household, since first she was brought to me at Farley Hill? But she has not been by me since my mishap, when the unfamiliar and rather forbidding nurse became my sole attendant until dear Betty, a godsend if ever there was one, commenced service at Dumbuck. Since then, if ever I do catch sight of Jane about the house it seems to me that her looks are cold, as if she too bears me ill-will.

But perhaps, as I say, all this is merely my fancy. I am plagued by dark imaginings so that sometimes I can't be sure if I dream or wake. Last night, for instance, taking my early retirement at John's urging, I heard a woman's laugh in the smoking room beside our chamber, but I knew that all the family remained in the drawing room and there was not the usual stench of pipe and cheroots that seeps into our chamber when the men are in the smoking room. The walls in this house are a feeble barrier and no door ever safely closed.

That laugh, a *woman's* laugh I could swear, stays with me still, though. I know it was not Bella's, and certainly not Mrs Colonel's, who dozes by the fire each night until she retires. Nor could it possibly be Margaret or Hannah's, as they keep to their own upper quarters and are of such subdued temperament that I cannot imagine such merriment emanating from either of them. In any case, no woman of the family has ever set foot in the smoking room, I believe.

John tells me that I must put my *setback* behind me; that it is indulgent to dwell on it. And I have tried to do so, even tolerating his renewed advances at night, despite the pain, until he rebukes me for grimacing *like a damned devil*. Afterwards, I take an anodyne to bring sleep but it prompts alarming dreams of being plunged in ice, paralysed and breathless. On such nights, it is almost a mercy when John shakes me awake, complaining that my breathing is so loud he cannot sleep, and that I am selfish to give no thought to his comfort.

* * *

I remained at the drawing-room window after John passed out of sight. This unprepossessing house faces directly on to the main road, with the Clyde beyond, while behind rises up Dumbuck Hill, that imposing eminence of rock and forest. I had wanted to scale the hill from the first time I stepped down from the carriage with Mother, it draws one so.

One fine day last summer, John had led me up the most accessible route to the top of the hill and the outlook did not disappoint, although I wish I had known then about the Rhymer's Cave that the Reverend has since talked of. As a child, I was enchanted by the ballad of Thomas the Rhymer, who was spirited away by the Queen of Elfland for seven years, *Thro weel or wae as must chance to be*. I recall puzzling over whether the bewitching Elf Queen meant good or ill to Sir Thomas, and whether the delights of Elfland would outweigh being outcast from home for so long.

But on that summer's day with John atop Dumbuck Hill, banishment could not have been further from my mind. We had looked down on Dumbuck House, dwarfed among its outbuildings like chicks clustered around a black-and-white hen, and the expanse of the busy Clyde glinted golden while overhead a skylark trilled his joyous song.

* * *

Carriage wheels on the puddle-rutted road. For a moment I thought that John had relented, returning for me after all, but then an unfamiliar trap drew up and a great-coated Reverend Jaffray emerged into the splashing rain. He turned back to offer a hand to someone else to descend – his wife.

He had never brought Mrs Jaffray on a visit before and I had only exchanged formalities with her after Sunday services, and not even that since my mishap has kept me at home. She has always given the impression, though, of being a woman of energy and good humour. As the daughter of one of the richest men in Dumbarton – a fact I had been astonished to learn, after meeting the Reverend – Mrs Jaffray might have some understanding of my plight, might even become an ally or confidante of sorts, in time. But I am racing far ahead of myself. At least her presence today might divert the Reverend from discoursing about the geology of Dumbarton or, worse, the mysteries of a beneficent Providence.

Betty, summoned from servants' dinner by the bell at the front door, ushered the Jaffrays into the drawing room.

Good afternoon, Mrs Geils, the Reverend said, *may I present my wife, Elizabeth?* He turned to his wife who swept past him, frankly extending a hand to grasp mine.

My dear, she said as she did so, *forgive our untimely visit – we took the liberty of leaving town a little before the appointed time for calls, due to a break in this terrible weather that we feared might not last. As has turned out to be the case, alas.* The lady pushed a rain-dampened bonnet ribbon back from her cheek with a merry laugh. *I am sorry, too, not to have visited long before now*, she went on. *I can only plead the season and its inevitable toll on the health of our family.* Her hand was firm in mine as she held my eye, but there was a kindness in both her tone and gesture that was almost more than I could bear in my current state. I bowed my head in return and gestured for her to sit, not trusting myself to speak.

She and her husband sat side by side on a chaise opposite me and the Reverend began to extemporise on the weather of the week past, comparing it to that of exactly a year ago based on the evidence of his private weather diary, which led him to offer a projection of the kind of spring we might expect, God willing.

While her husband spoke, Mrs Jaffray regarded him indulgently, but her upright posture and bright eye told me I was correct in my presumption that she was no milksop of a parson's wife. She seemed, too, to have the tempering effect on her husband's discourse that I had hoped; he soon stopped speaking and turned to his wife, as if acknowledging her right to share in the conversation, not a characteristic I had observed in him on previous occasions.

I am pleased to hear better news of your health, Mrs Geils, she said, with a slight inclination of her head towards her husband as if to thank him for his brevity.

Thank you, yes, I said, *I am much stronger.*

Is there anything you require in Dumbarton that we could send out for you? she continued. *I'm sure your family is taking all provision for you, of course, but perhaps a book or two from James's library? James tells me you are a great reader and this weather certainly lends itself to such an occupation. I fear it must have been a much crueller winter than you are accustomed to – in Berkshire, I believe?*

Yes, that's correct, I said. *Winters tend to be rather damp there, but without the excitement of the tempests and snow drifts we have had here.*

I did not want to talk of the weather, the Reverend already having done more than enough of that, but I could think of nothing else to say. Perhaps it was true that I was an ungrateful, selfish wretch – as John was wont to accuse me of late – unable to rouse myself to consider my guests, who had undertaken a journey from town when there was much to keep them there, no doubt. My mind was a painful blank, pierced only by self-reproach, yet I felt that if I could but speak to Mrs Jaffray alone, I might shake off this awkward reticence.

May I call for tea? I asked, making an effort to rally. Even though I knew it was early, the absence of the family emboldened me to alter the household's daily routine.

Thank you, that would be most kind, the Reverend replied, *but first perhaps I might speak to the servants? I gathered from the lassie that they are all still assembled at their dinner. I can pass on your request for tea directly myself, and I have some tracts that I want to leave with them.* He patted his pockets as he rose from his seat.

Reverend Jaffray had never expressed an interest in the servants' souls on his previous visits, seeming content to confine his concerns to the sitting room – although I had heard him, on one occasion, encouraging the Colonel to consider instituting family prayers for the household – and something in his speech seemed a little rehearsed so that I wondered if he and his wife had agreed on a plan before their arrival, to leave her alone with me for a time.

In any case he slipped away and Mrs Jaffray spoke again immediately. *I did not want to speak of it in front of the Reverend*, she said, *for all that James is a doting father who feels things most keenly and from whom I have never had any secrets about my own health. But I wanted to tell you how heartsick I was to hear of your news, my dear.*

I felt the tears well, then, and could only nod, melted by sympathy from a woman I knew to be mother to a large family.

Truth be told, I was touched as soon as I heard your name, she went on. *We lost a wee lassie named Frances, three years ago this winter. She was our youngest. We lost two others when they were just weans too, but Frances was a hard, hard loss to bear – just three months old, and such a bonnie thing. We are blessed to have another lass, though, and four strong laddies. Blessed, indeed. But I wanted to tell you of our Frances so that you might know that you are not alone in your pain. I don't hold with those who talk of "a false conception" for a loss like yours. Heartless talk, indeed.*

I could only nod again, my tears falling freely.

In our losses, James shared my sorrow. And my own kin were near to offer comfort, too. Mrs Jaffray paused then and her hint that I might be uncomforted in this house brought a stronger throb of affection towards this stranger, reaching out to an ignorant young Englishwoman who had imagined a happy life here based on little more than a brief summer visit and a skylark's song.

The Reverend then returned, accompanying Betty bearing the tea tray which she placed on a table close by me. Somehow, so cosy were we three over our tea that I was almost glad that John had deserted me that afternoon. My dark mood dissipated in the company of Mrs Jaffray and I eagerly accepted the good lady's invitation to tea at the manse next week, if John and Doctor Reid will allow me to venture as far by then.

Rev. James Jaffray

The Manse
Dumbarton
June 1839

Throngs of visitors have descended on Dumbarton, undeterred by the indifferent summer weather, to fill the inns on their way to Loch Lomond and its new attraction in the form of steamboat tours. Elizabeth has hit upon a fine plan to take the two English ladies of Dumbuck House on just such an excursion, to include an overnight stay in Balloch, now that Mrs Geils at last has the comfort of a visit from her mother.

My goodwife had intended to accompany me to Dumbuck House today to discuss final arrangements for the excursion in a week's time, Lord willing, but in the end I made my way alone. Elizabeth confessed to an enervation that has left her rather wan and listless, poor woman, and judged it best to remain at home. Nevertheless, she impressed on me to assure the ladies of her delight at the prospect of our pleasure trip.

It may have been a lingering sense of concern for my wife, so unusual was it to see her in a recumbent position during the day, that coloured my perception of the prevailing mood at Dumbuck House, but all did not seem harmonious on my arrival. I found Mrs Colonel Geils and Miss Isabella together with the two English ladies in the drawing room – all the men of the household being absent, as was frequently the case on my visits – and there was an air in the room like a gathering thunderhead, I would have said, although I am not usually given to fanciful constructions of that kind. Mrs Frances (as my wife refers to her, and I find myself following her lead, on the strength of our growing acquaintance) looked about from face to face with some vexation and Miss Isabella was quite flushed, while the two older ladies each frowned over the work occupying their hands.

I did my best, then, to distract them all with my news of the parish and was rewarded with a more temperate mood beginning to prevail. Mrs Colonel Geils nodded affably as I talked but I suspect that venerable lady does not hear so well as she did in former times because Miss Isabella sometimes needed to prompt her mother to reply to my inquiries.

I then turned my attention to Mrs Frances and Mrs Dickinson, conveying all the details of our excursion as instructed by my wife, as well as expatiating a little on the topography and vegetation of Loch Lomond and its environs that I surmised would be of great interest to the Englishwomen.

The rest of my visit passed pleasantly enough, apart from an awkward moment during tea. Mrs Dickinson held up the napkin she had placed in her lap, examining its frayed edge rather closely, causing Mrs Frances to reach out a hand so that her mother lowered her napkin again.

When, on my return home, I gave a report of my visit to Elizabeth she shook her head, detecting in my account evidence that Mrs Dickinson was not fully at ease with her daughter's new home and situation. *I wonder what might come of this visit?* she said, with an uncharacteristic frown. But as Elizabeth was still feeling a little feverish – her hand was warm and moist in mine when I took it – I put her suspicions down to a more clouded state of mind than was customary with her and thought nothing more of it. She will think differently in the morning, no doubt, after a good night's rest has dispelled her fatigue. I am certain next week's journey will restore the colour to her cheeks, as well as the good spirits of the ladies of Dumbuck too.

Jane McPhee

Dumbuck House
Dunbartonshire
October 1839

The kitchen claver is that your guidwife is to have a doon-lyin' before the spring. You have said nothing aboot it so I asked Betty, that mim quean, and she frooned like she was puir as the gowans in the haugh and couldna speak of such things. That Betty canna be trusted, maister. She is not loyal to you, but only to *her*, bi' fegs!

It is a week and more syne you nichted me. I will wait in the close, by the smoking room door, after I have seen Miss Isabella to her bed. J.

Mary Geils

Dumbuck House
Dunbartonshire
October 1839

20th October

My dear Mrs Dickinson,

I am sure my letter will distress you very much, and the only consolation I can give is to assure you that dear Fanny feels quite well today. She bids me to tell you so.

She had been in such good health and spirits of late but yesterday she was discovered unwell in her room and we sent for Dr Reid, that we might seek his advice. Upon his arrival, it became clear that an unfortunate occurrence had taken place.

Fanny really was wonderfully good about it all, not seeming to suffer so much as she did on the former occasion, but I am ashamed to say that I could not conceal the distress that I felt.

I need only add that our most affectionate regards are always with you, dear friend. The Colonel and Isabella also request their love to you, as does John of course.

Believe me,
Always affectionately yours,
Mary Geils

Frances

Dumbuck House
Dunbartonshire
October 1839

27th October

My dearest Mama,

As I am sure you would rather receive a short letter from me than none at all, I am determined to write you a few lines to assure you how much better I am. Except for some pains and weakness in my back I feel quite well. I think if I go on as well as at present, I will have got over this mishap very fairly indeed. With the laudanum, I do not suffer so much as you might fear.

The Doctor has assured me I shall in time be the mother of a dozen children! But I trust (however sorry I am for the mishap) to have a little liberty now, as really my health and spirits require it. The most agreeable place becomes a prison when one is long confined and I look forward with great pleasure to accompanying my dearest John again in all his walks and rides – I am sure wherever he is I must be happy. My course is simple, my end and aim very plain: to be able to please my husband and by making him happy to be so myself.

I had not intended writing so much and must really beg your forgiveness for this horrid scrawl. I will conclude, hoping you are quite well, and believe me, my dearest Mama,

Your most attached child,
Frances Geils

Catherine Dickinson

Farley Hill Court
Berkshire
October 1839

30th October

My dearest child,

I am delighted to receive a letter from your own hand and to learn that your recovery continues so well. How cheerful you sound! A mother must always keenly feel her child's situation and, after my summer visit to Dumbuck, you know the concerns I have held for you, even more so following the sad and untimely loss of dear Mrs Jaffray, your only true friend in those parts. And, since then, your own misfortune once more. I cannot help but fear that the various unpropitious circumstances at Dumbuck may have contributed to your mishap.

I long to see you, my child, and will brook no opposition to travelling north once more. I wanted to set out the moment I received Mary's letter but worried it might seem intemperate. It was foolish of me not to trust my own judgement on this matter, I now see. I have determined – after sober reflection – that my place is with you. I will write again from the road.

Ever your affectionate mother,
Catherine Dickinson

Rev. James Jaffray

The Manse
Dumbarton
November 1839

It has ever been a rule of mine not to meddle with private affairs, saving only as might come before the Session from time to time. On the first sabbath that Mrs Dickinson was back at Dumbuck House, however, I had taken as the text for my sermon: *He will wipe every tear from their eyes. There will be no more death or mourning or crying or pain, for the old order of things has passed away.* Looking out from the pulpit, I noticed that my words brought a moisture to the eye of the English lady, the only member of the Dumbuck household in attendance that day.

I have been turning to texts of this nature ever since my Elizabeth fell into the sleep that all must sleep – may the rest of the blessed be her portion! – and had felt the bittersweet consolation of a sombre spirit moving in the congregation that matched my own. The elders have counselled me concerning the need for a greater variety of topics in my sermons, but when I see so many weary and worn by the strife and tribulation of this fallen realm, I take heart that my words might provide healing balm until such time as we are all awakened to partake of the everlasting banquet of the saints in glory. *Amen.*

I reproach myself that I have not yet visited Dumbuck House to offer comfort to Mrs Frances in her latest travail, but some troubling illness of my youngest bairn has kept me close to home. Wee Louisa feels her mother's loss keenly, while the older lads manfully bear their dule. *The Lord is nigh unto them that are of a broken heart,* I remind my lassie many a time through the long nights, stroking her hair that is the very image of her mother's copper tresses.

So, on the sabbath, as I say, I approached Mrs Dickinson at the conclusion of the service to welcome her back to the north and express some words of comfort and it was then the floodgates opened, releasing a torrent of allegations and recriminations from the usually mild lady, directed towards the family at Dumbuck and her daughter's husband in particular.

Since her arrival some five days ago, she reported, she had heard Mr Geils quarrelling with his wife in the strongest terms, sometimes prolonged into the night; the situation of the couple's chamber on the ground floor and the close quarters of the house in general ensuring that his words and her tears might be clearly heard. *My daughter is broken-hearted, Reverend, and I never knew her do anything to blame,* Mrs Dickinson said. *The fault is all on his part, yet she repeatedly entreats him to forgive her!*

As a result, the lady said she felt herself to be an unwelcome visitor in the house and saw no other course of action than that Mrs Frances should accompany her back to Berkshire. To hear Mrs Dickinson, Dumbuck House offers none of the true comforts of a home, although I believe the English lady's maternal feelings might unduly prejudice her in this regard. Mr Geils, as might be expected, has refused to entertain the suggestion that his wife leave his father's roof, taking offence at Mrs Dickinson's concern for her daughter's welfare, so that there appears to be now a deep bitterness between son and mother-in-law.

Well, here was a state of affairs and, as so often, I wished that I could seek Elizabeth's counsel. Had my wife not foreseen discord at Dumbuck House? This report of Mrs Dickinson suggested that, indeed, the old Adam was in the ascendancy there. I had witnessed, once or twice, a profane tone of conversation amongst the younger Dumbuck men, none of them regular at kirk, but these were military folk, after all, hardened by generations of service in tropical climes.

In due course, would not the sweet influence of wives bring about a greater mellowing of word and deed in these young men? Does not the presence of a helpmeet soothe the roughest of us? The sins of the father – for which some amends had been made in providing a home for Miss Margaret and Miss Hannah Geils, persons of the greatest retirement at Dumbuck – need not be repeated by the sons.

The Lord does not change but the ways of man wax and wane, I told Mrs Dickinson, assuring her I would visit her daughter at my earliest opportunity. I further undertook to write a note to Lieutenant Geils proffering counsel during the difficult time resulting from his wife's recurring mishaps. I might have wished that the English lady had looked rather more comforted after our conversation, but a mother's concern, I reminded myself, knows no bounds, and with that my thoughts returned to my wee Louisa, and to her mother's empty chair by the hearth. *It is enough; stay now thine hand, Lord,* I prayed in my heart, as I made my way back to the manse.

Frances

Dumbuck House
Dunbartonshire
December 1839

The scene before Mother's departure was frightful, with John declaring that he now knew the source of his d—d wife's temper and that he would be d—d if he would allow his wife to return to the parental home from which it had sprung!

If it is the case that your daughter has not been provided for, he went on, *the blame lies with you as her mother—it was* your *duty to equip her with linens and suchlike before her marriage, Madam.*

Mother would not let that be, and was quite flushed with anger – dear, sweet Mother, who has never raised her voice even to a servant! She tried to say all the things she had observed that caused me misery, and that she feared had brought such serious consequences for my health, although I dearly wish she had not.

Take care, Mrs Dickinson, John then said – although he had been wont to call her *Mother* since the first days of our engagement – *I attribute almost every unhappy hour since my marriage to* you *and if you do not take care of your conduct you shall never see your daughter again!*

I truly feared what might then transpire and myself urged Mother to leave, promising her that all would be well if she would but go, but she wept and said she would never desert me and that I must accompany her home.

Home! I can barely allow myself to think of Farley Hill, to imagine approaching the dear old house at this time of year, when the scarlet berries on the roadside hawthorn catch the last, low rays of the sun, and the smoke from burning leaves mingles with mist in the hollows.

In the end, though, mother did not return south but has taken lodgings in Helensburgh, ten miles or so from here, and quite a congenial town from what I have heard. She would not leave me entirely unprotected in Scotland, she said, no matter what John might threaten. Mammy has said that Mother may return to us here whenever she wishes, and has written to Mother urging her not to *put so hard a construction on young people's manners*, a rather mild gloss on John's bitter temper!

Mother may now be but a carriage ride away at Helensburgh but I might as well call for a unicorn as a horse and a trap! I am utterly friendless here. I am left to take comfort from Betty, who serves me with more loving kindness than I ever had from Jane McPhee who, by the by, abruptly left Bella's service at Martinmas – almost a year since we had travelled back from Glenarbuck on that frosty night. I must not think of that either; a year of such disappointment and loss.

It was from Betty, too, that I learned more of the fate of dear Mrs Jaffray, on whom I had pinned such hopes of friendship until that sudden fever – that Betty calls an *eago* – took her in the summer. One day I expressed my surprise to Betty that the poor lady had not been laid to rest in her husband's kirkyard but Betty said that the reason she lies instead in her family's burial ground, among the ruins of an ancient chapel adjoining the grand home of the Dixons, is that the finer folk are averse to have their kin buried in Dumbarton churchyard on account of grave robbers! In one case, Betty said, the remains of an elderly woman were stolen, the theft only discovered on disinterring a grave for a new burial. Now, a watch is kept nightly by the men of Dumbarton, turn by turn. In this way, an attempt was foiled when a new grave was found scattered with herring scales, thought to emit a ghostly glow in the dark that would direct the robbers to their target! What *is* this place where I have come to dwell, and where my mother is driven out so cruelly?

Jane McPhee

Dumbarton
March 1840

The byre is a dreich place to wait for you in the rain. A kye watched me in an ourie way, until you came and pushed it away. Your hands were hot on my hurdies, cold as snaw aneath my skirt.

You like me to write like this, you say, for when you are alane and may read it over again. But I lippen nane to take this to you. I shall return anither time to push it under the smoking room door, drookit or not.

I count the weeks till Beltane when I am to return to your service, nae reason now why I may not. Nae living reason at all. J.

Frances

Auchendarroch
Argyllshire
May 1840

Oakfield: in my fancy, I imagined a baronial manor of mullions and stained glass beside a loch, and urged John to act on the recommendation he had received to secure the place for us for a twelvemonth. Surely at Oakfield I might become strong and clear-headed once more – a number of days' travel, by land and water, from Dumbuck!

Doctor Reid shared my faith in the restorative powers of the Highlands – I fear now that no new life will ever spring forth from me under the shadow of Dumbuck Hill – and, with his endorsement, Colonel and Mrs Geils reluctantly became reconciled to our departure. As the drenching rains lingered into April, even John seemed keen to leave his home and I began to doubt whether our darker moments had truly occurred. Could it be that my illnesses – and the stupefying draughts they brought – had disturbed my mind more than I had realised? Could it have been just troubled fantasy that woke me in the night, as though from a kick or a blow? Perhaps I have misinterpreted John's tone as cruel or mocking when he was merely vexed. With my more troubling symptoms subsiding – the fits of weeping, spasms and flow of blood, the disordered digestion – I determined to set aside the laudanum.

I was sorry to learn, though, that Betty was not to accompany us; she was needed at Dumbuck, I was told. Instead, John arranged for Jane McPhee to return to attend me at Oakfield. All the Oakfield staff are included in our lease but John said that he thought I might prefer a familiar face for my lady's maid. Another heartening sign of the return of his concern for me, I trust.

* * *

Leaving Dumbuck, our journey took us to the silent forests and vast lochs of the Trossachs – familiar to me only from Sir Walter Scott's fictional wayfarers. Among those brooding peaks and wild valleys, I could almost believe that I had entered an earlier time of divided loyalties and savage conflict of which I had read, were it not for occasional whitewashed homesteads with neatly-tilled gardens and shaggy cattle grazing.

John seemed unmoved by our journey, never commenting on the landscape, however sublime. It is his homeland, I suppose, but then again it is not quite three years since he left the scorching heat and monsoon rains of India behind – and surely the contrast between these two lands must impress itself on him? John never talks of India, unlike his father who talks of little else. Before we were married, I had once asked John to describe Madras and he merely shrugged and said, *Ah, where to begin? The heat, of course, there's that.* I had waited for him to continue but Pitt had come in with news of a whelping pointer bitch and John had followed him out to the stables without another word on the subject.

I have learned not to ask my husband his reasons for anything; John does not like discourse for its own sake. He is a man of bluntness or silence, with little in between. What I had taken as a pleasing plain-spokenness during our brief courtship now reminds me more and more of the little lord's curtness so that I wonder why it is that some men find it difficult to converse naturally with a lady. Whenever we stopped on our way to Oakfield, John would talk with ease to landlords or ostlers, anyone who might be a reliable source of information about the stock or game in the area. He even seemed to find time for a joke with Jane, if she sat on the box in fine weather while he rode alongside our carriage, but to me he said little. He kept to his own chamber during our travels, too, which I confess I welcomed.

So it was at the end of a stirring, if largely silent, journey, that we finally crossed a swing-bridge over the Crinan Canal and entered the gates of Oakfield, flanked by woodland. The house stood on top of a rise but instead of the soaring stone turrets of my fantasy, it was a modern house of pleasing symmetry, with banks of multi-paned windows running along the length of both storeys. Alighting from the carriage and turning to look away from the house, I saw the sweep of Loch Gilp beyond the canal, where the low tide had exposed dark sand and weed-strewn rocks.

On entering the house, we found assembled to meet us the butler and footman, the cook and kitchen girl, two housemaids, two dairy maids, two grooms, the gamekeeper, the head gardener, the laundress and even the girl under her. *Welcome to Auchendarroch*, Ross the butler said, the first time I heard the local name for this place. He then led me to a panelled sitting room of modest proportions, perhaps a morning room, where a small table was laid for supper and a fire flickered in the grate despite the warm day. Ross moved to draw the curtains but I asked him to stay his hand, captivated by a view I already knew I could never tire of, seeing a glint of silver in the distance, where the water had already begun to draw back into the loch.

John did not accompany me to the sitting room, however. He called Miller, the gamekeeper, to take him out to the grounds, later sending word for me to dine alone as he was detained. So I was served a simple meal of poached salmon and greens with a glass of hock before retiring to my elegant bedroom upstairs, directed by one of the Oakfield maids. I dismissed the girl and did not call for Jane. She had looked *palie*, as they say here, throughout our journey, not her robust self at all, so I sent word with the girl that I would not require attendance and Jane might retire early. I relished a rare opportunity to be alone in this way, that I might look closely at everything about me with none to observe, none to guide me like a child through my evening preparations: the unbuttoning, untying, loosening this, casting off that, and then the putting on again, buttoning and tying. The whole process put me in mind, sometimes, of Cook dressing birds for the table.

As I braided my hair – badly, not with Jane's touch at all – I stood at the window looking down through the trees to the loch holding the light at gloaming. A cuckoo called, despite the hour, from the thickest part of the Oakfield wood.

* * *

During the first peaceful weeks at Oakfield, I toyed with the idea of sending my impressions of this wonderful place to some journal or other. "A Lady's Highland Haven" might not be amiss in *The New Monthly Magazine*, I fancied. Not for the first time, I wished I had some gift for composing poetry, to best capture my new surroundings, but instead I contented myself with playing the rather fine old piano. My fingers began to lose their stiffness with regular practice and I amused myself by learning tunes from a miscellany of old Scottish songs left on the piano, singing them too when I was sure no one was near to hear my mangling of the words, awkward on my English tongue. *O waly, waly up the bank, and waly, waly, doun the brae*, I sang, laughing my way through the lament, in spite of my best efforts. But, even seated at the piano, my eyes would be drawn to the window, again and again, watching flecks of quicksilver on the loch's surface, between the trees, whenever the sun broke through.

Oakfield took its name (in both its English and Gaelic forms) from its ancient oaks, but in its dense woodland were also many larches and birches, sycamore and ash trees. A stream, criss-crossed with several narrow footbridges, ran across the estate before flowing into the canal, and I liked to walk from bank to bank, pausing to listen as draughts of cooler air stirred up by the flowing water set the leaves fluttering. The leafmeal was alive with hopping birds – robins and tits, whitefronts and blackbirds.

By comparison, Farley Hill now seemed a confected landscape where all roughness had been worn smooth, nothing untamed or untouched. I smiled to recall the 'wilderness' there that I had formerly treasured. Here was a more elemental beauty of tree and rock and water. But the wildwood was not my only haunt at Oakfield. The estate also contained an impressive walled garden, a veritable Eden in this remote northern place, under the care of the cantankerous Niven.

Like Sir Walter Scott's Andrew Fairservice, Niven maintained the first gardener's quarrel with women and was at first highly suspicious of my presence amongst his fruit trees and greenhouses. *I hope you'll not aye be crying for apricocks, pears and plums, summer and winter, Madam*, he said one afternoon, when I had praised the bounty I observed, neglecting my sketchbook to watch him at work. I reassured him on that front but, alas, I soon incurred the old man's wrath again, by remarking on how the lively bird song added to the beauty of his garden.

Och, he said, *blackbirds be damned! That's Miller's doing, trapping the gleds and gosshawks so the wee birds have nae fear, raucle as may be with my fruit!*

I had stumbled unwittingly on a spirited dispute between gardener and gamekeeper, so from then on kept my peace when visiting his garden until eventually Niven began to soften towards me. He no longer scowled when I opened the gate to enter, or tutted when I raised a hand to cup a still-green plum, warmed by the sun within the rugged stone walls.

John, meanwhile, spent much of his time with Niven's nemesis, Miller, familiarising himself with the estate and forming plans for shooting parties in due season. I would have far preferred to retain the place to ourselves, undisturbed by guests, but at least here there would be ample accommodation for visitors, and Mother might see her daughter happy in a more gracious home at last. John gave no overt signs, though, of missing his family in this new place, allowing me to indulge in a hope that perhaps someday we might break free of Dumbuck for good.

He began, too, to talk to me far more than he had since we were married. When we met for dinner in the evenings (he did not always return to the house for either luncheon or tea) he would be full of his day's activities, which I enjoyed hearing. Such were the healing powers of Oakfield that just as I became stronger and happier in this new place, so John became more gentle, or at least not so rough or brusque. Nor did he come to me every evening now, keeping a large chamber of his own across the corridor from my own. But sometimes, in our conjugal embrace, I experienced a strange sensation – a fluttering, quivering, that came warmly from deep within – making my heart beat fast, not with fear or faintness but some other feeling for which I had no name. It was like nothing so much as the impulse that rose within me when I stood over the flowing stream, breathing deeply of the earthy woodland, a sense that somehow I had merged with the wildlife flowing through this place.

Isabella Geils

Auchendarroch
Argyllshire
July 1840

I saw a good deal of my brother John and his wife during the first years of their marriage. In my opinion, the behaviour and language of Fanny to my brother was often of a very aggravating kind. She was of a restless spirit and it seemed as if she could not let him alone, whatever he might be about.

Upon my oath it is certainly not the fact that my brother was in the habit of silencing his wife, or objecting to her wishes, or in any unreasonable way imposing his authority over her. On the contrary, he was most forbearing towards her, as I witnessed repeatedly during my visit to Auchendarroch in the summer of 1840, on which visit I was joined by my parents and my brother Pitt.

On the second day after we arrived at Auchendarroch, I entered the breakfast room to hear Fanny say in a petulant tone, *What am I doing, Johnny dear?*

My brother gave no response to his wife, instead wishing me a warm good morning. Not a word to me from Fanny herself, snivelling over her untouched plate. Her mood seemed quite changed from the day of our arrival, when she had been all false smiles and graciousness as she sat at the piano playing *some Highland tunes to welcome you all to our new home*. You would have thought the house was her own possession and we mere poor relations partaking of her bounty. On and on Fanny played that evening, while John said nothing. I was sorry to see that my brother's indulgence in securing this residence for his wife had not led to any lasting improvement of temper – or submission – on her part.

It was just we three at the breakfast table that day, to the best of my recollection. Mother often took a tray in her room and I believe that Father and Pitt were already out at the stables overseeing the horses ahead of the day's excursion to the ruins of a place called Dunadd Fort – all Fanny's idea, of course, thoughtless of depriving the men a day's sport so soon into our visit.

I sat beside her in the carriage later that morning, facing Mother and Father opposite us, and thus had ample opportunity to notice her handkerchief raised repeatedly to her mouth, her frequent sighs. Her letters to Dumbuck had been full of extravagant claims about her health and the restorative life at Auchendarroch but she looked just as palie as ever. I quite envied John and Pitt the freedom of horseback travel and their ease of conversation as they rode alongside us. Such was their natural good humour that they did not seem to begrudge their lost day of shooting at all. Pitt, I recall, was particularly jovial that day, calling out to Jane – our Dumbuck maid who accompanied us, riding on the box with the driver – until the good-natured girl quite joined in with his jesting, her voice carrying back to us inside.

And what did we see when we finally reached the ruins on a rocky outcrop, high above the glen? Merely some scattered stones, partly overgrown with turf and moss, marked with lines or other shapes, barely visible. One, more noteworthy, contained indented footprints said to be where ancient kings were crowned when once they set their foot in that spot. Pitt insisted on stepping in, of course, to our great merriment – the only pleasure of the climb, to my mind. Fanny did not join in our laughter. She never does. Instead, from the expression on her face, I knew it could not be long before she began to recite poetry, so I took John's arm and said we should return to Mother and Father, for whom the climb had been too much and so they had remained below, in a sheltered place by the bridge over the burn, with Jane to tend them. Fanny was thus left alone with her fancies of ancient Scotland told to her by the *old gardener*, she had said, who assured her that this place was *sacred*!

So we five had a cheerful repast and Jane was beginning to pack away the remains of the victuals by the time Fanny returned, trailing her sketchbook in one hand, thoughtless as ever about inconveniencing others. She refused any food, taking only a small glass of wine that produced a shudder through her frame and caused her to drop her book near Pitt, where he was leaning back on his elbows on the grass.

Pitt looked down at the neglected book before raising his eyebrows at me and asking, *Any animals to draw today, Fanny?* I smiled at the recollection, then, of a day at Dumbuck when Pitt had found Fanny's sketchbook and, exclaiming, held up a drawing of a misshapen dog with a lolling tongue like a loaf of bread in shape and dimension. Pitt had put out his own tongue while pushing his chin down towards his chest, in such perfect imitation of the poor distended creature of Fanny's pencil, that John and I could not help but laugh.

In response to Pitt, however, Fanny merely shook her head and, leaving her book unclaimed, walked further away with some urgency to an apple tree at a little remove from where we sat by the bridge. I heard her retching. I tell you all this to show what a miserable and inconsiderate person she has ever been, and how much my brother has always had to endure, as have we all.

Frances

Auchendarroch
Argyllshire
September 1840

Gunfire from dawn to dusk. Even in the walled garden, I hear it.

When the men are not hunting, they are talking of it in the evenings over their whiskies – crowing over what they have bagged today, planning the next day's conquests. Friends of John come and go to join the adventure – some regimental chums but also Mr Molyneux Nepean, a baronet's son and Bella's intended, already a favourite with the family. Pitt seems positively inflamed by his sport; never have I seen him quite so wild as he has been here of late. On one occasion, I even heard John tell him to mind himself, and John normally indulges Pitt in everything. *Know your place and keep to what is your own*, were John's words, I recall, although I do not think he meant me to hear; to me, he never likes to acknowledge any flaws in his closest kin.

Bella and Mammy, too, talk of sport while the men are absent, driving me to seek the refuge of old Niven's domain, although it means passing an outbuilding where the stench of death lingers – row upon row of bloodied feathers, lolling necks, clouded eyes. Claws that will never more touch branch or earth hang limp and pale. Grouse, partridge, duck, pheasant, pigeon – whatever is in season, whatever may be brought to ground. No winged creature is safe from *the sportsman's joy, the murd'ring cry*.

Yet still the kitchen maids pluck and dress the birds, the dogs gather to lick the blood from the yard flagstones, and the wind whips feathers like snowflakes, hanging in the air or gathering in drifts. I cannot shake a morbid fancy that I am breathing in featherdown fine as gossamer, till my throat catches at the thought of it.

I have eaten no flesh for weeks now, despite the doctor's orders that I must keep up my strength now. When the plucked and roasted creatures appear on the table, I bite my lip to be sure that the blood I taste is my own alone. Only fish, from the clean waters of the loch, can I stomach.

The days of stag hunting are worst. Then, the men travel further and higher into the wild countryside so that no guns are audible, but I cannot prevent myself from imagining the innocent beasts walking the hills and glens oblivious to their impending doom. When venison is served at dinner, I beg John to excuse me from dining at the table, pleading the preservation of my health as the reason and entreating his mother to join me in persuading him that every precaution must be taken to ensure the blessed outcome this time. He once ordered me to stay at table and eat, reminding me before everyone that he is my husband, and I am ashamed to say that I disgraced myself in such a way that he has not done so since.

But I am not so weak and ill as I have been on previous occasions and as my belly begins to swell, so my hope rises. I trust to the silence of Mammy and Bella concerning my absences from the house during the day, which may be folly on my part, but I *cannot* remain inside. I dare not venture so far as the loch shore but sometimes I walk along the canal, where I imagine boarding a passing ship and travelling northwest to the rocky shores of Jura, where the only sounds would be crashing waves and the cry of wheeling seabirds.

* * *

Stag hunting took the men from home once more today, with the exception of Mr Nepean, who escorted the ladies to Lochgilphead to call on a distant connection of Mammy's, thus leaving me in peace. After walking to the canalside, I turned back into the woodland where I leaned against a mighty oak trunk, watching a swirl of leaves float down the stream, gold and scarlet against the black rocks beneath rushing water.

I cannot say how long I stood there, no hint of chill in the air to make me relinquish my post, absorbed by all I saw and heard. So I do not know how long he had been watching from the footbridge above when he called my name.

Fanny!

Startled, I looked up. *John! You are returned sooner than expected.*

What are you doing here? Jane said you were out walking but I did not believe her, knowing you are under strict instructions to rest. As he spoke, he made his way down from the narrow bridge. I wrapped my white shawl tighter around me, before pressing both hands back against the reassuring trunk as he approached.

I am feeling so well, Johnny dear, and I believe the air does me good on mild days such as this.

He stood directly in front of me, so that I could see the colour rising in his smooth-shaven cheeks and a thread of muscle twitching beneath one eye. He smelled of shot and pelts.

You feel? You believe? he said, leaning so close now that he was pushing me back against the tree, the pressure on my stout belly unpleasant. *What has that to do with it? You have been told what you need to do but you cannot obey, can you? Not even when your wilfulness has such dire consequences as you have suffered before!*

But you know that wasn't my fault, Johnny, Doctor Reid said so. Something went amiss, he said. I did nothing wrong.

Nothing wrong? Here you are, wandering for God knows how many hours. Jane said you had not been seen since luncheon. Are you really so selfish? After all the indulgence I have shown you!

He reached out a hand towards my throat then, pushing my head painfully into the rough bark, and as he did so, my foot slipped on a mossy tree root so that I slid down heavily. But he did not release his hand, instead kneeling beside me, and when I tried to raise my hands to loosen his hold on my throat, he grabbed both of them, pinning them by my sides so that my fingers pushed down into the soft dirt, among the rotting leaves and acorns. I gasped with the relief of breathing more freely but he kept pressing my hands further down into the cold dirt and leaning his weight into me so that I was pushed awkwardly to one side against the tree. My head struck something then – a rock or another tree root, I could not tell – causing a judder of pain that made me catch my breath and blurred my vision for an instant. In that moment, he managed to put both of my hands into one of his and pushed his hip roughly against me to force my knees apart. With his free hand, he began to pull up my skirts and petticoats.

I cried out, I think, for then he said, *Shut up, bitch! I have a right to what is mine and none shall gainsay me.*

I had to close my eyes, the look of savagery on his face more than I could bear.

The baby, Johnny. Please, no!

But he did not stop and I feared that someone might come to see what was happening if they heard us, so I clamped my mouth closed and, my eyes still shut, breathed in the smell of rotting leafmeal. *I thocht it was a trusty tree I thocht it was a trusty tree I thocht it was a trusty tree,* I said to myself, over and over, until it was done and he had gone.

* * *

Gloaming. A word I loved, signalling not the loss of the day but the arrival of some other dimension altogether, a softly darkening presence, full and gentle. Today it was cold and colourless.

I shivered, my hands chilled from the dirt that caked them. My fine shawl was filthy; it repelled me so that I could not bear to pull it closer. I would rather freeze. My only warmth came from the hot sting of abused flesh between my legs. But no sign yet of that deeper, tearing pain that I know so well. Beneath the folds of my dress, my belly felt firm to the touch, as if still inviolate.

In the growing gloom, I thought I heard the carriage return, bringing Mammy and Bella back from Lochgilphead with Mr

Nepean. What time was it? How long until my absence from the house was noted? And where was John now?

I roused myself but found I could not stand. Instead, I remained like an animal on all fours, sobbing to be brought so low in this place that had promised so much. Never before had John treated me so brutally. What could have provoked him? Could he really have been so enraged simply to find me in the woods?

A step on the footbridge above me. I crouched low, keeping quiet, but the steps came closer. I prayed it was not John returning.

Mistress?

Jane's voice!

I said nothing. I wished myself invisible rather than be found like this.

Mistress Geils?

She was upon me then, gripping me firmly in her strong hands to raise me so that her face loomed close, framed by the bleached kerchief she sometimes wore. Wretch that I was, I sobbed uncontrollably then.

She hesitated, no longer trying to lift me, but instead assisting me to a sitting position against that wretched oak. *Are you in a tender way?* she asked.

I lifted a weak hand to smooth back my hair, pulling free a leaf caught there, and felt my fingers brush an oozing scratch on my temple. *I fell, Jane; I fell, that is all. I fell, just a stumble. I am a little winded and quite dirty, that is all.*

I do not think Jane was deceived by my bravado. Her dark eyes took in my disordered appearance, the dirty shawl.

Sit doon a wee. She lightly patted my shoulder, a gesture I never recall receiving from Jane before. She who dressed my hair and laced my stays, arranged my undergarments and buttoned my boots, had never before touched me unless for some purpose, never for its own sake. She kept her hand on my shoulder as she turned to look towards the house in the distance. Through the trees, lamplight was visible from the windows on the ground floor.

I maun fesh Ross to bear you back to the hoose, Jane said.

No, Jane! You must help me. Only you. Fetch no one else.

But you canna walk, mistress. You maunna! You are wabbit oot – weak, I mean.

I stretched out a hand to grasp one of hers, putting all the strength I could into my grip. *Jane, you must help me to my feet and we will make our way back together.* I held her gaze until I saw her relent.

She raised me carefully to my feet, and I leaned back against the cursed tree while she brushed what dirt and debris from me she could, smoothing down my skirts and straightening the front of my dress across the bodice, where it rode high above my belly.

Take this, I said, pulling the shawl from me. I never wanted to see it again.

Jane bundled it up, tucking it under one arm. *Is there pyne, mistress?* she asked. I pressed her warm hand against my belly, shaking my head by way of reply. No pain within.

Do you nae mind ma curch? she asked.

No, not at all, Jane, I said, touched again by her uncustomary gentleness as she untied her kerchief and used it brush away the dirt that caked my palms and stuck to my fingers. Even in the encroaching darkness, I could see the kerchief quickly become filthy.

Jane persisted, though, and her efforts at least had the effect of restoring some warmth to my cold fingers so that I let her continue, despite my fear over remaining too long outside where we might be discovered.

When she stopped, no doubt realising nothing further could be done to improve my dishevelled state until I was safely upstairs, I felt a little stronger so we began our slow way back towards the house. Crossing the narrow footbridge, where the handrail could support me on one side, we then stayed close to the stand of trees at the edge of the lawn to provide some cover, although all the curtains had now been drawn against the evening so there was little chance of our being seen from the house.

I know I must have tired her, leaning on her as heavily as I did, but Jane's arm held firm around the back of my waist, enabling me to keep putting one foot forward, and then the other. All the time, I dreaded to feel that warm, sickening flow that might herald another bitter loss, but there was nothing yet, just a stinging burn between my legs.

Jane guided me to a side door, well away from the part of the house where the family and other guests would be gathering in anticipation of dinner, but the final effort of crossing the threshold into a warmer space brought on a wave of faintness. Jane must have helped me to a bench in the vestibule but suddenly she was gone and I sat, slumped and leaden as if stupefied. Through my blurred sight, though, I sensed an inner door being opened and the passage growing lighter before hands lifted me on either side, Jane's and another's, strong and firm. They spoke to one another in words I could not understand so that I was afraid I had lost my reason and the power of language entirely. I surrendered to the darkness.

Mary Geils

Auchendarroch
Argyllshire
October 1840

2nd October

My dear Mrs Dickinson,

The Colonel and I are to leave Auchendarroch tomorrow, with Pitt to accompany us. Bella is to remain here with Frances, who is taking the greatest care of herself and almost entirely confining herself to her room. She has had a cold for the past week after taking a chill outdoors and does not feel as well as she usually does but is generally in good health. Rest assured, the doctor reports no concerns on her behalf.

I hope you continue well at Farley Hill. The Colonel sends his love to you as does John.

Believe me, my dear Friend,
Affectionately yours,
M. Geils

Frances

Auchendarroch
Argyllshire
October 1840

Jane wants to throw away the spikes of purple hooded flowers, white at their throat, with toothed leaves like nettles but without the sting. I see them even when my eyes are closed. I breathe in their sharp, bitter scent.

A child came to my door – yesterday? – her brogue so broad and voice so soft as she spoke to Jane that I did not catch her meaning. Closing the door again, Jane had held the flowers at arm's length, frowning.

Wee Effie Niven, she said.

Who, Jane?

The wee lass. Jane shook the stems in her hand. *These come from her grandfaither, the auld gairdner. Sayed they are flooers – these weebies! Shall I toss them awa?*

No Jane, please put them by me, where I can see them.

Jane filled a tumbler with water and placed the humble blooms on the bureau by my bed, her disapproval evident. But then she shrugged, saying, *She's a douce wee lass, Effie. Auld Niven heard you war tak naeweel, she sayed.*

I thought of that strong grip, assisting Jane to bring me upstairs that night. Could it have been Niven?

I have not left my room since then. How many days? A week?

More? Only Jane and the doctor have crossed its threshold. I have heard Jane telling any who come to the door that I have taken a bad cold, perhaps an influenza, and all should *keep awa*. I have never known her so attentive; we are both quite immured here together.

I know not what the young doctor from Lochgilphead concluded when he first examined me. Jane had washed me and changed my clothing by then. I said only that I had had a fall outside. He did not challenge my account but visits each day, listening carefully to my belly. Am I to come through *unscathed* after all?

There can be no question of resuming my walks, the doctor says. I care not if I ever see the grounds of this place again. I do not even want to say its name. Indeed, merely to think of returning downstairs, taking my place at the table opposite John, makes my heart race and my hands tremble. I keep the curtains drawn too, despite the doctor recommending light and ventilation. He is quite modern in his ways, for a Highland doctor. But gone is my interest in watching the boats pass from my bed, mocking me with their freedom to sail quite away.

I would give anything to be *alone*. Or, no, not entirely alone I suppose, while my babe remains safe within me. And I could not do without Jane, even if her presence calls to mind that night and the uncustomary tenderness she had shown me then. I search her face, when she does not see, for a trace of her thoughts. Does she pity me? Or does my shame disgust her? I cannot judge but she seems changed somehow, subdued I might almost say, not a word I would usually think of in relation to Jane.

Last evening – I think – I was already dozing, having taken my evening drops from Jane's hand, when a sharp rapping began at my door. I quailed, thinking it was John, who had not come at all since—

I had been expecting, fearing, that he would tire of my absence after a few days, aware of how it must appear to his guests that his wife does not sit at his table night after night, whatever was reported concerning her health. But John would not normally knock, nor wait to be admitted to any room he wished to enter, and when Jane opened the door, it was Pitt on the threshold, flushed and dishevelled. She set her foot down to prevent the door opening further, something I never recall seeing her do before.

Ah, Jane, you are still diligently at your post, Pitt said.

Doctor says mistress is to have nae visitors, she said, moving as if to close the door, but Pitt put out his hand to hold it in place.

Now, now, now, Jane, I expect a warmer welcome from you, especially in the evenings, he said with a laugh. *And may a man not inquire after his ailing sister? I have been remiss in not doing so sooner.* He shook his head then in a gesture of remorse, his rather theatrical manner removing any doubt that he was deep in his cups. But this whole time he had made no attempt to look over to me, nor to speak to me at all, and when the vigour of his head-shaking caused him to overbalance a little, Jane seized the moment to close the door firmly and turn the key.

Pitt lingered a little longer outside, knocking once or twice and calling *Jane, Jane,* but then I heard other men's voices in the corridor and Pitt must have moved off with them because a few moments later all was quiet again.

* * *

It shames me to say so, after all her devotion these past days, but I begin to tire of Jane's constant presence. It might be pleasant to have that little Effie come back and sit by my bedside. I did not even see the child's face when she brought her grandfather's humble offering, but I feel sure that if she could sit and talk to me of all the garden herbs and their power to heal, I would be comforted somehow. Such a sweet little voice she had, at my door. Perhaps she might sing to me.

Jane would no doubt disapprove of any request to summon Effie and I have so little courage these days I dare not even risk my maid's ire! All I seem able to do is write with this pencil from my bed. I am not yet strong enough to sit at a table to use an ink pen. I want to write to Mother but I know she would be distressed to see my pencil marks and I do not want her to know what I suffer. Still, I wish I could describe to her the white throat and bitter scent of the woundwort. *Allheal*, I have heard Cook at Farley Hill call it.

Rev. James Jaffray

The Manse
Dumbarton
November 1840

19th November

My dear Mrs Geils,

This epistle comes to you not in my own hand but rather that of my second son, Jacob, who writes at my dictation. He is a good lad and has of late spent much time at my bedside, devoting himself to my correspondence with great care and discretion. He blushes at my praise but I insist he writes the words exactly as I speak them, before I fall silent forever. I do not expect that you will find me still in residence in this earthly realm by Miss Geils' wedding in the spring. Jacob frowns at this, dear laddie, but dips his pen again so I may continue. "Man that is born of woman hath but a short time to live, and is full of misery. He cometh up, and is cut down, like a flower; he fleeth as it were a shadow, and never continueth in one stay." These words will one day be read over each one of us, even as I hold it as certain that the dead will be raised incorruptible at the appointed time.

You asked my advice on a matter of the heart and I have turned your letter over in my mind for several days that I may speak the truth with wisdom. Concerning your wifely duties, I believe that the sacred role of helpmeet knows no limits. Any misunderstanding between a husband and his wife is but the consequence of the first couple's misunderstanding in Eden and, like theirs, will in time yield joy where there once seemed only sorrow.

But, dear Mrs Geils, the Lord not only takes away but gives of his loving kindness – blessed be the name of the Lord – and I pray that the hope of which you wrote may come to fruition in due course and that you may know the joys of maternal duty, the central purpose of marriage after all, with which my dear Elizabeth was so blessed.

It is a steep brae that I have to climb, as we say here – but you have been amongst us lang enough to know our phrases and ways. (Indeed, your letter quoted that true son of Scotland, Mr Burns, even if his poetical subjects are not always seemly.)

Remember me ever your faithful servant in the Lord,

James Jaffray

(from the hand of Jacob Jaffray).

Frances

Auchendarroch
Argyllshire
March 1841

Red deer red blood torn flesh. Snipes screech across the water.

Blitter, Jane says.

Most bitter cold burning.

Gleed, Jane says.

Coals on my feathered head. Bed. She is long fled.

Gled! Betty says. *See, it soars gledly!* Far from me, Betty and bird both.

All nests among the stars brought down. Falcons on fists. High become low. Low in the dust. *But first it bow'd, and syne it brak.*

Feathers grounded matted black underfoot. Mud on snow, blood on snow.

White breast. White throat. *Waly, waly.*

Most bitter blood. Feathered bodies in the blood shed.

Mud and blood across the stones, the floor, the stairs, the bed.

Darkness cold as earth. Snipes drum in the mud, they say.

The blitter frae the boggie. Burns. I burn.

Light again. *When day did daw* the doctor did craw, his fingers sharp as talons pulling, tugging, dragging. *Need a body cry?*

White breast. White throat. Woundwort. *Waly, waly.*

Torn flesh, thorn flesh. Blood *reekin-red.*

I clutch the nurse, her red, rough hand coarse as earth. Under I go.

First it bow'd, and syne it brak.

Split asunder.

Guid lass, one more, she whispers.

No, no more. Please, Johnny, no.

I am no one's lass less than whole born of woman full of misery. *A maid again I'll never be.* Please no more.

Dawn torn. *Need a body cry?*

Feather-soft breath, heather-pink flesh.

Smooth as an acorn cup.

White as snaw, warm as blood.

Smooth as an acorn cup.

O waly, waly, but love be bonnie.

Reading Mercury

Saturday, 20 March 1841

BIRTHS

On the 8th inst., at Auchendarroch, Lochgilphead, the lady of John Edward Geils, Esq., of a daughter.

3.

Foolish strife

(March 1841–December 1842)

Hugh Smith

Letters to Married Women,

On Nursing and the Management of Children

Sixth Edition

(London: C. and G. Kearsley)

There may be some cases in which it is not prudent for a mother to give suck; but these instances very rarely happen; and there may be some women who, although they are ever so desirous, cannot suckle; this however is but seldom to be urged. I sincerely sympathise with those unfortunate ladies who are thus deprived of a happiness only known to those who enjoy it. What shall we say under these necessitous circumstances? Shall we advise such mothers to employ a wet nurse? Much is to be apprehended from a child's suckling a strange woman; nothing less than absolute necessity would make me comply with it.

It is a shocking truth, but vicious inconstancy is become so universal, even among the lower rank of people, that many women offer themselves, and are daily employed as wet nurses, who are labouring under dreadful and infectious diseases.

There is yet a further evil to be dreaded: as it is through necessity alone that a woman will desert her own infant, and take another to her breast, she may be induced, by the advantage she gains, to conceal her being again with child.

Such are the melancholy prospects attending the present unnatural practice of wet nursing; for which a curse is oftentimes entailed upon a generation. How terrible soever these things appear, I esteem it my duty to acquaint mothers in particular, what a risk they run in thus hazarding the health and lives of their children, together with their own present and future happiness.

Oh! that I could prevail upon my fair countrywomen to become still more lovely in the sight of men! Trust me, there is no husband could withstand the fond solicitations of an endearing wife, would she be earnest in her desire of bringing up her own children. Rest assured, when he beholds the object of his soul cherishing and supporting in her arms the propitious reward of wedlock, it recalls a thousand delicate sensations to a delicate mind. How ardent soever such an one's affections might be before matrimony, a scene like this will more firmly rivet the pleasing fetters of love: —for, though a beautiful virgin must ever kindle emotions in a man of sensibility, a chaste and tender wife, with a little one at her breast, is certainly, to her husband, the most exquisitely enchanting object upon earth.

Frances

Dumbuck House
Dunbartonshire
March 1841

I feel it, sharp as a blade, each time Maria takes little Kate from my arms, leaving me alone once more. Alone, but without peace: all day, people pass in the corridor outside my door or cross the forecourt beyond my window; by night, the stench from the smoking room curdles my dreams. And whether within or without, John's new terrier, Fury, yaps and yelps. I have never before encountered a dog I could not abide but I would sooner stroke the rats she catches than that mean-tempered thing.

Doctor Reid says it is a pity that I journeyed back so soon after my confinement, with only Maria to serve me and the babe as we travelled. The monthly nurse was left behind at Lochgilphead but here, at least, good-hearted Betty may tend me once more while Jane McPhee waits on Bella again.

Bella's wedding next week is the reason for our return. And, as is the custom in Scotland, Kate is to be christened on the same day, while the minister is present at the house – no church, for either wedding or christening!

Nor is the officiating minister to be my old friend, Reverend Jaffray, poor man. Betty says that all of Dumbarton gathered for his funeral, the church overflowing, and his orphaned children are now dispersed to schools or relatives elsewhere, never more to know a home under their parents' care. And to think that less than a year ago Mrs Jaffray was comforting *me*; now she and her husband are both below the ground.

So, I suppose I must be grateful that little Kate grows strong on the milk of Maria McKichan, a hearty maid of the Highlands. Mother would not approve of Maria, though; she holds to the views of Mrs Wollstonecraft and Mr Smith that it is a mother's duty to nourish her own child. But my body was too weak. I almost died the very day I came of age, at risk of adding not another day more to my sum, just as the days of my babe began! John even brought the lawyer to my lying-in that I might sign my will on my birthday, though I did not recall that until Mr Patrick returned with further papers some days later and spoke of those already signed.

Katherine – always little Kate, to me – is now forever secure and it is the greatest comfort to know that she is protected in every way that she may be, both in health and fortune.

Jane McPhee

Dumbuck House
Dunbartonshire
April 1841

What a carfuffle last night from your guidwife after Miss Isabella's wedding! This hoose has seen naething like it! Still, you were wrong to say to me what you did this morning.

The night begun better than any Hogmanay, when you came to the barn where we folk were dancing, to take some of us, wi' your brother and your soldier friends, to Flora Currie's inn. You were a sight more cantie than at your ain wedding!

But then hame agin past midnicht, when mistress came out from her chamber skreeching and gowling, *What are you doing out with the servants half the nicht, Johnny?* And turning a mad eye to me as she yalled, bi fegs!

Still I stayed near, trusting that I might come to the smoking room after all, until that mim Betty appeared, like a ghaist in her muckle great nicht-goun, clucking over her blirting mistress. So you shouldna have sayed to me this morning that I was not to be lippened because I didna come to you. There is nae other. I am aye your ain Jane. J.

Frances

Dumbuck House
Dunbartonshire
May 1841

Not a word from John since he left. Mammy insists on sitting with me in the afternoons, reading out Bella's letters, which seem to come almost daily during her wedding tour. She blames me for her son's absence, I am sure, though what she knows of the night of the wedding she has never said. Certainly, Mammy knows nothing of what I hide from sight, though I press those two spots on my arm when I am alone, *here* and *here*, noting each day as they pass from blue to green to palest yellow. *Here* and *here*.

Two days after the wedding – days in which John spoke not a word to me if others were not by, nor did he so much as touch me again, never appearing in our chamber at night at all – he was gone, travelling north to Strathpeffer for his health, he said.

Mammy comes to me again in the evenings to ensure I take a *sleeping draught*, as she calls it. It tastes just like the laudanum I had after my mishaps. The bitter draught quiets the rustling in my head but does not always bring sleep, leaving me restless. Some nights I wander the downstairs rooms after all the household lies asleep on the floors above.

Never before tonight, though, had I ever entered the smoking room, through the queer short passage that leads from John's dressing alcove off our bedchamber. The room was smaller than I imagined it; some nights the men must be squeezed in uncomfortably, when guests are visiting. I pulled back the baize curtain covering the half-glazed outer door so that the moonlight, added to my candle flame, revealed decanters and glasses, boxes of tobacco and cigars, a rack of antique guns, a shelf of magazines and illustrated papers, some rather unsavoury. On a table by a low armchair was a stand containing the old Colonel's pipes. On one side of the hearth stood a small locked bureau where I knew John sometimes worked on estate matters, allowing him to refer to this room as his office.

The most striking feature in the room, though, its colours vivid even in the half-light, was an afghan rug in reds and blues draped over the davenport. Brought back from the sub-continent, no doubt, but by John or his father, or even his grandfather before that, I could not say. What had happened to John there, in his years in the regiment? Had he been happy? For surely he is *unhappy* now, desperately so, or he would not be so cruel to me. Had the heat broken his health in some corrosive way, mind or body, that he conceals? He has given me to understand that half-pay on health grounds is common practice for officers who have served in India, a mere form of gratuity he implies, but I no longer know that I can trust anything he tells me.

The sky already lightens beyond the glass door. I must return to my bed before the servants are up and moving about the house. Today Bella and her husband are due back from the Nepeans' seat in Dorset. Why the couple intend to reside with us in this crowded house, instead of taking a place of their own is a mystery to me. They will both, no doubt, miss John's presence, giving Bella a further grievance against me.

It is still some hours until I see Kate at eight o'clock. Maria brings her to me then each morning, even though Mammy says it is indulgent to summon a child from the nursery so early. When Maria places her in my arms and leaves us alone in my chamber, I watch as Kate's tiny red lips purse in her sleep, dreaming of being suckled by another. And when my babe at last opens her cornflower blue eyes and lifts her dimpled pink fingers to my face that I may kiss them, cooing and crowing all the while, I know I must endure anything for her sake.

Isabella Nepean

*Dumbuck House
Dunbartonshire
May 1841*

On my return from my wedding journey, I swear, to the best of my recollection, that Fanny was in full possession of her senses. She was in no way deranged by her confinement, with the exception of her excessive attention to the infant, parading it about in her arms and even bringing it into the drawing room to dandle on her lap!

Only one minor alteration in her demeanour did I detect, which I attributed to her remorse at having driven her husband from his home with her shrewish temper, and resulting in exhibitions of misery most irritating to witness. In every other way, however, Fanny remained as wilful as ever, persisting in an exaggerated sense of her own importance, most evident in her failure to acknowledge any change in my position as the wife of a baronet's heir.

Regarding the circumstances leading to my brother's return to Dumbuck: upon my oath, I played no small role in this outcome. One morning, I was alone in the drawing room at Dumbuck when Fanny came in and asked if she could confide in me on a most painful matter. I had barely inclined my head in response when she began to pour out a litany of all her failings, weeping all the while.

I do not see how we can continue to live in this way, Bella, Fanny said. *I fear that Johnny and I will never suit each other. I'm sure you understand now how vital it is that a husband and wife are in sympathy with one another. Perhaps it would be better if Katherine and I returned to Berkshire so that peace may be restored to this household and John may return home. Unless something – or someone – intervenes, I truly fear that this rupture between us may result in a lasting break.*

I need not say how alarmed I was by these words, and by the prospect of further distress for my brother John.

You must not contemplate such a step, I counselled. *Think of your child, if not your husband – or your own dignity. Your place is here.*

I gave an undertaking, though, to write to John directly, urging him to return home and telling him that he would find his wife much changed for the better and newly mindful of her duty. Fanny's gratitude was almost worse than her despair, although, as ever, I suspected the sincerity of her display, especially when she insisted that I stress her improvement of temper (which, against my better judgement, I subsequently did).

In my letter, though, I also thought it wise to suggest to John that, after his return, he might make some concessions for the sake of the whole family. Perhaps, I wrote, some alterations might be undertaken at Dumbuck, so that Fanny would have no valid grounds for complaint concerning her accommodation here. He might also consider permitting Fanny to travel to her mother at Farley Hill for further convalescence, in hopes her behaviour might become more fittingly submissive as a result.

I could not but concur with Fanny, for once, in believing that her absence from Dumbuck might result in a restoration of equanimity that would be welcome to all. *A small concession,* I wrote to my brother, *however temporary, might prevent a far greater injury to the good name of Geils.*

Frances

Dumbuck House
Dunbartonshire
May 1841

24th May

My dear Mama,

I delayed writing again until final arrangements were in place, but it is with a glad heart that I now say we will soon be on our way to you at last! John is far from well after his return from the waters of Strathpeffer, though, and dreads very much the trouble of another journey. So, you and I must do all in our power to make Farley Hill agreeable to him.

He is not at all in good spirits (this is of course *entre nous*). It is a pity that his time at Strathpeffer did not serve him better. But at least the presence of Mr Ffarington will provide him with some male company at Farley Hill. How fortunate that your invitation to him and his mother coincides with our visit! I spoke to Edmund (as I still think of him, having called him so when I was a girl) very little during their visit to Berkshire for my wedding but he struck me as a congenial gentleman. I well recall that his fondness for books as a boy endeared him to me, as did his manner of speaking to a girl quite as if she were a rational person like himself.

All here are quite well but Pitt's departure with his regiment has been delayed yet again due to his chest complaint and he now tries Ardrossan for the Hot Baths. I wonder sometimes if he will make it to India at all, if his health continues so variable!

The dear Baby is doing nicely. I only wish she was older and could have come but John says she must remain and the doctor concurs. I am so torn between my desire to see you and not to be parted from her, the poor little thing.

I shall write again from Town, when we stop to break our journey there.

Ever yours,
Fanny Geils

Jane McPhee

Dumbuck House
Dunbartonshire
May 1841

Fareweel, you sayed, barely a sennicht after you were back frae Strathpeffer! You pushed the curch back off my head so that my hair tummled aboot and said you would fetch me back *a canty wee hat*. But I've nae use for a Sassenach bonnet.

Dinna leave me here while you go back to thon southron place with hersel. Take me with you. J.

Frances

Farley Hill Court
Berkshire
June 1841

I can see the blue outline of hills, far beyond the park and the pine wood. When I raise the sash of the nursery window, the sunset song of the blackbirds flows in sweet and clear.

> *The blackbird in the summer trees,*
> *The lark upon the hill,*
> *Let loose their carols when they please,*
> *Are quiet when they will.*
>
> *With Nature never do they wage*
> *A foolish strife; they see*
> *A happy youth, and their old age*
> *Is beautiful and free:*
>
> *But we are press'd by heavy laws;*
> *And often, glad no more—*

It was Miss Mitford, I think, who taught me that Wordsworth poem, although I forget its name. Or perhaps it was Papa? He was a great reciter of poetry, according to Mother. He may have watched these same blackbirds at Farley Hill, or their forebears, I suppose. Did he once lead me by the hand beneath the trees where they now sing, or is that just a trick of fancy disguised as memory?

I barely recall him at all. A figure in the library, writing at his table while I was allowed to sit close by the fire with a book on my knee, turning thick pages until I came to a plate that caught my childish eye. A shape in the bed in his darkened room, the stern nurse by his side, the cloying smells of the sickroom forcing me to pass swiftly by, the door ajar.

Glad no more. I lean from the open window and look down on the stone terrace below. How often have I sat there with Mother on a warm afternoon, together with Miss Mitford or Mrs Anderdon? Drinking cup after cup of tea, sweet and strong, emptying Cook's generous cake platter while Mother and her friend talked on – lively conversation about dogs or books or London if it were Miss Mitford, or news of the neighbourhood or Italy, if it were Mrs Anderdon. When I tired of listening, or became too drowsy in the sun, I would call for Crab and run off across the lawn with him bounding beside me.

Two days past, we were quite a party there, Mr and Mrs Anderdon having come to dine on the last day of the Ffaringtons' stay. John has warmed to Edmund, even if he is not a military man like the other men of his family. I have found him pleasant company, too, talking to him of books almost as I would with dear Miss Mitford. The only gloom occurred when Mr Ffarington declined John's invitation for a fishing expedition on that final day, on account of the Anderdons' visit, so that John had gone alone and in a bad temper, not returning home until we were already at table.

The day after the Ffaringtons departed, mother and son, John also left for our Somerset estate, taking Webb with him to assist in the assessment of rents due at Queen Charlton this year. At last, Mama and I are alone here.

* * *

I lean further out the nursery window until my arms are at full-stretch, fingers hooked on the edge of the sill. I push my face forward, chin up, like a ship's figurehead. A fancy takes me that were I to let go, I would not fall but fly, gliding gently towards the nearest tree-top where I might land among those trilling blackbirds. Would their melodic song then cease, replaced by a call of alarm at an intruder among them? *Chink-chink-chink!*

There is Amy now, crossing the lawn to the rosebeds, with a trug on her arm. She is paler than formerly, her face white against hair the colour of late-gathered hay, just like her mother's. She has taken her mother's death hard, I think, as has her father, of whom there is talk of drink.

Amy bends her head to sniff the full-throated flowers before cutting their stems and laying them gently in her basket. I fancy I smell their fragrance rising all the way to me up here.

She has seen me! Her task complete, Amy looked up to the sky, stretching her neck as if it ached, and started when she saw me here in my eyrie. I felt chastened, as though caught out in a shameful act rather than simply admiring the view on a warm June evening. I withdrew from the window and sat in the wicker chair beside the small bed, my arms suddenly sore from the strain of stretching. A bluebottle bumped and buzzed along the pane of the closed window on the other side of the warm room.

John had been adamant. *Katherine is to remain in Scotland*, he said. Even Doctor Reid had betrayed me; after the babe's digestive issues, though relatively minor, a long journey was not to be contemplated for an infant so young, he judged. Far better she remain where she was in the care of her nurse. But, oh, how I wept as the carriage drove away from the house and Maria – who I had insisted bring the baby down that she might be the very last thing I saw of Dumbuck – turned back inside, clutching the sleeping child tightly to her.

Enough, John had said and I stopped my tears.

* * *

A soft knocking on the door before it opened to reveal Amy bearing a glass of barley water on a tray.

It is so warm, she said. *I thought you might be in need of some refreshment. It is yet more than an hour until the dinner bell.*

She placed the glass down on a low dresser beside my chair and I saw that the outdoor warmth had refreshed her complexion a little, a few curls of hair clinging damply to her neck where they had escaped her cap.

This room has been shut up so long, she continued, looking about her. *Would you like me to have it freshly aired and dusted? It would be a more pleasant place to sit, then, I think.* She smiled shyly, stepping back towards the door.

Thank you, Amy, I said.

We were so formal now, compared to former times, and I still felt shamed by that look of alarm I had seen on her face when she spied me at the window, sorry to be the cause of any further distress to her in her grief. The thought of *her* loss led my mind to the absence of little Kate once more. My babe felt as far from me as if she were in the underworld and I had been left to roam, forlorn and forsaken, in the sunlit realm above. Tears started in my eyes before I could brush them away.

Next time, Mis—Mrs Geils, Amy said, as if she knew my thoughts. *On your next stay, we will have all in readiness here for your dear child.*

Please, Amy, I said, *won't you please call me Fanny?*

And with a nod and another gentle smile, she was gone.

Amy Webb

*Farley Hill Court
Berkshire
July 1841*

I do not like the way he looks at me. How much more pleasant the house had been while he was away in Somerset with Father. I came upon Mr Geils today as he was returning to the house from the direction of the woodland, and I stood aside to let him pass, surprised to see him enter through the back quarters where only we servants are. He slowed his approach when he saw me in the corridor but came nearer than there was any need for, staring at me all the while. I wished I was still bearing the tray of polished silver I had so recently set down that there might be something between us but I could smell his stale shirt and feel the heat rising from him. He lifted a hand to my cheek and made as if to speak but then Jane, the Scotch maid, appeared from outside, too. I was grateful to see her, even though I do not like her much – she expresses her unhappiness freely about anything she considers too English or *southern*. I think that is what she says; I cannot always be sure. At least now I do not share a room with her, Mrs Dickinson allowing me to return to Lower Cottage in the evenings to sleep, since mother died, so that I share a bed with Lydia once more.

Ah, Jane, Mr Geils said, leaving his hand for a moment on my face before removing it. *Is all well with your mistress today?*

Such a strange look on his face as he spoke, like there was some joke in his words. But it was a simple question, and Jane's face registered nothing amiss.

Aye, sir, she said, quickly turning into the doorway leading to the kitchen and, saying *Excuse me, sir*, I squeezed myself as close as I could against the wall so that I might pass him and dart after Jane before he could call me back. How my heart thumped within my breast, as if it had until then been stopped dead.

I dare not say anything to Mrs Dickinson, and certainly not to Miss… Mrs F, if I may call her so. In any case, what could I possibly say to those ladies? I am not a child and no harm has been done. I cannot say, *he chills me when he passes*. And yet it seems sometimes that the ladies are themselves unhappy whenever Mr Geils is present. If I enter a room where the three of them are seated, it sometimes feel as cold as the buttery, however warm the day. And that sight of Mrs F leaning from the window the other day frightened me so. If ever I am out in the grounds now, I always look up to the nursery and am relieved to see the windows closed, the curtains drawn up there.

An odd thing occurred today when I returned to Lower Cottage at day's end, though. Mrs D had dismissed me early, as she sometimes does if they are to dine out in the evening, so that I may take supper with my family, and I found Father already in his chair by the hearth. Since he returned from Somerset with Mr Geils, he has been far less dejected, once or twice even hinting at a grander future for us all. (As if mother's passing had not robbed our household of all hope and joy forever, as I feel in my heart to be so!) John and Lydia had not yet returned home from their day's labours and as I set out the cold supper on the table, Father watched me without any of his usual chivvying about being quick about it. Then, as I passed him, he put a hand on my wrist – something he never did – and said, *Mind you take care around the master. They'll be away back to Scotland again in a week or so but, until then, keep your wits about you and pay him no heed.*

Frances

Dumbuck House
Dunbartonshire
September 1841

Dumbuck again. Dreary, dull Dumbuck. I don't know how I am to pass away the time here with only Colonel and Mammy now that the others have gone to Ross-shire. Not that I was tempted to join the Nepeans' shooting party: that self-important pair left yesterday to take the Highland steamer north while John and Pitt drove away today in John's dog cart. At least Dr Reid was able to confirm my suspicions before John's departure so that my husband could not berate me for indolence; once he knew that my fatigue was on account of an expected confinement, he was happy enough to leave me behind.

So here I must remain, where a rare letter to his parents from Thomas in Madras offers entertainment for several days, Mammy reading it aloud over and over, her increasing deafness ensuring that nothing distracts her from her recitations and no one may speak until she is done. Then I must listen to all her concerns about Pitt. One moment she despairs he will ever join his regiment in India; the next she expresses a desire that he will go on to Strathpeffer for the waters and remain there, on account of his weak chest.

At least here I have my sweet Kate, funny little rogue that she is, when she is not troubled by her teeth, poor thing. She is a great favourite with all, even the Nepeans. Mammy says her fair hair is quite the colour of John's when he was small but her eyes are mine. Already I cannot walk out with her each day, due to my faintness. She delights in going up Dumbuck Hill, just a little way at least, so I must leave her to her nurse and remain indoors. If only Kate and I could be at Farley Hill with Mother, instead of here, but even I would not risk such a journey in my current state.

* * *

Alas, alas, alas. It has happened again. That dragging feeling came upon me, then the spasms and the flow.

John was summoned home, at Mammy's insistence. I would far rather have left him undisturbed, imagining his displeasure when he learns my news. I pray that Dr Reid will tell John, on his return, that it was in no way my fault.

* * *

He is home.

In Mammy's presence, he says he is relieved to find me well and unharmed. When we are alone, however, he says I must have done something to bring it on, that I could not bear him to be from home with Bella and Nepean and Pitt and that I must have committed some dreadful act to put an end to his sport in this way.

How can I reason with such cruel untruths? Yet he speaks with such conviction as though he truly believes that *he* is the one who has unjustly suffered!

Weak woman that I am, I cannot refuse the sweet forgetfulness the laudanum brings, even if it means I can scarcely hold my pen to form these letters and the words are so slow on this page.

Jane McPhee

Dumbarton
December 1841

Do you think I'm some gowk lassie that disna see thon hizzy Maria? Mistress may be too dozent to see that the white bosie of her nurse is not the delight of her wean alone, but I ken why you call that nesty bitch Maria to the smoking room.

And so I am sent away – or was it because my wame began to grow roond as a pudding?

But nae sooner had I gone to work at Flora Currie's than the bluid flowed from me, with pangs far warse than that first time that came to naething. Flora, bless her heart, stayed by my side. What she took doon with her at keek o' day and put in the ash heap niver drew braith, I swear. Would she had taen me with it. J.

Frances

Dumbuck House
Dunbartonshire
February 1842

11th Feb.

My dearest Mama,

We are coming to see you! The time is not yet fixed, as John is so very busy. He proposes only staying a few days before returning to Scotland, and leaving me and Kate with you for some time until he will fetch us back again.

I have my reward then, it seems, for keeping quiet through the long winter after my mishap, remaining on Bella's good side, and doing anything John asks of me, even speaking sweetly to his beastly Fury.

John is gone to Edinburgh for a few days to see the Solicitor, Mr Patrick, about the estate he is so keen to buy, Barcaldine. So I am alone with the old people again and although it is infinitely dull it is preferable to the *Nepean reign*. (They are gone to Edinburgh, too.) Dear Baby is quite well and I hope she will remain so as everything must depend on her health, if we are finally to bring her to see you at Farley Hill. Only think how nice it will be! But speak not of it I beg.

Ever yours,
F. Geils

Elizabeth Campbell

Dumbuck House
Dunbartonshire
May 1842

I freely swear upon my oath, without any inducement offered or accepted, that I first entered the service of the family at Dumbuck on the fifteenth of May, 1842. I was betwixt eighteen and nineteen years of age when I went to live there as dairy maid. Mrs Geils was not then at Dumbuck. She was living, I believe, in England with her mother.

When I had been at Dumbuck about two or three days, Mr Geils began to take notice of me and talk to me. At the first, I recollect, he said something very indelicate to me but as I gave no answer he did not then repeat it. And after that he used to watch every opportunity of my being alone in the byre where the cows were, to come and talk to me. He very often tried to take improper liberties with me there, and at last he succeeded in getting his will with me, and had improper connection with me. That was in my own bedroom above the kitchen. After I had gone to bed, he came there to me. He had often made the attempt before in the cowhouse and other places where he got me alone but I had always withstood him till then.

From that time, Mr Geils used to have connection with me very frequently. It was continually happening, whenever he pleased and could get an opportunity. It took place sometimes in my own bedroom and sometimes in his bedroom, and once or twice in the cowhouse. It happened a good many times in the plantations at the foot of Dumbuck Hill for Mr Geils used to watch me as I took out the herd boy's dinner, the lad who was minding the cows that is, and to follow me there.

Frances

Farley Hill Court
Berkshire
August 1842

The babe tumbles within me, warm in her fleshy cocoon. We are both of us trapped, I suppose, in our own way. No walks for me, no carriage rides, no sitting in armchairs, until Dr Bulley says I may.

I should not complain. There is so much kindness here: books from Miss Mitford, cooling cordials from Cook, and an abundance of blooms from Amy, so that the bumble bees seek out my room through the ever-open windows, my chamber a veritable walled garden on high. We are quite chums again, Amy and I, although both of us are quieter in spirit now than formerly. She sits with me, hour on hour, most days.

The merry squeals of little Kate carry up to my room from the garden. She is flourishing like a hedgerow wildflower and grown big enough to totter on the lawns. It is too cruel that it is not *my* arms to which she staggers and reels: I hear Maria out there with her, the lilting tones of her Highland accent and little Kate babbling in response.

Today, though, it is not simply my immurement that puts me out of temper. John has written from Scotland with bad news: the estate at Barcaldine has not been secured. I feared this would be the result, seeing that no buyer could be found for Queen Charlton: it has been sorely neglected since Father's death, so any buyer would need to make great improvements there, as John himself has often said, no doubt affecting its appeal to buyers. John then wanted to borrow against Queen Charlton but Mr Jennings told us we could not, so ultimately John has been unable to raise the funds necessary for a substantial purchase like Barcaldine. Still, he blames me for the outcome, most unfairly. I have never even *seen* Balcardine but he was fulsome in his praise of it and I was willing to make a home there if it meant leaving dreary Dumbuck at last. But all has come to nought.

Dr Bulley advises that I am not to worry myself about business matters before my confinement – nor would I, if I did not fear John's displeasure now that he finds the Dickinson property does not allow him to do anything he wishes.

And, just as bad, the loss of the prospect of Barcaldine means I must eventually return to Dumbuck, after all. Must my two babies (may it be, please God) sleep in that narrow, dark room that passes for a nursery, little more than an upstairs corridor? Must I remain banished to the ground floor there? I cannot bear to think of it.

Amy Webb

Farley Hill Court
Berkshire
September 1842

What a summer we have had at Farley Hill – with Mrs F in residence and Mr Geils mostly in Scotland.

Although Mrs F's state has been delicate, of late Dr Bulley has allowed that she might recline on the sofa in the library, her favourite room in the house, some days. So I assist her downstairs, fetch books for her, and sometimes even write my little pieces there. Mrs F likes to see me writing. It brings her memories of happier times at Cavendish Square, she says, but she no longer asks to look over my pages as she used to do when we were young. None but my eyes ever see my words.

In truth, I have felt quite like I am on a spree, so light have my duties seemed, and such pleasure as they give me. Even when Mr Geils returns to Farley Hill from time to time, he spends most of the long days out of doors and never approaches me in any unseemly way.

Mrs Dickinson, too, has been as cheerful a mistress as any housemaid could want, no longer dejected in spirit as I have often seen her since Mrs F's marriage, especially in the evenings. So that I thought it most uncommonly cruel of Mr Geils' man, Muirhead, to stagger about the kitchen, with a tea-cup in hand, making a poor attempt to speak like an English lady and pretending to be Mrs D.

He has started a story that my mistress likes to help herself from a spirit cask, by way of a tea-cup, as if it were not the most absurd suggestion that *a lady would serve herself*! Anyone who knows Farley Hill Court knows this for the most terrible slander that it is. Not only is there *no* spirit cask here, merely a wine cask, but I do not believe that Mrs D would know how to get the wine from it, what's more.

But that aside, our pleasant days have far outnumbered the disagreeable ones. Until yesterday.

I had gone to the library to light the fire ahead of the time Mrs F came downstairs. She felt the cold most keenly on days when Dr Bulley had been to drain a little blood from her arm. He did so to ensure she avoid overexcitement, he told me, instructing me to be especially careful she remain quiet and calm on such days. I think he would prefer that Mrs F remain entirely in bed until her time comes upon her but he knows her so well – he attended at her birth, after all – that he sees no purpose in vexing her unnecessarily, and Mrs F *hates* to have the blood-letting. So the promise of an afternoon in the library afterwards helps her face her trial and I do my best to ensure she is as comfortable there as may be.

In the library, one of the windows, a round one, had been left ajar and after attending the fire I closed it, noting as I did so a wide crack in the timber frame that let in a draught. So I sought out my father to ask if it might be attended to in some way before I fetched Mrs F downstairs. I found him in the grounds with Robert Pillinger, a carpenter long employed at Farley Hill doing all manner of work. The three of us then crossed the lawns to the library window so the men could judge if the damage extended to the outside of the frame. Father and Pillinger, although old friends, were inclined to banter and bicker over any task, and so they did now, their faces bent close to the glass while I stood behind them. It was then that we three saw, inside the room, the door swing open and Mr Geils push his wife forcefully so that she collapsed like a rag doll onto the sofa. He then proceeded to call his wife a *damned bitch* and other fearful names while she wept and begged him not to treat her so. Neither paid any heed to us outside, never looking towards the round window at all.

It's as you said, Webb, Pillinger said.

Hush! said my father, before telling me to return to the house at once and find Mrs Dickinson. Horrified, I went straight to the China Closet and told the mistress that I had heard Mrs Geils in some distress in the library – saying nothing of her husband or what we had seen – and was relieved when that lady rose immediately to go to that part of the house in time to witness her son-in-law dash past her and pass out the front door.

I loitered in the hall outside the library, then, not knowing what else to do, and Mrs Dickinson soon reappeared, asking me to send a lad for Dr Bulley and to bring smelling salts to the library. It was an agony waiting for the doctor to come and not being permitted to remain in the library to tend Mrs F, after I had taken the smelling salts to Mrs Dickinson.

There was no meal served in the dining room that evening and Mr Geils did not return to the house that I saw. Someone said he had been seen riding away. Later, the doctor instructed father to carry poor Mrs F upstairs and I followed that I might prepare her for bed. I was relieved beyond measure to see her calm and unharmed, but she spoke never a word to me when we were alone, merely raising her arms or bending her neck meekly, as required to undress her. She was almost as one sleepwalking, so dazed and weak did she seem, and she closed her eyes immediately I smoothed the bedcovers over her. I remained until I observed the even rise and fall of her chest that told me she had fallen into a deep sleep, and went downstairs to seek out Mrs D once more, that I might receive any further orders or know if I were required to sit watch through the night.

Outside the closed library door, I heard Mrs Dickinson in conversation with a man, and thought at first it might be Mr Geils returned but soon realised that it was my own father's voice, although I could make out no words. When eventually Father came out from the library, he led me away saying, *Come now, Amy, we are done for the day here, missus says.*

What is to be done, Father? I found the courage to ask him. *May I not sit with Mrs Geils tonight?*

It is all in hand, he said, taking my arm more firmly now, but not unkindly, and thus we walked, arm in arm, out of the house and into the darkness towards Lower Cottage. But I could not think what remedy there might be that would protect poor Mrs F, or what might happen on Mr Geils' return from wherever he had fled.

Frances

Farley Hill Court
Berkshire
November 1842

I feel certain now that I have put that day in the library firmly out of my thoughts.

If I have found a way to bear what John did to me on that day Jane found me at O— I can do so again, shutting it away in another unvisited corner of my mind. There is no need to ever recall the pushing and shoving, the bitter words from John. All gone, plunged deep deep deep, where they need never resurface. Deep deep deep. Quite drowned.

The only part that I could not bury so readily was my fear of another mishap, being as far along as I was, but after some anxious days Dr Bulley expressed hope that I might escape unharmed after all.

With John gone back to Scotland, Farley Hill Court was quiet and calm once more. The only disturbance was a welcome one – little Kate was much in my chamber, cheering me with her boisterous ways and happy laugh. It was as if the presence of my lively girl was a kind of talisman, a token of safekeeping for the babe yet to be born.

And soon I was further distracted from any dark thoughts by the appearance of little Mary Lucy herself, a week ago today. The birth pangs were less frightful, with no need for instruments, and I was permitted by Dr Bulley to nurse my infant at my breast, under the watchful eye of the monthly nurse, who is venerated as a saint in many households in this neighbourhood. Dinah says that in all her service as a monthly she has never seen such a treasure as Lucy, and so she is – a merry, blue-eyed treasure in my arms.

The only shadow on my joy is that Lucy's birth brought John back to Farley Hill. When he arrived, three days past, subdued in manner if not remorseful, he took but little notice of his new daughter but continued to show his customary affection for Kate, liking to have her about him as he walks in the grounds, accompanied by Maria, of course.

John has at least conceded that I can remain at Farley Hill with my blessed babies until the spring, deferring to Dr Bulley's recommendation that I do so, but he plans to return home to Dumbuck before too long, taking Maria back with him. If it were within my command – which nothing at Dumbuck ever is – I would prefer to see Maria dismissed altogether now that I have no further need of her. Mother has complained of a degree of slovenliness and insolence creeping into Maria's manner since my confinement and the new English nursemaid, who comes with the highest recommendation from old Mrs Anderdon's daughter-in-law, is a kindly, cheerful soul who works without complaint. Still, perhaps Maria's behaviour is only due to being so long in a strange place; I well know how oppressive that can be. I suppose a servant might feel such things just as strongly as we do.

Amy Webb

Farley Hill Court
Berkshire
November 1842

I would never, never, do anything to distress Mrs F, especially now that Dinah has left her to my care once more. Yet I must continue to record here whatever I see and learn, painful though it be. Who knows but there might come a day when it will be well that I did? For now, though, Mrs F does not know what I have seen and my mind is uneasy, as if it is *I* who is guilty of some wrongdoing.

Two days' since, Mrs Dickinson summoned me to ask if I knew where on the estate my father was working that morning as she needed a message taken to him with some urgency. He had been complaining to me the previous evening of some problems that had arisen with Mr Geils' new horse, a source of some dispute between them ever since Father, as instructed, had bought a horse for the master during his absence. On his return from Scotland, Mr Geils had not been happy with Father's choice, saying the animal was vicious, although Father says the fault lies with the rider not his mount. I thought it likely, then, that Father might be in the stables or thereabouts as the matter still remained unresolved so Mrs D asked me if I would run to find him there, saying it would be quicker than seeking out one of the outdoor lads to fetch him.

When I reached the stable building, there was at first no sign of anyone about until I heard the unmistakeable babbling of little Kate, such a happy child she is, and then saw Mr Geils, standing within one of the empty loose boxes and reaching out – as I thought at first – to his child in her nurse's arms, before I realised that Maria's dress was open to the waist and it was not his child at all that Mr Geils was grasping. And then he leaned forward, closer to Maria, and in total disregard of the child that she held, put his mouth to that part where a child sucks!

I turned and fled back to the house, not stopping until I had closed the kitchen door behind me, and praying that the wicked pair had not seen me. Poor Cook thought I was having a fit of hysterics and sat me down by the fire to catch my breath. Not a word did I say of what I had seen, feeling my face flame with the shame of it rather than the heat of the stove, but instead telling Cook a story that one of the horses had given me a fright. But when I thought of Mrs F's innocent child and what she had been privy to between her *father* and her *nurse*, it was all I could do not to rush to little Kate's mother and tell all!

Cook, though, insisted on setting a glass of something before me, saying she could not let me leave her kitchen until she was certain I was quite restored, and it must only be on account of that dram that I was able, soon after, to go to Mrs Dickinson and say that Father was not in the stables after all, without giving any sign of my shock.

But that was not to be the end of the matter. The day after, I was taking up Mrs Geils' tray when I saw Father leading Maria into the dining room, where Mr Geils and Mrs Dickinson were still at breakfast. Something struck me as strange – I could not have said quite what – so I stood with my tray for a few moments and soon heard the master's voice, raised. Thus, when the dining room door was flung open and Mr Geils came out into the hallway, he saw me immediately and said, *Fetch your brother to me here at once*! before retreating inside and slamming the door once more.

My brother Jack? What could Mr Geils want with him, with such urgency? Jack was already out in the fields, so I could think of no reason that he might be of use or interest to Mr Geils. The glimpse of the dining room I had caught only added to my confusion. Maria was standing with her head bowed – a pose which should have confirmed to me that something was awry, Maria usually more than willing to meet any eye, chin held high. She was an excessively proud person for someone who spoke like a foreigner, worse even than that Jane McPhee. And standing beside her, my father had looked flushed, puffing out his cheeks in a manner that all at Farley Hill knew meant he was out of temper.

Ever since that September night – after that terrible scene in the library – I had had a strong feeling that Father knew more than I did about how things stood with Mr Geils, but in the master's absence I had held my tongue and not pressed Father on the matter, comforting myself with the thought that Mrs F remained safe and well here so long as her husband was away. But had something now come to light regarding her husband and Maria? That was my first thought.

As I still hesitated, confused, Mrs D then came out from the dining room, followed by Mr Geils.

I told you to summon Jack Webb, girl, he said to me. *What kind of devilish household is this? Not a single woman in it who will do as she is told! No, stay, send one of the men to find him and go tell your mistress she is wanted.*

I looked to Mrs Dickinson then, as that lady had not yet spoken a word.

Tell my daughter she is needed downstairs, Amy, she said, her face so pale that I feared she might swoon, but I had no choice but to obey and hurry upstairs.

I could give Mrs F no reason for her summons yet she seemed to read in my face that something troubled me as I supported her down the stairs. *Stay with me*, she whispered, looking frailer than ever.

The dining room was now empty but voices could be heard from the direction of the library. I wanted nothing more than to lead Mrs F away from whatever awaited her there. Instead, I helped her to a low armchair, alongside her mother's, and Mr Geils stood before the hearth, one hand raised to the marble mantle. Father, my brother Jack and Maria all stood beside him.

I turned to leave but Mrs F said once more, *Stay, Amy*. I kept my post behind her chair.

Clearing his throat then, Mr Geils said, *It is my sad duty to inform you all that this woman* – gesturing towards Maria – *has brought disgrace upon herself and is today discharged from the service of the lady of the house.* He inclined his head towards Mrs Dickinson, who looked as if she had been insulted rather than honoured.

It falls to me, Mr Geils continued, *to further resolve this matter by administering an oath to this woman so that she may declare before witnesses the father of her child.*

At this, I could barely breathe so fearful was I of the effect this would have on dear Mrs F to have her husband's shame thus exposed. Such was my concern for my lady, watching her so closely, that I failed to notice Father. If I had, I would have seen the fury mounting in his face. I should also have given more thought as to what had caused my mild-tempered brother to clench and unclench his hands, shifting on his feet like he stood on hot coals. But, as I say, all my attention was on Mrs F, waiting for the terrible blow to fall upon her when Maria spoke.

I do swear, Maria said, *that I am wi' child by Jack Webb and that he hae'na done the jennock wi' me by marrying me as he should.*

Jack Webb!

She lies! Jack said. *It is not true. I've never touched her – I've barely seen or spoke to her! Father, you know it is not true. And I will not marry her!*

Come, lad, where is your honour? Mr Geils said. *Why would the lass say what wasn't so?*

Mr Geils, my father then said in a riled tone I knew well. *You know that Jack has already denied any part in this. If my lad says he is not the father, he is not!*

Well, Maria, what say you? Mr Geils said, reacting not one whit but instead fixing his gaze squarely on Maria.

I've sayed my trowth, she said, meeting Mr Geils' gaze.

This is a bad business, Mr Geils continued, *but I can do no more. Mrs Dickinson, you must consider what is to be done with young Webb but, if there is to be no marriage, Maria must leave Farley Hill today.* And with that, Mr Geils was gone, with not so much as a word or a glance at his wife, who now gulped for air, her head bowed, her shoulders heaving.

Poor Jack! I had seen my brother talk to Maria once or twice but then Maria liked to talk to anyone, especially the men, when she could get free of the nursery for a time. I had not thought anything of it, just as I did not for one moment believe my brother to be guilty. If Jack said he had had nothing to do with the Scotchwoman then I had no doubt it was the truth.

But I could not stay now to learn any more as I needed to assist Mrs F back to her room. I was broken for her and wondered if she believed her husband's account but she only expressed her shock to discover the immoral behaviour of one who had had the daily care of her own sweet, unsullied child. Not a word about who she thought might have brought about Maria's state.

I stayed close to her for the remainder of the day, tending both my mistress and little Kate, whom Mrs F would not allow to leave her sight, so it was only when I returned to Lower Cottage that evening that I learned Mr Geils had privately offered Jack fifty pounds to marry Maria, even after Jack had denied Maria's charge. Jack had refused, saying *I'll not clean up another man's dirt*, and thought that Mr Geils might have struck him then if Mrs Dickinson had not returned to the room at that moment.

But *I* could have struck Mr Geils, never having believed that such cruel mistreatment could fall upon Miss Frances Dickinson of Farley Hill. Was there no advantage then in being a rich lady? And was the truth to be forever untold? Even Father kept quiet thereafter, though not out of any respect for Mr Geils, I was sure of that. But as long as I remain under the same roof as Mr Geils, I must keep careful watch.

4.

A stronger mind

(January 1843–February 1845)

Sarah Stickney Ellis

The Wives of England:
Their Relative Duties, Domestic Influence,
and Social Obligations
(London: Fisher, Son & Co.)

Characteristics of Men

And here we are brought at once to that great leading peculiarity in man's character – his nobility, or, in other words, his exemption from those innumerable littlenesses which obscure the beauty, and sully the integrity, of woman's life. From all their underhand contrivances, their secret envyings, and petty spite, man is exempt; so much so, that the mere contemplation of the broad, clear basis of his moral character, his open truth, his singleness of aim, and, above all, his dignified forbearance under provocation, might often put the weaker sex to shame.

And a sacred and ennobling trust it is for woman to have the happiness of such a being committed to her charge – a holy privilege to be the chosen companion of his lot – to come with her helplessness and weakness to find safety under his protection, and to repose her own perturbed and troubled mind beneath the shelter of his love.

What, then, if by perpetual provocation she should awake the tempest of his wrath! We will not contemplate the thought, for there is something as fearful in his indignation, as there is attractive in his kindness, and flattering in his esteem.

Nor, in return for this kindness, are we accustomed to feel gratitude enough; for take away from social life not only the civility, but the actual service done by men, in removing difficulty, protecting weakness, and assisting in distress, in what a joyless, helpless world would women find themselves, left only to the slender aid, and the tender mercies of each other!

Amy Webb

Farley Hill Court
Berkshire
January 1843

Mrs D has bid me watch closely over her daughter, who grows ever weaker with wakefulness. I spend my nights on a couch at the foot of F's bed.

Build up the fire, Amy, it is as cold as Scotland, F says, s*tay close by me.*

She often talks of that Jane McPhee through these long nights, hinting at some special kindness shown to her by Jane, before then railing against Jane's watchful eyes and sour temper, and *that* is the Jane McPhee I know well. Once I confess I had envied Jane, with her fine ways with hairpins and needle, thinking her a favourite of F's.

Odd it is that F has seemed to give Maria McKichan no further thought. She is convinced that some man on the estate had his way with Maria and that the girl falsely named my brother, knowing how well-regarded the Webbs are at Farley Hill, in hopes of lessening her shame. But I know F to be so clever – how can she not suspect the truth?

Meantime, I listen close for any sounds from the master's room next door. I don't mind saying that I am sore afraid of his temper, now that I have seen for myself what he may do to his own wife. His guilty secrets might drive a better man to behave badly. But, mercy of mercies, he has never yet troubled us.

I tell no one of all this, of course, and most of all try to conceal my state of mind whenever I come upon Mr Geils' man, John Leigh, who waylays me to ask about my mistress in a manner most indelicate. I had not thought Mr Geils could have a more odious manservant than that Muirhead but I dread going below stairs now lest Leigh seek me out. He is very free with his ways, standing too close, staring too boldly, so that he reminds me of his master. Just this morning, when I was leaving my mistress's chamber at the same time as he was coming from Mr Geils' room bearing his master's travel desk, Leigh hailed me again, but I scurried quickly away, descending to the kitchen while he went to his master in the library.

Mr Geils may leave his wife untroubled at night, but he is far from kind to her during the day. Yesterday, while the family were at supper and the last of the plates had been sent up, I was briefly in the servants' hall alone, from which place sound carries quite clearly from the dining room directly overhead. So it was that I heard Mr Geils railing at his wife, calling F a *devil* and a *damned bitch*. I was impatient, then, for Mrs D to ring the bell that dinner was at an end, so that I could go and assist F back to her chamber, leaving her wretch of a husband alone with his port.

When the bell finally jangled, I flew up the backstairs to find F paler and more downcast than ever. After I had prepared her for her bed, she told me that her husband was insisting they return to Dumbuck, saying that all the family was needed at home where his father was likely on his deathbed and that it was her duty to be there too.

I cannot go back to Scotland, Amy! she said.

My heart was quite breaking at the thought of her in that place with none to protect her but I soothed her as well as I could, saying that she must not fear, that perhaps she might yet be spared the journey north if Dr Bulley forbade it.

Then today, when I saw Mr Geils and John Leigh riding out in the afternoon in the direction of the Anderdons, I was seized by a sudden thought. Here was a chance! After I had made F comfortable, sitting in the China Closet with her mother, I slipped upstairs and into her husband's chamber, my breath coming so fast that my hands quite trembled. The travelling desk was atop the dresser where it usually stood. I opened it to find it quite stuffed with papers – I don't know what I hoped to find there, except that a man so boldly false as I knew Mr Geils to be might be careless about keeping hidden what should not be seen. But there were only letters from his family and that man Nepean, as well as notes of business and such, nothing of an improper nature that I could see. It was a foolish notion, I suppose, and I rated myself then for a silly, silly girl, putting the papers back just as I found them – my hands no longer shaking – before closing the lid of the desk.

But then I paused, my hand on the doorknob. On the back of the door hung Mr Geils' greatcoat, the one he had arrived from Scotland wearing, much mud-spattered, that had since been brushed clean. When I had seen him just now, he was wearing his shorter, blue jacket that he usually wore for riding and hunting when the weather was dry. I slipped my hand into one front pocket of the greatcoat to find a flask and a coiled length of leather such as might have been snapped from a riding crop. In the other pocket was a tweed muffler and a tobacco pouch, but as I was removing my hand, it slipped through a gap torn in the lining, and I felt the edge of a piece of paper within. I took it out to see that it was a rough page, containing just a few lines written in a weak, wild hand and signed with a *J*. Thrusting my hand once more carefully inside the torn lining, I found several other pages, bound together with string, in the same hand. I blushed to read them, these bold words of *Jane McPhee* – it must be, from what she said of Dumbuck, and Farley Hill, too.

So Maria is not the only one!

Could it be I have found a way to save my F at last?

Frances

Farley Hill Court
Berkshire
January 1843

I am saved! But what a cruel, cruel mother I seem to myself in saying that, since it is only by little Lucy being afflicted with a cold that we have escaped leaving Farley Hill. John and his man departed yesterday evening, sparing my children and me the journey north for the present – and that is all I care for now.

I hold no real fear for Baby's health; it was more a kindness of dear Dr Bulley's on behalf of his treasured patients at Farley Hill when he pronounced the child should not be removed at this unseasonable time. To my infinite relief, John accepted the judgement and so here I remain with my girls and my dearest mama – and my stalwart Amy!

I am truly sorry to hear that the old Colonel is so poorly, as is Mother at the prospect of losing another old friend. I forget sometimes that long before I first crossed the threshold of Dumbuck, the Colonel and his wife had been dear to both Mama and Papa. Now I cannot but think of John's parents as parties to my misery, and quite blind to the failings of their eldest son. In truth, I think that Mother no longer feels quite the same regard for her old friends that she did before my marriage. Mrs Colonel means well, I suppose, but she will never do anything to displease John, for which I blame her most heartily when I know she has heard the dreadful names he calls me and the way he orders me about at Dumbuck saying, *Am I not your husband?* until I could scream with vexation.

My reprieve, however, is only a delay at best – unless I can hit upon some way to vacate that wretched place for good, which is surely a hopeless ambition. John coming into possession of Dumbuck may even make matters worse. The house will remain as cold and poorly-arranged as ever; I can expect no latitude from him on that front, knowing how he rants so over any expenditures I propose. Nor would my becoming mistress of Dumbuck carry weight with anyone there. Mrs Colonel – Mammy, I should say – will not want to give up her home and I have no hope that Bella and Nepean might be kept from the door. Then there is the question of what might come to pass regarding the two shadowy ladies upstairs. But, above all, I know that I cannot expect any change in John, and that alone clouds every thought of the future most darkly.

In one way, however, his tyranny has been checked of late, and it is no small way. While he was here at Farley Hill, he made no attempt to enter my chamber. It is most strange – I have never gone so long without his attentions, whatever my state of health. I do not believe it was out of compassion for me, and even Amy's presence with me he might have easily overcome if he had been minded. Perhaps he is more distressed about his father than I give him credit for, but I have long since given up any belief that wifely affection might in time transform my husband into a kinder man. Those fleeting moments of tenderness I had with him during that summer at O— are so utterly obliterated, like a dream or something from a book. I *long* to lavish my affection on someone; I may no longer be the girl dreaming of a noble suitor but there is much within me that I yearn to express without being scorned as I am by the man to whom I have joined my life.

I wish I had not thought of that Highland place just now, but such memories rise unbidden of late, even from the distance of Farley Hill, and with them, Jane McPhee has been much on my mind, too. In my troubled sleep, I even dream of her at times, a dream in which she lies half-buried at the foot of that loathsome tree, wrapped in my filthy wedding shawl.

I talk to Amy of all this – not of my dream, of course, although once I said that I had a *presentiment* about Jane and she frowned and asked if that meant a feeling about a before time? And in a way it does; when I cast my mind back to all I have known of Jane, and my husband, and indeed myself since I first visited Dumbuck House, it seems the life of a stranger named Frances Geils, a sorry creature trapped in a place where nothing is as it seems and worse may be yet to come.

My only comfort – apart from my sweet babes – is that here with Amy I have some reminder of my former life. When I see her each day, I see the same trusting face I recall coming to my chamber every morning, bearing her heavy pitcher, when we were both little more than children ourselves. I marvel now that I was so eager to leave Farley Hill, believing that a better life lay elsewhere.

But even *here*, I sometimes fear that Amy is hiding something from me – she, who has ever been the picture of frankness and friendship to me! How could that possibly be? It must be simply a trick of my sad, weary mind, clouded by the fears and anxieties I cannot dispel.

But that Jane McPhee, now, she was always too knowing, wise beyond her station. She could pass for a lady, with the right clothes, with *my* clothes. As long as she remained silent, of course.

Amy Webb

*Farley Hill Court
Berkshire
February 1843*

When word reached Farley Hill of the death of old Colonel Geils, I could remain silent no more. Knowing that F would no longer be able to delay her return to Scotland, I could not bear her to go back in ignorance. So I have spoken to Father. It was such a relief to speak at last of what I had read in those notes signed *J* – by none other but Jane McPhee, I am certain!

I had long been in no doubt that Father held a low opinion of Mr Geils, not only for his false charge against Jack and his behaviour towards Mrs F, but also because of the high-handed way he treated him when at Farley Hill. Father had, however, tolerated all this in the belief that if one day Mr Geils and his wife took up permanent residence at the other Dickinson estate, Queen Charlton, he would have made himself so useful to Mr Geils that he might be made steward there, with an increase of income as a result. A man didn't have to like his master to like his money, Father would often say.

So when I approached Lower Cottage, where I knew Father to be at work on the accounts that morning, I could not be certain if he would take the ladies' side as I hoped, or cling to his grudging loyalty to Mr Geils in the hope of future gain. I could do no other than trust to his better nature in telling him what I had learned of the improper understanding between Mr Geils and Jane McPhee.

The *how* of what I had learned, though, was almost as bad as the *what*: I feared lest Father rate me for bringing any suggestion of dishonesty or thievery to the Webb name by tampering with Mr Geils' belongings. He had taken the slur against Jack hard, even though folk at Farley Hill seemed to hold nothing against my brother, such was the low regard in which Maria had been held here. Father, though, had begun to talk a great deal of the pride of the Webbs, telling Jack, Lydia and me how we were *better than our betters*, as he put it.

Far from provoking his anger, though, as soon as Father grasped my meaning, he leapt to his feet saying I had always been a good girl and that he wanted that devil to pay for the shame he had put upon Jack. *We must find Mrs D with haste*, Father said.

But there is more yet, Father, I said.

More? This is quite sufficient to be going on with, my girl.

But it concerns Maria McKichan. I saw them one day—

With a face like thunder, Father put his hand up before me. *Stay, girl,* he said. *By 'them' you mean Maria and—?*

Mr Geils.

Father nodded. *Daughter, half the estate saw them. Pillinger, more than once. But there is no gain in telling tales of that. For now at least. No, if you have seen letters, that is what the legal men call evidence. That's different from just servants' tales in the eyes of a judge – they set great store by writing, do judges. We will confine ourselves to this matter of Jane McPhee. Leave it to me. Mrs Dickinson may want to see you after. Will you tell her what have told me, with no hysterics but plain as plain?*

Of course, Father! I trusted my resolve now that I knew he saw no fault in what I had done.

And you will say nothing to Mrs Geils until I have spoke to her mother?

Yes, I said. *Have I not kept silent till now?*

You're a good girl, Amy, with the good sense your dear departed mother gave you. Away back to the big house now. And, taking up his cap, he went to wait on Mrs D while I returned to F's chamber, not liking to leave her too long unattended. I found the poor lady in a dejected state, sitting by her fire with her book unopened before her. I did not know what might come to pass from Father's conversation with Mrs D, nor how long before F might learn of it, but thought it best to do what I could to calm and comfort her till then.

Are you in need of anything, Miss Fanny? (for so she liked me to call her when we were alone and I no longer resisted doing any little thing that might please her). *Shall I read some more Mr Dickens to you, perhaps?* Since those long distant days in Cavendish Square, I had persisted with my reading whenever I could so that now I could read aloud to her passably well, when she was too weary to read for herself.

She held out her book to me with a weak smile and I sat across from her on the straight-backed chair placed there for such a purpose. I continued with the story, although thinking that perhaps the sad fortunes of Little Nell might not be so cheering as I would have liked, but I was not certain that F was even listening, her eyes fixed on the embers, until a knock on the door startled her.

Ruth the scullery girl said Mrs D wanted to see her daughter in the China Closet, if she pleased. Such was F's state of weakness that both Ruth and I together assisted her downstairs – so sad to see what has become of Miss Frances Dickinson, that strong, romping young lady!

Father looked awkward standing in the China Closet, as he always did whenever I saw him in that small space, with its little tables that would knock over if you so much as brushed them, and low, silk-covered chairs that I liked to run my hands over when no one was looking. Along the walls were glass-fronted cabinets filled with all those valuable things that I had once been terrified to dust, for fear of breaking them. Mrs Dickinson sat hunched as if in pain but F did not seem to notice her mother at all, sinking into the small divan to catch her breath while I smoothed her skirts and secured her woollen wrap close around her.

Mrs D then dismissed Ruth but asked Father and me to remain. *I am afraid, Fanny dear*, she then said, *that I have just received some very painful news that I need to impart to you.*

Was there ever a sadder task for a mother than to tell a daughter of her husband's treachery? But Mrs D told it simply, in terms that made it clear that Father had passed on almost all of what I had told him, and I watched F closely for any sign of faintness or extreme distress that the news might provoke. But F – after looking in surprise at me, when she heard of my part in it – seemed not to be brought low at all; rather, she sat up straighter in her seat, her eyes flashing bright, and questioned me on the particulars of what I had seen in the papers from her husband's coat. I told her about some of the Scotch words that sounded just like the way Jane spoke, and about what it said about meetings between Jane and Mr Geils.

Are you absolutely certain of that, Amy? Mrs Dickinson asked me then. *This is a matter of such extreme seriousness and, if you were mistaken, would put my daughter in great peril. I know you to be an honest girl but is there any chance you may have misunderstood the meaning of those Scotch words?*

I could see, then, I had no choice but to speak even more frankly about what Jane had written – about hands and skirts and such – so that I felt my cheeks grow warm. Mrs D breathed in sharply and put a hand to her mouth.

Even after hearing all this, though, F did not shrink and, when I had finished, she said, *Thank you, Amy, for your brave actions on my behalf. I only wish you had told me sooner, not sparing me the truth, even though I know it was your good heart wanting to save me pain.*

I bowed my head, flushing at her words. As if I would not do that and more again for her!

But Mama, F quickly went on, *how should we best proceed? There can be no question now of anything less than a complete separation but how are we to achieve this? The lawyers must be summoned—*

Fanny, my dear, Mrs D said, *only think. Perhaps we should not be so quick to discuss a matter of such consequence.* Mrs D looked to me and Father in turn and I thought she meant to dismiss us but F spoke again before her mother could say anything further.

No, Mother, you are wrong. There is every reason for haste but I confess I know nothing of the law on this matter. It is a pity that Mr Anderdon has ended his visit at his father's house. We could write to him at his chambers directly, though. Or should we send for Mr Jennings? We will require evidence, I suppose – it is a shame that Amy did not retain those vile notes.

Fanny! You cannot mean that Amy should have stolen *them from your husband? Think of the consequences, if he had missed them – not simply for her, but for all of us, from such provocation. You above all know what he is capable of.*

I thought, then, that Mrs D perhaps knew even worse of Mr Geils than I did, in speaking so to her daughter. But what could possibly be worse than what I had seen of him? Or read?

Something must be done, though, Mama! F said sharply, with a feverish air about her that alarmed me.

If I may, ma'am, Father then said. *You have only to say – any assistance that I can give in the matter, any inquiries I could perhaps make. Someone is sure to have seen something.*

F seemed struck by Father's words. *Yes, Webb, yes,* she said, *but it is Dumbuck, surely, where any further evidence could best be gathered. I cannot believe that John – at Farley Hill…*

She faltered and I stole a glance at Father, seeking a sign if he wanted me to speak further, about what I knew of Maria. I did not know what course was best to take. I had only thought that if F knew the truth, everything would come right, but it seemed she was far from safe yet. But surely, with all the money F possessed, and the important legal men she and her mother knew, she could find a way to stay forever at Farley Hill?

Father did not meet my eye, though, nor did he betray any eagerness in his manner, any sense of being a man hungry to avenge his son's honour, only looking down at the cap in his hands like a dutiful servant awaiting orders.

Fanny, dear, you must not distress yourself, her mother said. *Let us take some time to consider. A separation – almost as bad as a divorce! – is surely to be avoided if at all possible? I know you have been unhappy but think what may come from such a step. And what of your babies? You would have no claim over them, I fear. Have you considered that?*

But F only shook her head, scarcely seeming to listen at all. *Mother, what if we were to send Webb to Scotland?*

Mrs D frowned. *What do you mean, dear?*

Well, there can be no question of my returning there now – we can easily write that I am unwell. So we could send Webb, saying that he might be of assistance to John at this difficult time. There must be any number of business concerns arising at Dumbuck as a result of the Colonel's death, and you know how John has relied on Webb before, taking him to Queen Charlton on rent matters and so forth. I am sure you will know better than I the ways in which Webb might be useful to John. You could write a letter explaining it all, so that John would suspect nothing but your goodwill.

And what would that achieve, Fanny dear?

Well, Webb might speak to the servants and tenants, asking about Jane, or even find out where she is now, speak to her. Jennings could perhaps instruct us on the kinds of things that Webb should seek to learn there?

I wished, then, that *I* could be sent, that I could be the one to bring an end to all F's suffering at the hands of her husband. But I was just a maid. I could not make such a journey without remark, nor could I hope to sit in inns, talking freely to strangers about the master of Dumbuck and his doings, or discover the whereabouts of a former maid, as Father could.

Webb, what say you? Mrs D said. *Would you be willing to undertake this duty, on my daughter's behalf? On* my *behalf? You must not disclose to anyone what you are about. My daughter's future – and that of my grandchildren – may depend on your discretion.*

Of course, Mrs Dickinson, Father replied. *Anything for the ladies of Farley Hill. I start at your command.*

John Geils

Dumbuck House
Dunbartonshire
March 1843

1st March

My dear Fanny,

Webb left here by boat today for Liverpool.

Have you had any communication from Jennings about our rents being received and placed in the bank in your name? I hope you are running up no bills as I shall have some large payments to make this year and you know I told you particularly to ask me for money but to have no bills. I shall be most disappointed indeed if you have not attended to my direction on this point.

I hope to leave here on Tuesday next. I shall discharge all the house servants but one maid, and Dugald Macfarlane and his wife are to move into the main house from their lodge to tend it.

I have got lodgings for the poor creatures upstairs at Helensburgh and they go there on Monday night. I shall see my mother to Leamington, with Isabella to keep her company while Nepean is away. I will be with you the following Tuesday. I am very anxious to see you and the children. It seems so long since I was last with you.

I think if the horse is sent on Thursday to wait at the Reading Railroad Stables for me all will be right. In the meantime, Webb will have done something about a harness.

Ever yours,
J. E. Geils

Frances

Farley Hill Court
Berkshire
March 1843

These letters beside me – my fingers itch to throw them into the fire, to watch them blacken and curl and crumble to ash. I know almost every word of them by heart, roughly scratched by a hand that has sponged my skin, dressed my hair, arranged the clothes upon my body. I had never doubted Amy, but to receive this packet from Webb on his return from Scotland was to cross a threshold with a door closing fast behind me. *Ah, but to trap or release me?*

Dumbuck's smoking-room bureau had been the hiding place of these vile letters – as I had suggested to Webb they might be, telling him that John was the only one of the family to use that bureau for his business, and I knew it to have any number of keyed drawers. At last, the nooks and crannies of Dumbuck have been turned to my advantage! I had told Webb, too, to watch for a chance to enter the smoking room from the forecourt undetected and so it had come about, apparently.

But how strange that John had kept such evidence of his treachery – like trophies of his ill-doings, almost! More were found there, beyond what Amy had discovered in John's coat. What is it Jane says at one point, about John *wanting* her to write of their foul deeds together? I feel quite sick to think of it.

On arriving back at Farley Hill, Webb had placed the package on the table before me, assuring me he had never opened it (can that be true?). He then proceeded to tell Mother and me all that he had gleaned in the servants' hall and the inns of Dumbarton. It was common knowledge, he said, of night-time visits to servants' quarters, of maids, shoes in hand, discovered in the hallway near the master's quarters, during the time his wife was from home. The young cowshed boy had told him of seeing things that he would not dare to repeat to we ladies, Webb said.

But all the time he spoke, I could not take my eyes from those folded and tied pages. What did I care for the gossip of Dumbarton, now that they were mine? And what wild letters they turned out to be! They are scarcely *love* letters: it is not clear if their author loves or hates my husband. Was there ever a maid like Jane McPhee? To recall what *I* have suffered if I so much as question John's commands, while she writes as if she were *his* master! Do I almost *admire* her? No! For she has treated me most cruelly, knowing *what I have endured* and yet giving herself to the man who inflicted my injury. Yet there are her mishaps, too. And she knows something of betrayal as well – *Maria McKichan!*

I watched John accuse an innocent man, Jack Webb, when he himself was the guilty party! What a fiend I have bound my life to! I curse myself for what I failed to see from the very first. I, a clever woman, outwitted not only by my treacherous husband but by *my maids*.

So I must stay my hand, though the flames crackle and lick so hungrily. I shall tie the tape around the letters once more, place them back in my own writing desk, turn the key.

Below my window, Webb and Pillinger pass together across the lawn, talking all the while, their breath coming in white clouds, their footsteps outlined behind them in the lingering frost. I shiver, but not with cold.

When I heard John's arrival this morning, I sent word down that I wished to speak with him after he had taken his late breakfast. Almost an hour has since passed. I must go to him now.

* * *

Ah, there you are. Call for more tea, my dear, John said as I entered the dining room.

Not just yet, perhaps, I said. Thinking it best to remain on my feet, I grasped the back of a chair at some little distance from him.

What's that? I require more tea. Ring for the girl.

John, it is most urgent that I speak to you, I began.

It cannot be more urgent than your husband's tea, he growled, but giving me his full attention now. He stood then, walking to the bell to pull it, watching me all the while. By the time he had taken his seat at the head of the table once more, Sarah had appeared.

Tea, John said.

Sarah nodded and quickly withdrew.

Well? he continued.

I will wait until your tea is brought. It would not do to be interrupted once I had begun.

You will speak now, damn you! What possesses you this morning, Fanny?

Very well, I said. *I do not speak easily, but with great pain. I have come to believe that there are grounds – that you – that it is no longer possible that we continue to live together as husband and wife. I require a separation from you, John.*

This is how you greet me! This! After the journey I have had, when I cannot really be spared at Dumbuck after Father's death. You really are a devil of a wife and no mistake!

Sarah knocked again before entering with a tray and we waited in silence until she left the room, John then gesturing to me to fill his cup. It was all I could do to still my hands to control the stream of hot tea and set the pot down once more on the table.

Fanny, this is no time for your hysterics, John then said, having watched me closely, his manner less heated than a moment before, as if it had been just a passing flash of annoyance. I dared to hope, then, that he still had no idea of the loss of his letters; he could not retain any civility at all, surely, if he had missed them, if he knew that his perfidy was thoroughly exposed?

He resumed smearing butter on some broken pieces of bread

on his plate. *Grant me some peace at least before you begin your aggravations,* he said.

No, John, it will not wait. I know about Jane McPhee.

Jane McPhee! What has she to do with anything? He put down his knife but remained unruffled, apart from the dismissive frown that I knew so well, as if he found every utterance of mine an unreasonable imposition.

It is adultery, John. And that's an end of it.

He laughed then – actually laughed! *Jane McPhee – so that is what has caused this? Fanny, that girl is no better than she ought to be. One day she came into my dressing room and the job was done and over.*

No outraged denial or retaliatory accusation! I could never have imagined John speaking so coolly of his guilt.

So you admit it, then? I asked. *And we may summon Mr Jennings, and you shall write to Mr Patrick? Both lawyers, I suppose, will need to be consulted on the terms of separation.*

Fanny, Fanny, Fanny, John said. *You are such a child. I'm afraid you know nothing of men – or of maids, for that matter. It was but a single incident, long ago, and as you know Jane has left our service. I am not proud of the entanglement; I blame my youth and her persistence. I don't know how you have heard of this at last, but I am sure it is much exaggerated. And* that's *an end of it.*

He approached me then, pulling out a chair from the table for me to sit. And I did, so shocked was I by his demeanour, not to mention his brazen lies. The letters told me that this was no *single incident*, but a matter of *years*, from before we were married. Yet I could not indulge my righteous anger at his deception, I must remain vigilant, primed for a sudden change in his temper when I revealed what I knew further from Jane's letters. So I sat, attempting to still my racing thoughts that I might judge how best to proceed. I had been wise not to tell him all I knew, thus far.

He sat in the chair beside mine and reached for my hand, bowing his head to kiss it. The kiss stung like a slap and I started, causing him to laugh again, as if at the antics of a child or a simpleton, but he held my hand more tightly then and I dared not withdraw it. *Fanny, my dear wife*, he said, *will you forgive me?*

But what of Maria? I whispered, my voice betraying me now.

What? He dropped my hand and sat back in his chair. It was his turn now to be startled, but he quickly recovered himself. *What about her? She is no concern of ours now.*

I know about Maria McKichan, too.

Yes, yes, the girl was no better than she ought to be and should never have entered your service. You must attend more closely to your duties in the household, my dear, so that you do not make the same mistake in future.

I shook my head. *No, no.* You *and Maria...*

I? She was your concern, your wet nurse. The girl was nothing to do with me. Was she not recommended to you by the housekeeper at Auchendarroch?

Did you not have relations with her, too, John?

What nonsense is this! he said. *Where have you been gathering such ideas? Is it the gossip of that maid of yours, Webb's girl? Of course she would want to spread stories to absolve her brother from guilt but that my own wife would heed such slander against her husband!*

Now here I faltered. If I revealed that what I knew of Maria I had learned from Jane's letters, I would disclose my possession of them, which must in turn lead to how I had obtained them and thus implicate both Amy and her father, bringing John's wrath down on them both. It was true, too, that Jane had only written of her suspicions regarding Maria – but they had struck my heart with the clarity and certainty of divine truth, especially in the light of Maria's pregnancy and John's role in her dismissal.

Why had I not better prepared myself for this eventuality in our conversation? Because I had believed, even knowing the true nature of my husband as I now did, that charged with the truth of his infidelities, he would confess to them like a man of honour, or at least like a man with some shred of feeling or pity for the woman to whom he had pledged himself, the mother of his children. Foolish woman! He had wronged me most foully, and now he sought to brazen out my accusation regarding Maria, while entreating my forgiveness for a *single* encounter with Jane. His mock sincerity could deceive no one!

Now, Fanny, no more of this, he said. *You must make more effort to marshal your reason; it is your health that has weakened your mind, leaving you prey to the influence of your inferiors. I do not like that you spend so much time with that girl. And her father made a positive nuisance of himself at Dumbuck. I have been much misled about Webb. Your mother has made an error of judgement in placing so much trust in him.*

As to my youthful indiscretion with Jane McPhee, I have admitted it and it does you no credit, my dear, to linger on it so. It is most ungracious of you. And whoever has told you of it has done harm here, too. I will need to know more of that – but we shall say no more of it for now.

I froze then, the last of the fight draining from me: if my husband refused to acknowledge the full extent of his guilt, if he denied outright my request for a separation, I feared that the law would offer me no respite. John had out-played me, leaving me defenceless once more. And if I did not speak further of the letters, I might yet save Amy and her father from John's vengeance since he already seemed to have taken against them.

In any case, he went on, as if we were engaged in an unremarkable conversation such as any husband and wife might have, *I have been most keen to speak with you, now that you are to be mistress at Dumbuck. I confess that it has weighed on me of late that I may have been remiss in preventing you from drawing down more of the income allowed to you in our marriage settlement, for your own purchases of clothing, or books, or what have you. I acknowledge that it cannot have been easy for you, my dear, after you were used to having every indulgence from your mother – too much perhaps, as an only child, but let us not pursue that now.* He smiled again, taking my cold hand once more in a tight grasp. *And Dumbuck is always in need of expenditure, as you know, but now that the household is to be considerably smaller, we may proceed on a better footing, I believe.*

A smaller household? I asked.

Yes, Mother is to take up a residence of her own elsewhere when she returns from Leamington, probably at Geilston, to be nearer her people. And Nepean and Bella are to take a house in Argyllshire, I believe.

He proceeded to talk then of alterations that he planned and I was so weary with the effort of confronting him, and so broken in spirit at having failed so abysmally, that I let him talk on, uninterrupted. The nursery might be moved to a more spacious and salubrious position within the house, he said, there might be new paint and new papers hung, he said. And I only nodded, like the defeated thing that I was.

Then, even more remarkably, he poured me tea, something he had never done before, and proposed that we take a trip together, perhaps the Cheltenham races for a few days? Surely I was in need of diversion after my months of confinement at Farley Hill?

But, John – I rallied one final time to shake off the illusion into which he sought to draw me – *I have been most dreadfully wronged—*

Yes, my dear, I have acknowledged that, and the wickedness of the girl who drew me in, besides. But I have asked your forgiveness and you must admit, in turn, that your mishaps and frequent ill-health have been a trial that would test the most virtuous of husbands.

But it is adultery, John, the worst wickedness!

As I say, my dear, you have forgiven me, and so let there be nothing more said about separation. I am sure you will admit you have been a little hasty, have you not? You would surely not want to give up the children, knowing my claim to them as their father, nor bring disgrace upon them by any public shame that would fall on your name and theirs as well as my own, were you to insist on such a dreadful undertaking?

Am I not already shamed? I asked, my voice a whisper once more. *How many may know of this at Dumbuck?*

I saw, for a moment, a vision of myself returning to that place, subjected to knowing stares and sniggers from the servants. And what of the family? Had *no one* known? Or had they, rather, concealed it from me, indulging the eldest son – whose own father after all had behaved in an unseemly way in his youth! I recalled then hearing Bella once refer to Jane McPhee as *a favourite of the family* and the tea curdled in my stomach. If Bella had known, then

Nepean had known, for she told him everything – and neither of them had thought I deserved better than deception and betrayal!

Now, my dear, I can see you have tired yourself, John replied, resuming his disarming smile. *You should return to your chamber and rest. But give some thought to Cheltenham. I am sure it would benefit us both*, he said, assisting me to rise. Placing my arm within his, he led me from the room, where Amy appeared to help me up the staircase.

Take care of your mistress, Amy, he said. *She is not herself.*

Not myself? No. I was a mere husk, spent and lifeless. Leaning on Amy each time I raised a foot to the next tread on the stairs, I thought only of those letters safely locked in my room, letters that I had not breathed a word of to John, for now.

Amy Webb

Farley Hill Court
Berkshire
March 1843

As I led F away from her cruel husband, John Leigh appeared as if from nowhere and followed his master back into the dining room. Before we had passed out of sight at the top of the stairs, though, I saw Leigh leave again and turn towards the backstairs. Leigh's haste made my heart lift, thinking it signalled a plan afoot for Mr Geils' departure. But why had I not heard a violent scene in the dining room? Why had all seemed so quiet within? Surely Mr Geils would not have agreed to F's request without angry challenge?

F declined her bed in favour of sitting once more by her fire, which I quickly stoked back to a blaze. She asked that I seek out the nursemaid to bring the children down to her but seemed in no mood for further talk. When I returned, leading a lively Kate by the hand while Ninnie the nursemaid carried little Lucy, I found Mrs D already there with her daughter, the two ladies breaking off a sad conversation, to judge from their faces. I think F had shed tears since I left, though she turned her head to the window that I might not see.

Shall I stay, Mrs Geils? (for so I called her whenever Mrs D was present).

No, Amy. Take your dinner, now, and you too, Ninnie. Mother and I will mind the babies for a time, shan't we, Mama?

Neither lady looked fit to watch over the children, I thought, but of course I could say nothing further. What I wanted most to know I had no right to ask, so Ninnie and I went down, even though I had little interest in my dinner. Nor did I learn anything further that day. In the afternoon, Mr Geils accompanied his wife on her drive out in the carriage – something he never did! And when I dressed F for dinner, she only spoke of commonplace things, as she did later, too, when I prepared her for bed.

By then, Cook had told me that there were no changes for tomorrow in the household, no comings or goings expected, such as she would have to be informed of so that meals could be arranged accordingly. So it seems Mr Geils is not to depart, nor any legal men to come to the house. I could not understand what might have happened nor, after what I had risked for her, why F did not confide in me. When I had brushed out her hair, F said I might sleep in my own room tonight. *We shall talk anon, Amy*, was all she said, grasping my hand for a moment, and then dismissing me.

Frances

*Farley Hill Court
Berkshire
March 1843*

Oh, what is it I have done? Have I ransomed myself and my babies for some hollow words of contrition? For the promise of new furnishings, a new nursery?

Such a frightful scene we have had this morning, Amy and I. She was angry that I had forgiven John, even when I told her what Mother had confided in me later that same fateful day. Mama said that *my own father* had strayed from the path of virtue, that there was a daughter born out of wedlock, now a grown woman and married and living in London! Here was another sign of how men differ from women, husbands from wives!

When I asked Mother how she could have tolerated Father's sin, she had said, *Should a wife be obedient to a husband, whatever his actions or words? No, of course not. We are creatures of dignity no less than men. But women have ever been called upon to overlook some failings in their mate, for a higher good – the protection of their children and the continuity of family ties.*

But at what cost, Mother? I had said. *Did you not raise me to be free? Was I not always led to believe that the dictates of my own mind and conscience, as much as my inheritance, entitle me to follow my own path? And that I had a right, in turn, to expect just and fair treatment from others similarly prompted by conscience?*

Mother had shaken her bowed head then, before gently taking hold of my hand. *Fanny, would that it were so,* she said. *We are constrained by the feminine duties of motherhood and what is expected of us as wives, I am afraid.*

I dropped Mother's hand. *But protecting my children is precisely what I cannot do, in the eyes of the law! John made sure to remind me that his rights as a father would always prevail over mine. If I can never remove my babies from a father who would treat their mother so ill, how may a mother be said to truly care for her children?*

Fanny, dear, don't upset yourself so, Mama had said. *We must hope that John will be changed by the knowledge he now has of how his actions have grieved you. Think of how his own father made amends for his youthful indiscretions, through bringing the two young women to live in his own home, and himself living blamelessly ever after, I believe. You know him to have been a kindly man. John has made a start on reform, too, with his assurance of restoring your income.*

Seeing the conviction with which my mother spoke, in spite of what she had herself endured, I tried to believe that reconciling with John was indeed the right thing to do. If Mama believed in a man's capacity to change, then I could but attempt to follow her example.

All this I explained to Amy as frankly as I could – leaving out the part about my father, of course – the morning John and I were to leave for Cheltenham.

You are really not to separate from him, then? You are to go with him to Cheltenham instead? I will never forget what I saw through the library window – and I don't know how you can tolerate such treatment, even before this business with Jane McPhee and – such.

Amy, that is not for you to say! I was riled at such boldness on her part but she would not be silenced.

When I think of how you laughed at Lady Downshire's son and ran free about this place – and to see you now—

Stop, Amy. I will not be spoken to like this! I stood now, feeling at a disadvantage to be sitting while she faced me so passionately in her anger.

And what of those letters? she went on, unchecked. *Does he know you have them?*

Enough! I will not discuss this any further with you. I turned my back on her then, going over to the window from where I could see John below, leading little Kate about the lawn by the hand, watched by Mother and Ninnie from the stone terrace. Mother called something to Kate then, for the cherub looked back to her grandmother, her little face wreathed in smiles, and I saw John raise his head, too, as if laughing. I could not bear to think of Jane's letters at such a moment, locked in my desk close by. I wanted to believe in this idyll of a loving father and his merry little daughter, cost what it might.

There is yet one more thing I must tell you, I said in what I hoped was a calmer tone, turning to face Amy once more. *I know it will grieve you to hear it but you must believe that it is for the best, truly. For you, as well as for me, and Mother too.*

Amy remained quiet then, having no suspicion, I saw, of what was to come. *John is quite determined that your father must be dismissed, and Mother and I see no way to challenge his decision.*

But Father only went to Scotland at Mrs Dickinson's order! Amy said. *Is the messenger to be blamed for the bad tidings he brought?*

That is an end to it, Amy, I said. *I can do nothing further.*

It breaks my heart to see what happens here while I must say and do nothing! Amy broke out then. *And, unlike you, I cannot put any faith in Mr Geils becoming a better man. So, Mrs Geils, I wish to leave your employ.*

Amy! Farley Hill is your home!

Yes! As it is my father's too. But home does not mean what it did, it seems.

Come, do not be hasty. I am sure we will both feel sorry for what we have said here today.

I am not sorry, Mrs Geils – that name grating on me every time she said it, as I saw she meant it to do. *I cannot remain here if Father is to go. And I am afeared that one day Mr Geils will learn it was me who started all this when I first saw Jane's letters!*

But where will you go? Amy, this is really too foolish. I will forgive you everything you have said, if you will just take the time to reconsider your actions. I will not tell Mother a word of this.

As to where I will go, I don't know, she said. *With Father, I suppose. I will ask Mrs Dickinson to provide me with a character and I am sure that her good word will lead me to a position somewhere else hereabouts, soon enough.*

Amy's courage was a thing to behold. No longer was she the shy, half-ignorant thing she had been in our Cavendish Square days – I almost envy her now! She takes her orders for her wages alone; no vow of obedience until death binds *her*. And now she is apparently to do what I never could: leave Farley Hill on the terms of her own choosing.

Amy Webb

Farley Hill Court
Berkshire
March 1843

They have turned their backs on me, Amy! Father said. *After all their promises – and all I have done for them! Quite turned their backs on me.*

He has been permitted to remain a month more in Lower Cottage *as a kindness*, Mrs D said, but what kindness is this? Father is angry beyond anything I have seen, believing he had been promised a cottage for life, and an annuity too, but I can say nothing of that. I have never heard of being paid beyond your time of service; it sounds a thing Father may have misremembered from his drinking days after Mother's death. But for all that, he still speaks very freely around the estate about Mr Geils, and about Mrs D going back on her word to him. I wish he wouldn't.

Mrs Dickinson knows she is wrong to treat Father so, I am sure, for she acts as if to make it up to me, offering me Cook's place in the kitchen when the dear old thing goes to her nephew in the autumn. Lydia has been offered a new position in the big house, too – trying to win us both over with higher wages for the wrong done to our father! Jack is determined to go with Father and me, whatever Mrs Dickinson may do for him, but Lydia is not decided yet.

I should like very much to have the run of the kitchen at Farley

Hill, but how could I remain when my father is shamed and branded unworthy of Mrs D's trust?

Meantime, Father blames himself for a fool that he had nothing in writing from Mrs Dickinson. *Gentlefolks' word alone is worthless, remember that my girl, only what they put down on paper that a lawyer might see counts for anything. Well, we shall see about that,* Father says.

He told me then that on his return from Scotland, he had written down all he had heard there about Mr Geils, more than he had ever told the ladies, thinking he might wait to see how things lay before passing it all on to Mrs D. Now he brought out some pages hidden beneath his bolster and flung them into the fire.

There! he said, clapping his hands as the flames took hold. *Those ladies will never know all that Edward Webb knows! And on their heads be it!*

I always feared what might come of Father's going to Scotland, much as I wanted F to part herself from her wicked husband. From the moment Mr Geils found out his wife knew of his carrying on with Jane McPhee, I have feared him discovering my part in it. I have seen how he behaves with a lady of his own station. What harm might come to *me* if a man so false set his mind to it?

Frances

*Dumbuck House
Dunbartonshire
June 1843*

So strange to return as mistress to the now empty home of the Geils, although perhaps no stranger than a Farley Hill Court without Amy. My last days there were heavy ones indeed; Mother felt it so, too, weeping sorely when I left.

Then the long journey north again to this awful place. With the servants dismissed, only a dairy maid had remained – a girl of barely eighteen, to judge by appearances. I asked John why, since he had not planned to be away from Dumbuck for too long, he had not retained a footman or cook or housemaid, indeed anyone rather than a simple *dairy maid* during his absence. She was, in fact, no longer a dairy maid, he replied; she had commenced work in the house shortly before his father died, and besides, the Macfarlanes had remained as well.

It turned out that John had asked the Macfarlanes to move from the lodge to sleep in the main house because there had been reports of thieves in the area prior to his departure for Berkshire. I knew Dugald Macfarlane, the grieve at Dumbuck, to be a sensible man of many years' service and his wife Morag was also very capable, by all accounts, but they are back in their own place now, Morag only coming in to manage the kitchen in a simple way until the new servants commence at Whitsun quarter-day.

It was Morag who had described Lizzie to me as a dairy maid. I have no complaints about Lizzie's work; she is very willing and seems a quiet girl who, had I not known otherwise, I might assume had always done indoor work as there is nothing rough or clumsy about her. But something in her manner makes me uneasy. It is not sullenness or temper, such as I have encountered with Scotch servants before. Rather, she has what I can only call a somewhat haunted air, by which I mean she seems easily startled – not nervous or flighty so much as always on her guard against unforeseen peril. Perhaps, though, that simply comes from being accustomed to working among large, clumsy beasts whose hooves and horns require watchfulness, especially for a girl of small stature such as Lizzie.

Can I aid you in any way, Mrs Geils? she will say, with a look of concern on her pale, open face that I find almost touching. Sometimes she is at my elbow before I even know of her presence and more than once I have had to insist she go on to her own dinner, so reluctant does she seem to leave me. She has certainly made herself very useful, fitting up temporary quarters in rooms free from the smell of paint and paper glue, and even pitching in with the care of the children, sleeping nights in the nursery since Ninnie the nursemaid took to her bed with a severe attack of ague that shows no sign of subsiding.

Gradually, the house is being restored with the help of day labourers from Dumbarton. Gone are the dark tones and dull papers Mammy favoured, or at least had left unchanged. Where possible, doors have been moved to make spaces larger and lighter although the rooms, with their many passings-through, will never have the dimensions of Farley Hill. On one thing, though, John remains immovable. He will not hear of exchanging our ground-floor chamber for one of the newly-vacant upstairs rooms. I might redecorate them as I pleased, he says, but they must remain set aside for family and guests. He requires the convenience of a bed and dressing chamber easily accessible at all times, with his business room adjoining. He cannot always be running up and down stairs, he says. Futile was it to point out that other gentlemen manage their farms and indulge their outdoor pursuits while maintaining a sleeping chamber upstairs. I have learned that sometimes I must retreat from a sortie I cannot hope to win. So I resign myself to the hurly-burly of the ground floor once more.

* * *

Odd, too, has been receiving Mammy as a guest here. On her first visit after my return to Dumbuck, I made sure to tell her very plainly all that had happened with John at Farley Hill. There have been secrets enough in this family and I will no longer be blamed as the sole cause of John's temper or any other disharmony in the household. She seemed deeply shocked, poor thing, but when she described Jane McPhee as *violent-tempered,* even though I had often heard her praise Jane in the past as *a thoroughly virtuous girl*, I knew beyond doubt that I would never be able to rely on Mammy to see things as they really were if it meant condemning one of her own.

With the Nepeans, however, I will attempt no disclosure. The more I reflect, the more certain I become that they *must* have known about Jane McPhee, if not Maria McKichan. I cannot bear the thought of being on polite terms with them or welcoming them into my home when all along, I now believe, they have regarded me as undeserving to know what my husband was about, with no concern at all for my shame or that of my children. When I think of the times I have sought Bella's *sympathy*, pleading my own ignorance and failings as a wife, and she advised forbearance, praising John's devotion as a husband, I could scream with vexation.

Nepean has been here once, on his own, seeking Bella's allowance on her behalf – of course it would be money that brought him – but I avoided him entirely. He arrived late in the day and by pleading a sick headache I left the men to dine without me. Next morning, he had departed before I left my chamber. I do not know how long I can avoid them in this way; John disapproves of my lack of regard for his kin, persisting as ever in his belief – shared by everyone in this wretched family – that they are each of them the finest company I could ever have the privilege to receive.

In the absence of his family, though, the only real blot on my days are the evenings when I cannot forbid John from my chamber – *there* I hold no power whatsoever as mistress of the household. But I have hit upon a newfound method to endure what I cannot prevent by refusing to entertain any thoughts about the night to come during the hours of daylight. As these northern days grow ever longer, I have nothing to fear, or dwell upon, so long as it is light, I tell myself. Besides, John does not come to my bed so often as he used to.

I have also made plans for a holiday that offers some hope of diversion and distraction. John has accepted my suggestion and we will spend a month or so of the summer at the seaside at Ardrossan – a place that is near enough that he need not be alarmed at the expense of travel or the prospect of leaving Scotland. I have heard Mammy's Geilston relatives speak of its virtues and, in any case, proper sea air *must* be preferable to a dreary Dumbuck summer.

I have arranged for Ayrshire lodgings of modest proportion, in order to preclude any visitors joining us. There will be just John and me, the babies, my faithful Betty, recently returned to me, a temporary nursemaid (as Ninnie is not yet recovered), and the new cook, Bessie Bremner. John plans to sail a pleasure craft there, assisted by Dugald Macfarlane, rather than travel with us but he will not depart for a week or so after I go with the children. Nor does he plan to stay at Ardrossan for the whole of our holiday, but to return to Dumbuck from time to time to attend to estate business, he says. I would not doubt that such *estate business* may also include visits by any family members he chooses to invite. But no matter to me, so long as I have my babies about me at the seaside! Such are the small blessings to which I now must cling.

Elizabeth Campbell

*Dumbuck House
Dunbartonshire
August 1843*

I did not stay long at Dumbuck after young Mrs Geils returned from England. She came on the 15th of May 1843 and about the beginning of July following she went to stay at the seaside at Ardrossan. Mr Geils, her husband, did not go with her, not at the same time. He stopped at Dumbuck after her to get his pleasure boat ready.

I did not stay at Dumbuck while he remained. I had leave to go and see my family for eight days and I went the same morning as Mrs Geils was to leave for Ardrossan. When I got back to Dumbuck at the end of my eight days, Mr Geils had already departed.

On the 3rd or 4th of August, before she returned to Dumbuck, Mrs Geils sent a note dismissing me from their service. It was not owing to any jealousy of me and her husband that she dismissed me. I have no reason to suppose that *that* had anything to do with it or that she knew anything then or had any suspicion of anything having happened with her husband and me.

Rather, during the time the family was at Ardrossan, there were reports that noises had been heard about the house at Dumbuck of a night. I think it was Mrs Macfarlane who so reported it. I do not know why. The Dumbarton Captain of Police gave it for his opinion that it was only from "some sweetheart come after the girls" and as I was the only female in the house at the time, except a nursery maid who was laid up very ill, Mrs Geils blamed me and gave me my leave.

Up to the time of my leaving Dumbuck, Mr Geils had continued to carry on his said adulterous intercourse with me, from time to time. But Mr Geils never had any kind of intercourse with me from the time I left Dumbuck, the same day Mrs Geils departed for Ardrossan. Upon my oath, I never saw him after that.

Frances

Dumbuck House
Dunbartonshire
August 1843

11th August.

My dearest Mama,

I am exceedingly sorry to hear you are troubled by the continued presence of Webb at Farley Hill; it was so unlooked-for that he might choose to remain in the neighbourhood, telling bitter stories of his ill-usage to any who would listen. Who could have foreseen him marrying one of your widowed tenants? It is too, too bad when he had seemed so loyal to us for so long.

I, too, have had trouble with servants. I had to dismiss Lizzie (of whom I told you, the girl who had seemed so helpful when I first returned to Scotland) following word from the Dumbarton Police Captain (!) of intruders at Dumbuck who may or may not have been in intrigue with the maid. The grieve's wife believed so, in any case, and I know her to be a trustworthy woman. Of course, I could take no risk – but I had thought Lizzie a most respectable young woman. Scotch servants are the devil!

But I almost wish I had none but servants to plague me. My torments are of a more unbearable kind for only imagine my horror to find that, after I had departed Ardrossan by land, John sailed back accompanied by *Nepean* (and another man, a friend of the latter I had never seen before). I received them at Dumbuck with the most marked coolness but Nepean is a person totally devoid of all delicacy and so all is quite thrown away on him. Heaven knows how long these worthies mean to favour us but N's presence throws me into the worst agitation once more.

Returning to Dumbuck brings home to me again how solitary and forsaken I am in this strange land. It is hopeless to pretend otherwise. There is not enough new furniture in the world to reconcile me to my life here! I fear that John and I are coming nearer every day to talk of what should never be thought of. I tell only you this – to others I write happy letters, the easier to conceal my feelings, and beg you to tell no one of my true state. Ardrossan changed nothing; mere sea air can only do so much, it cannot change the nature of a man or the heart of a woman.

Now there is my health, too. I have a constant pain in my back, a sure sign. Would that I could have prevented it, and that John had never come to me at Ardrossan. How I miss you, dearest Mama! You cannot come to me soon enough. No one else but you can guess how unhappy we are. I keep up an excellent face, and must continue to do so during Edmund's visit, which will be all the easier knowing that you will be here too. Until then,

Ever yours,

F. G.

Edmund Ffarington

Dumbuck House
Dunbartonshire
September 1843

Sept 13. I am very glad to have exchanged my customary holiday at home at Woodvale for the glens of Scotland instead. The Isle of Wight, for all its beauty spots, has nothing to compare!

I doubt I ever received a more welcome letter than that from Geils, coming as it did in the dog days of the London summer, and renewing an invitation first issued almost two years past when we were both at Farley Hill. A fortnight of sport in the northern air, in addition to the lively company of John and Fanny, is certain to restore me before the law renews its claim on me again.

We are a small party, just myself and Mrs Dickinson visiting, with none of the extended Geils family or other houseguests such as I might have expected during grouse season. But when the company is congenial, and the forests and moors beckon, I require nothing more.

The sporting gods have smiled on us, John says. Spring apparently came late this year, delaying the nesting of the grouse. Nothing is so easy to shoot as grouse, it is true, when the birds are young and remain close to their nests among the old heather. Now they are so numerous that one need only load and fire, John claims. Still, when the birds fly slow and low it seems almost a cheat to bag them so freely.

Sept 14. John was impatient to lead me from the house directly after breakfast today but I owed it to Fanny and her mother not to neglect them so soon.

When last I saw Fanny at Farley Hill, I had been struck by the change in her – as noted in this diary, I recall. To behold the tearaway girl I had formerly known, and seen since only briefly as a distracted bride, now a married lady and mother was a striking alteration. None of us can ever remain the wild things we were at eleven and twelve, I suppose, but the quieter Fanny I had met with at Farley Hill had allowed me to observe the high degree of sense and good taste she possesses. Now, though, there seems *none* of the spark of former times in her manner. Instead, a tendency to melancholy colours her observations of things, coupled with an air of delicacy that suggests her health may be the cause of her altered spirits. Fanny Dickinson could never have been kept indoors by a mere wind squall. John, indeed, was not put off by such inclemency – choosing to spend his day out of doors alone before returning at tea with a half-brace of birds that he took me out to admire.

Sept 15. A day spent mostly in John's company, to make amends for yesterday being devoted to the two ladies. He had planned for us to travel with rod and gun to a small loch to the north, precisely the kind of expedition I relish, even if it means suppressing any misgiving I might have about Fanny and her mother sitting alone all day in a house which I find drearier than I had ever imagined it might be. (It cannot be considered a manor house at all, by English standards, more a grander type of farmhouse, but one very irregular in arrangement, both inside and out. It brings to mind what Miss Austen wrote of another unprepossessing residence: a scrambling place with as many roofs as windows, and none of them elegant in proportion or arrangement.)

John had promised me a choice of grouse or pike, recalling a conversation we had had at Farley Hill about our shared passion for angling. The loch (I do not know that it was large enough to have a name, at least John gave it none) could not have been more different than the flowing Solent, being as still and dark as night, and enclosed by a ring of hills – quite mountains to my southern eyes – so that the slightest sounds carried: the stirring of leaves, the lapping of water on rock.

We took up our position in the shade of a hazel hanging almost over the water, where John said the grouse might be taken unawares, knowing it to be a spot where the older birds led their young to the water's edge to drink, or to swallow the small pebbles they use to grind hard food in their stomachs. There was warmth enough in the day that our post was far from unpleasant, despite the absence of birds. Further along the shore could be heard teal and snipe and John said he had shot plovers here too, so he was altogether jovial at the day's prospects. He is a man of great energy and easy company when in his element, as he always seems out of doors, with no interest in talk of abstractions but only of all things practical – just the kind of companion I need to put all thoughts of Temple from my mind!

Perhaps our late arrival – John had been detained after breakfast by his steward (or grieve, as I believe they are called here) – accounted for the lack of grouse and, as we waited in the shadows, John grew restless, sending the beater off to scout for suitable places to cast our rods instead.

We can't send you back to London without a good tally and a story for your legal chums, he said. *I don't know how you bear it, shut up in an office or a courtroom, endlessly jawing when you are not poring over books.*

I laughed. *Needs must, John*, I said.

Nonsense. I'm surprised your father couldn't persuade you into the navy, like your brother. A life at sea would suit you, I'd have thought.

I shook my head ruefully. It was only to be expected that John, as a military man himself, would express a similar opinion on this subject as my father and brother.

Is there some London lass who keeps you to the task ashore, eh?
No time for that, I said.
Takes little time, John said, springing to his feet and striding

away from the water's edge, deeper into the shadows, to relieve himself. *Meantime*, he called over his shoulder, *I can find you company here, should you require it.*

I'm not looking to marry a Highland girl, I said.

John resumed his post beside me. *Who said anything about marriage? I'd not recommend* that *without a sizeable settlement, and there you would be better served in the south, where the money is. The son of a good family of military distinction, with a not altogether forbidding appearance – you should have no problem landing an heiress in Town, eh?* He clapped me on the shoulder then, in his easy way.

You're too kind. But there aren't many to match Mrs Geils, I imagine.

John raised his gun suddenly and fired. Two plovers crumpled, in a spray of feathers.

Very true, he said. *Come on. Where's that damned Donald gone with our rods?*

My tally: 2 perch, 5 snipe. An indifferent day.

Sept. 17. Rain kept us indoors again, a development that does nothing to improve John's temper. In fact, I am afraid to say that he is far from the man I had taken him for, in more ways than one. He treats Fanny most shamefully, so that I am made quite miserable to witness it. All the more remarkable is that John has no scruples whatsoever in quarrelling with his wife in the presence of the lady's own mother!

At breakfast alone with the two ladies, I was talking of the first numbers of *Martin Chuzzlewit* that they had not yet seen, when John burst in and began at once to rebuke his wife roundly. He had just come from the nursery, apparently, where he visited most mornings – a softer side to the man that quite confounded me, when considered alongside his manner with his wife.

Fanny looked alarmed. *What is amiss, dear? Are the children ill? The nurse has sent me no such report.*

Kate eats herring for breakfast! he thundered. *Herring!*

Yes? She loves it so, John dear, Fanny said.

But John would not hear of it, judging it an unacceptable risk to the child and charging his wife with the most extreme failings as a mother, the whole couched in language I had never heard a gentleman use before ladies before.

Poor Mrs Dickinson looked fearful and furious by turns but of course could not speak, while Fanny did what she could to placate her husband, telling him it should not happen again, and making as if to rise and remedy the situation immediately.

John, however, would not be pacified. *Stay, you devil!* he said to her. He had thrown the fish from the nursery window he said, and impressed on his child the mortal danger she had just escaped so that she had then refused to eat any breakfast at all, a sad outcome which he also laid squarely at the feet of his wife.

All over a herring for breakfast! Where was the harm if Kate was watched over by her nurse, as I am sure she was? Such a nourishing meal for a growing child!

The Ffarington children were all raised on fish, my friend, I intervened, in an attempt to deflect John's attention. *We might have cried in vain for anything else in* our *nursery*, I said, directing a smile to all, but the look that John turned on me then made me fear for his sanity, in truth, such was the flare in his eye, the flush in his cheek. Nor were the two ladies cheered either, looking just as abject as formerly. My speaking did, however, stop the flow of his tirade, as without another word he turned on his heel and was gone from the room, leaving Fanny to apologise for what I had witnessed.

Not at all, Fanny, I said, *but might there be anything that I can do?*

Please don't leave yet, that is all, she said. *And if, perhaps, you might find an opportunity to suggest to John another way of behaving – I do not mean that you should rebuke him, I understand of course that you could do nothing of that sort, and I would not presume on our friendship to ask such a thing. But he is fond of you, Edmund, he might listen to you.*

Of course I will stay, and see what might be done, I said.

Thank you, Edmund, Mrs Dickinson said, giving up on the cold tea in her cup. *We would be so grateful.*

My dear mother would never forgive me if I deserted you both, I said. *I am only sorry that I cannot do more.*

And I am sorry that your visit is spoiled by this endless rain, Fanny said, smiling weakly in a way that quite moved me.

Sept. 18. The strangest day yet in this unhappy place. No hunting or fishing yet again. Endless rain, quite in sheets, and lashing winds besides.

I thought to try what I could to accede to Fanny's request and sought out John's company in his business room – the weather keeping even him and his snappish little dog inside. It is the oddest arrangement, by the by, the ground floor here at Dumbuck. Fanny and John's chamber lies there, although there are empty rooms on upper floors from what I can tell. Stranger still, a communicating door leads from their chamber, via John's dressing room, to his business room, and in bad weather their bedchamber must be traversed in order to enter the business room as the only other door is an external one which provides no shelter from the elements at all.

It is a very objectionable if not improper arrangement, and one I know Fanny finds trying. She told me last evening that she had fitted up rooms on a floor above, where she had thought to have a dressing room and sitting room besides, with similar spaces for her husband on the other side of a spacious bedchamber up there. The suite of rooms had formerly been occupied by John's sister and her husband, Fanny said, but there had been a falling-out with them and while she no longer wished to receive them in the house, John insisted on calling it *Bella's suite* and keeping it set aside for this purpose only.

John's business room, though, is really the only place in the house I have seen him as comfortable as when out in the open air – not pinched and snappish as he seems with the ladies. Joining him there, I adopted my best air of *bonhomie*, as if nothing was amiss in the house, and he needed little encouragement to confide in me then, discoursing at length about his many grievances: the unreasonableness of his wife, the endless demands she made on him to go to England, the inadequacies of her settlement that he believed had been intended from the outset to make him beholden to her. Worst of all, he continued, was *their sending down that damned bailiff to uncover my doings with a maid. It has given them a hold over me I can never shake off – were there ever such a pair of bitches? I shall never be free of them!*

I do not know what kind of man John took me for but such an admission was not the kind of thing I was accustomed to hear between two gentlemen – more like something I might read in a court proceeding of the most salacious kind. Fanny had already discreetly revealed to me the deepest cause of distress arising from her marriage and I had had the painful duty to point out that her continued cohabitation with her husband after her discovery of adultery was considered by the law a *condonation* which, once given, could not be withdrawn, so that a party could not subsequently cite the adultery as a ground for separation.

Fanny, it transpires, had only imperfectly understood the situation she had placed herself in by deciding not to separate from John when first she learned of his vile behaviour. She appears to place an unwarranted faith in some documents in her possession – I do not know what they are, nor did I think it best to inquire – that she believed could be presented to a lawyer should she ever wish to renew her quest for a separation. She knows enough to comprehend that the question of the children remains the biggest hurdle to separation, unless both parties reach an amicable agreement on the matter (and even that would be no guarantee against a father's subsequent claim to custody, according to the law) but she had mistakenly believed that she still held *the means of freedom in my own hands*, as she put it. To disabuse her of this fantasy of liberation was a sad thing indeed; and it dawned on me for the first time that marriage might seem little more than a tyranny to a lady so unfortunately situated.

Listening to John plead *his* powerlessness in our smoking-room discussion, therefore, was an ordeal to be endured as best I could, much as I longed to come to the defence of the two ladies so slandered. Nay, I even went so far as to provide some faint echo of his sentiments, towards Mrs Dickinson at least, in the hopes that so long as he perceived me as an ally, I might in time persuade him of a better, kinder course of action. From all I had witnessed already, I sensed that nothing could be gained by outright defiance of his views, however ill-founded or deluded they might be. Rather, John Geils was a man of such self-regard that he judged the world as either for him or against him and stubbornly maintained such lines of loyalty once drawn. So I reasoned that, if I were ever to offer any real service to Fanny and her mother, I must bide my time and even speak falsely for now, that truth might triumph in the end.

Sept. 20. Was there ever such an interminable fortnight? Not only does the weather continue to curtail our sport – I returned soaked this afternoon, after a few hours' fruitless vigil with John on a boggy hillside – but I remain torn between the duty owed to my host and hostess, respectively. Geils can still be a model host when it suits him, and is certainly a cheerful companion in riding out or walking the glens hereabouts whenever the blasted rain subsides. He may not be a man for books or introspection but can speak with good sense and great enthusiasm about the things that engage him, so that his listener catches his interest in turn and forgets, for a time, the petty abuses and insults he heaps upon his wife.

Sometimes I think if he were a man who had never married, who lived entirely among men – as he had done in his regiment, perhaps – where he might feel free to talk at length of game or farming or horseflesh, he might have an altogether different character. Instead, he seems consumed with a corroding bitterness, chafing at any slight he perceives at feminine hands so that one might think he had married a monster, the offspring of a she-devil!

This unfortunate couple become quite changed creatures when they are in a room together: John cruel and tyrannical, Fanny weak and querulous. Even their shared affection for their children fails to unite them. John seems devoted to his eldest child, taking her out to the farmyard and the plantations when the weather lifts, although I have seen him show little interest in the younger baby, but that is not perhaps singular among even the most virtuous of fathers. Fanny, of course, quite dotes on her girls, just as any mother would.

Today I discovered that she expects another confinement. We had been talking over tea in the room where she and her mother like to sit and which reminds me most of Farley Hill of any of the rooms here, all Fanny's doing, I believe. Mrs Dickinson was writing letters at a table, while Fanny and I sat closer to the fire. Despite the teeming rain outside, John had not followed me in on our return from our failed sport and had just passed by the window, in conversation with his man, while the little brown dog who rarely leaves his side jauntily trailed along after, albeit rather muddy and bedraggled.

At the sight of John, Fanny sighed and turned back to gaze at the blazing coals.

He treats you like a dog, Fanny, I said in a low voice that I hoped Mrs Dickinson might not hear.

Fanny smiled. *I wish he did. Have you seen how he favours Fury?* she said.

Fanny, I really must entreat John to let you return to England with me, especially now, Mrs Dickinson then said, clearly having overheard us.

Fanny looked at me then. *Yes,* she said, *I need to be under the care of our medical man there, dear Dr Bulley, until the middle part of next spring. But Mama,* she continued, *I would rather you did not speak to John. I must find a way, in my own time.*

Or Edmund, perhaps you could speak on Fanny's behalf? Mrs Dickinson then urged. *She does not like me to speak for her because she fears it only provokes her husband and I must say that such fears are not unwarranted – I may speak plainly before the son of such a dear friend, knowing too what you have witnessed here. John has said very hurtful things to me in the past when I have tried to plead my daughter's welfare.*

So here was a task set before me: to persuade a husband that it was in his wife's best interests, and the interests of his unborn child, that she *not* remain under his roof! But I had no doubt at all that the ladies were right in their aim and that Fanny would be best at Farley Hill. I gave my word, then, that I would broach the topic with John at the first opportunity.

Midnight has struck. I have sat with John in his business room once more tonight, as he smoked and stroked the dozing Fury, listening again to all his imagined slights and complaints. And in reply I said not a word to any purpose. Courage, Ffarington! Tomorrow it must be done!

Sept. 21. I have spoken to John, urging him in the strongest terms to consent to his wife going to Farley Hill on account of her health. He was reluctant, saying that he would be unable at this time to accompany his wife but I easily rebutted this excuse, given that Mrs Dickinson was on hand to travel with her daughter and take command of the maids and children. Of course, John's reasons were a mere cover for a petty stubbornness which seems to oppose any measure that he perceives his wife favours and I wondered anew at how a man and wife could come to such an *impasse* when, as Fanny had assured me, *she* at least had begun with nothing but wholehearted and sincere affection towards her husband.

Sept. 22. As if I were not already determined to assist Fanny in her aim in any way I could, the events of late last night – or the small hours of this morning, I should rather say – have spurred me on, so that I have persisted in bringing John round on the matter.

My room being nearby Mrs Dickinson's, I was familiar with the hour of her retirement and, by her own admission to me, I also knew she was a great advocate of black drops to ensure an undisturbed night. So when I was awakened by sounds in the passage outside my door some hours after I had fallen asleep, I feared something amiss. A soft knocking could be heard on a door not my own, followed by what sounded like Fanny's voice, although in lower tones than customary. I rose and donned my robe before opening my door to see Fanny, clad only in a white nightgown – I could just make her out in the dim hallway – and weeping as she knocked on her mother's door.

Fanny? Are you in distress? Do you require a doctor? I called.

Sh! Edmund, please – no, I simply need my mother, but I cannot rouse her. And she continued knocking, a little louder now, and bending to the keyhole to call *Mama! Mama!* in a hoarse whisper.

Fanny, will you not let me help in some way?

No, Edmund, please, I beg you, go back to bed. I am sorry to have disturbed you.

Well, how could I obey such a request? But before I could form any clear resolve, Mrs Dickinson's door opened a little so that Fanny could put in a hand.

Mama! Please, it's only me, your Fanny, let me in, won't you?

The door opened wider then so that Fanny could slip through. When it closed again, I heard the key turn in the lock.

I returned to my bed but did not settle at first, fearing there might be some medical cause that would yet require assistance before the night was out. But all was quiet and I must have slept again for when I woke it was fully daylight and I dressed quickly before descending to breakfast to find Fanny alone.

Good morning, Edmund, I hoped you would join me, she said. *Mother takes a tray in her room. I am so sorry to have alarmed you last night, please forgive me.*

There is nothing to forgive, I said, *I was merely concerned for your health. You are quite well this morning?*

Yes, perfectly so, she said, although the brightness of the room emphasised the pallor of her face, the dark crescents below her bright eyes. *John is out with Macfarlane in the far fields this morning, I believe.*

It is a painful matter, she continued, *but you are such a confidant of the family that I feel I can say to you that it was due to John treating me so ill last night that I could not bear to stay in my chamber, and wanted to sleep with my mother instead.*

I understand, I said, although I did not, nor did I wish to encourage any further revelations on the matter from Fanny, for both our sakes, and was relieved when a maid entered with a fresh chafing dish, putting our conversation temporarily at an end.

After the girl left, we talked of my journey home tomorrow and other minor matters until John sent word that he awaited my readiness to walk out to our final day of sport.

My tally: one brace and a half of grouse.

Mary Geils

*Dumbuck House
Dunbartonshire
October 1843*

I recollect the circumstance of my daughter-in-law leaving Dumbuck in company with her mother and attended by two female servants in October 1843, at the time of my stay there. It was on account of her health that she returned to England with her mother. But I most certainly do not recollect my son saying to me that he was "glad that they were gone" or anything to that effect. And I will positively swear that he did not on the occasion allude to or at any other time refer to his wife and her mother and their two servants "that they were four whores together." It is a decided falsehood.

In the first place, I do not believe that he expressed himself glad that they were gone for he was always sorry to part with his wife and children (for they accompanied their mother). And then, in any event, he never would have made use before me of gross language of the kind suggested.

Upon my oath, I have never heard the fact to be that Jeanie Anderson, a servant in the house at Dumbuck at the time, swore to having heard my son say such a thing. It is entirely a fiction from beginning to end. Indeed, I believe that Jeanie Anderson had been detected stealing provisions from the kitchen just a short time before this, and my son had rebuked her for it. So the woman, Jeanie Anderson, might have had an inducement to say or swear anything to my son's disadvantage. But, in any case, the woman was not present on any occasion of the kind. It is all false.

It *is* the fact, as you have suggested, that I am very deaf, but for what earthly reason could my son have used such words, if it was not intended to be addressed to me, or for my hearing? It could not possibly have occurred that such words had been uttered by John in my hearing and I not have remembered it. Had I ever heard him say such a thing, I never think to have forgotten it!

His wife used to accuse him of addressing coarse language to her, but I always told her that it must have been under great provocation on her part for we never heard him use bad language. He *never* did make use of abusive or scurrilous language before us.

Frances

Farley Hill Court
Berkshire
November 1843

The light of a fiery sunset caught the ruddy beeches and bramble canes, the thorn berries red as blood, lining our way as we approached Farley Hill at last. Village women were collecting acorns in their aprons along the avenue, their little children clamouring as they scrabbled for beech nuts, while older boys gathered armfuls of fallen leaves to feed their smoking bonfires. On turning into the park gates, robins and wood pigeons could be heard in the coppice – the same coppice that Miss Mitford always says *is a place to live and die in*, such delight she finds there in any season.

The mildness of the approaching evening was such a contrast to the morning mother and I had driven away from Dumbuck, a day of such biting chill that my little ones had fretted and cried until they were soothed to sleep by the regular motion of the conveyance. Truly a cold departure in every sense – John handed me brusquely into the carriage before turning back into the house, not a word to Mother and scarcely an acknowledgement to his own children. When I had raised my hand in farewell to Mammy, looking out from the drawing-room window, he appeared beside her. Mammy's smile froze, then, and she turned to John as if startled. Then I saw them both no more.

I had not dared set my hopes on the promise that Edmund had

extracted from John, that I might return to Farley Hill with Mother until my confinement. After Edmund had departed and October wore on, John would allow no firm plans to be made and Mother began to contemplate a solitary journey home after all. In desperation, then, I had written to Mammy at Geilston, begging her to visit us that she might entreat John on my behalf, and she had agreed to come directly.

I would not have put my trust in Mammy in that way if she had not so recently written me such a strange letter. In my previous to her, I had frankly confided that I feared a separation was inevitable before too much longer and, in reply, she had sent me *two* distinct letters, concealed under the cover of one. The first had expressed only commonplace sentiments that John might see (as he so often asks to read my letters, both written and received), while her second letter acknowledged John's failings as a husband and expressed a comforting solicitude for my troubles. Nothing could have surprised me more than to see his own mother forced to exercise such deception! For all that I knew she would never challenge John directly, this secret letter gave me at least some crumb of consolation.

Once Mammy was at Dumbuck with us, John became a little more circumspect, a little less belligerent, and we three ladies began to talk openly of my travelling back to Farley Hill as if it were a certainty, so that John at last accepted its inevitability, pledging to follow me in a few weeks' time once his mother had returned to her Geilston home.

* * *

Through the window nearest me, I see the solitary old thorn in the distance illumined in the last rays of another bright day so that every jagged, twisted branch seems brought close. Dr Bulley has today declared me delicate but in no danger and I am not to be confined to bed! So here I sit, rejoicing, as the fire casts flickering light and shadow on the library's curved walls that so enchanted me as a child. Yes, I have taken possession of this room once more, determined to reclaim it from its horrid associations, dwelling instead on happier recollections here.

But not everything is as it was in former times. So many have gone; old Matthew dead, Cook gone to her nephew, and Sarah married to a tenant farmer with Lydia Webb moved up into her post. Quarrelsome Pillinger has been dismissed and become something of a vagrant, by all accounts, reliant on the charity of Webb, now the landlord of 'The Hare and Hounds'! I have a new maid here, too, Janet Gibson, a woman with the strength and cheer and sound sense of Amy but some ten years older. I grow fond of her already.

Mother's ever-faithful Hester is now almost the only familiar face remaining here of the folk below stairs, apart from Lydia, who would tell me nothing of Amy when I inquired, claiming she could not recall the address of her sister's new employer, only that it was in London. I knew this could not be true but had not the heart to challenge the girl, so weary am I of trouble and so uneasy in my heart over the treatment of old Webb. Mother and I should never have given in so easily to John, in his insistence that Webb must go; Amy was right to challenge me and now she is lost to me. I can hardly blame her sister's sullen manner towards me, though it is painful to see her feeding her discontent against things that are past and beyond our control.

What an old woman I sound, embittered by fate. Yet some things *do* endure, providing comfort. The Anderdons have visited, with all their customary amiability borne of long acquaintance. Old Mr Anderdon comes alive when he speaks of wintering in Rome, shaking off the frailty of age that has delayed their departure thus far. Italy sounds quite a place of magical renewal, despite its antiquity! Today, too, a letter from Edmund has cheered me considerably, confirming he is to come and stay a few days with us.

Most of all, though, I must treasure the new life within me. I *pray* this will be my last confinement and, for that reason, I have determined that she will be a new Frances (or Francis, I suppose, if needs be). A new *Frances Geils* – that would truly be a fresh and precious life!

Edmund Ffarington

Farley Hill Court
Berkshire
December 1843

Dec. 2. I find matters just as formerly between Geils and Fanny – an *appearance* of civility that I fear will not withstand any scrutiny. What has grown far worse, though, is John's contempt for Mrs Dickinson, in her own home! After the two ladies had left the table this evening, he indulged in the most vehement abuse of our hostess, the least of which was his repeated assertion that he *should like to trample over the Old Devil's grave.*

I had already decided, on the journey down to Farley Hill, to continue the strategy I adopted when last we met at Dumbuck, namely, to appear to echo John's grievances, the better to retain his good graces in the hope of serving Fanny's interests in the future, should I be called upon to do so.

So, this evening – to my shame do I record it here – I said in reply, *Oh Geils, she can't live for ever*, or something to that effect, which brought a cruel laugh from him but succeeded in turning aside the conversation. Assent to his views seems to soothe him, at least for a time, where dissent merely inflames and prolongs his obsessions. So I was much relieved when he began to talk of his intention to pursue some plans for development at Queen Charlton, seeking my advice on a legal question regarding tenancies there. I could shed no light on the matter, and we then rejoined the ladies with but little enjoyment for the remainder of the evening to anyone present, I believe, myself included. Observing Mrs Dickinson to be as thoroughly amiable and ladylike as ever, and recalling to what expressions I had been led by her unrelenting son-in-law, I am anxious about how long I can persist in my duplicity with John. Fanny barely spoke but at least looks to be in a satisfactory state of health, given her condition. I will hope for a better opportunity to converse with her tomorrow.

Dec. 3. John rode out early alone, leaving me to breakfast with the two ladies. Both were in indifferent spirits, I judged, and we confined our talk to mere pleasantries. I can't help but observe how far more salutary the surroundings are at Farley Hill than at Dumbuck House – a graceful elegance throughout the rooms, with the warmth of genuine English hospitality besides.

John returned as I was writing letters in the library, while the ladies sat at their needlework in the China Closet. He insisted we immediately set out in pursuit of pheasant, saying a man he had encountered on his ride had told him they were in particular abundance on the eastern fringe of the estate, where the stubbled fields give way to an adjoining wood. I could not refuse and, leaving my letter, we were off, not returning until the tea tray had already appeared in the drawing room.

My tally was unimpressive but not shameful – a half-dozen pheasant and the same of partridge. John had greater success, as usual.

Fanny did not reappear after tea, being indisposed, and so at dinner I was caught awkwardly between Geils and Mrs Dickinson. I did not sit late with that gentleman, however, and finding Mrs Dickinson had already retired from the drawing room, I took my leave, too, pleading my unfinished correspondence.

Dec. 4. My final day at FH. John hunted alone today; I cried off on account of the ladies who had asked me to stay behind, as they expected a visit from their neighbours, the Anderdons. As the eldest son of that family is a distinguished man of the law visiting from London and known to me previously only by reputation, I needed little encouragement to remain. The visit was indeed a pleasant one, with Mr Anderdon QC and his wife, in addition to his amiable father and mother, on the eve of their much-delayed departure for Italy.

Fanny has seemed in better health and spirits today. In the few minutes we were able to converse alone, she showed none of the dejection that had so alarmed me at Dumbuck. The poignancy of her situation struck me anew, however, knowing her to be in the family way, and with all the anxieties that any woman must confront at such a time, no doubt amplified by the infelicitous marriage in which she finds herself.

I, of course, reiterated my willingness to offer any support I could, a hollow enough offer, I concede. But she held my eye fearlessly with her own of striking blue, and said – words that I commit here verbatim, so strong was the impression they made on me – *I would be most grateful to call on the support of such a trusted friend as you, Edmund, but I believe that I may yet surprise many with what I am able to achieve on my own behalf.*

We shared no further private words and I have called for an early horse in the morning so do not expect to see her again before I leave.

Frances

Farley Hill Court
Berkshire
January 1844

A new year begins with but little promise of new beginnings – with the sacred exception, of course, of what I pray will be the safe arrival of my child of the spring. I think of her whenever I am tempted to despair and, really, when Kate and Lucy are brought down to play merrily before me, I can almost fancy myself happy.

Edmund's return once more for his promised New Year's visit did not turn out quite the pleasure I had anticipated. I am coming to rely on him so much for his sound and steady judgement, as well as his sympathetic friendship, that perhaps I expected too much of his short stay. John, however, monopolised much of Edmund's time, being starved of male company whenever he is at Farley Hill. And thus I came to learn more of what John feels and thinks, thanks to Edmund's reports. I am grateful for Edmund's loyalty to me in this way but, oh, how I wish what he conveyed was not such a source of pain – to learn that John speaks openly of his contempt for my mother and of his frustration at what he views as the concerted effort of Mama and I to thwart him at every turn! It makes me fear that when once I depart Farley Hill this time, John's irrational fear of collusion against him may prevent me from ever returning.

On what foundation might I build any hope of delaying my return to Dumbuck indefinitely, beyond my confinement? *I will not think of that place*, I tell myself countless times, but yet it intrudes even on to these pages. Perhaps I must even renounce the comfort of expressing my thoughts in this way, straying as they so often do to what I dread to contemplate.

Illustrated London News

April 1844

BIRTHS: 27 April. At Farley Hill, the residence of her mother, Mrs Charles Dickinson, the lady of J. E. Geils, Esq., of Dumbuck, of a daughter.

Edmund Ffarington

Middle Temple
London
June 1844

June 10. How can I continue in the intolerable position in which I find myself with Fanny and John? Tonight cannot be repeated – to see such disappointment on Fanny's face, when I told her I was unable to remonstrate with John on her behalf, was almost more than I could bear. And yet what that poor lady *must* bear, and bear alone…

The dinner at Ibbotson's Hotel to toast the safe arrival of little Frances Clotilde Geils, occasioned by the couple being in Town with old Mrs Geils, who is on her way back to Scotland after greeting her new grandchild, promised an agreeable enough occasion. But Fanny was a ghost of her former self, pale with hectic eyes, and John restless and out of sorts. Old Mrs Geils was indisposed and did not join us at all so we were a sombre group of three at table, the movement of the waiters coming in and out almost the only sign of life among us. I seemed to taste nothing and Fanny barely touched her plate.

Before dessert was served, however, a message was brought to John from his mother, causing him to excuse himself to go to her. No sooner had he left the room than Fanny, the spell broken, poured out to me her distress, saying that John had behaved most savagely last night after they had retired to their chamber, apparently provoked by some remark she had made about his family in Scotland and how they seemed to have so little regard for her.

I knew of John's fierce loyalty to his family but could scarcely believe what Fanny told me: how he began by abusing her but quickly became physically menacing, eventually forcing her to her knees to demand she beg his forgiveness and retract what she had said of his family. He also reverted to his ravings about Fanny's mother, that I had witnessed myself when alone with John, threatening his wife that if anything should happen to separate the couple, their children should never darken Mrs Dickinson's doors again. Fanny was so shaken simply retelling what had occurred that I feared she might swoon away and I wondered if I should summon help.

But she did not swoon, instead rallying to implore me to speak to John to say he must never again lay a hand on her. I see her now, such a vivid impression did the poor lady make upon me in her desperation: burning spots of colour in her cheeks, her hands stretching towards me across the table as if she would cling to me for safety, yet her eyes darting again and again to the door where she feared her husband might return any instant.

And did I rise from my seat and go to her? Did I kneel by her side and swear to protect her? No, coward that I am; I did not. I maintained the proprieties, so that if John returned he would see nothing amiss in my behaviour. I sat, unmoved, offering the sad creature only platitudes of sympathy until I saw her shoulders sag and her head bow. Placing her hands in her lap, she twisted and twined her fingers as if unable to control their movement, but said nothing further.

It must perhaps have been a full ten minutes of silence between us then – or at least it seemed so – before John returned, saying his mother had apparently been troubled about some matter regarding her early departure in the morning. Somehow the rest of the evening passed and I was never so glad to be outside on Vere Street once more, breathing the close London air of a warm spring night. I waved away the hansom cab summoned for me, choosing to walk home instead, and haunted by the final words Fanny had spoken to me, when John had been momentarily distracted by attending to his cheroot.

You are a witness, she had said. *Remember what you have seen.*

I pressed her hand in leaving but I did not have the heart to tell her that, in the eyes of the law, I had witnessed nothing of any value as evidence that evening, that all I had was her own account of events. As plain as her suffering was to any who would but see, what John had done to her was invisible as far as justice was concerned. I can do *nothing* to protect her.

Frances

Dumbuck House
Dunbartonshire
December 1844

Christmas Day

My dearest Mama,

This is Christmas Day and as dull and miserable a one as you can well conceive, dreary in and out of doors, although I have now somewhat recovered from the bad cold that has plagued me since my return. I have quite lost all my colour and I am sure you would think me looking quite ill. Kate is far from well, too, and everyone sees that she is thin. It is evident this place does not suit her but to say this to John is treason!

The only tolerable way I pass my time is being alone and busy with my own occupations but that is quite impossible while the house is full of visitors. The Nepeans are here with Mammy, but so far the Ns are monstrously civil and by mutual consent we avoid each other as much as we can. Mrs N, in particular, seems much improved, doubtless as sly in reality but never saying one word objectionable to me, and Mr N plays and sings in a first-rate manner, it must be conceded. Perhaps the presence of our other guests, the Misses Noble from Geilston, relatives of Mammy's you may recall, play some part in maintaining the polite cordiality that prevails in the house, and for which I am grateful, even if their company is hardly diverting.

I remain hopeful, too, of travelling to Glasgow and Edinburgh early in the new year, if I can persuade my beastly Bear to go to the parties and balls and concerts to which we are again invited. Such a change will be *so* welcome, as I am sure you may imagine, and Mammy is more than happy to remain here with the children during our absence. I will miss the dear little ones so much but I *must* have some diversion, something beyond this place. Amongst the throngs and sights of those cities, I will not be so thrown on John's company, nor his moods that are so hard to escape at Dumbuck.

I hope you are not dull, dearest, but I fear this season must make you very melancholy. I am sure it will be a comfort to you to hear that Lucy and Baby Frances are going on better than I might have expected, and please have no fears for Kate – she is not as well as when at home with you but still shows wonderful sense and observation. I hear most kindly from many friends, including Edmund F.

Ever yours,
F. Geils

John Geils

Dumbuck House
Dunbartonshire
January 1845

Tuesday, Jan. 21.

My dear wife,

I should indeed be sorry that you should think me a jealous husband, and still more to think so myself; but to avoid being called a cuckold, which, report says, is the same as to be one in reality, I must beg that you do not take me again into public until you can assume a less familiar manner with other men, as I witnessed on our final night in Glasgow.

As I have no moral power whatever over you, I adopt this method of being forced to write to you, in black and white, concerning my observations as a husband. Your extreme confusion, and the unwarrantable familiarity in look, manner, and bearing of your admirer last evening, surely warranted an instant explanation had it not been for my unwillingness to take issue with a total stranger.

On reflection, I cannot but think that your own bearing could alone have authorised such open and unlicensed attentions from a stranger in a public theatre; and as I have a weakness about my being looked on in general as a cuckold, I must desire that you refrain from any more of this sort of thing whilst under my roof. If your thirst for admiration is ever so strong, I call on you to reflect how dear the purchase should the slightest breath of impropriety attach to your fair frame.

J. E. G.

Frances

Dumbuck House
Dunbartonshire
February 1845

He will scrag me, he says.
   Twist round my neck.
   Knock off my damned little head.
   He will not end without leaving a mark on me, he says.
   I am a lying bitch.
   I am a damned lying bitch, he says.

5.

The day of trial

(March 1845–April 1848)

Elizabeth Lanfear

Letters to Young Ladies
On Their Entrance Into the World;
To Which Are Added,
Sketches From Real Life

(London: J. Robins and Co)

On the Conjugal Duties

When the dark clouds of adversity are gathering thick around, man's haughty soul is ofttimes brought low; his spirit fails, his courage is subdued; like the forest-tree uprooted by the tempest, he falls to rise no more. Woman, on the contrary, resembling the lowly shrub, over which the storm sweeps, despoiling but not destroying, often raises her drooping head, and, with a firm mind, meets with meek submission those troubles which she could neither foresee, nor, foreseeing, avert.

In the hour of affliction or misfortune, female fortitude is peculiarly requisite, and, when properly exerted, must ever ensure respect. In the time of distress, the day of trial, a virtuous and sensible woman endeavours by her example to infuse courage and magnanimity into those around her; and, should adverse circumstances or pecuniary disappointments render it either necessary or prudent in her to give up luxuries, or even comforts, to which she has been long accustomed, she parts with them at once, readily and cheerfully, without repinings, without reproaches, not wishing to increase by her weak and unavailing regrets the difficulties of her situation, or, by her helplessness, add to the weight of woe, which may already press too heavily on those whose peace of mind is to her of more value than all the goods which vanity may covet or prosperity bestow.

Catherine Dickinson

Farley Hill Court
Berkshire
April 1845

I was present on one occasion when Mr Geils behaved with great personal violence to my daughter. It was at my house at Farley Hill, in the early spring, soon after my daughter and her husband had returned for an extended visit. I cannot from memory speak to the exact date but I know it was around Easter, the time of the Reading Ball, I recollect, for the dispute on the occasion arose out of something connected with that.

The circumstances were these. A friend of mine, Mrs Pigott, wanted us to attend the Basingstoke Ball on the Friday in the same week as the Reading Ball was to take place (on the Tuesday). My daughter wrote to decline the invitation, on the grounds that Mr Geils did not like going out and was likely to object to attending a second ball in one week. In her note to Mrs Pigott, however, my daughter suggested that Mrs Pigott's husband might ask Mr Geils in person when they met at the Reading Ball, and try to persuade him about the Basingstoke Ball. And Mr Geils happening to see the note, chose to take offence at it, though in truth there was really no cause for anything of the kind.

My daughter was in the round room, the library of the house, when Mr Geils began to find fault with her about the Ball business, and after some words in which my daughter expressed her regret that he should have such an objection to going out, he got into a violent passion and ordered her to leave the room. I had known him order her out of the room on similar occasions but this time my daughter, who was naturally irritated at such treatment, refused to leave. Her husband then seized hold of her with the intention of turning her out of the room, trying to force her out, which my daughter resisted as well as she could. In the scuffle, she caught hold of a shelf and held to it as tight as she could. And such was the force Mr Geils used in dragging her from her hold that the shelf was actually broken.

My daughter at this time was, as was well known to Mr Geils, in the family way again, being at least five months gone. And I was frightened lest Mr Geils by his violence should do her some injury. I begged him to desist, laying hold of him and saying, "You will kill her." But he persisted, swearing he would turn her out "though he did for her." I recollect well his using that expression.

In the end, he succeeded in forcing her from the room and I followed my daughter out, finding her much agitated. Her dress was much discomposed. I recollect observing that the ruffles at her wrists were torn. One of her hands had been injured in the scuffle in some way and was bleeding. And the hook of a golden ornament called a chatelaine, attached to her waist, was broken. The hook of the ornament was thick and strong and could not have been broken without considerable violence.

Edmund Ffarington

Farley Hill Court
Berkshire
June 1845

June 11. Farley Hill once more. Fanny and John seem on better terms than when I saw them last, at that dreadful dinner at Ibbotson's Hotel a year ago.

A military chum of John's from his Dragoon days, a Mr Draper, is staying here too and rarely leaves John's side so that may go some way to account for John's good humour – as of course do the Ascot races, the reason bringing both Mr Draper and myself here. At least, speaking for myself, the *stated* reason for my visit.

I do not care for Mr Draper, and nor do the ladies, I perceive. He is of a type that I have observed among some former military men: considering every other occupation inferior and never quite reconciling to civilian life. They therefore fail to adapt their manners to suit a drawing room rather than a barracks or a ship's mess. He makes John cheerful but that does not make him good company for the rest of us. Still, I have heard no quarrel between husband and wife since I arrived and for that I am grateful, on poor Fanny's account.

June 14. My final day here. John and Draper to Ascot again, excited as schoolboys. I have had my fill of horseracing and remained behind with the ladies.

Fanny looks fatigued after the past couple of days but really so much stronger and brighter than the last time I saw her in the family way. We have had only brief opportunities for private conversation but there has been no mention of an imminent separation. I rejoice to think that she may have become reconciled to her marital state; indeed, nothing could cheer me more, nothing at all, especially if I have played any small part in such an improvement through my tempering influence on John, slight as it may be.

Such is Fanny's general health, in fact, that she and her mother talk of travelling to the Isle of Wight after John departs for Scotland next week, if Dr Bulley judges Fanny fit for the journey.

The sea air for all concerned – both ladies and the children – would, I am sure, be of great benefit. I have given my wholehearted support for the plan, all the more as it may coincide with my own visit home to Woodvale in July, long promised to my mother, to whom Mrs Dickinson has already written, she tells me.

Frances

Cowes
Isle of Wight
July 1845

1st July.

My dear John,

Your letter arrived last night and I am sorry to hear your journey home was so disagreeable. We are all very well and the weather most favourable. The Solent is calm as a lake, which does not please the Ffarington sailors but makes them regular visitors, to our delight. They were here again yesterday, Admiral and Mrs Ffarington, their eldest son, Walter (the poor man lacking an arm, as you may recall hearing, following a sailing accident, but really he fares remarkably well), and Edmund, of course. They invited us to dine at Woodvale, two days hence. They truly are the kindest friends to us.

Mostly we continue in our quiet way, Mother and I. Kate delights to gambol in the garden here, such colour in her cheeks now. Mary Lucy and Frances grow fatter each day, the dear angels.

I do not think you should plan to leave Dumbuck again so soon as you mentioned, since Dr Bulley is of the belief that I may not be confined until the beginning of August. Mother and I talk of extending our time here if all continues as congenially as at present. You well know, dear John, that until the shooting begins, you will have nothing to amuse you at Farley Hill, although I am sure I regret your absence beyond measure.

I hope my letter reassures you of the benefits to me and the children of remaining by the coast. You said you loved me when you wrote, and now allow me to return the compliment.

Ever yours,

F. Geils

Reading Mercury

Saturday, 26 July, 1845

BIRTHS

On the 21st inst., at Farley Hill, at the residence of her mother, Mrs Charles Dickinson, Mrs Geils, of a daughter.

Mary Geils

Geilston
Dunbartonshire
July 1845

31st July

My dear Fanny,

Thank you for your note yesterday in reply to my congratulations on the birth of little Cecile. I assure you I think daughters to any amount are most desirable, being well calculated to brighten the evening of your days, whilst sons are seldom companions to their mothers after they reach the age of fourteen.

I am sorry to hear you have experienced a check in your recovery. Your doctor's prediction for an August confinement having proved wrong (so fortunate that you returned safely to Farley Hill in good time and did not extend your time away), I hope that you feel you can continue to trust his judgement in all other matters. But I am sure your dear mother would not allow him to continue your care if she did not have full faith in him.

Pray kiss my *four* granddaughters and accept my thanks for adding to my store of little lambs. God bless you, my dear Fanny. My love is with you all.

Believe me affectionately yours,
M. Geils

Frances

Farley Hill
Berkshire
August 1845

A little stronger today, walking on the lawn as far as the pines and back. To be finally released from my chamber and able to take the fresh summer air is freedom indeed. I almost swooned in the heady delights of the roses beyond the terrace! Ninnie then brought my two biggest girls out to me in the dappled shade of the lime walk, where I could sit and watch them weaving in and out among the trees. Such a paradise here – at least until nightfall.

I will not think of that. Only of damask roses and blackbirds and the laughter of children and the strawberries they have been promised for their tea.

Still a month and more yet until we are to leave for Somerset. I cannot see how it can be put off, not when we are to host the annual muster of the Yeomanry Cavalry at Queen Charlton! With John as Honorary Commander this year, I had at one point even hoped that the event might herald the beginning of us making a real home there at last, if John could but find some purpose and occupation in Somerset to lure him from Dumbuck.

Now I can only think of home as any place where John is not. A chill steals over me when I think of our planned departure from here and I wake in the early light each day wondering what can prevent it. Is it weakness or strength that will serve me best?

I have not told Mother what has been occurring each night. In the brightness of day, it seems even to me that it cannot be so. To speak of such a thing would be to bring it to life from the shadows where John says, *Don't tell.*

Catherine Dickinson

Farley Hill Court
Berkshire
September 1845

One day, in the early part of September, 1845 (I am not able to speak to the precise day), I was walking in my garden with my daughter, when she put the question to me, "Mama, what is sodomy?" I explained to her what I understood it to be, that is, that it is the love of one man for another, and then she put the question to me, "Can such a thing be done to a woman?" I expressed my ignorance on the subject, but said that I never heard of such a thing.

Nothing more passed then; but the same night, after I had gone to bed, she came to my bedroom, and said she must speak to me; and then, referring to the conversation (just described) which had passed between us in the morning, she said to me, *Mama, my husband tries to do that to me*, or *does that to me*, I forget what her precise expression was then. She did not further explain the nature of her husband's conduct, but she represented that she had not been able to understand her husband for some time past; that he had made attempts which she could not understand on several different occasions, and that a recent attempt on his part had been, as she described it, *more undisguised and disgusting than any before*, and that she was determined to learn whether she was obliged to submit to be so treated. She seemed very much distressed in making the communication and remained in my room for the rest of the night.

The following day, her husband being out shooting as usual from an early hour, my daughter and I talked further about the matter. We formed the intention of consulting with Mr Anderdon, QC, as we knew he was down from London on a visit to his father at Farley Hall.

Oliver Anderdon, Q. C.

Farley Hall
Berkshire
September 1845

I was on a visit to my father's house, little more than a quarter of a mile from Farley Hill Court, the residence of Mrs Dickinson. There is a great intimacy of longstanding between our families. On the afternoon of Friday the 12th of the said month, a private interview took place at my father's house between myself and Mrs Dickinson at her instance, during which she made a certain communication to me. In consequence of such communication, a further private interview with Mrs Geils took place, as she had accompanied her mother to Farley Hall. That interview proceeded upon the footing of, and in reference to, the communication so previously made to me by Mrs Dickinson.

In consequence of these communications with Mrs Dickinson and Mrs Geils, I went up to Town the following day (Saturday) and communicated with Mr Jennings of the Temple, their family solicitor. And on my return on the same day through Reading, I communicated with Dr Bulley, the medical advisor of the family. I then returned to Farley Hall.

The following day, I saw Mrs Dickinson again and afterwards had an interview with Mrs Geils. At her request, I gave her certain advice as to her demeanour towards her husband until his intended departure from Mrs Dickinson's for Somerset. My advice concerned the manner in which the lady should conduct herself in the presence of her husband.

Ann Wigley

Farley Hill Court
Berkshire
Sept 1845

I have been in service to Mrs Geils as a nursemaid for over a year, both at Farley Hill and at Dumbuck, and so I am able to swear that I observed a great change in her manner towards her husband in the late part of summer that year. I observed that she kept out of his company as much as she could, so much so that I knew her more than once leave the room directly as he came in. It was when I happened to be in the drawing room with the baby one day that I saw that there was something wrong between them, so that she left the room directly. I recollect that after, I remarked on it to Mr Geils' servant, John Leigh, who said that he had also observed something amiss between Mr and Mrs Geils but that he did not know what the cause of it was any more than me.

I recollect, too, that around this same time, Mrs Geils moved into a different bedroom, not her regular bedroom, that is, the room in which she had been recently confined due to her fourth child. She requested me to sleep in the adjoining room to hers. Her new chamber was an inner room and mine the outer room leading into hers. And no one could go into her room but through mine. She never left her room of a night. All the time that I slept there I used to keep my door locked at night. That is my habit. So that nobody could have come in or out of my mistress's room without my knowing it. She retained that bedroom until Mr Geils left Farley Hill.

Frances

Farley Hill Court
Berkshire
September 1845

Mr Anderdon says I must by no means allow John to touch me again. When he speaks so, he offers a glimpse into a realm where one might allow – or disallow – a touch, a grasp, a thrust, a blow; a strange realm where one might say, *No, that is beyond the bounds of your power, sir,* and be heeded.

I wonder how long John will permit me to sleep in the chamber alongside Mother's, watched over by Ninnie in the anteroom? I barely sleep, fearing he might somehow break through and overpower me in the night. And, were he to do so, would Mr Anderdon think that I had *allowed* it?

* * *

Mr Anderdon says that we are to retain an air of normality here until John's departure for Queen Charlton but we must then be ready to act quickly. I am tortured by the prospect of John questioning what takes us so frequently to the Anderdons these past days. As much as I can, I avoid my husband in the house so that my face may not betray me in some way, under this weight of secrecy I bear like guilt.

This morning, the last but one before John is due to leave for Somerset, I had no milk for Cecile. So piteously did she cry that I feared all she sucked from me was fear and shame, poisoning her little body so that she arched her back and flailed like a desperate thing. Ninnie carried her away then and I was left alone, spent and trembling.

* * *

Mr Anderdon says I must write a statement for him about what John has done to me. But how can I do such a thing? It would not be like these pages, written for myself alone, but for the cold scrutiny of the law. I doubt that there is any way a man might truly comprehend a woman's words on such matters. How can ink on a page tell what cannot be *shown*, what cannot be *felt* except by she who has endured it in her *flesh*?

* * *

It was that farewell kiss, about which John made such a performance before his man John Leigh, that did it. The brush of his cold lips on my colder cheek – false, all utterly false, both my submission and his affection! But it was like a spell had broken. I remained stock-still on the house steps as he whipped his horse and the trap jerked forcefully forward, Fury yapping beside him all the while, but within I felt my pulse quicken, my anger rise to fire my purpose.

I turned back into the house, closed the library door behind me, and wrote like a creature possessed, scarcely looking down at my pen on the page, telling my tale as though it was the story of some other poor benighted creature, not myself at all.

This was done. And then this.
And then it happened again.
And again.

When I was finished, I dared not read the pages back over but folded and sealed them as fast as ever I could, impatient now to give them into Mr Anderdon's hand when he calls before leaving for London, there to pursue matters further on my behalf.

* * *

Mr Anderdon took the sealed envelope from my shaking hand, impressing on me that the utmost secrecy should be observed on the matter for the present.

That I do not need to be told. I am very good at keeping silent on what should never be spoken.

He also advised against committing to letters anything that can be communicated in person. Written words are to be weapons, from now on, wielded with the greatest care lest they wound those in most need of their protection.

Mr Anderdon then asked if there was someone I trusted sufficiently to act as my intermediary, someone who might be dispatched to Somerset to negotiate terms of separation in person with my husband, now that John's actions have given me fresh grounds to pursue such remedy.

There is but one person I can trust with such a perilous task.

Edmund Ffarington

Middle Temple
London
September 1845

Sept. 19. Mr Oliver Anderdon's note summoning me to Lincoln's Inn at *your earliest convenience on a matter of great urgency and delicacy* immediately alarmed me about Fanny. The absence of any detail only increased my certainty that it must concern her, especially since he had never previously had cause to communicate with me since we met at Farley Hill Court.

With haste, then, I abandoned the case papers on which I was engaged to walk the half mile to Mr Anderdon's chambers. Nothing could prepare me, however, for what he conveyed, first by his own brief spoken communication and then by Fanny's written statement – a document the like of which I never thought to see in that fair lady's handwriting. I do not confide to this diary what I read therein. To think that I had ever befriended the monster capable of such villainry!

No sooner had I understood what Mr Anderdon requested, on Fanny's behalf, than I agreed to depart forthwith, let my chambers' master say what he might. By the afternoon, I was on the train for Reading, where I was instructed to meet with Dr Bulley, Fanny's doctor. Mr Anderdon gave me a note to present to Dr Bulley and also undertook to send word to Mrs Dickinson, in hopes she might meet me in Reading also.

From Reading Station, I took a conveyance to Dr Bulley's and was immediately ushered into the good doctor's library. It was Mr Anderdon's view that greater knowledge on the matter from a medical man might prove necessary to equip me for the meeting with Geils in Somerset. Before I had left my chambers, I had written a note to Geils, alerting him to my intention to visit him while in the county on some legal business, I said.

By the time my unpleasant talk with Dr Bulley was concluded – unpleasant only in its subject, the old doctor could not have been more solicitous on Fanny's behalf – Mrs Dickinson had arrived in her carriage. She had come to escort me back to Farley Hill, she said, after consulting herself with Dr Bulley. She could not be prevailed upon by Mrs Bulley to take a cup of tea before the two of us departed once more, such was the dear lady's grim purpose. I never wish to see my own mother in the state of affliction that poor Mrs Dickinson seemed to be suffering, her noble face quite ghostly beside me in the carriage. I believe we passed the entire journey in silence.

Indeed, it was all I could do to keep my own composure whenever my thoughts strayed to the details of Fanny's document, in which she had spoken of a *twelvemonth* during which she had endured unnatural approaches from her husband – without a word to her mother or anyone. A twelvemonth in which I had often sat in her company – *and his* – with not a hint of understanding the enormity of what she was suffering, the fear and loathing she was forced to conceal! Not for the first time I marvelled at the unseen fortitude some ladies must command, when all the while they are never secure in that most sacred place – their *home*.

At Farley Hill, Fanny awaited us in the drawing room. I had feared to find her weak or ill-disposed – as she had every right to be – and while I was not altogether reassured by a hectic glitter in her bright eyes, she gave no indication of giving way. She insisted on calling for tea although it was past five, no doubt seeing how much in need of sustenance her mother was by then; I fear I scarcely looked more robust. It was but a poor showing of refreshment that we three made when the tray arrived but I did at least see a little colour return to Mrs Dickinson's face after she had drained her cup at Fanny's urging.

The tray removed, Fanny proposed that she and I withdraw to the adjoining China Closet, where we might remain in sight but out of earshot of her mother who, after the urgency of her journey, now sat unmoved like a figure in a *tableau vivant,* her gaze fixed out into the park. Fanny's self-possession, premised as it seemed to be on her confidence in me to achieve her purpose, made me then hasten to assure her that Geils would surely accept the terms of *amicable separation* – what a mockery that term was in the current circumstances! There could be no doubt, I said, that he would want to save himself from what I considered *destruction*, the inevitable consequence of his vile crime coming to light, and therefore agree to live quietly in Scotland upon the funds granted to him by the marriage settlement, leaving Fanny in peace at her mother's home with the custody of the children.

Yes, she said, *you must threaten him with exposure outright, and if he refuses my terms you must tell him that I will seek to have the marriage settlement set aside in its entirety, and bring the whole thing out before a court, or to that effect.*

Fanny, we cannot blackmail *your husband,* I said, regretting my choice of words as soon as I saw her recoil as if stung. I could see her blood was up now and was deeply sorry not to have been more mindful of her desperate state, despite her admirable appearance of resolve.

Blackmail is originally a Scottish *word, is it not?* she said, sharply. *That is not at all my intention, Edmund. But can you blame me for hoping to avoid public exposure of these most shameful events? And do you not think that, at your urging, John might even be persuaded to quit the country entirely to avoid the shame – or worse – of my charges against him?*

Of course I had to counsel Fanny in the strongest terms, then, that my standing as a barrister precluded me from issuing any such threats or inducements to John as those that she, in all innocence no doubt, pressed on me. I did my utmost to persuade her that the law was worthy of her trust and that she must not in any way seek to take matters in her own hands; nor could I, in good conscience, assist her to do so. I could see that my words displeased her and I did not like to be a source of disappointment in her hour of need but what else could I do? I hoped, I said, that she knew I wanted only to secure a brighter future for her, and without the security of a legal separation she would never be safe from any future claims from John – on her money *and* her children.

Well then, he may have his twelve hundred pounds a year from me, she said. *I give it up to him, a ransom in perpetuity, in return for my freedom. He should be exultant to have such an offer, when the threat of absolute disgrace is his only alternative!*

She sat back in her chair, then, and I could see the effort our conversation was requiring of her. Her breath came in shallow gasps and livid spots of colour appeared and quickly faded in her cheeks, by turns. My heart was moved to see her suffering so and not for anything would I have contributed to its increase at such a time.

Fanny, the position you find yourself in is deeply unjust, I said, *as any reasonable person must acknowledge, and as those who care for you must feel with great sorrow on your behalf. You know, I trust, that I no longer harbour any illusions about John's character and temper. All friendship between he and I must be at an end hence forward, whatever claim to it I shall be forced to feign tomorrow in order to mediate this cause between you.*

But your own knowledge of the man must tell you that we must proceed with the greatest care, even to the extent of appearing to concede at least some of his claims as a husband, in order to achieve the greater good of your freedom, as you so rightly call it. And if he does not agree, you must prepare yourself for the fact that the law will not perhaps extend to you the full justice you seek. The natural justice that you are due is not always within the purview of human courts, alas.

She seemed, then, to surrender her anger, nodding once or twice as she considered my words and looking more sorrowful than she had since my arrival.

Of course, Edmund. I concede I have no real knowledge of what the law allows, and indeed I am sorry if I have seemed to tell you how to proceed when the statute books are your daily reading. I did not mean to seem high-handed in this way. I am sure you will know how best to handle John; I trust you entirely. And I owe you a heavy debt for coming to my aid that I cannot begin to express, much less repay.

We spoke no further of distressing matters and Fanny and her mother soon after left the room together. I am sorry that no formal leave-taking took place between us then, as neither lady was strong enough to dine with me and I took a simple repast alone before retiring. At dawn I am to leave for Somerset.

Sept. 20. It will be long ere today's events fade from my recollection, I am sure, but I must commit them to this page, lest at some future point I am called upon under oath to recount the odious conversation. I have already penned a hasty letter to Mrs Dickinson, knowing how eagerly she and Fanny would be awaiting news from me, but I spared them details that I reveal here.

After travelling the final eight miles from Bath by fly, I passed through the stone gateway of Queen Charlton. Anxious as I was with the prospect of my task, I was struck by the fact that the manor house was altogether more imposing – with its lofty grey stone gables and large Georgian casements – than I had gathered from Geils' representation of it to me. He always spoke of it as little more than a ruin, not fit for his family to inhabit without substantial expenditure, if not complete rebuilding. It is true that the gardens to the front were unkempt but there was an elegance and proportion to the house that could readily be made good, I believe, and signs of improvement were already in evidence, such as the new road through the estate that my fly sped so smoothly over.

From an expansive tiled entry, I was led by a servant through an inner, timbered hall to a drawing room occupying a great part of the western wing on the ground floor, but I was not left long to survey the somewhat scant and faded furnishings.

John entered, followed by a panting Fury, and extended a cold hand to me. *Edmund! Your note did not lead me to expect you in Somerset quite so soon. I was just heading out on foot for an hour or two's sport before dinner when the servant found me. You will stay to dine?*

He then gestured for me to sit in one of the two high-backed chairs before the unlit fireplace. *As you may see, things are behind hand here; I never use this room when I am alone, as that damned man should know who let you in. My man is still back at Farley Hill, that he may travel down with my wife when she comes. The folk here are little better than useless. They seem to resent having their idleness interrupted by opening the house for their master!* He sat down opposite me, no hint in his demeanour that he detected any change in my manner towards him as yet, and pushed Fury aside when the creature sought to sit her haunches on her master's boot.

I am very sorry to say, John, that I have been to Farley Hill and am now come upon a most unpleasant errand. Mrs Geils will not be joining you here.

Yes, yes, she says she's not well enough to travel, I know. That damned Bulley is too soft on her, if you ask me. Damned inconvenient, too – there is the Yeomanry trooping, you know.

John, your wife has made an accusation against you that involves your personal safety, I said, unable to delay any longer revealing my purpose for this visit.

What's that? My safety? I don't take your meaning, old fellow.

Your safety in the eyes of the law, John, arising from an accusation of – an unnatural crime.

I do not understand what you mean, he said, still betraying no hint of alarm, or even astonishment at my opening our conversation in this serious vein, which I found very odd indeed.

An unnatural offence against your wife, I said, and we regarded each other in silence for a few moments. I had braced myself for an explosion of temper but was more unnerved by his apparent composure in response to my extraordinary disclosure.

The law knows no such offence, he said finally. *A man may do what he likes with his wife. There is some old judge has laid it down as law.* Mulier est omnino. *You know your Latin no doubt? Woman is cunt all over, as we used to say in the Dragoons.*

My bile rose to hear him refer to Fanny in this way.

You wife wishes to secure your agreement to a separation henceforward, I said, with more warmth than I had intended.

He sprang up then, so that Fury yelped from the unwelcome contact with her master's foot once more.

Ha! So you have come on my wife's bidding then, Ffarington? A fine commission for a gentleman to come as spy and traitor to his friend!

I come precisely as a friend, and in the role of mediator, if I may. I had regained my composure, knowing how much depended on my keeping an air of rational civility between us, but John merely shook his head, laughing hollowly as he paced about the chamber.

I see now why you did not follow your father and brother's profession, he said. *You're not a Miss Nancy, are you, Ffarington? You do seem to prefer the ladies' company, I've noticed. Draper said as much, too.*

Let us not stoop to personal insults, John. Am I to understand, then, that you deny the accusation?

Speak up, man, I can scarcely hear you, he said. *You are not helping your cause by whispering like a girl. It's a mistake, that is all. A woman might be mistaken on such things. Any man knows that.*

Geils, there is no mistake in the matter. Besides, Dr Bulley has confirmed it and I also understand you have attempted it before.

Bulley! You have spoken to Bulley? Damn you all! What kind of conspiracy has been going on behind my back with you and those bitches, eh? How long has this been brewing? He was beginning now to work himself up into the kind of rage that I had expected from the first but the effect on me was quite other than he might have wished: the more he seethed, the calmer I became, watching as the enormity of his situation seemed at last to dawn fully upon him.

Besides which, he continued, *it was she who asked me to take it out of one hole and put it in the other!*

So let me understand you, John, I said, suppressing my revulsion as best I could but, in the process, sacrificing the coolness of my temper. *You begin by saying that no such crime exists; then that Fanny is mistaken about what happened, as is her doctor; and then that it was your* wife *who made this unnatural request of you. Which is it – an invention, a mistake, or your wife's initiative? They cannot all be true. You would do well to hit upon a defence and stick to it – or better yet, be truthful, man!*

The force of my words was such that John ceased his pacing to stare at me for a moment. *She must have read such things in the newspaper*, he then said, but I was in no mood to listen to his weak excuses any further.

I come to you today, John, authorised by your wife to obtain your agreement to an amicable separation to the effect that you consent to live in Scotland apart from her, and you allow her to reside with her mother and to have the children in her care under her mother's roof. In return, your wife will consent to you retaining the whole of the twelve hundred a year granted to you by her marriage settlement. If you agree, nothing more will be said about what we have discussed here today. In my capacity as a legal man, it is my unequivocal advice that you accept these terms.

John paced in a more desultory way than previously, and I judged it best to give him time to consider my proposal before speaking further.

I should like to consult Nepean, he said after a time, not bothering to turn to face me from where he had come to stand before the large window looking out over the grounds to the front.

I would advise against that, I said, knowing the antipathy that existed between Fanny and the Nepeans and seeing no hope of the situation being improved by involvement from that quarter.

Silence fell between us again, John maintaining his vigil at the window while I remained in the chair by the cold hearth.

I think, then, he said, *that you may tell my wife that I defy her – and her mother, too – and that they may do their worst. And if they pursue this matter through the courts, you may rest assured, Ffarington, that I shall summon you as a witness on my behalf.*

It pains me greatly to hear you say so, I said. *I should rather go abroad than appear in such a case as your witness, should that ever come to pass. But am I to understand then, to leave the matter in no doubt, that you do not deny the original charge I laid before you today?*

Of course I deny it, man! It is all a mistake, as I have said, and I have no fear in that regard. Neither do I fear the marriage settlement being overturned, should my wife be foolish enough to carry her threat into action – for that is what it is, a hollow threat to secure my relinquishment of what is mine, both my money and my children!

John returned to me, then, placing a hand on my shoulder in what he imagined was a friendly manner, evidently not sensing my inner recoil from his touch.

Come, let's put an end to this unpleasantness, he said. *You must take a glass of wine with me before you depart.*

And to my eternal shame, and wanting nothing more than to flee his presence for good and all, I did indeed partake of refreshment with him before I left Queen Charlton, although there was no further suggestion of dining. I can recollect nothing of what we may have spoken of, for words must have been exchanged over that glass. I even shook his hand once more on my leave-taking, such is our easy reliance on the forms of courtesy, even when in the presence of one we hold in the deepest contempt.

John Leigh

Farley Hill Court
Berkshire
September 1845

I forget the precise day on which my master left Farley Hill to join his Troop of Yeomanry on the understanding that Mrs Geils and the children were to follow in a few days to join him at Queen Charlton. Mr Geils' groom had gone over to Reading with the saddle horse and so I had to accompany my master in the dogcart. Just before we started from the door my master said to my mistress, "You'll come down in a day or two and bring Kate with you." (Kate was their eldest child.) And my mistress said to him in answer that she would if she were well enough or to that effect.

They kissed each other at parting, I recollect. My master, after he was up in the dogcart said to my mistress as she stood by to see him off, *My dear, I have forgotten to kiss you*, and he got down and kissed her. There was nothing on her part that I noticed but what an affectionate wife would do in parting from her husband with whom she was on the best terms.

It was only after I had come back from taking my master over to Reading in the dogcart, that I heard from Ninnie (the nursemaid, Ann Wigley, that is) that Mrs Geils was not to go to Queen Charlton after all. *There's something the matter*, Ninnie said to me, either on the stairs or near the pantry door, I don't recall exactly. *I don't think*

Mrs Geils will go to Queen Charlton. She told me that something was up but she did not know what.

Then it was two or three days following that, that Mrs Dickinson called me into the dining room and asked me if I wished to leave Mrs Geils' service. And I said, no, I had no wish to do so. And she said that it might be as well to tell me that something would come out about Mr and Mrs Geils but she did not say what.

Mrs Dickinson explained to me that I had been Mrs Geils' servant, that it had been Mrs Geils who paid my wages, and she asked if I would continue on at the same wages but as her (Mrs Dickinson's) servant and I said that I had no objection.

It never was put to me in any way to choose whether I would be Mr Geils' or Mrs Geils' servant. I was merely asked if I wished to leave Mrs Geils and when I arranged to be Mrs Dickinson's servant, I did not know but that Mr Geils would be coming there as before. If I had known then what I afterwards learned I never would have consented to stop.

On the following Wednesday after Mr Geils had left, and the day after Mr Ffarington had stopped overnight, Mrs Geils left Farley Hill with Mrs Dickinson and the children, as well as Ninnie (Ann Wigley that is), Janet Gibson and Hester Byars. And I did not see Mrs Geils from that time. I do not know where she went to. Her boxes and things were sent up to the office of Mr Jennings in London.

A day or two after that, Mr Geils and Mr Nepean, his brother-in-law, arrived at Farley Hill. They stayed, it may be, no more than half an hour. Mr Geils asked me if Mrs Geils were there and I told him no. And I told him, as was the fact, that she had told me to tell him if he called that she was very poorly. I mentioned to him too what Mrs Dickinson had said to me regarding her being my mistress and he told me that I could do as I chose, that it was no odds to him.

They did not come in the house beyond the lobby. Mr Geils' clothes had been packed up by Mrs Dickinson's orders and put into a box which stood in the hall. By Mr Geils' instruction, I gave him some of his shirts out of the box. Mr Nepean asked for a glass of beer, which I gave him. They went to look at the horse in the stable too. That is all they did that I recollect. I noticed that

Mr Geils looked pale and ill but I did not notice anything in his behaviour to mention.

Mr Geils asked me, I recall, if the children were there and I told him, "No." And he said "Are you sure?" and I said, "Yes, I am sure they are gone." And he asked me when they went away and I told him. He asked where they were gone to and I told him I did not know. He made no further observation respecting the children that I recollect. Not a word was said to me or in my hearing, as I believe, as to the reason of Mrs Geils being gone. I am sure of that.

I deny on my oath that I, on that or any other occasion, said or declared to any person that, during their visit to Farley Hill, Mr Nepean had clapped Mr Geils on the back and said "that it was the happiest day of his when he got rid of his wife," or to that effect. Or that Mr Nepean or Mr Geils, speaking of Mrs Dickinson, said that they would drive the old woman out of the family or to that effect. Or that they would get the "children and then the damned little bitch would soon break her heart" or to that effect.

That same day, after Mr Geils and Mr Nepean were gone, I wrote a letter to Mrs Dickinson. Mrs Dickinson had directed me to write her word by her solicitor, Mr Jennings, if Mr Geils came and to tell what he said and I did so.

In that same letter, I told Mrs Dickinson that I would be leaving her service to re-enter the service of Mr Geils. When I had thought over the matter, I could not help but think that, notwithstanding what Mrs Dickinson had said, I was really Mr Geils' servant, seeing that when he had first left Farley Hill for Somerset he had left his things and one of his horses under my charge here. And though certainly he told me, when he and Mr Nepean called, that it did not matter to him whose servant I was, I did not think on reflection that I was acting fairly by him to leave him in that way. I was afraid, as well, that I might get myself into trouble if Mrs Geils should think of making a go-between of me. For, as I have said, she and Mrs Dickinson had desired me to write of everything that went on to them. And I did not like the job.

Francis Henry Dickinson, MP

Kingweston
Somerset
September 1845

I am acquainted with Mr and Mrs Geils. The latter (Mrs Geils) I have known from a child. She is my father's second cousin. My father was her trusted advisor. Since his death, I have been so. I have also been her trustee since her marriage.

My acquaintance with Mr Geils commenced with his marriage and I was on friendly terms with him up to the date of their separation. I never liked him much but I had no reason for thinking that he disliked me. I am not aware so far as I can remember that I ever had occasion to observe that his feelings towards me were not of the most friendly kind. I would observe, however, that I always thought him an odd fellow and could not understand him. And therefore, on that account, dislike may have grown up between us.

On or about the 28th of September I received a letter by post from Mr Geils announcing that a friend of his would call on me. On the following day, I then received a visit from a gentleman (a stranger to me) who represented himself to be Mr Nepean, Mr Geils' brother-in-law. The separation which had then recently taken place between Mr and Mrs Geils was the subject of the said interview between Mr Nepean and myself and, amongst other things, mention was made of the charge made against Mr Geils of having had a guilty connexion with his wife.

Mr Nepean, on behalf of Mr Geils, denied the imputation put upon him (Mr Geils) in that respect. Mr Nepean suggested circumstances which he seemed to think might account for the grounds on which that charge was made. He intimated that in consequence of its having at one period given Mrs Geils pain to have connexion with her husband in the natural way, he (Mr Geils) had at her desire performed the act (to use Mr Nepean's own expression) "*a posteriore*" and that it was *that* probably which had led her to the mistake as to there having been a connection between them of an unnatural kind.

Immediately afterwards, I wrote a full account of what had passed between Mr Nepean and myself at this interview and, on that basis, I provide here the substance of what transpired on that day.

Frances

Cavendish Square
London
October 1845

I wonder now what I imagined freedom might be. Certainly not this: constantly beset with gentlemen who all take great pains on my behalf – good Mr Anderdon and Mr Jennings; my cousin and trustee, Frank Dickinson, and Mother's old friend Mr Clive; and even Edmund's father, the Admiral, come up from Woodvale to offer his assistance, he says. And, not least, Edmund himself, of course. They solemnly troop in and out of the drawing room, talking to us endlessly of allegations and suits and statements and articles and interrogatories.

Sometimes as they talk, I push my fingernails deep into the flesh on the inside of my wrist, that I might remind myself that it is of *me* they speak, and what I have endured. Yet not a one of them can tell me how to erase the vile ways John has used me or how I might put myself beyond his reach *now, here, forever*. All the time I try to attend to them, I am half-listening for a sharp knock at the door, or a rap of a crop more like, that would announce John has come for me at last.

When Leigh had written to Mother from Farley Hill to say that John and that wretch Nepean had been there seeking the children, I understood anew the danger I had placed my girls in, simply by seeking my own safety. What a topsy-turvy world is this, where a mother who wants to keep herself free from harm must risk the surrender of those in her care, even more powerless than herself!

It was then that Mother and I had a long and bitter quarrel. I wanted to flee. I had wanted to do so when first we left Farley Hill, to take my girls deep into the countryside and lodge somewhere unknown to John. Mother had talked me round, however, persuading me we would all be safe at Cavendish Square, close to those working on my behalf, who well understood my need for protection. But after Leigh's letter arrived, I told the maids to pack at once, heedless of Mother's urgings to calm myself. She said we must continue to mind the advice we had been given and pursue the law's protection for the children, and that required us staying in London, for now at least.

I think I was a little out of my wits that evening, as it was only when I saw the fear on Mother's face that I grasped how close to unreason I was, flying about the house and calling to Ninnie and Gibbie to *make haste, make haste*! Mother at last took me by the hand and led me down the stairs to the front door that she might show me the footman turn the key in the lock and take up his post there, commanded by Mother to remain there all night so that I might leave the children undisturbed in their beds and allow the maids to retire.

* * *

Today I had a rare outing – to a church in Paddington I had never visited before, for little Cecile's christening. I could only be persuaded to go, leaving the other children at the house, when Edmund offered to remain behind as custodian in my absence. Admiral Ffarington accompanied Mother and I, together with Ninnie and the babe, to the church, where Frank awaited us to stand as godfather. Some arrangement had been made with the curate, the details of which I was spared, that nothing might be considered amiss with the father being absent from such a sacred ceremony, and it was soon done and I could hurry home once more, relieved beyond measure to find Edmund undisturbed at his vigil. A brief glass of sherry to wet the baby's head followed before everyone left, dour as funeral mourners.

I had no private words at all with Edmund today, nor have I in fact since we came from Berkshire. I do not quite know why we may not talk as we did formerly, except that Mr Anderdon insists that the strictest proprieties must be observed at this time. I can no longer judge what is a reasonable precaution and what might arise from my own disordered thoughts, but so many instructions and cautions do I receive that it is like I have become a child once more. Would that I *were* still a child, romping with Amy Webb in those attic rooms where my own babes now sleep!

What would Amy say to know that I have separated myself from John at last, as she had urged me years ago? I know not where she is now – gone from her post as cook for one of Miss Mitford's London friends who I heard fell on hard times and was forced to break up her household, discharging all her servants. Is she still somewhere in this teeming city? How passing strange it is to think that Amy might, this very moment, be stirring her fire, making her pies, dressing her birds, in a house not unlike this one, while I sit idle and afraid.

Edmund Ffarington

Middle Temple
London
October 1845

Oct. 6. On leaving Cavendish Square following the christening, I accepted Mr Dickinson's invitation to take Father and me to our respective destinations. Father alighted in Warwick Street at his lodgings and Mr Dickinson then suggested that I accompany him to his appointment with Mr Anderdon.

In Mr Anderdon's chambers, the chief order of business under discussion was a bill to be brought before the Chancery Court to petition that Fanny's children be made Wards of Chancery.

It is my strong belief, Mr Anderdon said, *that as Chancery is known to look favourably upon protecting the pecuniary interests of children, sometimes even at the expense of a father's right to guardianship, we should make haste to secure the children of Mrs Geils in this way. We should not hope that any future suit for separation in the Court of Arches might prevail to Mrs Geils' advantage. The atrocious allegations she brings may, by their very extremity, be met with incredulity there, I fear. Eh, Mr Puckle?*

Here Mr Anderdon turned to a gentleman sitting in a corner of the room and partially concealed by the wingback of his chair, who had not acknowledged our entry and who I had therefore assumed to be a clerk or scribe of some sort due to the notebook open on his lap. But, now addressed by Mr Anderdon, that gentleman turned to

Mr Dickinson and myself with a wry smile – in lieu of any formal greeting – that seemed to say that though he had reason to find the ways of the courts sadly wanting, he was not downhearted by their folly. *Indeed, Mr Anderdon, indeed,* this gentleman said. *Arches is not known for its generosity to lady petitioners, it is true. But, if I may be so bold, sir, I would also discourage any undue optimism regarding Chancery, as poor Mrs de Manneville found when my Lord Chancellor ruled against her.*

But de Manneville v de Manneville does not apply here, surely? I then said. *The suit Mr Anderdon proposes would simply request the children be made Wards of Chancery, rather than seek a ruling on the marriage, or the children's custody explicitly, as Mrs de Manneville did. Providing the children with some financial protection against any unreasonable demands made by their father, through the appointment of trustees, is entirely consistent with Chancery, I would have thought.*

Mr Puckle, who gave a start when I began to speak, had then fixed me with a steely gaze between narrowed eyes that almost disappeared beneath his ginger brows and seemed to weigh up the merit of each word I uttered.

Ah, Puckle, what do you say to Mr Ffarington then? Mr Anderdon said, in a tone that suggested the two men were accustomed to sparring over legal niceties. *Mr Puckle is quite a loss to the Woolsack*, Mr Anderdon continued, now addressing myself and Mr Dickinson. *Not only is he without equal in seeking out witnesses, whatever lengths they might have gone to in order to conceal themselves, and extracting evidence they did not know they had to offer, but he devotes his remaining time to attending court sessions, near and far.*

During the latter part of Mr Anderdon's speech, Mr Puckle had been shaking his head vigorously and chuckling. *Nay, nay, sir*, he said, *you have me wrong there, although I do confess I find a day in court more diverting than any night in the theatre. But I stand corrected by Mr Ffarington, for placing too much weight on my observation of the manner and behaviour of men such as the Lord Chancellor when on the bench, and not enough, perhaps, on the case books wherein their judgements are transcribed, and where studious men like Mr Ffarington decipher their implications, no doubt with greater enlightenment as a result.*

This is all very well, Anderdon, Mr Dickinson said, betraying an impatience with the digression of the conversation. *If it is your advice that this course of action be taken, then let us be on with it. I will agree to stand guardian or trustee to the children – whatever the appropriate term is. What more is required?*

I could see that Mr Dickinson's breezy disregard was not lost on Mr Puckle, who now turned his attention to Fanny's relative with a pronounced alteration of expression so that his impressive eyebrows quite rose to his hairline, both of which were a ginger or russet colour flecked with silver that reinforced the rather avian impression he made on me the more I regarded him. I judged Mr Puckle to be a keen student of human behaviour and, but for the openness with which his face registered his reactions, I could well imagine that his facility with witnesses might be everything that Mr Anderdon had claimed.

Well, given that Chancery will be chiefly concerned with questions of property and inheritance, Mr Anderdon said, *it is my belief that we would do well to avoid connecting the children's interests – in every sense of the word – with the marriage settlement, to avoid unnecessary complications that could arise. Instead, I have already proposed to Mrs Dickinson – and she has given her assent on the proviso that you, Mr Dickinson, also approve – that she place a sum of money in trust for the children as the foundation of the suit. I would then append her name as guardian alongside yours, so that my Lord Chancellor may see that the situation of the children is kept free and clear of any of the entanglements connected with the marriage or – God forbid – its subsequent dissolution.*

God forbid? I said. *You think, sir, that the marriage may not go to the Court of Arches for a legal separation after all?* I was alarmed at this hint of prevarication from Mr Anderdon, after what I had endured at Queen Charlton.

That is not for me to say, Mr Ffarington, he said. *My concern is purely with the Chancery matter at this point as the most pressing for Mrs Geils. I will continue, of course, to consult and advise her in any way she chooses but I would say that, for now, I advocate caution in proceedings on that front.*

Sir, do you not think it is of the greatest urgency to ensure that Fanny secures the separation she so justly deserves, without the least delay?

Patience, Ffarington, patience. Reason, caution and patience must be our watch words in our dealings with Mrs Geils, Mr Anderdon said, drawing attention to my slip in speaking so familiarly of Fanny. *Any other – passions – must be kept firmly in check.*

I felt his rebuke, with its implication that I was motivated by more than a friend's concern or a lawyer's commitment to justice, but bitterly swallowed my response. Little did I expect, though, to be thrown a morsel of comfort by the puzzling Mr Puckle who, leaning towards me said almost *sotto voce, wheels are in motion, sir, wheels are in motion.*

And what of Geils in all of this? Mr Dickinson continued, once again seeming to ignore Mr Puckle. *Is it really the case that we can seek a ruling on the children in Chancery without informing him of the suit?*

Indeed we can, Mr Dickinson, and I would advise we do precisely that, Mr Anderdon said. *With Mrs Dickinson's funds in trust, we present the Lord Chancellor with a relatively simple suit to protect the children's legacy, and the appointment of guardians will offer further security in the matter.*

When once the children have been made Wards of Chancery, there will be time enough to tell their father – and I will ensure it is done, to check any foolish claims he might envisage once he learns that the children are beyond his reach, at least in monetary terms.

I think I am correct in my assumption, such have my years in this profession hardened my view of human nature, that without the hope to claim further on the inheritance of his children, his interest in securing their custody may also wane, Mr Anderdon concluded.

Do not underestimate the capacity of a bitter and spiteful man, I could not help but interject, and was again rewarded with what I took to be a glance of approbation from Mr Puckle.

There I am sure you may be right, Mr Ffarington, said Mr Anderdon. *On that front, we must watch and wait.*

Well, Anderdon, let us then proceed exactly as you have advised. Are there papers to sign? Or that I need take away with me to peruse? Mr Dickinson asked.

Yes, yes, I will have my clerk bring them, Mr Anderdon replied, but before he could ring a small bell on his desk Mr Puckle was on his feet saying, *Allow me, sir*, and moved swiftly towards the large outer office where a row of clerks were bent over their high desks.

I will take my leave, then, gentlemen, I said, rising, and after a cordial shake of the hand from both gentlemen, I turned to go just as Mr Puckle returned bearing a sheaf of papers which he laid on Mr Anderdon's desk.

Thank you, Mr Puckle. We shall send word in due course on any next steps, Mr Anderdon said, before turning his attention back to the papers.

So it was that Mr Puckle and I left Mr Anderdon's chambers together, and it was only as we walked down the stairs to the street door, side by side, that I fully comprehended the short stature of the man who had commanded such a presence from his corner of Mr Anderdon's room. He barely reached my shoulder but was of a rather wiry build that conveyed considerable strength and energy. I could not determine his age but, as we walked, he spoke of Puckle Junior so that I gathered his son was just beginning in his father's profession and I found an image come to my mind of a person as small again in comparison to his father as Puckle Senior was to me. I cannot say how such an absurdity presented itself to me, given the seriousness of the matters just discussed in Mr Anderdon's chambers and my anxiety for Fanny's safety, but any such frivolity was soon driven from my head by what Puckle said on parting, as I turned in the direction of Temple while he seemed headed west towards the Strand.

Begging your pardon, sir, are you familiar with the Chancery case of Rex v. Greenhill?

I was not, I told him.

Well, sir, the plight of your Mrs Geils reminds me very much of Mrs Greenhill.

In what way, Mr Puckle?

In that, like your Mr Geils, Mr Greenhill seems not to have been all a husband ought, despite his wife's fortune, and so Mrs Greenhill settled property on her children and sought to make them Wards of Chancery.

And was she successful?

She was not, I'm afraid. But something in Puckle's manner led me to think this was not the end of the story – or at least, I hoped it was not, as it would otherwise seem a poor exemplar to offer any friend of Fanny's.

And what did that lady do then? I asked.

She fled, sir, Puckle said, his voice dropping so low that I strained to hear him above the street clamour.

Fled?

He nodded and leaned closer, touching my sleeve. *Took her three children and left England. A fugitive, you might say. In exile. Location unknown.* And with that, he tipped his hat and walked briskly away.

Frances

Cavendish Square
London
October 1845

He is so long coming. The clock has already struck three, meaning three hours have passed since I read Mr Anderdon's note and, shortly thereafter, sent one of my own to Edmund, telling the boy to wait for a reply. I know Edmund is a man of occupation and that I must not be unreasonable in expecting him to set all aside at an instant for me, but what else am I to do?

Mr Geils has commenced a suit for the restitution of conjugal rights, Mr Anderdon has written. *I am unfortunately detained today, as also is Mr Jennings, but we will both come to Cavendish Square tomorrow, at your earliest convenience. This step was to be expected; do not be unduly alarmed, dear lady. Yours &c. O. A.*

Alarmed? How could I not be? With the Chancery suit awaiting a decision, leaving my girls still entirely at the mercy of their father, and now the commencement of proceedings against me – why had I listened to counsel and not brought my own suit, ere now? What time has been lost? And with what consequence? I could not help shedding tears of frustration on receiving Mr Anderdon's note, not least at my own shameful ignorance of the whole hulking edifice of the law ranged against me.

What I would not give to know *for myself* what is to be done! Mother is as much at sea as I, but she allows herself to repose all trust in the gentlemen who advise us, whereas I – who can I trust now? What might have transpired differently these past seven years if I had not, from the first, assumed in my innocence that all was as it appeared, that none I encountered could meet my eye and tell me falsely? What a child I have been, and what it has cost me!

Oh, *where* is Edmund? Mother has left me alone. We have, of late, lacked patience with each other, she and I, each worn down by our fears and uncertainties. I know she means me nothing but kindness but, left to ourselves, we have both been curt and out of temper, perhaps seeing in each other's face the worry that we long to set aside but can never cast off.

Ah, the outer door at last! But two gentlemen's voices – Edmund is not alone?

* * *

Well, the oddest interview has just taken place! I can scarcely say if my nerves have found comfort or merely been wound to a higher pitch that enlivens me with daring purpose. All I know is that my anxious despair has been replaced by a head full of plans.

When the door opened on Edmund, I scarcely had a moment to steal a look at his face that I might be calmed by his steady gaze, before he stood aside and gestured to a smaller gentleman who accompanied him, thin of frame with reddish whiskers and hair that quite stood up on his head.

Please allow me to introduce Mr Puckle, Fa... Mrs Geils, Edmund said. *He is assisting us on your behalf, and comes with the highest recommendation of Mr Anderdon.*

Mr Puckle bowed quite low in response, before lifting his face to show a wide grin that I might have found a little alarming if not reassured by Edmund's words, and by the respect evident in his manner to the little man.

A privilege and an honour, Mrs Geils, Mr Puckle said, *despite the circumstances of our acquaintance.*

We all three took our seats and, without unnecessary preamble,

Edmund sought to explain to me the process by which John had been able to bring his suit forward. John's action would in no way place me or my cause at a disadvantage, Edmund said: I had the choice to respond to John's suit, or to bring forward my own *Defensive Allegation*, by which I could propose a petition for separation on my own terms, according to the provision of *a mensa et thoro*, as had already been outlined to me by Mr Jennings and Mr Anderdon on an earlier occasion.

While Edmund was speaking, Mr Puckle nodded from time to time in assent, and then looked to catch my eye as if to show the pleasure he took in Edmund's clarity. Forcing myself to look away from Mr Puckle – whose animated visage was distracting if also peculiarly comforting – I must have frowned because Edmund soon paused.

What is it, Fan... Mrs Geils? he said.

I am, of course, glad beyond measure to hear that you do not think that John's suit presents any unexpected impediments to us, but are we not left somewhat unprepared? When might we face the judge? Must there not be many documents prepared before then? I'm sorry for my ignorance, Edmund—

You may consider me, Mrs Geils, Mr Puckle interjected, *quite the representative of Dr Addams, who I believe is to be your counsel in the Court of Arches and is a man of commanding experience – quite a leading figure in that place. I may say that I enjoy the full trust of Dr Addams and will be off in quest of witnesses the very moment I receive instruction from him, on your behalf.*

I must have looked confused, perhaps even a little flustered, by this, because Edmund then put a hand out to the sleeve of Mr Puckle, as if to curb his enthusiasm somewhat, leading that gentleman to offer a profuse apology that Edmund in turn quietened in good humour.

What Mr Puckle says is the very best tidings I could bring you today, Fanny. Rest assured that there is only need for your counsel to announce your intention to respond with your own allegation and then we begin in earnest to assemble your case. It could be months before the thing is argued before a judge. I know it asks so much of you, Fanny, but we must be patient. All your legal men will meet with you tomorrow, I believe – is that not right, Mr Puckle?

Indeed it is, Mr Ffarington.

And they will tell you more – and better – than I can. You are in the safest of hands, believe me – you and your children, Edmund said, smiling reassuringly, but the magnitude of all I had learned thus far today did not easily assuage my rising fears.

Mr Puckle, I said, *this Dr Addams – I have heard his name mentioned by Mr Jennings, or it may have been Mr Anderdon perhaps. He is truly the man to take my case in the courtroom, you believe?*

Oh, indeed, Mr Puckle replied, with a rather grand sweep of his arms. *He fears no judge, although I believe one or two of them may sit decidedly less comfortably on their bench when he stands before them. Dr Addams is quite the foremost man in Doctors' Commons, you will find, and renowned too for his published reports and commentaries besides. Is that not so, Mr Ffarington?*

Indeed it is, said Edmund. *You are in quite the best position it is possible to be, under the circumstances, Fan... Mrs Geils.*

At this, Mr Puckle shifted in his seat and gave a discreet cough.

Ah, yes, said Edmund, as if he knew Mr Puckle's meaning. *Now, Fanny, I want you to know that, in terms of the procedure regarding the trial for separation, you can have full faith in the power of the courts to protect you, and in the abilities of your legal men on your behalf.*

Again, Mr Puckle adjusted his posture but made no sound.

However—

However, what, Edmund? The anxiety that had begun to subside was instantly reignited. *What is it?*

Edmund looked at Mr Puckle, who seemed to take it as permission to answer in Edmund's stead.

Well, you see, Mrs Geils, while we – all of us, on your behalf – will be doing our mightiest to bring together the strongest case we can (and I will have many questions that I shall crave your indulgence in answering on another occasion, very soon, if I may), in the meantime there is a need for great care regarding the children.

The children? What is it? I could scarcely keep my seat now, such was my growing sense of dread.

Now, now, Mr Puckle went on, *while we await the result of Mr Anderdon's Chancery bill in particular, but also in the lead up to the commencement of proceedings in the Court of Arches, we must guard against the Producent – by which I mean Mr Geils – somehow taking custody of the children.*

I felt the blood drain from my face – was this not what I had feared all along? And yet here I had remained, against my own instincts to flee!

I have been told that Mr Geils has been to Farley Hill Court seeking the children, Mr Puckle said. *But he has not appeared in London, to your knowledge?*

No, I said weakly. *I keep expecting it since he knows well where to find me, I should have thought.*

Mr Puckle nodded. *Quite so*, he said. *He may be heeding wiser advice, or may simply not have found the opportunity yet. But, as you know, Wards of Chancery cannot be taken out of the country, and we would not want to prejudice your case before my Lord Chancellor by so doing, before his judgement is handed down.*

Yes, yes, so what am I to do? I asked.

Fanny, please do not upset yourself so, Edmund said. *It is Mr Puckle's suggestion that you might go into retirement somewhere, where John would never think to seek you out – you and the children – and that you might remain there until the Arches proceedings are underway, or at least until the Chancery bill is decided, which we all believe it will be, in your favour.*

Again, I couldn't help but notice that Mr Puckle stole a sideways look at Edmund.

Yes, that's the thing, Mr Puckle continued. *Retirement. Not abroad, mind. No. But somewhere out of the way. Leaving here quietly, so that it may not be readily apparent that you have gone at all.*

I entirely see the benefit in what you propose, Mr Puckle, I said. *I had an inkling that such a thing might be needed but allowed myself to be persuaded otherwise, I'm sorry to say, although I know that those who advised me meant well. I would gladly gather up my girls now and summon the carriage this instant, but of course I must needs give some thought to our destination first. One other thing that concerns me, though, is that, if I leave Town, I shall thus be removed from the ability to meet so easily and frequently with my legal advisors. Surely that is a problem with your plan, sir?*

Now, Mrs Geils, no, not at all, if I may be so bold as to contradict a lady, Mr Puckle said. *I can travel far and fast, be assured, and I undertake to come to your aid, or to bring you word, at a moment's notice; and without detection, moreover.*

Edmund? What say you? I asked, contemplating for the first time what it might mean to remove myself from the chance of regular conversation with such a dear and trusted friend as he had proved himself to be in my deepest need.

I have no doubt whatsoever, he said, *that Mr Puckle's advice is beyond reproach on this matter. And that you may rely on him just as you rely on me. Nay, more so – for I doubt that I could fly to your side with the speed or secrecy with which I believe he could.*

Neither gentleman could remain for tea, such were the calls upon their time elsewhere, so our interview drew to a hasty conclusion, Edmund promising to return tomorrow evening. By the day after that, I hope to have left Cavendish Square.

Edmund Ffarington

Middle Temple
London
October 1845

Oct. 20. Just returned by foot from Cavendish Square where I have bid farewell to Fanny. Such a dank, foggy evening, exactly matching my mood, so that only a long walk home would do. I avoided the larger thoroughfares, bright with lamps and busy with the traffic of men and horses, the night-time hawkers and those sorry, painted creatures beckoning from doorways. In the quieter squares and side streets, my footfall rang out like hammer on anvil, such are the uncanny tricks the fog plays with sound. If not for the evening's chill, however, I would still be walking, so reluctant am I to sit here alone with my thoughts.

Earlier in the day, Fanny and her mother had been escorted by Mr Anderdon, along with Mr Jennings, Mr Puckle and myself, to the chambers of Dr Addams, where he was formally introduced to her as her advocate in the Court of Arches for her suit for separation *a mensa et thoro*, in response to Geils' suit against her. Mr Puckle was right to stress how distinguished a figure he was; Dr Addams has the commanding voice of a born orator combined with the upright posture of a military man, albeit one of silvered hair. In another setting, I might have taken him for a retired general, a man accustomed to issue orders that would be promptly obeyed. Yet when I looked to see how Fanny was receiving him, concerned she might be alarmed by something of fierceness in his manner, I saw that far from being cowed, she seemed reassured, almost comforted, as if in the presence of a protector. It was then I surmised that the true source of his authority – besides his formidable legal mind of course – was his capacity to project what others most needed to behold in him, bringing to mind what I had read of the great Kemble at his prime on the stage.

Dr Addams had confirmed to Fanny that he intended to pursue her case on three grounds – cruelty, adultery, and unnatural connection – and that witnesses would now be sought in earnest to provide evidence on any of these three grounds. But Fanny had had so much to take in at this interview, she confided to me this evening (not least the stirring presence of Dr Addams, I suspect), that she still did not fully understand the procedure in the Court of Arches concerning witness testimony. So I explained to her that no one was to appear in court in person before the judge except the legal men on both sides. All witnesses, as well as the parties to the suit (namely herself and her husband), would be represented solely through their written statements or depositions, consisting of a sworn account of their evidence as well as the interrogatories put to them in writing by the opposing counsel, in response to those sworn accounts. She had been much taken aback to learn there would thus be no process of cross-examination of witnesses in the courtroom, such as there might be in a criminal trial, until I pointed out that she herself would thus be spared the ordeal of the witness box.

Dr Addams had further impressed upon Fanny that it was vitally important that she provide a full list of anyone she could think of who might bear witness to her husband's ill-treatment of her during the course of their marriage, telling her that in such cases it was frequently the servants of a household who provided the crucial evidence. Wasting no time on this front, shortly before my arrival this evening, Mr Puckle had been dispatched to call again in Cavendish Square to collect a list of names that Fanny and her mother had drawn up together in the interval since they had returned from Dr Addams' chambers.

Do you not think it shameful, Edmund, that so much is to rely on the recollections of those who have been about me each day? Fanny then asked. *I am accustomed to servants being about one, of course, but I do not like to think of their eyes upon me in the manner that Dr Addams described, noting and judging my behaviour.*

But it is John's *behaviour that will be on trial here, Fanny,* I assured her. *I am certain you have nothing whatsoever to reproach yourself with. I have seen for myself, remember, what you have endured from him, even in the so-called public rooms of the household.*

Will you be called upon to provide evidence, then? she asked. *I had not thought to add friends to my list, although I understand that mother will of course be called upon to submit a deposition.*

And so I had disclosed that it was highly likely that I would be deposed as a witness but, for that reason, we should not now be discussing her suit at all.

But why? Surely I can rely on the comfort and knowledge of a dear friend, and a man of the law himself, in this way? What harm does that do?

I explained, then, the likelihood that the opposing legal men would ask each witness if they had been coached in their answers, or conferred with other witnesses regarding the evidence they were to give, only hinting to Fanny the severe legal penalties that could be incurred, for fear of giving her any unnecessary alarm at this time. As painful as it was, I also needed to tell Fanny that I would not be able to correspond with her on anything pertaining to her case while she was away, since any such letters could be seized. At the very least, I might be questioned about our correspondence during any future deposition I might provide.

It grieved me to see the stricken look on her face then, and I strove, in the time remaining us, to turn our talk to brighter things, little as I could think of anything of a cheerful nature when I contemplated that I would no longer sit in this manner with my favourite conversant, no longer behold her blue eyes brighten when I greeted her.

But I had brought Fanny a parcel of books as my parting gift and I encouraged her to open it now that I might see if I had judged aright what might please her and thus end my visit on a happier note.

I had included the latest efforts by Mr Disraeli and Mr Patmore, knowing she had not yet read either, together with another I hoped might prove a valuable resource, Mr Redding's *Illustrated Itinerary of the County of Cornwall*. The perusing of these books aided us to make merrier talk for a time and Fanny seemed to summon some excitement at the prospect of her journey to a part of the country she had never before seen, renowned for its natural beauty. But when she opened to a striking illustration of Land's End in Mr Redding's book, she drew a deep sigh and I think I may say that, for us both, it seemed as if tomorrow she were truly to depart for the ends of the earth.

What a brave soul she is, having endured so much already, and now venturing forth alone to shelter her children in a strange place, with but two maids to accompany her. May God bless her in her travels.

Frances

Polperro
Cornwall
November 1845

Polperro is squeezed between high cliffs and rocky hills, above a narrow harbour entrance where the waves beat and dash unceasingly, covering the rocks with snowy foam. The village, therefore, consists of narrow streets of houses terraced one above another, so that one ascends and descends interminable flights of steps, picking one's way carefully among the debris of discarded fish. I am sure I shall never eat fish any more, after seeing how it is thrown about in these dirty little streets, cod's heads and conger eels alike, in wait to slip up the unwary.

But the climate – how deliciously mild! Here are roses and carnations and passion flowers, still in bloom at the start of November. I had come prepared for winter weather, but shed layers on my daily walks, such power does the sun possess in this southernmost corner of the country.

Can it be only two weeks since we departed from Paddington Station? Foggy London was then left behind, as Swindon, Bristol, Exeter, passed the train carriage windows in turn. As we approached Dawlish and the railway came close to the estuary where the river Exe flows to the sea, I began to shake off the sadness of leaving all that was familiar behind – though, of course, what is most precious of all accompanied me on this journey.

The train then passed through a series of tunnels, revealing in between stretches of dramatic coastline with the green sea surging beyond, in a variation of scene that quite captivated me until we reached the termination at Teignmouth, when everyone aboard surged as one onto the platform to crowd about the luggage van. Such a hubbub of activity as trunks and carpetbags and hat boxes and even a bird in a cage were desperately sought, and called for, and tussled over, and carried off in triumph, with little regard for toes or small children underfoot. At first, I had stood within the roiling mass, transfixed, trusting to Ninnie and Gibbie to keep the little ones safe, but it was only when the crowd subsided that we could look about ourselves and find, miraculously, that all our luggage had been safely unloaded by a guard, who had piled it to one side where it remained undisturbed.

Then next we must find our way to the stagecoach for the remainder of our journey, loading what had just been unloaded, before ensuring that each of the children were securely, if tightly, wedged between Ninnie and myself, poor Gibbie having to ride on the box alongside the coachman. Of the night in the inn at Devonport, and the following day's travel, I retain but a jumble of impressions – of deep woods and secluded valleys, streams running between stands of colouring trees, picturesque harbours and bays – and a deep gratitude for the fortitude of my girls in bearing up so bravely through all the turns and twistings, the steep ascents that the horses crawled up like rats, before dashing us perilously down the other side. The two babies, indeed, slept through almost all of the journey, lulled by the motion, but Kate and Lucy were wide-eyed and wondering at all that we passed. At last, though, we arrived at the little slate-roofed, whitewashed house secured for us, perched high above the harbour where it caught the brilliant sunshine and looked out upon the sparkling sea.

In those first days as Mrs Frances Vickris Dickinson, a poor widow left with her four angels, I sought to live as quietly as possible among my new neighbours and knew almost nothing of what was happening in the world beyond the scope of my little house and the nearby alleys and lanes. But then I began to familiarise myself with this place in long, solitary walks into the countryside beyond, during which I was often beset with feelings of melancholy and foreboding about the chances of keeping my children concealed here, and ruminating obsessively on future ills that may yet lie in store for us. At such times, I wished for the presence of that dear friend who of late had brought such comfort and reassurance. He did not write; letters being a luxury I could not often expect here, not simply due to the isolation of my refuge but the dangers of committing to paper anything pertaining to my suit.

So when, this morning, I received a note from Mr Puckle asking me to receive him sometime this afternoon in Polperro, I knew not what to expect. What had already been a day out of the ordinary – being little Lucy's birthday – became even more so, and I was glad for the distraction of making paper crowns for the children, and overseeing the little feast we had planned for their tea, to pass the time until Mr Puckle's arrival.

It was another of those days here almost like August in its warmth, although the woods were increasingly splashed with red and gold. The children were in high spirits – even little Cecile crowing with delight – so that when at last Mr Puckle appeared, I prayed that he had not come all this way bearing bad news. And so it was! For he brought glad tidings of Chancery: my four angels were now Wards of the Lord Chancellor, as their mother once had been, too. Nor was that all, he said.

When once Mr Puckle had been ushered into the tiny sitting room by Gibbie, away from the festivities in the equally small dining room so that he and I could speak undisturbed, he said that he had just returned from Scotland, where he had been to seek out witnesses. *She is found,* he said. *Lizzie Campbell, as was, is found and is willing to stand a witness in this cause.*

I did not at first understand why Mr Puckle's manner seemed to suggest that the discovery of Lizzie Campbell was a significant one, since she had only been in my service at Dumbuck for such a comparatively short time before I had dismissed her. I knew that, like any other servant at Dumbuck, she had probably observed, or heard, instances of John's unpleasant behaviour towards me, but surely she might not be kindly disposed towards me, given her dismissal at my hand?

I then observed in Mr Puckle's face a glimmer of comprehension at my puzzlement. *Oh, Mrs Geils,* he said, *I see that I have caught you by surprise.*

A little, Mr Puckle, I said, *for I cannot see how Lizzie could advance my case in any material way. She was on my list because you asked for the names of* all *the servants who had been present at Dumbuck during my time there, but I should probably have told you more about her dismissal – it's just that time was so short in our final meeting in London...*

Yes, I can quite understand, Mrs Geils, he said. *It is all clear to me now. I am afraid, then, madam, that you should prepare yourself for learning something unpleasant. Or rather, while unpleasant in itself, it is of great value for your cause, which is what you must bear in mind. It is the kind of thing – a deposition such as this – that could win your suit outright.*

I'm afraid I still don't take your meaning, I said. *What has Lizzie said that is so helpful?*

She has said, Mrs Geils, and given her word that she will depose as a witness, that Mr Geils had adulterous connection with her throughout the time she was in service at Dumbuck.

My vision clouded and I must have fainted clean away, something I had never done since my weakest days in the north. When I returned to myself to find Gibbie hovering with the smelling salts and the room filled with maritime breezes now that both windows had been thrown wide to assist my revival, I saw that Mr Puckle remained unmoved in his post.

Now then, Mrs Geils, you have given us quite a fright, Miss Gibson and I, he said in a more gentle tone than I had heard from him before.

Gibbie helped me to a more upright position in my seat, fussing all the while, and retaining hold of my hand.

Thank you, Gibbie, I am quite restored, I said, although without the bracing air blowing about my face, I fear I might have slipped under once more. But as Mr Puckle spoke encouragingly to Gibbie, approving her endeavours to make me more comfortable, I gradually felt my senses sharpen and my head clear and, with that, the force of Mr Puckle's revelation returned, sending my thoughts racing away with the consequences of this knowledge.

Evidently, more tea had been called for as Gibbie returned with the tray and performed the duties I would normally have done. The aroma of the freshly-brewed cup placed before me made me seize upon it with relish and, as I drank, I thought back to those days of disarray at Dumbuck with little Lizzie constantly saying, *Can I be of service, Mrs Geils?* Her manner could not have been more different from Jane McPhee's and yet, if what Mr Puckle said was true – as I implicitly believed – what might that say of Lizzie? And of John?

What must be done next, Mr Puckle? I asked, at last.

He shook his head then, with that strange abbreviated chuckle he sometimes emits, and said, *In all my dealings, Mrs Geils, I have never encountered a lady such as yourself – if you don't mind my remarking so. Such terrible news as I have delivered and you are already wanting to get on with matters.*

But he took me at my word and proceeded to explain the need for me to return with him to London, in order to amend my Allegation and sign it accordingly, just as soon as it could be arranged for my mother to travel down and remain here with the children during my brief absence.

My heart sunk, then, at this prospect – so recently installed here in our rocky refuge and already I must leave my cherubs! – but every day, every task, that hastens my case is a day nearer a happier future.

Elizabeth Campbell

Lincoln's Inn
London
14 February 1846

Elizabeth Millar (formerly known as Lizzie Campbell), wife of William Millar, block cutter, of Main Street in the city of Glasgow. Aged 22 years. A witness produced and sworn upon oath deposes and says:

It was Mr Puckle applied to me first to become a witness in this cause. It was in the month of November last, I forget the day of the month, at the house where I then resided in St Ninian Street in Glasgow. It was by word. I have seen no one relative to my evidence but Mr Puckle. I have not seen or received any letters or messages from Mrs Geils relative to my evidence. I have not seen or heard from her since I left Dumbuck.

Mr Puckle came and saw me more than once in the month of November last. It was at the said house in St Ninian Street. No one else was present. I do not recollect how many times I saw him. He questioned me about what passed between Mr Geils and me, and I admitted to it, and he questioned me further and wrote down my evidence. He said, I think, that he had learned it from some of the other servants. Mr Puckle then explained to me that I would have to go down and be examined in London.

I have never communicated my having intercourse with Mr Geils to any person either by letter or word until I told it to Mr Puckle in November last. And again, when I have told you today. I knew it was the truth and therefore I thought it better to own to it when Mr Puckle questioned me rather than that others who knew me should be speaking about it and tell it of me. I did not communicate the fact voluntarily, not until Mr Puckle put the question to me.

He did not use any threats or persuasions but when he asked me the question whether there had not been an improper intercourse between me and Mr Geils, I could not deny it. And I told him it was so. And then he put further questions as to particulars, and I answered his questions according to the truth.

I have no reason or motive for coming forward as a witness to prove my own shame, except that I would rather tell it myself than have my fellow servants telling it of me. I have never denied that I had had carnal intercourse with Mr Geils but nobody ever put the question to me until Mr Puckle did so. I used to think that my fellow servants suspected it but they never named it to me.

I have not received anything beyond money to pay my expenses down from Glasgow and I have not been promised nor have I any expectations of anything besides, except that I believe I shall be paid for my trouble and loss of time in coming here. I have had as yet six sovereigns. I have received no money from Mrs Geils since I left her service.

I have come from Scotland expressly for the purpose of being examined. I am lodging at the house of Miss Burrows of No. 19 Soho Square. I came down from Scotland alone. My husband is in Glasgow. He knows nothing of Mr Geils or Mrs Geils. He knows of, and consents to, my coming here as a witness. He does not know what I am come to swear to. He does not know that I am here to swear to my own shame.

Frances

Brandenburg House
Hammersmith
London
April 1846

Once more, a house close by a waterway. This river, though, flows from the very heart of England before continuing east through the metropolis and the Kentish flats to the North Sea. None would seek Frances Dickinson in Hammersmith!

Our apartments here are light and spacious but I must admit I miss the higgledy-piggledy lanes and alleys of Polperro, the wilder walks beyond, and the surging, soothing sea day and night. Have I done right in returning? Everyone – by which I mean chiefly Mr Anderdon and Mr Puckle – reassures me that we will be safe here, and that watch is kept over this place on my behalf.

Mr Anderdon yet thinks I might avoid the dreadful exposure of the Court of Arches, that John might still see reason and spare us both that fate. Did not *The Times*, just last week, report in horrid detail on another separation case? To have such personal misery perused over the family breakfast table! If I, as the innocent party, fear the shame of publicity as akin to being led naked through Trafalgar Square, how much more must John tremble at the prospect? Scotland, after all, is not so far away as to be beyond the reach of the newspapers.

Such an array of witnesses have already come forward on my behalf, too, prompted by the indefatigable Mr Puckle, and not merely folk at Farley Hill but even more from Dumbuck. I might have thought loyalty to, or fear of the influence of, the Geilses in that district would have kept tongues silent, but no – depositions on my side already secured from *nine* Dumbuck servants! And at Farley Hill even old Webb has put his grudge against Mother and me aside, it seems, to swear testimony on my behalf, thereby proving that his antipathy to John surpasses all in his bitter old heart. But I do him an injustice. From what Mr Puckle tells me, not only has Webb testified against John, but he has also been instrumental in persuading others to do so as well, going so far as to assist some to journey from Berkshire to London to take their oath.

Yet the stronger my case grows, the greater the possibility that John might be pushed to more desperate measures. At every turn, he exerts what power he can, such as refusing to return my possessions from Dumbuck – my few remaining clothes and a larger number of books. Of more value to him, no doubt, were the stray papers I left in an old writing case, and which may yet be used against me, I suppose, for so often there my only relief was to commit my thoughts to paper. Isabella, I am certain, would welcome the opportunity to rummage among my things, seeking anything to her brother's advantage.

When it is not my fears of what might be used against me that keeps me wakeful, I toss and turn with dreams of intruders coming to steal away my girls in the night. I cannot even ease my mind by walking, as I did so freely at Polperro – I only walk at dusk here, and that brings its own dangers to ladies. When I look out upon the Thames, I try to imagine a time when I might imitate its motion, and at last be carried away from England across the Channel and to the Continent. Then what a world might open before me! But so much is to be endured before then.

Mother has been but seldom to Hammersmith, and only once has Edmund accompanied her, although now that he has been deposed, I hope that he might feel freer to call on me, even if the visit of any friend here presents an opportunity for my discovery by those who wish me ill. Still, I pass my time in reading and have resumed my language studies, taking advantage of the many language masters who reside in Hammersmith and who may, without remark, visit the home of a solitary widow, as I continue to style myself here.

* * *

When Mr Puckle first told me of Lizzie, I was won over by his optimism and eagerness to pursue my suit. But over subsequent days my courage began to fail me and I wished I could hide myself away in Polperro forever, as the shrinking widow I claimed to be. To learn that John had behaved so with Lizzie *after* the trouble over Jane – so little did he fear any consequences of his actions or feel any contrition for his infidelity – was a devastating blow. There was truly not a shred of goodness in the man at all, he had deceived me again and again. By turns I pitied and despised young Fanny Dickinson, so poor a judge of a man and his affections had she been, so willing to shackle herself to an unworthy mate. But my heart went out to Lizzie Campbell, who had risked so much in coming forward, and for no gain whatsoever other than to assist a lady who had believed the worst of her on hearsay and discharged her accordingly.

Well, what could I do in the end but determine to persevere with more resolve than ever? As Mr Puckle says, only from painfully-extracted ore comes the refined metal of truth. And so my whole story must now be paraded before the eyes of the world, by way of the Court of Arches; my name will forever linked with Jane McPhee, Maria McKichan and Lizzie Campbell besides!

Would that *I* might speak on my own behalf, face to face with John, and only the judge alone with the two of us to determine what is true from what is false. I know I would prevail in such a contest, no longer in fear of the blows and shoves and kicks – *and worse* – that ever sought to silence me. But I cannot speak, just as I cannot ensure that all who come forward are bound by the sanctity of their oath: John and his family, and whoever they enlist on their behalf, are free to say what they like of me, revelling in the opportunity to bring me low. What vicious falsehoods might be spun into perjury by those who have much to fear from my victory?

But I must have faith in Dr Addams. He, surely, will not allow falsehood and treachery to go unchallenged. If I cannot speak for myself, it is best to have an advocate of such courage and conviction as he seems to be! He is the father of daughters himself; he knows their inestimable worth, their precious purity, and will do everything in his power to protect mine, he tells me. But can even *he* know what it is like to know that nothing stands between me and my enemies, should their wish to harm me be strong enough to defy the law? That in an undefended household of women and children, there can never be perfect assurance of safety?

Enough! I will calm myself with Italian conjugations ahead of my *conversazione* with Signore Agnello this afternoon. Just yesterday, I was greatly diverted by little Kate picking up my Italian grammar book from my lap and asking why the words looked so strange, as she could not make out a single one – such a look of surprise on her little face because she already considers herself a first-rate scholar (as she *is*, the precocious treasure). When I explained it was another tongue altogether, she clamoured for me to teach her some Italian words and later I heard her skipping in the paved garden, singing *mi chiamo Kate, mi chiamo Kate*, over and over, echoed by little Lucy trotting beside her chanting *micky-mo Kate, micky-mo Kate!* When I think back to those dark Dumbuck days when her father would parade our firstborn before the Nepeans like a little doll, all three laughing when she parroted back to them *damn, damn, damn* – the sweet babe knowing not what she said but delighting in their corrupting praise – how she and her sisters lift my heart now with their innocent play, safe in our riverside hiding place.

* * *

Some hours have passed since I left off here, first due to my pleasant time with Signore Agnello, a charming elderly gentleman who quite beguiles me with his praise of my efforts so that I forget all my troubles for a time. No sooner had he departed, though, but Gibbie came to tell me that a young woman was asking to see me – I noticed she did not say *lady* – and that she was going to turn her away, as it was my tea-time. Gibbie well knew my standing instructions that any strangers coming to the house were to be refused, so something made me ask, *Do you know who she is, Gibbie?*

Yes, ma'am. She says she's Amy Webb, ma'am.

Feeling Gibbie's eyes upon me, I sought to disguise my shock at her words. *You may show her in,* I said, *and bring the tea tray please, Gibbie.*

When the door opened again, it was Amy herself who appeared, Gibbie evidently expressing her displeasure with a former maid being received in this way by refusing to show Amy in. So it was that my old friend and I were once more together, almost three years to the day since I had last spoken with her alone.

Mrs Geils, she began, *I hope you will forgive a visit in this way, as I thought it best not to write to you first.*

But how on earth did you find me, Amy?

I went to Cavendish Square, ma'am, and your mother was kind enough to tell me, knowing, she said, how we were once chums – not that she put it quite like that – and when I told her what I had just done, she said that she thought you would be very happy to receive me.

Well, here was a strange betrayal of sorts – my own mother giving up my refuge to one who had turned her back on me!

And what is it that you have done, Amy, that is apparently enough to make amends for ending our friendship, and swearing your sister to silence, too, that I might not even hear from her where you were?

You know how it pained me to part from you and from Farley Hill, ma'am, she said. *But I have today been at Lincoln's Inn, and from there went straight to Cavendish Square, Mr Puckle saying I might since I had completed my deposition.*

You have sworn testimony as a witness, Amy?

Yes, of course, ma'am—

Please do not call me that, Amy.

What am I to call you then, ma—? I do not feel entitled to anything more familiar.

I suppose, then, you must call me Mrs Dickinson – that is the name I intend to use once this trial is over and done with. Indeed, I use it already, truth be told.

A sharp rap at the door, not Gibbie's usual gentle tap, brought the tea tray in, and I gestured to Amy to sit while Gibbie set the tray down before withdrawing, evidently still in a bad humour, judging from the rough manner in which she closed the door behind her. The tea preparations helped to ease the air of discomfort between the two of us, though, even if my hands were a little unsteady.

Extending a cup to Amy, I said, *I am most grateful that you have come forward in this way. And your father, too, I believe?*

Yes, she said.

I do not want to retrieve the painful past – that seems all I ever do, with worse yet to come, I fear. But I must say that the loss of your friendship has been a considerable source of sorrow to me and, in return, I am very sorry if, in any way, I caused you or your family pain.

Let us not talk of my family, Mrs Dickinson, if you please, Amy said, *other than to say that I know that Lydia remains content in your mother's service and that is sufficient for me.*

And your father is well, and still presiding over his public house?

Yes, together with Jack and his growing family, Amy said, before pausing. *I don't believe that you know that I was myself in the neighbourhood of Farley Hill for a period of time last year?*

What? I was led to understand that you had a position somewhere in London.

Indeed, yes, I am Cook for Dr Steele in Camden Town. But last year, circumstances arose that, for my health, I needed to take leave from my post, so I returned to my father's house from March to September.

You were there when I was too, yet you made no attempt to see me? I asked, although Amy had every right to avoid me, I know.

As I said, Mrs Dickinson, it was my health. And Dr Steele, a very good and kind man, allowed me to stop away for that time.

Amy looked me full in the face then, as if to give me to understand something in her words that I had not yet deciphered. And then I knew.

Oh, Amy, I said. *Are you now in good health?*
Yes, indeed. Very strong, thank you.
And are you – is all well?

It was a trying time, before I returned to my post alone, she said, her voice catching a little on that final word. She put down her cup then and sat up straight in her chair, regarding me in that frank way I knew so well. *But when Mr Puckle sought me out, and I reflected on what I knew, and on what I had heard from others last year while I was at Farley Hill, and in light of what I had endured myself, and how I understood far better now something of what* you *have suffered – how could I do anything but swear an oath on what I knew to be the truth, if it might help your cause?*

I rose from my chair, then, to kneel beside hers, and we both shed tears as we joined hands, until I laughed to recall how often I had clasped those strong hands before, in the vigour of our youth when we tumbled and wrestled together, as carefree and innocent as my own babes.

Startled by my laugh, Amy said, *What is it, Miss Fanny?* So I told her of my thoughts and she said, *What was it you used to call us in Cavendish Square? Berkshire rustics!* And she laughed then, too, and tightened her hold on my hands.

Amy Webb

Lincoln's Inn
London
April 1846

Emma (known as Amy) Webb, spinster, aged 27 years.

Cook in the service of Dr Steele of No 47 Great Camden Street, Camden Town, in the County of Middlesex.

A witness produced and sworn upon her oath deposes and says:

I was asked to become a witness in this cause. It was by word, when Mr Puckle called upon me at my master's. I have received no letters or messages from Mrs Geils or Mrs Dickinson about my evidence. I have seen no one in reference to my evidence but Mr Puckle and him only that one time I have referred to. I believe Mr Puckle wrote to my master for permission for me to come to be examined today.

I was five years and a half a maid in Mrs Dickinson's house. During the time Mr Geils was at Farley Hill with Mrs Geils I used very often to hear him quarrelling with her. And in their quarrels I often heard him "damn her" and call her names, very bad names, such as "damned bitch". I heard him call her that several times. A good many times I should say. I used to hear him quarrelling with her in the Dining Room when I was in the Servants' Hall which was underneath: and sometimes when he raised his voice loud I could overhear his words, and then it was that I heard him call Mrs Geils those names.

It also happened at times in my presence, when I happened to go into the Dining Room with a message or to take anything in or to lift Mrs Geils, which I had to do night and morning, and sometimes in the day beside. It was when Mr Geils was in a violent passion that I heard him abuse and call Mrs Geils those bad names. But I have also heard him "damn her" and tell her she was a Devil and the like when he was not in a passion but only sulky and surly with her as he used often to be. Sometimes he would be pleasant enough with her; but more often I saw him sulky or surly, and sometimes very cross and harsh to her. I have often heard him say to her, "Oh you be damned."

Mrs Geils always appeared fond of him, but also afraid, too. I have never said that she was as bad as he was, or anything to that effect. If ever I said she was as bad as he was, it was not on account of her temper, but because of her having been so determined to part with him on account of his conduct with Jane McPhee and then, as soon as he got back from Scotland, to be friends again with him almost immediately.

Her conduct to Mr Geils was, whatever I saw of it, always kind and forbearing, very much so indeed. I do not mean to swear that she was always right and never to blame and that he was always wrong and alone to blame in whatever differences happened between them. But this I will say, that generally whatever I saw, the quarrels were of his making. No woman could shew more fondness for her husband than she did for him.

Mr and Mrs Geils were, however, the cause of my leaving. At least I left on my own account, but after having told Mrs Geils about those letters of Jane McPhee's, I was afraid to stop in the house. I was afraid because of what I knew of Mr Geils' violent temper.

That was the reason I gave for wishing to leave and it was the real one. It was not, as suggested, on account of Mrs Dickinson and Mrs Geils going back on a promise to my father of an annuity of £50 and a house rent-free, although I was upset at my father's dismissal, it is true. I only know that after I had told about the letters, and Mrs Geils said that she intended to be parted from Mr Geils, she said that "let what would happen, my father should not lose his situation." Why she did not keep her promise I cannot say.

I can solemnly swear that I have never found Mrs Geils false or not to be trusted. And I believe I could say the same of Mrs Dickinson. If I have said otherwise it has been perhaps when I have been out of temper. I certainly will swear that I think Mrs Geils and her mother thoroughly trustworthy and I would believe anything either of them told me.

I was back in the vicinity of Farley Hill between March and September 1845 for I was at that time at home ill, at my father's home that is. But I was not at Mrs Dickinson's. Nor did I see Mrs Geils to speak to her nor Mrs Dickinson either.

Edmund Ffarington

Woodvale
Isle of Wight
&
Middle Temple
London
September 1846

Sept. 14. I must take myself in hand. The summer has slipped away and yet here I remain at Woodvale, neither taking up that shooting party invitation in Gloucestershire, nor returning to Temple to serve any useful purpose there. If I thought that exchanging this place for London might provide opportunities to undertake pleasant visits to Hammersmith, I would have roused myself ere now. But Fanny has been absent herself much of the summer, first at some relative of Anderdon's in Buckinghamshire for a time, and after that I know not where, except that it was not Farley Hill. The poor creature has not felt safe to return to her own home for *a full year* now.

But, in any case, what would be the purpose of a visit to Hammersmith? All is frustration there; Fanny's case suffers delay after delay and she turns to me so trustingly to explain the arcane ways of the law which only brings her further disappointment. I *cannot* explain it to her satisfaction, of course, and when last I saw her there – can it really have been in June? – we almost quarrelled, such was her vexation with her plight. She spoke as if I, too, were part of the forces of the law ranged against her. She is grown embittered, I fear, with the constant anxiety for her children and her dismay at what she calls her *homeless state*.

Today I learned, from a note from Puckle, who is most assiduous in keeping me informed (although his notes err on the side of brevity bordering on the cryptic, so wary is he of committing any word to paper), that *Geils v. Geils* has failed to be listed for Michaelmas term. I hope it will not fall to me to be the one to tell Fanny of this latest delay. Puckle was, he said, on the point of departing once more for Scotland, ostensibly still pursuing further witnesses but I would be much surprised if he does not also go to learn what he might of how the other party and his legal men are progressing. There is little, I believe, that Mr Puckle might not winkle out, if once he puts his powers of discovery to work. I envy the man on so many counts!

Sept. 27. I am returned to Town and must now shake off the shameful lethargy that has left these pages untouched so long. Let Mr Puckle be my example: he came to my chambers this evening not realising his luck in finding me here, since I had arrived back a mere two hours before he appeared. He was as neat and indefatigable as ever; I have never once seen him show any signs of his labours, always as well-presented and nimble, in his humble way, as an opera dancer, who must stand quietly by, not detracting attention from the main actors on the stage but ready in an instant to perform his part with vigour. In the time since I last wrote here, while I took my ease at my parents' home, Puckle has been to Scotland and back, stopping in Leeds along the way to pursue witnesses for some other suit on which he assists Dr Addams.

But Puckle's report that it would be some time yet before the suit appears in the Arches' Court has disturbed me, as have his disclosures about the murky links between Geils' side and the court itself. I had already known that Nepean, husband to Geils' sister, was related by marriage both to the man acting for Geils, Herbert Jenner, and to the judge likely to preside, *who was the same Jenner's father.* In Scotland, however, Puckle had heard talk of social visits to Dumbuck by various Jenners involved in the case. Here was an unseemly development indeed!

I asked Mr Puckle if he intended to inform Fanny of what he had discovered and he fixed me with that sharp gaze I have come to know so well. I take no offence at such scrutiny, far from it. To come under the eye of Puckle in this way impresses on a fellow the need to consider carefully the worth of every word he utters.

Well, Mr Ffarington, Puckle said, *what would be the gain, I wonder?*

But you must know, I said, *how Fanny feels any attempt to withhold information from her as a slight, rightly so I may say, when her life and the future of her children are at stake?*

I understand, Mr Ffarington. Mrs Geils strikes me as one of those remarkable women who do not regard their sex as a natural limitation on their knowledge, much less their actions. But she is also a lady in much distress and so my question is, why should we add to it in this way, when nothing can be done?

Is that so, Mr Puckle? Is there really no legal recourse to such obvious nepotism?

Ah, you sound now like one of the editorials in our radical press, Mr Ffarington, railing about the shameful shortcomings of the Court of Arches.

I am no radical, I assure you, I said. *And I notice you have not answered my question.*

Puckle gave a short, barking laugh. *A hit, a veritable hit, sir. But of course the matter is far from a humorous one.* He tented his fingers then, lifting them to his lips for a moment before speaking again. *I believe I shall wait to be guided by Dr Addams in this matter but* you, *Mr Ffarington, are of course free to act on your knowledge as you think best – none having the confidence of Mrs Geils in quite the manner that you do, I believe I may say.*

I did not like what Puckle seemed to be implying and I fear I may have flushed in response.

Now, young sir, Puckle then said before I could speak, *I would not offend you for anything. But I would caution that Mrs Geils remains in a perilous situation – we may speak freely here, I think – and I fear that any friends who care for her must risk seeming to care* less *for her, to show* less *solicitude for her, whether in the frequency of their visits or in their expressions of comfort, than their natural feelings of sympathy might otherwise prompt.*

I could not but concede that Puckle was right, much as it pained me to acknowledge.

When he spoke again, his voice was lower, scarcely more than a whisper. *And, dear Mr Ffarington, you know as well as I do the limits that apply even to those whose suit carries the day in the Court of Arches, if we may tempt fate by thinking ahead to such an outcome. Separation is all that court can allow. I know you take my meaning, sir, and will bear me no ill-will for speaking in this manner.*

Damn that Puckle and his perspicacity, was my first thought. But I knew my wise friend was right; I had spent much of my summer by the Solent turning over the same thought, fruitlessly and frequently, to the point that I had come back to Town with the intention of investigating a future posting to the Northern Circuit, removing myself in this way from Fanny's orbit, when once more – as I hoped and believed would soon come to pass – she enjoyed the freedom to dwell in her own home, whether in Berkshire or London, if not the freedom to set aside her marriage absolutely.

Frances

*Brandenburg House
Hammersmith
May 1847*

I wonder, sometimes, what Fanny Geils might be doing now, what her life might look like, if I had never confided in Mother, that September day, what John had done to me. Or even if having done so, we two had not sought out Mr Anderdon's advice and thus set in motion all that has since unravelled. And yet *motion* is not quite the word. It has been more than one year and a half and we are no nearer to any resolution, the wheels of justice stuck fast.

Motion, though, precisely describes the life of my poor vagrant children and myself. To think that, before my marriage, I was heir to two estates and now can rest my head in neither! Instead, it is a borrowed house here or lodgings there; a brief visit to a kind friend, unknown to my husband; or a stay with a friend's relative whom I had never met until my carriage rolled up to their door. My four girls, my two maids, my books, my trunks – these are the only constants in my life this year and more.

Today, however, I have been forcibly reminded what Fanny Geils might be enduring still. On a rare summons to Lincoln's Inn, I sat with Mr Jennings and Dr Addams, as his clerk read out documents and then recorded all that was said in response. My cheeks burn at the recollection of hearing the deposition of a medical man that

John's legal counsel has taken. *This* is knowledge, these *fanciful ideas* of what a woman's body feels and endures?

I was at first so shaken by hearing this so-called testimony that I asked Dr Addams if we should, after all, abandon the suit. I could live in hiding for the rest of my days, if needed, I said; it could be borne.

By no means, Mrs Geils, Dr Addams replied. *It is in the very nature of adversarial proceedings that each side will differ and dispute what is alleged. This is why I have judged it necessary to subject you to what I understand must be a painful interview, in order that I may better persuade the judge of the credibility of your allegation.*

But what judge would listen to me, I asked, *against the testimony of a respected surgeon? And you say there may yet be other medical men brought by John to testify, along the same lines as this? Why do we not put forward more doctors, besides Dr Bulley of course? There must be some who can support my testimony on this matter?*

But Dr Addams dismissed my concerns, reminding me that this allegation was but one of the grounds on which my suit was based. *We should not allow ourselves to be unduly obsessed with one ground in isolation,* he said.

Obsessed was an odd word; it rankled me, as nothing else Dr Addams had ever said in all our conversations had, such was his ability to always say the right thing, to offer the sagest advice. Until now. How could it be termed *obsessive* to take issue with such a false representation of what I had endured? What would be the right kind and degree of interest to give to the forcible entry of one's body by one who delighted in the suffering so inflicted?

On my return to Hammersmith, still distressed and out of temper with Dr Addams, I called for Gibbie to fill my bath, despite the late hour, and while I waited for the kettles to be brought, I sat alone without candles, seeing no one, not even the children, whom I could hear complaining pitifully that they could not say good night to their mama.

At least the newspapers will never be able to publish the details I heard this afternoon, too shocking and extreme to be relayed in that way. My girls need never learn of it. And while I remain a homeless sojourner, hidden away in modest retirement, I have had no hand laid on me against my will this year and a half. My bed is mine alone. I rise each morning unsullied and do not shrink from myself in the glass. My flesh is without bruise or graze.

Thomas Callaway

Doctors' Commons
London
May 1847

Thomas Callaway, of Wellington Street, London Bridge, Southwark in the County of Surrey. Surgeon. Aged 55 years.

A witness produced and sworn upon his oath deposes and says:

I am one of the principal surgeons of Guy's Hospital and in extensive practice as a surgeon. I have had no consultation with my said fellow witnesses upon the subject in relation to which my evidence has been taken. My evidence does wholly emanate from myself, unless so far as this that I have asked other persons what their opinion was upon the question raised and so strengthened the opinion I had previously formed myself. My evidence has been in no way pre-arranged. It has in no sort been given in concert with my fellow witnesses, except that I was aware of their opinions on the point being in accordance with my own, as being my colleagues at the hospital, the one as anatomist and the other as Physician Accoucheur. I put the question to each of them, but merely in the way of conversation, to learn their opinions, and I was happy to find that their opinions coincided with the opinion I had myself previously formed.

In my opinion, unless actual force is used by the man, and the woman is wholly deprived of all power of resistance, it is physically impossible for a man to have connection with a woman without her consent. I do not say without her assistance. Her consent in such case would be necessary but not her assistance. My opinion is that while the woman had the power of volition, the power of exerting those muscles by which resistance would be made, it would be impossible for a man to accomplish such his object without her consent.

I am prepared to say absolutely on my oath that in my judgement (assuming even the case suggested of the woman having, at the age of twenty-five years, suffered five miscarriages and being the mother of four children, the youngest of which she had been delivered barely a month before), it would not be possible for even a powerful man (sleeping, passing night after night in bed with a woman in the delicate state one so circumstanced might be presumed to be) in the course of the night to effect a penetration *in ano* of the woman without the use of force (downright violence) by him towards and upon the person of the woman.

I conceive the parts of the patient would naturally be to some extent in a state of relaxation. There would be a want of tone to all the muscles after so recent a delivery. But still I consider that there would exist sufficient power of resistance in them to prevent the accomplishment under such circumstances of the man's object.

A lubrication of the parts of either or both (the man and the woman) with oil or Pomatum or other unctuous matter would doubtless greatly facilitate penetration. But still in my judgement, it would not facilitate it to that extent as to render the penetration feasible with little force, or in fact at all feasible without the woman being a consenting party.

Frances

Brandenburg House
Hammersmith
November 1847

It has begun. Cecile, but a nursling in my arms when first we fled, now capers about the room to little Fanny's playful commands, while the older two sit beside me, over their shared book. My four little loves have no idea at all what momentous event has commenced in a chamber at the heart of this great city. Mother, however, sighs in her seat by the hearth. I fear she makes little progress with the woolwork in her hand.

This morning we both shed tears over *The Times*, where my story – names and places and dates – was spread across columns and columns devoted to the first day of proceedings.

She despised him from the bottom of her heart, terrified by his threats and violent behaviour.

Adulterous connexion.

Everyone in Scotland said what a hell of a wife he had.

We will need to conceal all the newspapers from Kate for the duration; she sometimes pores over them, liking to make out what words she can. She would be sure to spy her own name *Geils* there. Mother says we should not take the papers at all during the trial but I *must* know what is said of me.

Yesterday, when he came for tea, Edmund said that I should prepare myself for the worst that could be put into print. He looked strained, poor man, and it was kind of him to make the journey out to us here, but his manner to me is not what it was, I fear. Whether the reserve that has grown up between us of late is due to what he has been shown of all the depositions I cannot say, but while we still talk of books and such as we always have, his gaze is not so frank as formerly. Does he look upon me differently, seeing only what has been done *to me*, not who *I am*? Or am I perhaps grown too sensitive, under the forced isolation of the past year and more?

Changed for the better, though, is dear Amy, who visits on her half-days, although I do not like the thought of her spending her precious leisure time travelling the great distance from Camden Town to Hammersmith. Gibbie has become reconciled to Amy's visits and my girls have grown very fond of her so that sometimes we are quite the community of ladies once more, just as we were so long ago at Farley Hill.

Mother likes to talk of when we all return home – she would like to spirit Amy back to Farley Hill, too, although Amy is quite the Londoner now, I think – but I do not allow myself to dwell too much on that. After so long away, what would strike me more? My memories of childhood innocence? Or the shame and suffering I endured there? Better never to return than face that.

Or I might go to Queen Charlton, Mother says; but so long as John retains his share of my income, as he must under English law, I would not be free to make the kind of home for my girls there that I would wish. More and more I dream of a different life entirely, a fresh beginning in parts unknown. Have I been so long a wanderer that to stop in one place now seems a surrender? When Signore Agnello talks of his beloved Florence, he reminds me of old Mr Anderdon's raptures over Rome, and I feel a quickening sense, a desire to walk ancient streets under southern skies, imagining myself a lady traveller who pens her adventures, something akin to Mr Dickens's delightful *Pictures from Italy*.

Ah, but there is that taunting creature, *Hope*, raising her head once more. I must dispel such fancies of myself and my girls, riding in a carriage past cypress groves and ancient ruins. Edmund has warned that the judge may not deliver his ruling until next spring, such are the slow ways of the Court of Arches. And who can yet say what the outcome will be?

So the year dwindles away, the leaves piling, brown and sodden, along the pavements by the swollen river while here I sit, like Mr Tennyson's Mariana in her moated grange. *Aweary, aweary.*

The Satirist; or, the True Censor of the Times

November 28, 1847

Editorial:
Chaste Case in the Court of Arches

The suit we allude to, Geils v. Geils, was instituted by the husband for the restitution of conjugal rights. The evidence given proved that the parties led a quarrelsome sort of life but the result of the union was the birth, amidst all their bickerings, of four children – daughters – with seven declared miscarriages on the part of the wife.

The pleas which Mrs Geils puts forth, in resistance to his plaint, are of a threefold character, alleging cruelty, adultery, and sodomy, on the part of her husband. Her counsel, in his statement, alleged various acts of violence by the husband, in knocking his wife about, using opprobrious epithets, and customary ill-treatment, in support of the alleged cruelty; and related various acts of adultery with servant girls and the lady's wet nurse; but the gravest and last charge, the one which led to the wife's final separation, the counsel thus detailed, on the statement of the wife, that during the *last year* of cohabitation Mr. Geils made, at intervals, repeated attempts to have a connexion with her against the order of nature, from which she *always* recoiled, feeling them to be criminal (but utterly unsuspicious in what degree), and imploring him to desist; *until*, in September, 1845, on suffering an attempt, or assault, of the kind, more offensive as to the *means*, and *more successful as to the end*, than any which had preceded it, she became so disgusted and alarmed that she disclosed to her mother the abuse to which she had been subjected and learned from her, and the family medical attendant, the nature of the crime, in the commission of which Mr. Geils had endeavoured to make her his accomplice; upon which she finally separated from him; and further, that Mr. Geils had *admitted* that he had had an unnatural connexion with her. Mr. Geils, of course, flatly contradicts these allegations, asserting that they are brought up in consequence of his refusing to part with his children, &c., &c.

What a pretty specimen have we here of the morals of people of thousands per annum! We know not, neither do we care, who Mrs. Geils is, but we do hope there are not many of her sex, mother of four living children, and who admit to seven miscarriages in a disturbed union of eight years, who could have it in their power to make such a disgusting charge!

Frances

Dorset Square
London
21 January 1848

I mean to show that her story is true, Dr Addams said, according to *The Times'* account of yesterday's proceedings. But who will believe my true story, besieged as it is by lie after lie from John's side?

Dr Addams spoke of my letters given in evidence as *the history of her whole life, exhibiting her in the most amiable colours, as the fondest and most devoted wife, and the tenderest and most affectionate mother*. Yet later he told the judge that *Her terror of her husband had taught her artifices which were quite foreign to her nature*. So is my life in my letters? Or is artifice my history? Will my words be judged to speak for or against my cause?

I understand, of course, that Dr Addams must stress the importance of my letters in order to rebut the evidence – if it can be called such – of Isabella, who has gone so far as to make the ludicrous claim that my letters are littered with mistakes in spelling, despite the fact that those very letters are before the court showing no such thing! Dr Addams spoke of *wilful and corrupt perjury on the part of Mrs Nepean, that cast doubt on all her other assertions in her deposition*. I hope and pray it may be so understood by the judge as she has said the most egregious things, repeating that diabolical gossip that Mama had some intrigue with Webb before I was born, and questioning my paternity as a result. As Dr Addams said, it is *a foul, false, infamous and atrocious lie*!

Even Mammy – or she who I once called Mammy but never will again, so cruelly has she abandoned me, thinking only of her son – has stooped to the most blatant untruths, saying that Jane McPhee was *illiterate*, and so could not have written the letters attributed to her. Illiterate! When I have myself seen Jane pen a receipt at Mrs Colonel Geils' instruction, and heard the old lady praise that wicked strumpet as a *good, clever girl* on viewing the result!

Poor Cousin Frank, who attended court yesterday, that he might report back to me, must have been deeply shamed to hear such a series of calumnies. Nor was that the worst said of Mother – John and his fiendish family have invented a vile story that Mother made advances to my bridegroom before we were married, when John first visited Farley Hill. *Anything so atrocious and disgusting never came out of the mouth of a woman*, Dr Addams said, *and the conduct of Mrs Colonel Geils and her son showed that it was altogether an invention; for they had suffered Mrs Geils to visit such a mother for months together without her husband, and had both of them written affectionate letters to Mrs Dickinson down to September, 1845. Could anyone doubt from this that the whole was a fiction?*

Fiction, lies, stories, history: all are swirled together and printed, column upon column, day after day, for all to read.

Dear Edmund, too, has been traduced as a deceitful person, *worming his way into Mr Geils' confidence*, in the words of Dr Jenner, John's counsel. I do not understand how a learned man of the law, such as I must believe Dr Jenner to be, could stoop to such false statements about a fellow lawyer. Dr Jenner accuses Edmund of playing some conspiratorial role with Mother and I, trying to thus dismiss the evidence of Edmund's diary as sheer fabrication, so that I fear for the consequences for Edmund. I do not know that even Dr Addams can retrieve Edmund's reputation after Dr Jenner's attack, in which he made much of Edmund staying to drink wine with John at Queen Charlton and shaking his hand on departing from their final meeting there.

What was presented in court went far beyond what Edmund had written to Mother directly after his visit to Queen Charlton, quite sickening me when I first became fully acquainted with it.

Dr Addams read out to the court the part where John rendered a Latin quotation about women into English, using the exact word that Edmund had reported of John, quite the coarsest of words but one I have heard from my husband's lips more than once.

A noticeable effect was produced in the court, *The Times* reported, visibly shocking the judge, but Dr Addams went on: *Ay, I do not mind; I will read it all (repeating the words); I am horrified at being obliged to go through this disgusting case but the fault is not mine.*

To which the judge replied: *I can hear no more, I am disgusted. It is quite disgraceful to the court, the public, and the profession. The manner in which this case had been argued is disgraceful.*

But Dr Addams – ever my champion – would not let such a statement go unchallenged, saying, *I protest against your observation, sir; and I treat it with disgust.*

Will I not forever be shunned as the wife who brought such things into the light of public exposure, things that I have been told, over and over, should never have been spoken of, things that I should not even *know* of? As if it is *my knowledge* rather than *John's crimes* that are subject to judgement?

* * *

Edmund has not come today, as he had intended. I cannot attribute his absence to the winter weather; the day has been unusually bright and mild, allowing the children to take a rare outing to the park this morning. But, really, we have seen less of Edmund here than we did at Hammersmith. After our discovery there by John's emissaries, I had thought that taking lodgings closer to Town might make it easier for our loyal friends to call, albeit under the usual precautions to avoid detection. But our circle of acquaintance grows ever smaller; even some of our oldest neighbours sent no Christmas greetings to Farley Hill this year, Mother wrote, having returned there for a time alone. I could not bear it if one so loyal to the friendless as Edmund should desert me at the end.

Edmund Ffarington

Middle Temple
London
January 1848

22nd January

My dear Fanny,

My apologies for not coming to call on you yesterday. I was unavoidably detained here in chambers, having received word by Saturday's late post that requires me to travel north later today.

You may recall my hopes of being appointed to the Northern Circuit? Well, I have received my summons to Manchester and expect forthwith that my time will be divided between Temple and, chiefly, the courts of Manchester and Preston. I am sorry not to bid you farewell in person but hope to return to Town in a few weeks' time, in this first instance, and will ensure I pay a call to Dorset Square, or wherever you may then be staying, if you will let me know.

I hope you are heartened by the most recent reportage of the proceedings. Addams made a strong impression, I thought, in drawing the court's attention to the dearth of witness statements that John's side had procured at Dumbuck, and hence that side's dependence on the entirely unreliable depositions of his sister and mother. Strange that there was no word from Nepean, which bears out the bad character you have always attributed to him, just as Mrs Nepean's frightful assertions betray hers, also. By contrast, you have secured such a very strong set of depositions from among the Dumbuck servants that I am sure no judge could set them aside.

I will continue to follow the newspapers' accounts in the remaining days of the case, although there may yet be a considerable delay before the judge delivers his ruling (and hope you will therefore prepare yourself for a further demand on your much-tested endurance).

I am sorry that, given my summons to the north, we are unlikely to spend as much time in company together as we have sometimes enjoyed in the past, but I must speak frankly, Fanny, when I say that I believe this is for the best, all things considered. Looking ahead to the summer, I know that it is Mother's intention to invite you all to Woodvale, where I would hope to join the party for a short time, but I repeat that I think our friendship should proceed on a somewhat different footing, and I trust to the confidence established between us to ensure that you will not take this amiss but understand that the terribly unfortunate events in which you have been enmired – and, to a far lesser extent, in which I too have been caught up – can, alas, never be fully cast aside.

The ways of the world are ever a constraint on the natural feelings and inclinations of many who, in a more innocent state of civilisation, might enjoy greater freedoms than modern society allows. I write so, not to cause you any pain but rather, inspired by the transparency of our relations thus far, unsullied by any hint of transgression and entirely motivated by a sense of brotherly friendship, I take my departure with the clearest of conscience and with an enduring regard for one who has ever been a model of feminine rectitude, forbearance, and tenacity, in the face of unimagined adversity.

Believe me, Fanny, I remain ever your devoted friend and humble servant,

E. F. F.

Sir Herbert Jenner-Fust

Court of Arches
London
April 26, 1848

GEILS v. GEILS – Suit brought for judgement before Sir Herbert Jenner-Fust for restitution of conjugal rights, by the husband against the wife, in reply to which the wife pleaded cruelty, adultery, and unnatural practices upon herself, on the part of her husband, and prayed a separation on the three grounds.

Sir Herbert Jenner-Fust rules as follows:

It is quite impossible for the Court to hold that the ground of cruelty has been proved, there being no evidence, but a mere allegation of the fact. This disposes of the whole question as to cruelty; and leaving this part of the case, I proceed to the next charge, that of adultery. The adultery charged against Mr Geils with Elizabeth Campbell (now Millar), which was deposed to by several witnesses, including Campbell herself, was established, and consequently the condonation of the adultery with McPhee was removed, and Mrs Geils was entitled to a sentence of separation on this ground.

...

This brings the Court to the consideration of the third of the three grounds of the case, pleaded in the 31st Article, which everyone must regret that it should have been thought necessary to bring before the public. The question is, whether, under the circumstances which have been deposed to, there is proof that Mr Geils committed, or attempted to commit, unnatural practices with his wife, in the manner in which it is laid in the Allegation.

...

According to this article, repeated attempts of this kind had been made, at intervals, during the last year of their cohabitation. The purpose for which those attempts were made, Mrs Geils says, she was aware of, though she was not aware of the precise and exact nature of the crime, and consequently, as she alleges, though she recoiled from them, she submitted to them without complaint or mention to any person, partly from her husband's injunctions not to tell, and partly from her fond reluctance to expose him to censure, though she felt the attempts to be criminal, hoping that he would desist.

Now her plea is that she submitted to these attempts, though she recoiled from them. If she submitted, what prevented their being successful? They were not successful until September; they were made, she recoiled from them, and yet submitted. This seems extraordinary conduct for a lady who had been married nearly seven years, and had had four children and several miscarriages; it is extraordinary, I say, that she should be a person of such "childlike simplicity" as that, when these attempts were made upon her, she should not have been aware of their nature. It is difficult to believe so great a degree of ignorance on the party of a lady acquainted with French and Italian, and who, according to Mrs Col. Geils and Mrs Nepean, had read books not suitable for a lady to read.

Her own plea is that she suffered during the last year of cohabitation repeated attempts of this kind; that she knew they were criminal, but did not know the nature or degree of the criminality, and she never thought of inquiring; that she submitted to these attempts until, in September, on suffering an assault "both more offensive as to the means and more successful as to the end" than the preceding, she became "so disgusted and alarmed" that she made a communication to her mother, and from her and their medical attendant learned the name and nature of the crime.

I confess this does appear to me a most extraordinary story. I must say that, if an accusation of this kind is brought against a person, he ought to have the fullest means of defending himself; the particular "means" alleged to have been used, ought to have been disclosed, which were more offensive, but in the end more successful, than the other attempts. But it is left in loose and indefinite terms, and the Court is to conjecture what is the difference between the previous attempts and the last attempt.

I must say this is a mode of pleading hardly consistent with the grave nature of the charge brought against this gentleman, and on which this Court, though not sitting as a court of criminal jurisdiction, is called upon to adjudicate, and by its sentence, drive him from society.

I cannot for the life of me believe that Mrs Geils could have understood the meaning and the extent of her plea. As I understand, it was attempted to be argued that the party has committed a criminal offence, formerly a capital offence, and for which he would now be liable to be expelled from the country. Under these circumstances, the court must have proof which would leave no doubt whatever upon its mind that the crime was committed; not merely that an attempt was made, but that the crime was committed and consummated. And upon what does it depend? Not upon an examination of the *particeps criminis* (or 'partner in crime' in more common parlance), if Mrs Geils may be so called, when she might have been subjected to cross-examination as to all the circumstances; but upon her answers, submitted in the form of written depositions, in which she simply denies that it is an invention by her, or that the facts are untruly pleaded by her, without any test being applied to her story by cross-examination.

...

I am not satisfied in my own mind that the charge is established against Mr Geils, and that the crime has been committed; and if I was satisfied, I should feel most extremely reluctant, for the sake of Mrs Geils herself, to pronounce a sentence which would declare that she had been a partaker in her husband's guilt, for a partaker in his guilt she must be, if her story be true – not guilty with a full and complete knowledge of the crime, though she admits that she knew it was an offence of a criminal nature. I should be most reluctant for Mrs Geils's own sake, and for the sake of the children who are descended from these parties, to pronounce that Mr Geils has been guilty of this crime.

But the most material part of this evidence, as it appears to me, is the medical and surgical evidence; and looking at this evidence, given by Mr Callaway, as well as subsequently by Mr Cooper and Dr Lever, gentlemen of eminence in their profession, they prove that it is absolutely and physically impossible for such an unnatural connection to take place without the passive consent and acquiescence of the woman, inasmuch as the least motion on her part would prevent it, and unless actual force was used – that is, actual violence, or the woman deprived of all power of resistance – they are of the opinion (at least, that is the result of their evidence) that such a connection could not take place. That she may have been mistaken, as suggested by Mr Geils, is, I think, very possible.

I must in justice to her, as well as to Mr Geils, say that the proof is not satisfactory to my mind. However disgraceful it was for Mr Geils to enter upon and discuss the subject, and speak in the manner he is said to have done, this is not sufficient to justify the Court in pronouncing him guilty of the grave offence laid to his charge. Suppose the case had come before a jury, would a jury have been of the opinion that the evidence was sufficient to convict? It must be recollected that there has been no cross-examination of the witness as to the expressions attributed to Mr Geils, upon which his confession and admission is founded.

Being of this opinion, without going into any recapitulation of the facts, I am of the opinion that Mr Geils has been guilty of adultery with two persons, McPhee and Campbell (McKichan having testified to deny any adultery on her part), but I am not satisfied that Mrs Geils is entitled to a separation on the grounds of cruelty. I pronounce that Mr Geils has been guilty of the crime of adultery, and that, on that ground alone, Mrs Geils is entitled to a sentence of separation.

Frances

Farley Hill Court
Berkshire
June 1848

May I say, dear Mrs Geils, what a delight it is to see you once more at Farley Hill? Mr Anderdon said.

Indeed, you may, I replied, *but the delight is mine in welcoming you and your wife back here at last. You may well imagine what joy it brings me to have been restored to my first and true home – owing to you, dear sir, in no small part. But may I ask that you call me by the name by which you first knew me here, Dickinson?*

Mr Anderdon inclined his head. *Of course, Mrs Dickinson; understood.*

And so began the most delightful afternoon that saw gathered in the gardens of Farley Hill Court some of our oldest friends – the Anderdons (although both the old man of Farley Hall and his gracious wife have both passed since last I was here), dear Miss Mitford, Dr and Mrs Bulley among them. I had not thought to make such an occasion of my homecoming, having crept back at first: such is to be my fate, I fear, now that my name is forever linked with notoriety wherever newspapers are read. But Mother urged me to celebrate my return with those who still wished me well and I found I could not disappoint her.

Dr Addams, Mr Jennings, Cousin Frank and his wife, and the Woodvale Ffaringtons sent their apologies to Mother's invitation, as did Edmund – now a man of Manchester, mostly – but I inferred no ill-will from such responses, accompanied as they were by warm expressions of genuine feeling. An invitation was also sent to Mr Puckle, asking him to enjoy the hospitality of Farley Hill if he could spare a few days from his labours, and of course included Mrs Puckle, too, although I had never encountered that lady. In truth, I found it hard to believe that such a person could exist, were it not for the fact that I knew there to be a Puckle Junior following in his father's professional footsteps, but Mr Puckle's note of acceptance had said that *while she was grateful beyond measure, Mrs Puckle must decline to travel to Berkshire as it was ever her intention to keep the sacred hearth of the Puckle home unsullied by any knowledge of, or acquaintance with, her husband's clients.* This response, too, I chose not to view as a source of shame, and not only because of my overwhelming sense of gratitude towards Mr Puckle both for his efforts and his open, honest manner with me at all times. If his life's companion preferred to keep her attention from being drawn into the world of wrong-dealing that was her husband's bread and butter, it was not for me to insist she be reminded of it.

Mr Puckle arrived alone yesterday, then, striking me at first as a fish out of water in the countryside: he seems a man born to traverse city streets, to pass unremarked there that he might better observe and detect what he seeks. But I saw him walking the grounds before dinner last evening, and this morning after breakfast I again spied him from my window stopping to engage in conversation any person he encountered, as if gathering information was his pastime as much as his profession, so that I suspect by the time our guests arrived this afternoon he knew more of Farley Hill and its folk than I now do.

Indeed, there was one matter remaining on which I longed to draw out his knowledge and that I hoped his visit might give me an opportunity to raise with him. Despite my immense relief at the verdict, I still smarted under the harsh words about my testimony in the judge's ruling. A visit from Mr Jennings to sign some papers regarding money matters had also forcibly reminded me that though I might call myself *Dickinson* and return home safely with my girls, I was still bound by the terms of my marriage settlement, meaning that John would retain £1200 per annum as his reward for securing my hand. Twelve hundred a year denied to me and my girls that he might spend as he wished, until his death! Now that the case was resolved in my favour, I felt the injustice of all that I had sacrificed more keenly than ever.

It is indeed a gross oversight that you have no recourse in English law, Mr Puckle said, when in the course of the afternoon's festivities he and I wandered away from the others, crossing the lawn to the shade of the lime avenue.

You have touched on the precise matter I wish to ask you about, I said. *What of* Scottish *law, Mr Puckle?*

He stopped his strolling then and fixed me with his attentive gaze. *But you are an Englishwoman, Mrs Dickinson, and were married in an English church?*

Yes, but to a Scotchman, and domiciled in Scotland for most of my marriage. I asked Mr Anderdon about this once and he urged me to confine myself to English law, but now I wonder...

Mr Puckle nodded. *You wonder?*

Well, it is not for me to say, Mr Puckle – and I would not so much as imply this to anyone but you in whom I have the greatest trust—

Go on, dear lady, he said, encouragingly.

Well, to be blunt, I wondered if Mr Anderdon was as familiar with Scottish law as with English. I was struck, in living there so long, how woefully ignorant even educated English people may be about how different things are there.

And I declare myself one among them, Mr Puckle said. *I admit I was much enlightened by the Scottish proctor in Glasgow with whom I conferred on your behalf. There are, indeed, significant differences in law, as you suggest, but the problem may be one of jurisdiction. That would be why Mr Anderdon advised you as he did, no doubt; believing that your case would be considered one for the English courts, concerning as it did an Englishwoman, a marriage in the English church and, perhaps not least, English property.*

I see what you mean, Mr Puckle, I said, *but amongst all the grand deceits of Mrs Nepean and her mother in their depositions was one that always puzzled me, so unnecessary did it seem.*

Mr Puckle smiled encouragement, nodding once more.

Both ladies repeatedly gave the impression that I was a mere visitor at Dumbuck House and exaggerated my absences at Farley Hill during my marriage when, as you know, John was ever reluctant for me to leave Scotland at all.

Mr Puckle's eyebrows had quite miraculously lifted as I spoke, in a way that would have been comical if I did not believe that such a response suggested he had come to a realisation that might be to my benefit.

Ah! he said. *You suspect, dear lady, that such an emphasis was deliberate? In response, perhaps, to legal advice that sought to put your claims beyond the reach of a Scottish court, where a full divorce might be granted?*

Is that too far-fetched? I asked.

I confess I had not considered that aspect of their evidence in that way, he said, *but you are quite right that those ladies were at pains to paint you as not really a denizen of Dumbuck, a ploy that I attributed entirely to their ill-feeling towards you, wanting to ostracise you from the family, as it were, once and for all. But you would not countenance further proceedings, Mrs Dickinson?*

I sighed then. *No, probably not, Mr Puckle. I doubt I have the stomach for any further exposure, even were Dr Addams to take on further efforts on my part. And yet, if I could in fact be granted a full divorce, giving me sole possession of all my income once more, and allowing me to take my girls abroad without fear of being considered a fugitive from the law—*

Little Kate, shoeless and with her hair flying free from her discarded cap, then came running out from between the limes, flinging herself into my skirts and wrapping her arms about me. I could feel the heat rising from her little body as she lifted her flushed face to me.

Mama, have you seen Badger? He ran away from me when I was taking him to Miss Mitford. She said she wanted to meet our new dog. He is so naughty and I have run ever so far and I took off my shoes and the grass is so lovely that I run and run!

I put a hand under my little girl's chin, delighted to see her face already grown a little fuller and sun-freckled since our return home.

Now, my darling, what a wild one you are! What will Mr Puckle think of my giddy Berkshire girls? I said.

He will think that they are the merriest, luckiest of girls, Mr Puckle said, with a chuckle that brought a shy smile from Kate in reply.

She then took my hand and submitted to strolling with us, a measure of how far the child had tired herself that she willingly slowed her pace to ours, stealing a glance at Mr Puckle from time to time, on each occasion bringing another nod and *that's the way!* from him in turn. In the distance, we heard a bark and a grey and white pup loped across the park into the stand of pines on the far side.

Badger! Kate said.

Never mind, dearest, I said, *let him run free on his own for a time. We shall go back now, I think. You must be wanting some lemon barley water, you are so warm?*

Yes, Mama, the child replied, *I would. And Mama?*

Yes, my love?

Please may we go to Italy now we are free? she said. *Miss Mitford says there are ever so many cats and dogs in Rome. And may we take Badger?*

Real history

(July 1875)

Frances

Villa Cetinale
Siena
July 1875

After a stifling rail journey from Florence, followed by the dusty carriage ride here yesterday, I woke at dawn to the peace and cool of the Sienese *campagna*. Can it really be more than twenty years since my first summer in Tuscany? Such heat then! Impossible to venture out before four or five o'clock without risking a *coup de soleil*.

Florence had been unusually quiet that year, I recall, the people all afraid of war and decamping to Rome for safety. To my English eyes, though, the streets and squares lining the Arno had still seemed so romantically picturesque – myself included, I suppose, bedecked in an immense flapping hat of Leghorn straw, as was the style at the time. A City of Flowers indeed! Everywhere pots of geraniums and roses, bouquets of vari-tinted carnations, and the scent of heliotrope and jessamine heavy in the air.

My girls, too, were enchanted by all they saw, especially *cara* Lucy; such a child of the south she became, so quickly! Of all my children, she seemed born to travel, neglecting her story books for her *Murray's Handbook to Rome*. I have it still, battered and dog-eared, and folded within its leaves a childish map of our first route from Lucca to Rome in Lucy's hand. (*She was her mother's joy and pride*, reads the dear child's headstone in the Eternal City.)

It is no coincidence, I am certain, that my two youngest have chosen a life far from the land of their birth, Cecile and Franny each marrying a marquis – one of Spain, one of Italy. Unlike their mother, though, my clever girls married men of character and distinction.

* * *

The exterior staircase at the rear of the villa takes me down to the cypress-lined lawn walk. Through gates at its end, a path leads up through the Holy Wood to a hill-top hermitage, the path's steepness intended to symbolise moving closer to God. But I will not pass beyond the gates this morning; earthly paradise is enough.

Turning around, I look back to the villa, the colour of honey in the early light. Servants come and go from the ground-floor doorways leading to the kitchens and store rooms. Behind the cypress avenues, work is beginning in the olive groves, in the corn fields and orchards, but no sign of life yet on the villa's *piano nobile*; the shutters of my room the only ones standing open there.

But there goes Angelo now, speeding down the steps – on his way to the stables, no doubt. My grandchild bears no trace of the Dickinsons in his colouring or bearing: Italian, through and through, the very image of his father, the Marchese, with a profile worthy of a Uffizi study. I hope he will not ride out too long this morning; it promises to be another scorching day.

* * *

At the front of the villa, clouds of dusty brown butterflies are already at work in the *limonaia* and the first of the cicadas start up their sawing; later their pulsing song will carry clear inside the house, easily penetrating the shutters closed against the heat. A low myrtle hedge surrounds the neat rows of lemon trees, releasing its soothing scent when I run my hand along the glossy leaves.

The rest of the summer lies before me, in the company of my dear Franny and her family once more, a time to read and write at my leisure, before resuming my travels in the autumn. I still marvel at my good fortune when, following the unexpected success of *The Diary of an Idle Woman in Italy*, Mr Chapman proposed a sequel, providing a reason – if one were needed – to return to the south once more.

Where might an idle woman like to go next? my indulgent publisher had asked.

Sicily, I had replied, without hesitation. Even dear Mr Dickens, in his *Pictures of Italy*, I said, had never ventured so far!

* * *

So I have Mr Chapman to thank for expelling from my mind an idea for a different kind of book altogether that had come to me after rereading Sir Walter Scott's *Waverley*. I had spent a soggy spring alone at Queen Charlton but I can't say exactly what had possessed me to turn back to Sir Walter, as I have long made it a rule to read nothing emanating from that venerable author's homeland. As I came towards the end of the story once more, though, I was struck anew by the sad fate of the two ladies of *Waverley*: confinement, by one means or another. By contrast, the once-feckless Edward Waverley closes his tale having:

acquired a more complete mastery of a spirit tamed by adversity, than his former experience had given him; and… entitled to say firmly, though perhaps with a sigh, that the romance of his life was ended, and that its real history had now commenced.

I could not help but reflect anew, then, on my desolate years spent north of the Tweed, and wonder if I might at last be ready to tell the story of the end of my own romance, the commencement of my own *real history*. I began to gather together all my papers from that time, that I might ship them here to Villa Cetinale and devote the summer to assembling my story; the light and warmth of this place more than enough to counter the dark past that I proposed to resurrect.

First were the thousands of pages devoted to my lawsuits – beginning in the Court of Arches and then continuing in the Scottish court and finally the House of Lords (obtaining a full and absolute divorce had taken longer than the seven years of my marriage, and cost me much besides!). Next into the trunks went my own writings and correspondence from those years, and the pages from newspapers

I had kept among them; then the poisonous packet of notes from Jane McPhee (I never did burn them); the extracts from dear Edmund's diary (copied out by one of Dr Addams' clerks); the papers sent to me by Jacob Jaffray (after Mr Puckle had tracked down the kind Reverend's son, in his quest for possible witnesses); and, most valued of all, the papers bequeathed to me by Amy Webb, in her Farley Hill grave these many years now. A truer testimony of friendship and devotion I could never ask for, nor deserve, than those pages that Amy had first begun to write, at my urging, in Cavendish Square, and continued beyond the time we were reunited at Hammersmith.

Into the trunks went it all, but no sooner had the trunks left Somerset ahead of my own departure than I began to reconsider my plan, even before Mr Chapman's urging of a sequel led me to drop it entirely. One of the last pages I had cast my eye over before closing the final lock was from the Scottish Court of Sessions, and it was that, I think, that prompted my second thoughts. In his ruling, the Scottish judge had written that:

John Edward Geils ought and should be divorced and separated from the pursuer, her society, fellowship, and company, in all time coming; and has forfeited all the rights and privileges of a lawful husband; and the pursuer is entitled to marry any free person she pleases, in the same manner as if she had never been married, or as if he, John Edward Geils, was naturally dead.

It was that term applied to myself – *the pursuer* – that particularly gave me pause. What in fact *was* I pursuing, in contemplating this melancholy project? If I were truly to live as if that man were *naturally dead*, what gain, what life, would there be in retelling the story of those years of painful immurement?

Now that my words are read by thousands, and I possess the freedom to roam where I choose, why should I not tell new tales rather than old ones? If I embellish a tad here or conceal a little there, what then? The words are my own, the stories mine to share as I determine: no judge to gainsay them, no one needed to speak on my behalf.

Besides, some things are best consigned to the darkness, unseen and unexamined, so that light and warmth might prevail.

* * *

From my room, so cool after the gravel paths of the *limonaia*, I see Lisetta, the cook's daughter, passing below, carrying a tray with a pitcher, clay cups and a covered plate. Two young men are at work in the garden; I have heard the clip of their shears and snatches of talk as I write at my table. Lisetta approaches the nearer of the gardeners and he looks up, passing an arm across his forehead and putting down his tool, before greeting the girl. The other gardener, further away, then calls, *Eh, Lisetta! Perche non mi servi prima?* But before Lisetta can reply, the first youth calls *Aspetti, aspetti!* to his co-worker and the two men banter good-naturedly while Lisetta stands by, laughing.

I know Lisetta to be a girl of lively temperament and great skill. When last here, I watched her one day in the kitchen, preparing a delicate Sienese pastry that she makes better than any I have tasted in the city. She had, at first, seemed shy to be so observed but, absorbed in her work, soon forgot my presence. She had kneaded and folded, rolled and cut, shaped and decorated, her long fingers and strong arms making me wish I had the aptitude to draw her. When she brought me the product of her labour, still warm and smelling of spice and citrus, it had melted on my tongue. *Squisita!* I said, and she had smiled with the pride of an artist who knows her worth.

But what do I really know of Lisetta, or any of the servants at Villa Cetinale, even though I speak their language, or observe them closely? Is it folly on my part to imagine they are freer and happier than their British counterparts? I have never forgotten the depositions of the servants of Dumbuck and Farley Hill, how in testifying what they had observed on my behalf, they also disclosed so much of their own lives – their losses and fears and hopes and quarrels – all wholly invisible to me while I lived among them, distracted by my own suffering.

To one servant in particular, of course, I owe a debt that can never be repaid. Whatever I endured was rivalled only by Lizzie Campbell, and yet, despite my own treatment of her in dismissing her so unjustly, she had come to my aid when discovered by Mr Puckle. She had not lied like that false Maria McKichan but spoken the truth. *And it set me free.*

Poor Lizzie, preyed upon so mercilessly by the man to whom I had joined my life; I never did learn the consequences of her testimony for her. All I know is that by the time my case finally came before the House of Lords four years later, Lizzie – like Jane McPhee – was dead.

Without Lizzie, I could never have gained a verdict in my favour. *Her* words had power, not mine, the judge having utterly dismissed my testimony of ill-treatment.

Without Lizzie, I would not be here, watching Lisetta and her two *corteggiatori* in the garden below on a summer's day.

I would be Frances Geils yet, perhaps.

* * *

Into my mind now comes something I wrote about my very first winter in Rome, so long ago, after a tour of an artist's studio. Lamenting my inability to make a self-portrait by my own hand, I had concluded then that *I must leave my readers to make their own sketch of me.* And so I must.

Author's Afterword

In November 1898, an obituary recorded the death in Siena of the 'author of *The Diary of an Idle Woman in Italy* and other works.' This obituary, as well as the one that soon followed in *The Times*, described Frances as the mother of four daughters from her marriage to John Geils. No mention was made of her divorce.

Both obituaries also offered faint praise of her literary achievements, noting that although her books 'met with considerable popular approval… they are not likely to occupy a permanent place in the literature of the time.' And so it has transpired. Despite the success of her *Diary of an Idle Woman* series of travel books (with volumes on Sicily, Spain and Constantinople following her first on Italy) and other books on Italy, France and Spain as well as four novels, few have now heard of Frances Dickinson – or Frances Elliot, the name under which all her books appeared. Fewer still have ever read any of her work.

I first came across her name while doing some research on Charles Dickens. I found that Frances had been a friend of Dickens from the 1850s, with the two exchanging frank and amusing letters up until Dickens' death. They also had a professional connection, due to Frances regularly submitting essays and stories to Dickens' literary magazine, *All the Year Round*. I've long been interested in Victorian women writers so I wondered why I had never heard of Frances before.

Part of the answer is that her first literary efforts in the 1850s were published in magazines under a pseudonym ('Florentia'). It was not uncommon for literary magazines to publish anonymous or pseudonymous articles at this time but Frances had good reason to keep a low profile after the publicity that the case of Geils v. Geils had received. Her brief obituary in *The Times* bore no resemblance to the detailed and salacious coverage the same newspaper had given to her case in the Court of Arches, the ecclesiastical court that was the only recourse for those seeking a marital separation in the 1840s. The case was covered extensively in many newspapers across the country – often printing almost verbatim each day's court proceedings – so that anyone interested in discovering the sordid history of the Geils' marriage can easily do so now through online archives of nineteenth-century British newspapers.

These newspaper accounts were my starting point in unearthing Frances' story, and they made for painful reading. A woman of only twenty-five when she first courageously exposed her abusive marriage, Frances was variously accused – both in court and in newspaper editorials – of deception, derangement, arrogance, ignorance, immorality, violence and rage. No true lady, it was said, could have made such allegations against her husband; a virtuous woman would not even know of the existence of such acts.

* * *

In the 1840s, the most secure means of gaining a legal separation was through proof of adultery. Although it was permitted to bring a case on the grounds of cruelty (in which charges of violence might be included), judges were inclined to see such allegations as exaggerated by the victim or to be sympathetic to a husband 'provoked' by his wife. By the time her case came to court, Frances knew beyond any doubt that her husband was a repeat adulterer but she chose to pursue two other counts against him as well: cruelty (detailing his many acts of physical violence, verbal abuse, and coercive control); and sodomy.

It was this last charge that attracted much of the attention to the legal proceedings, even as the newspapers had to avoid too direct discussion of such an 'unspeakable' charge. Reading Frances' account now, it is clear that what she was accusing her husband of was rape; anal rape, specifically. But there was no legal recognition of rape in marriage in the 1840s (or indeed for a further 150 years in the UK!) and so her allegation specified sodomy, still technically a capital offence at this time (in which both parties to the act were considered criminally liable). In response to Frances' allegation, counsel for John Geils sought to show that Frances was either mistaken (after seven years of marriage she supposedly couldn't tell what orifice her husband was penetrating) or that she was lying. The judge concluded that it was most likely the former (relying heavily on the 'expert' testimony of three doctors that it was physically impossible to anally rape a woman unless extreme physical force or stupefying drugs were used).

In fact, the judge in Geils v. Geils discounted *everything* that Frances testified about the abuse she suffered during her marriage. The only evidence he found compelling enough to grant a separation came from the deposition of a former servant, Elizabeth Campbell, who testified to repeated sexual coercion and violation at the hands of John Geils, further corroborated by circumstantial evidence from the depositions of other servants who had seen Elizabeth in compromising situations with her employer. How was it possible, I wondered, that a servant woman's testimony could be taken seriously in a court of law when that of a lady of status and wealth was not?

Further questions and complications arose when I read the 31 witness statements presented by both sides of the case, now held in the archives of Lambeth Palace Library. In a trial like Geils v. Geils, no witnesses appeared in court. All evidence was submitted in the form of written depositions compiled in advance of the trial by the respective legal teams. Witness statements were transcribed and then subjected to further questions from opposing counsel, such 'interrogatories' constituting a written form of cross-examination, in effect. Of the depositions I have read, 21 were from servants, former servants, or those employed in other working-class occupations: housemaids, cooks, shepherds, gardeners, nursemaids, man servants, farm labourers. Even more surprising, of that 21, *only four* testified in a manner advantageous to John Geils, although the majority were from those employed by the Geils family at Dumbuck House.

Much of the 'evidence' on John Geils' side reads now as almost laughably flawed – were it not for the seriousness of the allegations. His barrister accused every servant who testified against his client of drunkenness, dishonesty, or sexual impropriety (often all three), in order to discount the veracity of their testimony. His case therefore relied almost entirely on the depositions from Geils' mother and sister, which were riddled with inconsistencies, if not outright deceptions, and also clearly the result of collusion between the two. (Neither Isabella's husband, Molyneux Nepean, nor any of the Geils brothers gave depositions. Maria McKichan testified to deny she had ever committed adultery with John Geils. There is no deposition from Jane McPhee.) The depositions by Mary Geils and Isabella Nepean also included allegations of drunkenness and sexual impropriety against Frances' mother, Catherine Dickinson, bringing Frances' paternity into doubt by the insinuation that she was the child of a liaison between her mother and Edward Webb (the bailiff – that is, estate manager – at Farley Hill Court), as well as alleging that Catherine had sought to seduce John Geils during his engagement to Frances!

All the depositions make for gripping reading, far from dry legal documents (even though some, like that of Mary Geils, are over 30,000 words in length). What I had not expected, however, was such a poignant insight into the lives of servants. In the process of disclosing what they had seen and heard in the marriage of John and Frances Geils, the servants laid bare their own precarious lives – lacking basic privacy, subject to the power (or whim) of their employers, and beset by the ill-health, over-work, and tragic losses that poverty inevitably brought at that time. The preyed-upon servant girl berated and ostracised by her fellow servants for being a slut, the alcoholic gardener deserted by a wife who chose a life of prostitution in the city over remaining with him and their three children – these were stories that at times threatened to distract me altogether from the story of Frances Dickinson.

Even the act of giving their testimony was a demanding and intimidating process for working-class witnesses, having their every word interrogated by legal gentlemen, their motives subject to hostile challenge. Many witnesses made a long journey to London especially to give their statements (needing the permission of their employers to do so, of course). Some of their depositions are only signed with an 'X' or a very weak hand (although Amy Webb's is signed in neat copperplate); some testified that their original statements were never read back to them before they were told to sign them. All were quizzed extensively on the seriousness of the oath they had sworn, and explicitly threatened with eternal damnation as well as perjury if they did not speak the truth (although none of the upper-class witnesses were threatened in this way).

* * *

Despite the emotional power of the servants' stories, however, *An Idle Woman* focuses on the early life of a wealthy, privileged woman. I was drawn to Frances' story as an opportunity to explore issues that continue to dominate too many women's lives, whatever their social status: the 'blurred lines' of sexual consent, gaslighting, and coercive control.[1] In recreating the story of Frances Dickinson, especially her seven years as Frances Geils, I have gone back to a time before modern legal definitions of abuse and modern psychological theories of trauma to try to understand how an abused

---

1. It is still less than a decade since coercive control was formally defined in legal terms (for example, in the UK's Serious Crime Act in 2015). Understood as 'a repeated pattern of behaviour designed to undermine the autonomy of another individual' (Barlow and Walklate, 2022, p. 2), coercive control involves 'intimidation, isolation and control', with or without physical abuse (Stark 2007, p. 2). Research shows that coercive control is mainly perpetrated within heterosexual relationships where men 'use social norms of masculinity and femininity... to impose their will' (Stark 2007, p. 6). 'Gaslighting,' though not a legal term, can be one particularly insidious form of coercive control, undermining a person's ability to trust their own perceptions or name their own experience, when subjected to relentless denials, accusations, deceptions, or reframing of events by their abuser.

woman might have made sense of her experience then. I wanted to know how it was possible that an abused and traumatised woman might have eventually found the resilience to say *no more*, and to maintain her resolve even while she was subjected to public scorn through the reporting of her divorce proceedings.

I did not, however, start from the assumption that people in the past were really just like us, in different clothes. Frances Dickinson was a victim of sustained and brutal spousal abuse but she was also a privileged heiress, taking for granted that she was entitled to a life of comfort and that servants would do everything for her (although she also fondly recalled childish romps with her maid in the attics). Her views on race would not stand up to any modern scrutiny either – not only as evidenced in her later travel books, but also based on her comments about the illegitimate Anglo-Indian daughters of her father-in-law at Dumbuck House.

If she was not immune to the prevailing views of class and race of her time, however, how was it that Frances was able to repudiate equally pervasive assumptions about wifely submission and feminine self-abnegation? Frances was clearly an intelligent and well-read young woman but she lived at a time when a wife had no legal claim to bodily autonomy, custody of her children, freedom of movement, or control of her wealth. As the novelist George Eliot, writing just a few years later, summed up the powerlessness of wives: 'An unloving, tyrannous, brutal man needs no motive to prompt his cruelty; he needs only the perpetual presence of a woman he can call his own.'[2]

Despite such apparently insuperable obstacles, Frances made repeated attempts to gain an amicable separation from her husband and when that failed, she pursued every legal means available to end her marriage, through courts in both England and Scotland. Granted a separation in the Court of Arches 1848, it was only in November 1855 that Frances was able to write, in a letter to her cousin, that she was completely free of John Geils and he had renounced any claim to custody of their children.

---

2. Taken from 'Janet's Repentance,' one of the stories Eliot included in *Scenes of Clerical Life* (1858).

* * *

Much of *An Idle Woman*, then, is taken directly from the court documents relating to the case of Geils v. Geils in the Court of Arches; the witness depositions as well as a large number of letters that were given in evidence by both sides of the case have provided essential source material. In addition, I have referred to newspaper reportage of the court proceedings and accounts of the case in legal casebooks, including the judge's final ruling.

I have, of course, also drawn on Frances' own writings, such as 'A First Visit to the Court of Queen Adelaide' and 'Adventures of a First Season,' which appeared in *Bentley's Miscellany* in 1852 and 1853 respectively, her 'Polperro' series of essays published in *New Monthly Magazine* in monthly instalments between 1854 and 1855, and a number of essays on her extensive Italian travels (many of which she later collected and revised for *Diary of an Idle Woman in Italy*).

Census entries helped to fill in some details of the inhabitants of Farley Hill Court and Dumbuck House, both upstairs and downstairs, further fleshed out by a wide range of reading on the novel's locations in the 1830s and 1840s, from Mary Russell Mitford's *Our Village* to the 1845 *Statistical Account of Scotland* (where the entry on the parish of Dumbarton was written by Rev. Jaffray). Mary Russell Mitford's letters (in *The Life of Mary Russell Mitford, Told by Herself in Letters to Her Friends*) were also an indispensable source of information on the Dickinson family and Farley Hill, as she was a lifelong friend of Frances' mother, Catherine Dickinson. Historical information about Oakfield/Auchendarroch estate was found in *A History of The MacConnochie Campbells of Inverawe*, compiled by Diarmid Campbell and privately printed in 2014, which includes a brief memoir by Harriet Archibald (wife of Alexander Archibald, who owned Auchendarroch in the 1830s–1840s), describing life on the estate (including Niven the gardener). *The History of the Manor, Queen Charlton* (2012), by Jean Manco for David Streatfeild-James, provided background on Frances' second estate that she inherited through her father. Charles St John's *Short Sketches of the Wild*

Sports and Natural History of the Highlands, published in 1846, was helpful for Edmund's accounts of hunting in Scotland with John Geils. The Italian context in the Epilogue was also aided by Edith Wharton's *Italian Villas and Their Gardens* (1904), which includes a description of Villa Cetinale.

More broadly, a wide range of Scottish literature has left its mark on my rendering of Frances' life in Scotland, from John Galt's *Annals of the Parish* (1821) to Walter Scott's *Rob Roy* (1817) and *The Bride of Lammermoor* (1819) and J. M. Barrie's *Farewell, Miss Julie Logan* (1931). Lewis Grassic Gibson's *Sunset Song* (1932) influenced Jane McPhee's idiom. Poetry by Wordsworth, Byron, Burns, Hemans, and Scott is quoted throughout, reflecting the breadth of Frances' reading as well as prevailing literary tastes.

The extracts quoted in the novel – from William Buchan's *Domestic Medicine* (1834 edition), Hugh Smith's *Letters to Married Women: On Nursing and the Management of Children* (1774 edition), Sarah Stickney Ellis's *The Wives of England* (1843), Elizabeth Lanfear's *Letters to Young Ladies On Their Entrance Into the World* (1824), as well as the editorial from *The Satirist* – have only been edited for length.

One of the more mundane difficulties in writing about a true story is the tendency for common names to recur. To avoid unnecessary confusion to the reader, therefore, I have changed some first names to avoid having multiple Marys, Elizabeths, Johns, Williams, etc. With very few exceptions (in the case of minor characters only, none of them narrators), all of the characters are based on real people, although Edmund Ffarington is a composite of two men, both family friends of the Dickinsons, who assisted Frances in trying to extricate herself from her marriage. The diary of Edmund Ffarington (himself a barrister) was referred to in courtroom exchanges but does not appear in the archive of Geils v. Geils.

The vast majority of the letters that appear in the novel are based on actual letters, occasionally expanded to add necessary context for the reader or conflated for concision. While the discovery of Jane McPhee's letters to John Geils is mentioned in depositions – and involved both Amy Webb and her father in the way described in the novel – the letters themselves are not included in the archived case files. Thomas Callaway's evidence (one of three eminent doctors who testified for John Geils) and the judge's final ruling are both extant, merely edited for length.

* * *

Nat Reeve provided meticulous and enthusiastic assistance in accessing the archives at Lambeth Palace Library on my behalf, when Covid restrictions kept London out of reach for me.

I will always be grateful to Liam McIlvanney for mentoring this project, for keeping my spirits up when they flagged (which seemed often), for introducing me to that most extraordinary novel, *Sunset Song*, and for patiently pointing out the many significant differences between Scotland and England in the early Victorian period.

Any remaining errors, misrepresentations or infelicities, however unintentional, are my responsibility alone.

* * *

In *The Times* in 1871, the anonymous reviewer of *Diary of an Idle Woman in Italy* wryly remarked:

The reader, who for two volumes has been wondering when the idleness vaunted on the cover was going to begin, for he has seen none of it, must… think that her truer title would have been… 'The Indefatigable Woman in Italy.'

I can only sympathise with this reviewer's puzzlement; Frances Dickinson remains an enigma to me in many ways. And there is still much more to be told about her story. I don't think she is done with me yet.